HUNGRY

GRY

H. A. SWAIN

SQUARE
FISH

FEIWEL AND FRIENDS • NEW YORK

SQUARE
FISH

An Imprint of Macmillan
175 Fifth Avenue
New York, NY 10010
macteenbooks.com

Square Fish and the Square Fish logo are trademarks of Macmillan and
are used by Feiwel and Friends under license from Macmillan.

Square Fish books may be purchased for business or promotional use. For information on bulk
purchases, please contact the Macmillan Corporate and Premium Sales Department at
(800) 221-7945 x5442 or by e-mail at specialmarkets@macmillan.com.

Library of Congress Cataloging-in-Publication Data Available

ISBN 978-1-250-06308-3 (paperback)   ISBN 978-1-250-06184-3 (ebook)

Originally published in the United States by Feiwel and Friends
First Square Fish Edition: 2015
Book designed by Véronique Lefèvre Sweet
Square Fish logo designed by Filomena Tuosto

10 9 8 7 6 5 4 3 2

LEXILE: HL760L

For my father

HUNGRY

PROLOGUE

"Surely the apple is the noblest of fruits."
—Henry David Thoreau

In the ghostly branches of a hologram tree, light winks off the shiny side of something red and round. I hesitate to reach for it. It's just a projection of the past onto the present after all, but it looks so real that I can't help myself. I raise my arm. My body feels hollow and slow.

"Hey, who are you? That's not for you!" someone calls.

I try to tell this stranger my name, *Thalia Apple,* but the words burble up from my throat and pop like bubbles in my mouth with a taste that's faint and far away. My jaws work, unable to grasp the last word sitting smugly on the tip of my tongue. So I pluck that red and shiny thing from the tree and shove it in my mouth, feel it slide down my throat then watch as it falls out of a perfect empty circle carved from my hips to my ribs. I try to snatch it before it hits the ground, but it changes shape and flitters away on delicate wings, too fleeting to catch.

I must find something to block this opening where my belly button used to be or everything I want to say will fall out. I pick up a pillow, my favorite soft blanket on the ground beside me, then the dark and loamy dirt—like what my grandparents dug their hands into when they were young—but it all falls through, making a mound at my heels. I inhale deeply, catching the slightest whiff of something sweet, something desirable, as red and round as my name, and I moan.

PART 1

INNER LOOP

"... comfort me with apples, for I am sick of love."
—*Song of Solomon*

"What's the matter, Thalia?"

I wake up with a jerk. Squinting into the light, I see Mom zip past where I'm sprawled across the couch clutching a pillow to my belly, moaning. I try to clear my head and get my bearings. I'm not under a tree. There is no dirt. I poke myself in the stomach to make sure there's no hole. When I sit up, my head feels too heavy, so I flop back on the living room couch. My arms feel like spindly strings attached to my shoulders. My legs are wobbly. My belly is concave.

"Why were you in the dark?" Mom asks over the yapping of her personal cyber assistant Gretchen, who runs through today's junk mail on the main screen.

"Today only . . ." Gretchen announces.

"No," says Mom. Bonk, Gretchen deletes the message.

"Save big . . ." Gretchen says.

"No," says Mom. Bonk, goes Gretchen.

"Cyber sale!" Gretchen announces.

"Send to Thalia," Mom commands. *Ping!*

I roll away from the noise but can't get comfortable on the stiff couch because the backs of my legs stick to the wipeable surface. I pull the heavy pillow that smells strongly of synthetic citrus cleanser over my head to block out the fracas. I wish I could dive back into my dream and find that thing I was searching for. I inhale deeply, but the biting lemony-lime scent is not the smell I want. The smell I'm after is less pungent. More subtle. Not yellow or green but warm and earthy brown.

Mom's heels clack against the tile, then she slips a cool dry hand under the pillow and presses against my forehead.

"What are you doing?" I swat her away with the pillow.

"Checking for a fever."

"You're a doctor for god's sake," I grouse at her. "Why are you touching me?"

Mom crosses her arms and sticks a hip out to the side. She's all points and angles. "If you had your Gizmo with you, I could read your vitals from over there." She points across the room. "But since you don't, I have to do it the old-fashioned way." She holds up her hand and waves her fingers at me.

"Gross," I mutter.

Mom snorts. "That's how doctors used to do it. They even used their hands for surgery." She makes a sick face at the thought of digging inside someone's body. "Why are you on the couch in the middle of the day anyway?"

"I just feel . . ." I try to describe it. "Weird," I say because there is no one word I can think of.

"Weird is a relative term," says Mom. "Be specific."

"Hollow," I say. I could tell her more. Details like how it starts in my belly. Between my ribs and hips. Above my navel but beneath that springy muscle, the diaphragm, that makes your lungs expand and contract. How it's a strange yawning feeling, like my insides grew a mouth and that mouth is opening. I push a finger into the spot, but all I can say is, "Empty."

"Are you achy?" She cocks her head, and her hair shifts like a black cultured Silkese curtain across her narrow shoulders.

I shake my head no, which makes me dizzy for a moment as if my noggin is a balloon tethered above my shoulders.

Mom switches into full-on MD mode, picking up my arm with two fingers at my wrist, checking my pulse.

"Next you'll cut off my leg with a rusty saw and no anesthesia," I mutter, uncomfortable in her grip.

"Your historical medical references are hilarious," she deadpans. "You should work as a reenactor at the Relics. Did you have your Synthamil today?"

"Of course," I grumble.

"And water? Sixteen ounces of each this morning?"

"God, Mom, yes."

"Have you urinated?"

"Would you like a specimen?"

"Don't get smart." She drops my arm, which flops to the couch. I feel like I'm made of Just-Like-Skin. "Your Synthamil has been precisely calibrated, and if you don't . . ."

"Jeez, Mom." I sit up and hold my head in my hands. "I know. I drank it all and I had water on schedule and I peed. Okay?"

"Well, you're certainly grouchy," she mutters.

I glare at her through my fingers as she clacks away and returns gently shaking a bottle of blue Synthamil with my name embossed in gold across the label. "Maybe we need to recalibrate. Your metabolism might have shifted." She twists off the cap and hands me the liquid. "Maybe you're having one last growth spurt."

I roll my eyes at her before I take a swig. "I'm seventeen, not twelve."

She shrugs. "It's been known to happen. Sometimes people in their twenties grow a few more inches. Especially when they enter the Procreation Pool and their hormones surge." She's off again, clicking through the hall to her home office.

I chug the Synthamil then wipe the back of my hand across my mouth so I don't have a blue moustache.

Mom returns a few minutes later with a patch and an antiseptic swab. "I'll monitor you for twenty-four hours and see how everything is looking. Lift up your shirt."

"I don't want that on me."

She tugs at the back of my shirt anyway. "It's only for a day. It'll give me more info than just your Gizmo, which you never have with you anyway." She manages to expose my lower back. The swab is so cold it makes me jump. "Hold still. You won't even know it's there." She peels the ultrathin two-inch patch off its backing and presses it firmly against my skin, rubbing around all of the edges to make sure it's good and stuck. Then she takes her Gizmo out of her pocket and establishes a link with the patch.

"Doesn't have a locator, does it?" I scratch at it.

She swats my hand away. "Don't pick. You could break a circuit." She checks the connection then slips her Gizmo into her pocket. "And it's not an affront to your personal liberty. It only collects internal data."

"As if that's not personal?"

Mom's eyes narrow and she frowns, which makes her look just like her mother.

"That's your Nguyen face," I tell her. She gives me the eyebrow. "For real, you look just like Grandma Grace when you're mad at me."

For my biology class, we've been mapping the genomes of our four grandparents, our parents, and ourselves in order to figure out where our traits come from. I'm convinced there must be a humorless gene that comes straight from my mother's Vietnamese side because Grandma Grace is the most serious woman I've ever met, which is probably why she's such a good hematologist. There's nothing funny about blood.

Mom pushes off the couch. "I'd be happy to find a specialist to go over your data and make a recommendation."

It's an idle threat and we both know it. Specialists are the last resort, only called in when all the existing science has failed and the only thing left to try is some experimental treatment a doctor is hoping to patent as the latest breakthrough therapy. "As long as it's Papa Peter," I say.

This actually makes Mom laugh. She looks like her father when she's happy, with his broad smile and bright eyes. My whole life, I've heard stories about what a gentle and sweet pediatrician he was and how he sacrificed part of his family's rations for food and medicine to save starving children during the wars. That was a huge point of contention between my hard-nosed grandmother and my bleeding-heart grandfather that almost destroyed their family. My mother says it's an example of an old-fashioned cultural divide—Asian versus African American. Since Papa's black, she claims he had a family history of looking out for the most vulnerable. But that never made much sense to me. I think Grandma and Papa are just different sorts of people no matter what their cultural backgrounds may have been.

"Papa Peter's hugs and stickers won't recalibrate your Synthamil formula if something's off," Mom says as she finishes tidying up the mail, because she can't stand anything unnecessary junking up our waves. "By the way, Gretchen sent you some VirtuShops," she tells me. "You need new pants."

"I have plenty of jeans and skirts." I get off the couch and tug my miniskirt down around my thighs.

She gives me the eyebrow again. "Thalia, we discussed this. You can't keep wearing old stuff like that." She points to my corduroy mini. "What's it made of, anyway?"

"A vintage natural fiber called cotton, thank you very much."

She looks to the ceiling as if the solar lights will recharge her patience with me. "I know what cotton is, Thalia. You have an Interpersonal Classroom Meeting this week. You can't wear Grandma Apple's old clothes to an ICM. What will your instructors think?"

"Who cares what they think? Anyway, it's not a real class. More like four hours of product placement combined with a thinly veiled focus group, if you ask me. Not that anyone ever does."

Mom shakes her head and sighs. "A, that's not true. And B, your father and I care what your teachers think."

"Teachers?" I snort.

"Thalia—" she starts, but I cut her off.

"Dad doesn't mind," I tell her, and she doesn't say anything because she knows it's true. "I'd rather go real-time shopping anyway."

"Should be called waste-of-time shopping," Mom says and chuckles at her own dumb joke. "If you don't like what I put in your box, then design your own."

"But I don't know what I want until I see it and touch it."

She stops what she's doing to look at me. "Seriously, what century are you from?" This is her favorite question. One she's asked me since I was little and preferred to look at real books than have tablet time. "But if that's how you want to do it, fine. Just do it. Get something decent and make a good personal impression."

"I like the feel of cotton," I tell her as I sit down to browse my message center on the main screen.

"Chemically, Cottynelle is virtually the same," she says.

"Virtually," I reiterate. "But not really."

"Don't start."

"Your clothes are grown from bacteria and yeast in a lab."

"Enough." She gives me a warning glance. "Why don't you let Astrid cull the news for you?" she asks, motioning to how I'm manually going through headlines.

"That would necessitate finding my Gizmo."

"You don't know where it is?" She looks at me as if I'm missing an appendage.

"Around here somewhere."

"You're as bad as Grandma Apple."

"How bad am I?" Grandma Apple bops up from the basement, her gray curls bouncing. She carries a ball of string and two pointy sticks.

"Never mind," says Mom and goes back to her conversation with Gretchen.

"Gizmo," I mouth to Grandma, who twirls her finger in the air as if to say whoop-de-do.

I snicker, which makes my mom's back straighten, although she pretends to ignore us as she pockets her Gizmo then announces, "I'm off to the lab again."

"But it's Friday," says Grandma.

Mom glances up. "So?"

"Family time," Grandma says hopefully, but I see her shoulders slumping in anticipation of defeat.

"Did you schedule it?" Mom asks.

"But Lily, it's every Friday," says Grandma.

"Well if you don't schedule it . . ." Mom trails off. "It's not hard, Rebecca." Mom has a habit of speaking to Grandma as if she's talking to a small child who doesn't understand the great big scary Interweb. "Thalia or Max could teach you in two minutes. You just tell your PCA, what's her name?"

"Annie," Grandma says dryly.

"Just tell Annie one time to coordinate all our calendars with a repeating event. Then we'll be synched up, and when Gretchen checks my daily calendar to generate my to-do list . . ."

"I know how to do it," Grandma clarifies. "Just seems unnecessary."

I blink off the main screen. "We can do family night without Mom," I tell Grandma, hoping to avoid another awkward conversation about family life between the two of them.

Grandma smiles at me, but I see the tiredness around her eyes. "Of course, lovey." She holds up the ball of string. "I'm going to teach you how to knit."

I catch the tail end of my mom's eye roll as she swings her black Silkese jacket around her shoulders. Before she leaves, she says, "Schedule family night. We'll do it next week."

"Sure thing," I call after her, knowing full well that will never happen. "You, me, and Dad?" I ask Grandma after the door wheeshes closed.

"I doubt it," she says, pointing to the flashing video-message indicator on the main screen with my dad's network photo.

I accept and Dad pops up on the screen. He's in his office, slouching at his desk, surrounded by gently buzzing blue walls. "Hey, you guys, sorry I can't make family night. I've got to work late." Then he sits up tall and smiles. "But wait until you see what we're working on! It's almost done and you'll be the first to have it. Promise." I close Dad's message and ask Grandma what she thinks the surprise will be.

"A robotic head for when you're tired of thinking for yourself."

"The latest craze," I tell her. "You should have been a designer."

"Missed my calling, huh?"

"Oh well, not everyone can change the world one nanoprocessor at a time."

We both giggle at our stupid jokes, mostly because no one else would appreciate them.

"Let's go knit," I say. "With these." I hold up my hands and wave my fingers like my mom did earlier.

"Subversive," Grandma says with a chuckle.

⚜   ⚜   ⚜

Since it's just the two of us, Grandma Apple and I cozy up in her living room, which is in the basement of our house. I love her place with all the fluffy throw pillows, warm quilts, and soft worn rugs, the old-fashioned wooden furniture, and best of all—the books. Mom can't stand to come down here. She says all the microbes in the natural fibers make her sneeze. Not that that should surprise anyone. Sometimes I think my mom would rather live in her lab where every surface is smooth, cold, hard, and antibacterial.

I curl up next to my grandma on the sofa with my feet tucked beneath a hand-crocheted blanket her mother made a hundred years ago on their family farm.

"Used to be you could get yarn made out of natural fibers like cotton or wool," she tells me as she loops the slate-gray string, the same color and texture as her hair, around a knitting needle.

"What's wool again?" I ask, trying to mimic her motions with my own ball of red yarn and silver needles.

"The hair from sheep. But there were lots of other animals that people used for yarn, too. Goats, alpacas, rabbits. Each one had its own texture, and some of it was so soft and warm, you wouldn't believe it now. Real yarn was nothing like these synth fibers." She frowns down at the rows she's knitting.

"Which did you raise?" I ask.

"Goats," she tells me for the millionth time, but I can never remember the difference between a goat and a sheep. "Not the woolly one that said baa. The ornery one that would eat anything." She laughs at some memory I'll never understand. "But ours ate mostly sweet hay and clover, so their milk was delicious. And the cheese! There was nothing better than fresh goat cheese. Except for warm bread to put it on." She sighs. "Ahh, the smell of fresh-baked bread. I keep telling your father he should make an app for that! Then I'd have a reason to use my Gizmo."

I chuckle, then we're quiet for a few moments while she corrects my yarn. Once I get the hang of the knit stitch, I say, "Tell me about dinner again."

Grandma draws in a deep breath. "Well," she says, thinking back. "That was the real family time, you know. Not for everyone, I guess, but in our family, since we were farmers, we wanted to sit down together and enjoy the food we'd raised."

"That was before the wars."

"Yes, but even during the wars, we did the best we could from what little we were able to grow, even if it was just bitter greens and a few chicken eggs."

"And you had lots of people who came to eat with you, right?"

"At first," she says. "But when things got scarce, like everyone, we hid what we had."

I shake my head. "I don't want to hear that part. Tell me about when dinner was good."

Grandma grins. "Alright." She lays her knitting in her lap and thinks for a moment with her eyes closed. "I'll tell you how to make a roasted chicken."

Grandma takes her time, as if she's back in a kitchen, preparing each ingredient. She tells me about melting butter in the microwave and pouring it over the chicken. Then sprinkling on salt and pepper and fresh herbs that grew right outside her back door in a little pot filled with rich dark dirt. She explains how her mother put the chicken in a pan with onions and carrots and potatoes dug from her garden, and then stuck it all in the oven for hours, only opening the door to brush the juices over the chicken's skin every once in a while. I close my eyes when she talks about food, and I try to imagine how it was. My mind drifts and blurs through vague images, but it all fades into words because I have no idea what she's really talking about. And, to be honest, some of it sounds gross. Like the part about eating something dead.

"The fragrance of that roasting chicken would permeate the whole house, and you knew when it was done the skin would be brown and crispy and the meat would be tender and juicy."

As she says this, a sound, like a yowling animal trapped beneath my rib cage, roils up from deep inside of me. "Oh my god!" I say, sitting up straight.

Grandma blinks at me.

"That keeps happening," I tell her. "It's so embarrassing! It happened the last time I was at a PlugIn with Yaz. Luckily most people had on their Earz so not too many heard. And the ones who did thought it was a weird ringtone."

Grandma laughs.

"It's not funny!" I clutch myself around the middle as if that will stop the noise from coming out again. "This doesn't happen to anyone else I know. Something's wrong with me. I'm a freak."

"I don't know about that," she says calmly. "It sounds like your stomach is growling."

I must look horrified as I picture some rampant parasites in my guts, shrieking for blood.

Grandma lays her hand on my leg. "It's just what used to happen when people were hungry. Our stomachs would growl like that."

"For god's sake, don't tell Mom!" I almost shout. "She would never forgive me."

Grandma snorts. "Even the best inoculations can't fight the power of a good roasted chicken!"

"That makes no sense," I tell her. "I don't even know what a roasted chicken is."

"But someplace deep inside, your brain does," says Grandma. "And my description was so powerful that it woke up the eater in you for a moment. I mean, come on, human beings ate food for hundreds of thousands of years before the inoculations. It's a normal, natural response, Thalia. Nothing to be ashamed of."

"Easy for you to say. It's not happening to you."

"Oh, you'd be appalled by what noises we used to make when we ate. Burps and gurgles and farts!" she laughs. "Your grandfather Hector could belch his full name after a few beers."

"Disgusting," I say.

"Actually, a well-timed, rip-roaring fart could be quite funny, if you ask me."

I shake my head. "Oh, Grandma."

"Anyway, Thal, I wouldn't worry too much about that noise from your tummy," she says with a wink. "I'm sure it will go away." She looks down at the square of material I've knit. "In the olden days, this would have been called a pot holder."

"What'd you do with it?" I ask, trying to figure out any use for something so small.

"You used it to pick up hot pots so you didn't burn your hand."

"I always forget that food was warm." I size up the thing in my palm then laugh at how absurd the world must seem to Grandma. "Now it'd have to be a Gizmo holder."

"What a good idea!" My grandma, ever the resourceful one, takes it from me and folds it in half. "Add a strap and it would be perfect."

From upstairs, I hear pinging on the main screen. "Ugh," I groan. "Probably Mom sending more VirtuShops. She thinks I need new pants."

Grandma frowns. "I love your little skirts and jeans."

"Of course you do—they were yours."

"When I wore them, they were just farm-girl clothes, but you have such a wonderful independent sense of style." The screen pings again. "Could be a message from your dad or a friend," Grandma says. "You know it's okay if you bring your Gizmo down here."

"I like having one place with nothing yapping at me."

Grandma nods, because more than anyone else, she gets me. Mom says that's because I'm an old lady at heart, which I take as a compliment.

"I should probably go check it," I tell her with a sigh.

"That's fine, sweetie," says Grandma. "Thanks for doing family time with me."

"I'll be back," I say, but she just smiles down at the long chain of stitches gathering on her lap.

✢   ✢   ✢

Upstairs, I see Yaz's network photo blinking on the main screen, so I slide across the slick tile and accept the call. "Hey, what's going on?"

"Where have you been?" she gripes. "I pinged you, like, a million times."

"I was downstairs with my grandma. Are you on your PRC right now?" I point to her new HoverCam, which floats above her left shoulder.

"Not live," she says. "Just recording. I'll edit you out later." She flicks the camera, which sends it on a lap around the room where half the contents of her closet are scattered on the floor.

"Did you change your eyes?" I ask, studying her face, trying to pinpoint what's different today.

"Yes," she says, blinking bright blues at me. "You likey likey?"

"It's okay. I can't remember your natural color anymore."

"And my hair." She fluffs the platinum blonde streaks that used to be two-tone blue and purple. "Hey." She squints at me. "Are you on your family's main screen?"

"Yeah, so what?"

"Why can't you use your Gizmo like everybody else, so we can have a private conversation?"

"I'm not incapable," I tell her, quoting my grandmother. "Just uninterested."

"But that means I'm being broadcast into your family's living room for everyone to see." She spins and strikes a pose in black bra and panties then shouts, "Hello, Apples!" I see a new temp-i-tat of a multi-colored double helix stenciled around her midriff.

"First of all, I'm alone. And second, you're the one who now streams every moment of your life onto your Personal Reality Channel," I point out.

"Leave my PRC out of it," says Yaz. "Besides, that's different. I choose when to expose myself based on what it'll get me. Right now, I'm just exposed." She dramatically wraps her arms across her body, feigning modesty.

"Like you care," I say with a laugh.

"That's actually why I'm calling," she says as she goes back to picking through clothes. "I got a new product placement—if I can find it— and I want to wear it while I broadcast from a PlugIn. Come with me?"

"Not a PlugIn again." I slouch down and sigh.

She stands, feet wide, hands on hips, eyes boring twin holes in my forehead. "You won't go to the Spalon. . . ."

"Boring."

"You don't like EntertainArenas. . . ."

"Too crowded."

"You can't stand TopiClubs. . . ."

"Old hat."

She snickers. "The only thing *old hat* is your impossibly outdated lingo, Miss Apple."

"Got it from my grandma," I brag.

"No!" She widens her eyes in mock surprise.

"Fo' shizzle," I tell her, which reduces her to a fit of giggles.

"You did not just say that."

"Straight from the Relics," I admit. "We could go there and watch old 2-D movies."

"Those things give me a headache. Anyway, can't we do something relevant to our own demographic?"

"You only think those things are relevant because your algorithm says you'll like them."

"No, Thalia," Yaz says slowly, like I'm an idiot. "My algorithm says I'll like Spalons and EntertainArenas and PlugIns because I do. Most people our age do."

"Well, there's the problem," I tell her. "I don't like most people our age, so . . ."

"You don't give them a chance."

I slump down further on the stool. "They think I'm weird."

"That's because you are weird," she says.

I ignore her and lean close to the Eye. "Have you ever thought you might like something the algorithm doesn't even know about?"

"Like what?" she asks with a snort. "Reading books?"

That cracks me up.

"Come on, Thal," Yaz whines. "I'm sick of being home. My mom is driving me bonkers, and I want to get this product placement going, and there's a new game that just launched and . . ."

I cross my arms and stare at her. "Give me one good reason I won't be bored off my ass there."

"It's new! Jilly, send Thalia info about PlugIn 42," she tells her cyber assistant. A live video feed from the PlugIn pops up on the corner of my screen. I glance at it, see nothing of interest, and command it to close.

Sensing my lack of enthusiasm, Yaz says, "It's in the West Loop. You'll like that."

I sit up a bit because she's piqued my interest. "I thought it was just a bunch of abandoned buildings around there."

Yaz plucks items of clothing from her pile and tosses them over her shoulder as she says, "Isn't that what you like? Old abandoned crap that nobody cares about anymore?"

"You make it sound like a bad thing."

"I heard it was a retail area. Restaurant equipment and textiles or something. You could probably find lots of weird stuff. Oh, here it is!" She slides her legs into a black jumpsuit then stands and zips it from ankle to neck. "It's made from recycled inner tubes." She steps back and models her outfit for the camera. "How do I look?"

"Tired." I snort. "Get it? Tired? Like you're made from tires!"

"Really?" she says, but I can see that she's trying not to grin.

"Okay, not my best material," I admit.

"Just come with me, would you? Maybe you'll like this one."

"Fat chance."

Yaz siddles up to the HoverCam and cradles it in her palm. "Thalia, my little kilobyte, if you never leave the confines of your home, how can we have any fun?"

"I have fun," I say.

She swats her camera away. "By text chatting with a bunch of cyber ninja freakazoids? You guys don't even use video."

"That's to protect our privacy, and anyway the Dynasaurs are not freakazoids," I say, but then I reconsider. "Okay, so a lot of them are pretty strange. But they're my friends."

She rolls her eyes. "Friends are supposed to be fun, Thal. Look it up. It's part of the definition. Which is why I . . ." Yaz does a goofy dance in the middle of her room. "Am the best friend there ever was!"

I can't help but laugh. Yaz has always been amusing if nothing else. "That may be true, but we have a different kind of fun in our little cyber group."

She drops her arms. "No you don't. All the Dynasaurs do is talk about how great things used to be and how everything sucks now, then they try to figure out how to break stuff so the rest of us can't have fun either."

"There's more to it than that," I argue, but only halfheartedly because basically she's right.

Yaz shoves some stuff in her bag and says, "Anyway, would you just come with me? Hack the PlugIn security if it makes you happy." Then she looks at me, forlorn. "Please? I don't want to go alone."

"Okay, alright, save it." Our friendship has been the same since we met in toddler social time, where she constantly dragged me away from dismantling toys in a corner so she would have someone beside her. Plus, at heart, I think she believes she's doing me a favor. That someday I'll actually like something she drags me to. And sometimes I have to begrudgingly admit that I do enjoy myself, which is probably why I eventually give in. "Fine," I say, acting way more annoyed than I am. "I'll go with you. But it better be interesting."

"Oh goody!" she squeals and dances. Then she stops and stares at me for a moment. "And try to wear something less embarrassing."

"Hey!" I protest but she disconnects, leaving me yelling at a blank screen.

ψ   ψ   ψ

In my bedroom, I command the screen into a mirror and study my reflection, wondering if Yaz and my mom could be right about my clothes. They think I should be embarrassed by the way I dress because it's different, but the truth is, I don't want to look like everybody else. Especially when the rest of me is totally ordinary. My skin isn't dark or light, just plain warm brown. My hair isn't straight or curly, just long dark-brown waves over my shoulders. I have Grandma Grace's narrow eyes, but mine are green like Grandma Apple's. And when I'm happy, I have Papa Peter's big smile just like my mom. But my chin with its little cleft and the dimple on my left cheek come from my dad, which Grandma Apple says is a carbon copy of my other grandfather, Hector, the only one in my family who didn't make it through the wars.

I could cut my hair into some asymmetrical chop like other girls my age. Change my eyes or my skin or get some body art. But I'm sick of the holes and implants and ever-fading temp-i-tats everyone is obsessed with. My body's not a screen. Beside, the inocs are bad enough. I don't want anybody else poking me to rearrange my genetic makeup. Plus, the ways kids my age try to distinguish themselves just makes them look more alike to me.

Another tiny yawp burbles up from my stomach. I wrap my arms around my belly and press my lips closed to try to stop it, but I can't. It's like a speedboat motoring up my alimentary canal with noise from the engine echoing off my inner organs. My skirt isn't the thing that's going to embarrass me, so why should I bother changing clothes?

I turn off the mirror and figure I better find my Gizmo if I'm going to leave the house. "Astrid, wake up," I command since I know it's buried somewhere in my room. Within two seconds, the muffled voice of my PCA is begging for attention. I yank at the tangles of my comforter and clothes piled on my bed until my Gizmo drops to the floor and Astrid declares, "Sixteen new items!" while persistently flashing her screen. I don't totally get the draw of a twenty-four-hour personal cyber assistant. To me they're just nanotech with personalities more artificial than most humans. Which is why I reprogrammed mine to speak only when spoken to.

"Show messages," I command. Astrid pulls up my message center and runs through new assignments for biochem, lit, and recent history (which I tell her to save for later) and a bunch of crap, especially Mom's VirtuShops, which I run through so I can get rid of them.

"Lame," I mutter when Astrid chirps, "You'd look great in these!" and flashes pix of me digitally modeling a pair of navy blue PolyVisq pants. "Did you lose weight?" she coos over my virtual self in slick red ElastiVinyl leggings. As if I would be caught dead in those. And the gaggiest of all: "Girl, those make your butt look scrumptious!" she says about my pixilated rear end in purple Teflon trousers. "Delete! Delete! Delete!" I command. When that's done, I tell Astrid to go to sleep.

It's not that I hate technology, just the kind that never leaves you alone. Like Yaz's new HoverCam. So, as soon as Astrid's happily snoozing wavy gray lines across my Gizmo screen, I switch to a stealth server so I can log on to the Dynasaurs network, using my hacker name, HectorProtector.

My dad is the one who showed me how to access these private, hidden channels without being traced. When I was twelve, he took me to an electronics graveyard, where I stood in disbelief at the mountain of motherboards, cascade of keyboards, and sea of screens. We picked through the surprisingly well-organized piles of digital detritus until we had everything we needed to build an old-fashioned homemade tablet from scratch, which dad called a jalopy because it reminded him of the beat-up old cars that guys like his great-grandfather built and raced way back in the 1950s. Next, Dad showed me how to access the Dynasaurs chat room so I could take my jalopy out for a spin without being traced. When I asked him why he was showing me how to talk to the enemies of One World, he said he wanted me to understand that One World's appearance of total market domination was only as good as everyone's acceptance.

These are the skeptics, he told me. *The ones who will question the system and keep it honest if it becomes corrupt.*

If One World wants complete freedom on the Web so they can dominate the global marketplace, then they have to let everyone else have access, too. Which is why it's legal for the Dynasaurs to exist, even if what they do sometimes is against the law. *Their existence is a prime example of why Libertarianism works,* Dad told me. If there were no outlets for the skeptics One World would be perceived as a corporate dictator and more people might rebel. It just so happens, One World is very good at distracting most people from questioning the system by keeping everyone's belly full and brain entertained. Except for the Dynasaurs. Their greatest source of entertainment is throwing wrenches in One World systems. And that means people like my dad are continually trying to outsmart the Dynasaurs by creating better cyber security. Honestly, I think my dad likes the elaborate chess game he's playing with these guys more than he likes making new products.

Now when I log on to the Dynasaurs network, I don't use a jalopy like I used to. Instead, I figured out how to crack the operating system of my Gizmo and reconfigured it to hop from stealth server to stealth server all over the world. So, within seconds of logging on, I'm having an untraceable conversation with my pal AnonyGal.

> Hey HP was that you who pranked the ProPool Meet-Up
> Site last wk?

Unlike a lot of hackers, I work alone and I don't leave signatures. This is a point of contention among some Dynasaurs who think that not signing your work is cowardly. I think those people get some weird kind of rush off the cat-and-mouse game they play with cyber security. Constantly changing servers, wiping cyber lives clean, and re-creating online identities seems like a lot of rigmarole for a little infamy. Personally, I'd rather stay under the One World radar, but I don't mind recognition in the Dynasaurs forum every now and again, depending on who's asking. And since AnonyGal has been around on the chat boards for a long time, I feel safe texting back.

What makes you think it was me?

AG writes,

> Had all the hallmarks of an HP smack. Clean, elegant, and hilarious.

I never thought about my pranks having personality, but AG is kind of right. The hack was supersimple but had big results. I found a back door in the Procreation Pool Meet-Up Site system, then changed a few lines of the algorithm so that instead of being paired up with someone who shares the majority of your interests, you'd get a request from someone who was completely different. I write,

> Grandma always said that opposites attract.

AG sends me a smiley face with the message,

> Wish I could have been a spybot on some of those dates! ☺

The thing is, I wasn't trying to be unkind. I really do think it's more interesting to meet someone who is different than yourself, and I'd like to believe that maybe my hack made at least one match in digital heaven before my work was undone by security agents.

As I browse around the general topix board, I see that earlier tonight AnonyGal posted a call to action:

> Anybody see the new product launches in this week's ICM dox? Looks like fruit ripe for the picking? Who's in?

I haven't bothered to look at my ICM dox—I never do—and I don't like to join group hacks where people band together to find loopholes and back doors in the code of new products, so they can sabotage them before the launch. Some of the time it works, but most of the time One World finds and fixes the problems before the Dynasaurs act. I respect how AnonyGal works, though. She's a master at delegating tasks to find holes in One World code. Basically, the reverse of how I work, which is probably why I like her. That and the fact that there are very few girl hackers my age.

I figure she must be young because she doesn't sign off like the old-timers with the Svalbard symbol—a tiny sprout emerging from a seed above the word *Remember.* For the longest time I didn't know what I was looking at when I'd see that symbol. To me, it looked like a weird alien fetus escaping from a pod. But then my dad explained the symbol and told me that it's in honor of the Svalbard Rebellion, which happened after the last remaining seed vault near the Arctic Circle went belly up. World governments fought long and hard over who would control the seed vault until One World swooped in and promised to feed any population that capitulated to One World controlling their food supply, including the vault. One by one the governments agreed to let One World take over in order to save their starving masses.

Then twelve years ago, there was a rumor that One World destroyed the vault and all its contents, which sparked a rebellion. Of course, that ended badly when One World retaliated against the protesters, which drove the movement underground. My dad says lots of people who took part in the rebellion have a tattoo of the symbol somewhere on their bodies. Since lots of older members in the chat rooms use the symbol in their signatures, I assume the old-time Dynasaurs are a legacy of that rebellion.

Then there are the newbies like me and AnonyGal. No tattoos and sign-off symbols for us. Just some girls looking for a place to hack in peace. I bet AnonyGal never worries about what she wears, either. I finish cruising the chats, and since there's nothing else of interest going on, I log off for now and get ready to meet Yaz.

✤   ✤   ✤

Before I leave the house, I pop into the basement to say good-bye to Grandma.

"Heading out?" she asks.

"Yaz talked me into going to a PlugIn," I tell her, feeling a little bad for abandoning her.

But Grandma smiles brightly and says, "Good! You should spend more time with people your age."

"I have no idea why people go to those things," I admit. "Anything you can do there, you can do at home."

"They're like restaurants or coffee shops were for my generation," Grandma says. "You could make the same stuff at home, but some-times it was nice to go out and be around other people."

"If you say so."

"I made you something." She holds out my red pot holder trans-formed into a Gizmo-sized pouch with a long gray strap.

"This is great!" I grab it and slip it diagonally across my body. "Look, it's perfect!" I tuck my sleeping Gizmo inside.

"One of a kind, just like you, my dear."

I rub the soft fibers between my fingers. "People used to make stuff all the time, didn't they?"

Grandma nods. "Mostly because they had to, but sometimes just for the sake of art."

"Art," I say, relishing the word. "Sounds fun."

"It was," she says. "But your generation finds their own ways to have fun, don't you?"

"According to Yaz, we do." My stomach makes the weird yodelly sound again. I look at my grandma, who's trying not to laugh as I clutch my belly. "Do you miss it?" I ask her.

"Miss what, honey?"

"You know, eating, cooking. Food, I guess." The rumbling in my stomach threatens like the first rolls of distant thunder.

"Well, as your mother says, foodless nutrition is for the greater good." Grandma gives a little shrug. "So it's silly to pine away for something we can't all have. But between me and you?" She holds my gaze for a moment, then she whispers, "Yes, I do."

I hesitate by the door, my stomach gnawing at itself as if groping for something it can't quite reach. "If you could eat anything at all," I ask my grandmother, "what would it be?"

She thinks for a moment. "That's a hard question," she says. "Sort of like asking a mother to pick a favorite child, but . . ." She nibbles on the side of her lip. "I suppose if I had to choose, I would say an apple."

"An apple?" I ask with a laugh. "Like us?"

"No," she says. "The real thing. A perfect, red, round, crisp, tart apple."

I lean down and hug my grandmother good-bye. I know that kind of interpersonal touch is weird and anachronistic, but it's something that she and I like to do. She says it reminds her of the past, and being held by her makes me feel good in a way I can't quite explain. Almost like I'm a little kid again and nothing in the world can hurt me.

"Thank you, honey," she says, patting me on the back. "Have fun and be careful."

❧   ❧   ❧

"West Loop, PlugIn 42," I tell Astrid when I climb into my Smaurto.

"Got it," she says perkily then connects herself to the Smaurto navigator. My seat belt fastens, the doors lock, and the garage opens. "PlugIn 42, here we come!" she announces as the car pulls out of the driveway. "So, what do you wanna do?" she asks.

"Nothing," I mutter, which of course doesn't compute with a nano brain.

"Music?" she asks. "Movie? Game? Networking?"

"Open the window," I say, and my window goes down, letting in the cool evening air. Since it's nearly spring, the hologram trees on our block have been programmed to bud. Dad wants to change them to cherry trees this year, but Mom is voting for magnolias. The last time magnolias were programmed, Grandma wrinkled her nose and said, *Too cloying. Nothing like the real thing.*

"Music?" Astrid asks again. "Movie? Game? Networking?"

"No," I tell her. "Be quiet."

In the silence, I gaze at the half-moon perched above the rooftops with their whirling Whisson Windmills pulling water out of the skies. A few stars send their fuzzy light across the continuum. What was Earth like when that light was being generated? Lush and green and teeming with life-forms Grandma talks about. The furry, the feathered. Some armored like small tanks crawling over moss and rocks and fallen logs. Minuscule carbon-based helicopters buzzing flower to flower. Every creature on a genetically encoded mission to propagate. Now all that remains is the light of stars snuffed before the animals and plants died out. And the moon, a sterile rock. Just the kind of place my mother would love.

The Smaurto rounds the corner toward the highway and takes the entry ramp. The stars begin to fade from view, pushed out by the giant glaring screens along the road. Newsfeeds and ads flash by. Then Astrid pings awake, which I've programmed her to do when certain people call. "Your dad is calling!" she cries. I have to find a way to de-perkify her.

"Accept," I say.

Dad's face fills the onboard screen. I can see that he's in his Smaurto, too. He's got the seat reclined, so mostly I see his chin, which is covered with graying stubble. "I was just heading home," he tells me. "I saw that you were in transit."

"I'm going out with Yaz," I tell him. "How was your day?"

He sits up a bit and smiles at me. "Good. Busy." Lines, like sunbursts permanently etched in stone, crinkle at the edges of his eyes.

Grandma Apple calls these crow's-feet and says my grandfather Hector had them, too. Hector died trying to protect their family farm so I never met him, but she's told me so much—how he could coax green shoots from the earth and cultivate crops when others had given up—that I feel as if I know him.

"We're in the final phase of our new product," Dad says proudly.

"What is it?" I ask, feigning interest because if I don't, our conversation will be very short.

"Can't talk about it over the waves," he says. "But I'll bring it home soon. We'll be a test family."

"Mom will like that."

"You might, too."

"Maybe."

"What did you and Grandma do for family night?"

"She taught me to knit. We made this." I lift up the Gizmo holder. "See, now I won't lose Astrid."

Dad laughs. "That's perfect for you. Old-school meets nanotech."

"Exactly," I say, happy that he gets it.

"All right, then," he says through a yawn. "Have a good time."

We both sign off just as my car takes the ramp toward the old West Loop.

⚜   ⚜   ⚜

Astrid finds a parking space on a street full of abandoned buildings with dark windows staring like the vacant eyes of starving masses I've seen in historic pix at the Relics. I look up and down the street, wondering if Astrid got it wrong this time, but then I spot Yaz, her newly blonde locks twinkling like starlight amid the stark surroundings.

She waves at me and hurries over, her HoverCam close behind. "Thank god you're here!"

"I don't want that thing on me." I point at the camera.

She grabs it and shoves it in her bag. "This place gives me the creeps!"

"Looks kind of interesting to me."

"You *would* like this." Her eyes roam up and down my outfit. "I thought you were going to change."

I hold out my arms so she can get a good look. "Same ol' me."

"Someday I'm dragging you to Fiyo's Spalon for a makeover," she threatens as we walk toward a flashing green 42, which is the only light nearby. "God, there's nobody around for miles."

"We should go explore."

Yaz pulls her Gizmo out of her bag and asks, "Jilly, what's around here?"

Jilly, Yaz's cyber assistant, is quiet for a rare moment, then she says, "PlugIn 42 looks interesting." Yaz raises both eyebrows at me.

"Jilly only knows what someone programmed her to know. She has no idea what's waiting to be discovered. Out there." I point down an empty street. "In the real world."

"This is plenty real for me," Yaz says and yanks on the manual door under the flashing 42.

As soon as we're inside a dimly lit hall, Jilly starts yapping about everyone Yaz knows who's inside and everyone who she might like to know based on some Venn diagram of interests.

"Why don't you let me crack your OS and reprogram that thing for you," I propose for the millionth time so I don't have to compete with Jilly while I'm with Yaz.

"No way. I like her," Yaz says for the million-and-first time, but she turns down Jilly's volume to appease me.

"Don't you think it would be fun to do what our grandparents used to do?" I ask as we walk down the hall. "Like when they'd go someplace and meet random new people they knew nothing about?"

"Why would you want to slog through intros and small talk just to see if you might—what are the odds, something like five thousand to one—that you'd even like a real person you meet at random?" Yaz asks. "If you'd turn on your locator, Astrid could narrow down your options before you put any real effort in. Think of it as efficiency."

"But all that gets you is more of the same. If you take a chance on that one person in five thousand, you might meet someone totally unexpected who's had entirely different experiences than you. They could open you up to a whole new world and convince you to try something you've never done before. Or something you think you hate but that you end up loving!"

Yaz grins at me.

"What?" I ask.

"You just described you and me," she says. "We like totally different things, and I'm constantly begging you to try something new."

I start to argue with her, but I can't because she's right. The funny thing is, every time I think Yaz and I are growing apart, she surprises me. Like when she decided we should join a retro-team to play real-time hide-and-seek in abandoned schools or when she organized a scavenger hunt for dragons in an area once called Chinatown. When she comes up with stuff like that, I wonder if she's got a secret side lurking beneath her every-girl exterior.

"Wow," says Yaz when we turn the corner and enter a huge cavernous room. Even I'm impressed. "I've got to turn on for this." She digs the HoverCam out of her bag and launches it. I stay well behind her so I'm not in the frame as we walk inside.

The ceilings are at least fifty feet high with a maze of old exposed duct work around the perimeter. Along the walls and in the center of the ceiling are large screens running ads for new games and chat rooms and movies. At least thirty escalators are scattered around the room, each leading to landings where people sit on plush, multicolored settees, jabbering away at their screens.

"Vertical. Layered. Integrated," I say, nodding at the clever design.

"Where should we sit?" Yaz wonders aloud.

We walk around, our necks craned upward, looking for a spot to park ourselves, but the place is packed. "Up there," I say, pointing. "Fourth level on the right."

"Good thing I'm wearing my One World Rugged Life MicroFiber Boots." Yaz kicks up a heel as she steps onto the escalator. "They're perfect for a long flight of stairs," she says directly to her camera.

"You're not walking," I say loud enough for the HoverCam mic to pick up.

She gives a fake laugh and tosses her hair then runs up a few steps. Her dumbed-down Personal Reality Channel persona grates on me. She's smarter and more interesting than she appears from all the useless fashion chatter. But I get it. More viewers equal more products equal a better shot at a good corporate gig. It's a game, one that I'm hopeless at playing.

We pass each landing where people interact with their screens, sometimes laughing out loud or rearing back when an avatar bites it in a virtual battle. They only glance up at us if their cyber assistants ping them when we walk by. On the fourth landing, we wind our way through six back-to-back seats to a spot near the rail. I motion at the HoverCam.

Yaz bags it and grouches, "Why do you have such a thing about PRCs? You're my friend. You're part of my life. You should be on my channel."

I give her my standard retort. "I value personal privacy."

"So antiquated," she mumbles. "Which way do you want to face?"

"Out," I tell her, pointing to the side of the empty S-shaped couch that faces the railing, not the wall. "I like to look down on everyone."

Yaz snorts.

"Not like *that*," I say. "I mean I like to watch people."

"That's called lurking," she says. I don't argue the difference be-tween real-time people watching and virtual lurking, because to Yaz, those boundaries are blurry. She plunks down on her side of the seat and docks her Gizmo next to the big screen then blinks into the Eye to log on. "Want to play a new game called Master of Minions: Death Date with Hellfire."

"Sounds horrible."

"Don't know until you try." She slips on bright pink Earz that have been molded to the exact shape of her real ears.

"Are those new?" I ask.

"They're made from Just-Like-Skin and are so comfortable!" She mugs for her camera then remembers that she stashed it and she re-laxes. "What do you think?"

"Cute," I have to admit. "The color looks good with your hair."

"I heard they're coming out with a line that looks like the ears of extinct animals, with fur and everything."

"Creepy," I say with a little shiver.

"Speaking of creepy, did I tell you that Miyuki Shapiro's parents are applying to have a second? Can you believe that?"

"So?"

"So? They're old. I mean Miyuki is our age. Well, sixteen, but still. Isn't that weird to want another baby when you already have one kid?"

"People used to have more than one kid all the time," I say.

"And we all know where that got us," Yaz says. "Anyway, Miyuki is freaking out. She's like, 'Am I not good enough? Why do you need a second?' And what if her parents die and she has to take care of the second and pay for all its Synthamils and inocs for the rest of its life?"

"I'm sure they have enough money, and they're not going to die soon," I say.

"Oh please, my mother said childbirth nearly killed her," says Yaz. "I don't know why anyone ever gets pregnant anyway." She turns around and scrolls through the list Jilly has generated of the people from Yaz's circle who are plugged in.

"Um, propagation of species," I say.

"Yeah, yeah, but you get fat, then it hurts like hell, and as a reward you have to take care of a squalling baby."

"They add Arousatrol to your Synthamil when you enter the Procreation Pool. It adjusts your hormones so you want to, you know . . ." I blush a little. "Plus, once you give birth, your body naturally produces stuff like prolactin and vasopressin and oxytocin so you attach to the kid."

"Paging Dr. Apple," Yaz says and shoots me a withering glance, which means I'm being too geeky for my own social good. "I can think of fifty horrible things I'd rather do than have a kid."

"Really?" I ask, wrenching my body around until I'm facing the same direction as she is. "You never want to enter the Procreation Pool?" When Yaz and I were little, we thought it was an actual pool where grown-ups swam around, looking for a mate.

"I didn't say that," she says. "I want the Arousatrol so I can fall in love, but I'm definitely requesting birth control." She glances over her shoulder at me. "Do you want a kid?"

"Not right away. Mom and Dad want me to wait to enter the Procreation Pool until my late twenties, after I'm done with all my coursework and I have a good job. But, I'm the last Apple. If I don't have a kid, there won't be any more of us on Earth."

"There are plenty of people in the world," says Yaz. "And most of them are online right now."

"Yeah, yeah," I say, uninterested.

"Remember our motto," says Yaz in a mock serious voice, "'One World, One Big Human Family.'"

I laugh. "You'd never take a shot at One World that way if your HoverCam was on."

"Of course not," she says. "I wouldn't get any product placements if I was a smart-ass on-screen."

"But you'd be so much more entertaining that way."

"Only to you," she says with a shrug and turns away.

⚘   ⚘   ⚘

I don't blink on to the PlugIn network like everyone else at 42 has done. Instead, I use my Gizmo to find a stealth server, which takes me into the system through a back door some other Dynasaur has left open for people like me. Now I can hack around manually without the system recognizing my voice or tracking my preferences via Astrid while I lurk around legit One World sites for a while. After a half hour of cruising games, scrolling through movie rooms, and my half-assed attempt at joining a virtual DiaLogOn under the name Xerxes about whether the letter *X* should be eliminated from English (to which I post, "Excising the letter X would exacerbate the inexorable extinction of text!" but no one finds it funny except me), I've had enough.

I have no idea why every night thousands of kids my age sit around PlugIns in every population center around the world, doing the same dumb things—making avatars and playing games and chatting about the insular little worlds we've created—but never really interacting. Grandma says humans are not much different than herd animals. *Give them some grass,* she says, *and they'll graze.*

I hack into the Relics archive and search for videos of herd animals to see what they were like. I find old footage of sheep, fluffy white critters with kind black eyes, huddled together on a thick carpet of green. They contentedly snack on the grass, chomping away, no cares or thoughts about what's going on around them, and for a moment, I think it might be nice every once in a while to put my head down and be part of the flock. But then out of the left corner of the screen, another animal zips into view. It's a black-and-white dog running low, which startles the sheep. They charge, cloudlike down the side of the hill with the dog zigzagging behind them. And I think, *I don't want to be part of that herd. I want to be that dog.* And that gives me an idea.

Quickly, I hack around until I find the PlugIn admin pass and crack the security code with a program I wrote. It's illegal to use programs like these to play games for free or download proprietary content without paying, but I have no intention of stealing. As my dad says, *OW owns the content not the conduit,* and anyone can use the conduit, if they can find a way in. So what I'm about to do isn't technically illegal. I'm simply exercising my right to free speech. Or so I tell myself.

Once I'm in, I upload the video of the sheep onto the PlugIn server, which controls the ads being projected onto the ceiling and walls. Then from my Gizmo, I temporarily take over the PlugIn server, and I type, "Look Up!" The message appears on everyone's screen simultaneously. People rear back like startled sheep and lift their eyes to the ceiling where the grazing herd is being chased by the dog.

People look at each other and back at their screens, which they smack and curse. They shout voice commands to stop the video that now appears on every screen in the room, but I've set it on a repeat loop with a classic Dynasaur quote scrolling across the bottom:

> George Washington said, "If the freedom of speech
> is taken away then dumb and silent we may be led,
> like sheep to the slaughter." Don't be sheep!

Yaz glances over her shoulder at me and scowls.

"What?" I ask innocently as I disconnect and slide my Gizmo into my pouch.

She slips off one of her bright-pink Earz. "Someday you're going to get caught and slapped with a big-ass fine."

"Ewww, I'm scared," I say.

"Laugh now, but I heard some kid got caught hacking at the

EntertainArena, and his parents couldn't pay his restitution so now he's in jail."

"Your honor, I did nothing but help people engage in meaningful real-time conversation," I say in my imaginary defense as I point to all the people unplugging and talking to other people near them about what's happening. I know the chaos will only last for a few minutes more before security dismantles my work. By that time I'll be gone.

"You wouldn't think it was so great if your family couldn't pay and you got locked up," Yaz says.

"But first they'd have to catch me. And good luck with that."

On Yaz's screen, I see that security has managed to freeze the video loop on the dog in mid-stride, tongue out, looking as happy as can be, which makes me laugh. "Guess they outsmarted you," Yaz says when the dog is replaced by a spinning multicolored wheel in the center of the now black screen.

"Took them long enough."

All around us, people slip their Earz on again and settle back down to resume their virtual lives, which is my cue to get the heck out.

"Are you leaving?" Yaz asks when I stand up.

"I'm going to walk around the hood a little," I say then my stomach gurgles. I press my elbow into my gut to stifle the sounds escaping and echoing around the maze of metal in here.

Yaz blinks at me. "Was that you?"

"Was what me?" I ask, hoping to sound innocent.

"That noise. Did that come from you? Or is something wrong with these things?" She taps her Earz.

"I didn't hear it," I lie, but my cheeks flush. Forget about being caught for hacking. The worse thing I can imagine is everyone turning around to find the freak who's yawping and yowling like some long-dead sea creature come back to life. But Yaz doesn't seem too disturbed by the noise because she's already busy trying to relaunch her minion into its death date. Over the past few weeks, I've learned that the only thing to do in a situation like this is to cut out before my stomach acts up again.

"Have fun in hell," I tell her.

"You, too!" she says and waves good-bye.

⚘   ⚘   ⚘

I love exploring little abandoned pockets in the city where there are no cameras and no screens. No twenty-four-hour newsfeeds and ads. Not even the whirl of Whisson Windmills disturbs the quiet. I head south and imagine what it used to be like when people walked down sidewalks with animals on leashes and stopped at cafés for something to drink. I look in the black dusty windows, hoping to find an old abandoned real-time shop filled with things I could pick up and touch. Usually these places have been looted, but every once in a while I stumble on something strangely preserved. Like the time I found a store called Pottery Barn that had no pottery or farm animals, just dusty couches, disintegrating baskets, and rotted wooden chairs. I was disappointed because I wanted to find an antique mug, like the old green ceramic cup Grandma keeps beside her bed. She used to drink something called coffee from it as part of her morning routine—*an empty ritual*, my mother would say.

Used to be, you could pick up all the things in the store and weigh them in your hand. Compare the different colors and shapes made by some hopeful person who had to guess what other people might want instead of having people decide exactly what they want before it's produced. How funny and upside down the world used to be. *Wasteful*, my mother would say. That's what led to all the trouble. Waste and inefficiency.

I turn a corner, down a narrow street hemmed on either side by tall buildings made of metal and glass that somehow went unscathed through all the bombings. Grandma told me once that it used to be un-safe to walk around alone at night. I thought she meant during the wars, but she said no, just in life. *Wild animals?* I asked, imagining big-fanged creatures prowling the streets for food. She laughed at that. *Not in the cities,* she said. The big animals died out fast. Rats lasted longer. Some-thing called a cockroach sometimes still skitters in the darkest places.

Mostly it was other people that were the problem. They usually wanted money, she said, but sometimes other things. Sex. Or vio-lence. For protection the government forced the citizens to pay for lots of police who were out in the open looking for criminals so they had to make up laws to keep themselves busy. You could get arrested for things other than violence or fraud, like selling drugs or parking in the wrong place. *What was the matter with people?* I asked when Grandma told me this. She struggled for an answer. Finally she just shook her head and said, *That was the human condition.*

I turn another corner down an even smaller street between old brick buildings, what my father would call an alleyway. There are no big storefront windows back here, just doors, shut now, and old stair-ways and ladders called fire escapes zigzagging down from the roofs. Maybe these were apartments where people lived and in the summer they opened their windows and you could hear everybody talking, laughing, yelling, crying. You could smell what other people were cooking and see their laundry hanging out to dry. It would have been a big hot mess of humanity, as my mother would say, teeming with germs. Once I found an old cartoon at the Relics of a cat sitting on a trash can in an alley, singing under a full moon. A person got mad because the cat was interrupting his sleep, and he threw a boot at it from an open window. That was supposed to be funny back then.

I have no idea where I'm going, but I don't want to go back to find Yaz yet. I'd much rather be alone, following a tug I feel inside of me that comes from the place where that yawning hollow spot is starting to wake up. It's almost like I'm being pulled along by some invisible string. One time I found an abandoned house when I was snooping around an empty neighborhood in the South Loop. So much of the space was dedicated to eating. The place where they cooked with all its bulky gadgets and cupboards full of dishes. A separate room just for eating. Not to mention the toilet rooms. How primitive that big round open bowl seemed. Nothing like our sleek urinals of today. The thought of sitting there squeezing your insides out made me blush. Grandma told me that the hardest thing to get used to after the inocs and nutritional beverages was not using the toilet anymore. For the longest time, her body would think it needed to eliminate, but of course it didn't. There is no more waste. Efficiency in everything.

The alleyway comes to a T. I look right and left. Both are vacant stretches of cement, brick, and metal. A few long-forgotten signs hang crooked from their rusted bolts—SWANN DRY CLEANERS, FRIEDMAN'S FIX-TURES, RUG DEPOT. The left tugs at me harder, so I turn that way, happy to go farther into the abandonment. I slow down and lift my face. Something is in the air. A scent. At first it's faint. I wonder if there's a hologram park nearby, but the smell is not from synth trees or flowers. I sniff, letting my nose lead the way.

The smell gets stronger. I see a sliver of light sliding out from be-neath a door on the right side of the street, which is odd. I didn't think anybody lived down here anymore, and there's certainly nothing re-tail. Above the door, I can make out a faded red sign that says FLAV-O-RITE. I suppose it could be a lab or a manufacturer, but why so far away from the industrial center? I tiptoe to the door, which is slightly ajar. The smell surrounds me now. It's complicated with a light and flowery scent (like the elusive odor I was chasing in my dream), lay-ered over a darker, heavier smell that pulls me forward. I want to get closer to it, find its source, put my face near it so I can drink it in. The urge is so strong that I slip my fingers in the crack of the door and pull it open. Light washes over me as I step inside the building. Then, my stomach makes the craziest, loudest, most heinous noise I've ever heard. It roars, it yowls, it groans, and it gurgles like a gigantic sinkhole pulling everything nearby into its depths. I double over and grab my belly to make it stop.

I hear a crash and something scrambling. "Is somebody there?" I call, mortified that someone may have heard me. I peer into what looks like a lab. In the center, a long stainless steel table separates me from a guy, about my age, who is tangled in the legs of an overturned stool. I'm dying. More embarrassed than I've ever been in my life. I literally knocked this guy over with my freakishness.

"Sorry!" I call. "I didn't mean to scare you." He scrambles away, kicking himself loose from the stool, then gets to his feet and almost crouches behind the table as if he's ready to spring. "I saw the light, and there was this smell and . . ."

"What do you want?" he barks. His eyes are as dark as his hair, and he's dressed all in greens and browns like a tree.

"Nothing. I mean, I was just taking a walk and . . ." On the table between us, I see books, real books with paper pages. Some are fanned open. Others are stacked four or five high.

"Who are you with?" he asks, still eyeing me suspiciously, hands clenched into fists.

"No one," I say, and for the first time I feel scared. Could there still be the kind of dangerous people my grandma told me about? I slip my hand into my Gizmo holder.

"What are you doing?" he asks.

I pull out my Gizmo so he knows I can call for help.

"Don't!" he yells, pointing at the Gizmo in my hand. Then he softens. "Please."

"Then stop yelling at me!" I tell him.

He runs a hand through his messy hair, making it fall in soft curls around his ears. "You just surprised me, that's all. Nobody ever comes down here." Then he looks at me for a few seconds. "What are you doing here? What do you want?"

"I followed a smell," I tell him. "It smelled so good that I had to find it." I hang my head, embarrassed, but when I look up and see that he looks relieved, I get curious. "What are you doing here? What's the smell? Who are you?"

He licks his lips like he's nervous and says, "My name's Basil."

"Basil?" I can't help but laugh a little. "Basil what?"

He shakes the hair away from his eyes and says, "Just Basil. What's your name?"

"Tha—" I start to say, but then I decide to play his game, and I say, "Apple."

"Apple?" He lifts his eyebrows. "Apple what?"

"Just Apple," I say with a little smirk, and I think he nearly smiles.

I glance down at the table of books between us and see pictures of food. Some of it I recognize like the green, red, and yellow fruits and vegetables from old-timey children's books, the deep glossy brown of cooked meat from ancient advertisements at the Relics, and photos of puffy golden loaves of bread, like the ones Grandma showed me when I was little. Suddenly my mouth is full of saliva and my stomach goes ballistic, like that singing cartoon cat in the alley. I'm half afraid Basil will throw a boot at me. Embarrassed, I press my hands over my mouth to stop the torrent of noise coming from my insides, but Basil comes around the table and touches my arm. We stare at each other, and I shiver when he whispers, "You, too?"

 ✳ ✳ ✳

 41

Basil and I sit next to each other at the table. Between us are a stack of books and a little whirring device connected by a thin coil of hose to boxy stainless steel cabinets lining the wall.

"So I'm not the only one?" I ask and feel the kind of relief that I imagine survivors coming out of bunkers after bombings must have felt during the wars.

He nods.

"How long has it been happening to you?"

"A while," is all he says.

"And are there others?"

Again he nods.

I struggle to grasp that there are other people walking around with yowling bellies just like me. I wonder who they are, where they are, and what they do when it happens to them. But my biggest question is why.

"My mom's a researcher," I tell him. "She says my metabolism probably shifted." I lift the back of my shirt. "She's collecting data on me right now."

He winces when I show him the patch. "I would never let someone put that on me," he says, and I assure him it doesn't hurt. "That's not what I mean. You shouldn't be made to feel abnormal, like you're the one who needs to change." He sounds aggravated.

I lower my shirt. "But there has to be an explanation. Don't you want to know why?"

"I know why," he says.

"You do?" I lean closer, ready to be wowed by the answer. "Tell me."

"Because we're human."

"Oh that," I say, unimpressed. I pick up the funny little machine on the table. It's boxy with slats on the top and some kind of scanner thingy on the bottom but no screen anywhere. "What's this?"

Basil grabs it from me and puts it on his lap out of sight. "Just a thing."

I pull a book closer. "Where did you get all these?" I flip the heavy glossy pages. Not only are there pictures of food, most of which I've never seen before, but also instructions for how to make everything. "Half cup minced onion," I read. "One clove garlic. One green pepper." I laugh. "Sounds like a magic potion."

Basil reaches over and slams the book closed.

"Hey," I say. "I was looking at that."

He stacks all the books together and pushes them away from me. "Listen," he says, nervously. "You should probably get out of here. Won't someone be wondering where you are?" He points to my back. "They might come looking for you."

I touch the patch through my clothes. "It doesn't have a locator," I tell him. "And I told my Gizmo to go to sleep. I hate people knowing where I am all the time. It's an affront to my personal liberty."

He barks an unexpected laugh.

"You think that's funny?" I ask.

"Well, yeah," he says. "You just took One World's legal justification for everything they get away with and turned it against them."

"'Corporations are people, too!'" I quote OW's favorite defense. "Most people don't get that." I smile shyly, wondering if he might secretly be a Dynasaur.

"Most people are stupid," he says.

We grin at each other, but I have to look away and pull a book from the pile to stop myself from reaching out to touch him, which is what I suddenly feel like doing. It makes me nervous.

"Is this what you do when your body makes that noise?" I open the pages and stare at the pictures. "You look at these? Does that make it stop?"

Basil ducks his head and averts his eyes, but then he looks up at me through the soft curls across his forehead. "Sometimes it makes it worse."

"Then why . . ."

"How long has it been happening to you?" he asks.

"A few weeks. Maybe more." Then it's my turn to be embarrassed. "It's getting worse," I nearly whisper.

"It's been happening to me for longer than that," he says.

"Maybe you need your Synthamil formula recalibrated...."

He stares at me for a moment then shakes his head and says, "*Re*calibrated?" as if incredulous.

"Yeah, they can tweak your personal formula to optimize—"

"Believe me," he says, turning away. "I've seen what they do to the others like us, and it's not about calibrating optimal formulas. First you'll bounce around from specialist to specialist who'll claim they each have the answer, but nothing works. They'll say it's all in your mind. They lock you up. Drug you. Make you think you're crazy. But we're not crazy." He stares at me defensively. "Being hungry is the most natural thing in the world."

I flinch at the word *hungry,* my mother's least favorite in the English language.

"But sometimes..." Basil trails off with almost a wild look in his eye. "Sometimes, it's so bad that I have to do something. I just can't help it." Sheepishly, he pulls the little machine out and opens one of the books, which is different than all the others. This one has pictures of food, but underneath each photo an old-fashioned QR code has been pasted to the page. Delicately he turns the pages until he comes to a two-dimensional photograph of a tall round thing. It looks almost like a fancy white hat decorated with pink and purple flowers and curlicues.

"This is a cake," he says. "People used to eat it to celebrate their birthdays." He runs the machine over the QR code. The device whirs and clicks, then slowly a subtle scent floats out from the slats on top. I have to sniff several times to catch it. First it's sweet. High in my head, almost like the smell of hologram flowers that are programmed too strong. But there's something else in the smell. Something deeper, heavier. I don't have any words for it, but it makes my mouth go moist.

"This is incredible!" I say and grab the book from him. "What else do you have in here?" I flip the pages until I come to a plump brown bird-shaped thing. "Is this a roasted chicken?" He nods, and I hold out my hand for the machine, but Basil won't give it to me. "Come on," I plead. "Please."

He relents and hands it over. I do what he did, slowly scanning the QR code, then I close my eyes and wait while the smell is released. "Oh my god," I moan. "It's sort of salty, like the Simu-Sea at One World, Vacation World," I say. "And smoky, maybe? Like it's been over a fire." I pull in a deep breath. "And there's citrus and HoloGrass. And something else." I sniff again, uncertain. "I don't know how to say it, but it makes me think of my grandma's hug. Like the smell of her warm neck when I'm sad."

I open my eyes and see Basil watching me with a broad smile, which changes his face entirely. Instead of a heavy furrowed brow and brooding eyes under those dark curls, his eyes are wide and sparkling, and his smile flashes. A new feeling ripples deep in my stomach. Like going over a hill too fast in my Smaurto. I squirm a little.

"Want to smell something even better?" he asks, and I nod eagerly as he flips the pages. "This is called a chocolate brownie." He passes the scanner over the code under a photo of a flattish brown rectangle.

I close my eyes and inhale. "Oh my god," I say and move my face closer to the machine.

"I know," he says.

I get even closer, pulling in the amazing smell, trying to find a way to describe what's happening in my nose, my mouth, the pit of my stomach, but I have no words. No way to categorize it except to say that I want more. It starts to fade, and I shoot forward, wanting every last remnant of the scent. I lean closer and closer until Basil and I bump heads. We both fall back, rubbing our foreheads and laughing nervously. He reaches out and touches my scalp.

"You okay?"

His touch makes all the little hairs on the back of my neck stand on end.

"Yeah," I say quietly, biting my lip. "I'm okay. You?"

He takes his hand away and his fingers seem to tremble. "I'm fine."

"That was incredible," I say. "What was it called again?"

"A brownie. It was made with chocolate."

"My grandmother told me about chocolate!" I say excitedly. "She said it was like nothing else."

"Everything I've ever smelled with chocolate in it has been mind-blowing."

I turn the little machine over to study how it might work. "Where did you get this thing?"

"I made it," he says.

My mouth drops open. "You made it?" He nods. "How?"

"You really want to know?"

I nod eagerly.

Basil gets up and opens the door to one of the stainless steel cabinets mounted to the wall. Inside are hundreds of small upside-down brown bottles, stacked ten high and held in place by metal clamps. Tubes run from each bottle to a series of larger hoses, which all connect to the coil snaking out the bottom of the cabinet to the device on the table. "I think this was a food lab," he tells me. "All of these bottles contain aroma compounds and flavorants that they used to create different smells and tastes."

I stand beside him to get a better look at the labels on each bottle: diacetyl, benzaldehyde, limonene, ethylvanillin, ethyl maltol. "But how do you know which ones smell like what?"

"I found something called the SuperScent database at the Relics, which tells me exactly how much of each compound to use to create a specific scent, like chocolate. Then I collected all these old cook books with recipes and pictures of food, and I built this scanner and..."

"Oh I get it!" I say, holding the scanner in my palm. "You made a QR code for each picture, which tells the machine how much of each compound to release into the tube...."

"Exactly!" he says. "So I just run the scanner over the code, and the machine mixes up the smell."

"This is amazing!"

"Not really. Most of the smells probably aren't right. I have to guess a lot."

"Basil. I'm serious. This is the coolest thing I've ever seen. People would flock to this. It's better than anything you can do at an EntertainArena or PlugIn! People could come here and put together an entire menu!"

"No," he says and shuts the cabinet door. "This is not for the general public." He unplugs the device and starts stacking up the books on the table.

"But why?" I grab the rest of the books and follow him through a door on the other side of the lab.

Basil ignores my question as he fiddles with a small key to unlock a cupboard. One by one, he slides the books carefully onto the shelf. I hand him my books, too. Then he takes the machine out of his pocket and locks it in a drawer. When everything is put away, he leans against the counter, crosses his arms, and stares at me with that dark, brooding look from earlier.

"Did you really just stumble in here?"

"Of course. How else would I have gotten here? It's not like it's on a map."

He studies me for a moment, shaking his head. "I might be an idiot, but I think I believe you."

"Good," I say. "Because I'm not lying. Who do you think I am, anyway?"

He bites the side of his thumb. "I don't know, but I don't think you're an Analog, are you?"

"A what-a-log? Is that anything like a Dynasaur?"

"What's a Dynasaur?"

"Never mind," I say, disappointed.

"Listen, there's a group of us. . . ." He turns and opens another drawer then takes out what looks like an actual sheet of paper and an old wooden graphite pencil. "If you want to learn more about what we do . . ."

Excitement tingles over my skin at the thought of meeting more people like us.

He writes something down with his hand and gives it to me.

"Is this real?" I caress the smooth surface between my thumb and fingers. He nods. "What I am supposed to do with it?"

"Read it."

I stare at the words printed on the page.

Analogs
Friday
6:00 p.m.
1601 South Halsted

"What's it mean?" I ask.

"Information about a meeting."

"But where?"

"The address is there."

"I don't know where that is," I tell him. "Which Loop is it in?"

"You'll have to head west."

"Can't we just link Gizmos?" I reach for mine.

"I don't have one."

I almost drop the paper. "What do you mean? How's that possible? Everyone has a Gizmo."

He raises one eyebrow. "Not everyone."

As if in protest, my Gizmo pings and we both jump. "Sorry, probably my friend." I fumble with the knit holder at my hip, cursing Yaz for interrupting me, but when I pull out my Gizmo, I see that my mom has sent me a text.

> Where are you? Can't reach you by vid and your vitals are
> all over the place. Locate now!

"Crap!" I say as I text back, *Taking a walk.* "I have to go," I tell him and blush at the disappointment in my voice.

"Hey wait," Basil says. He grabs the paper. "You can't take that with you."

"Why not?" I tug on it. "You gave it to me."

He pulls harder. "Who are you really? And who's pinging you?"

I yank the paper and we both stumble backward, half a sheet in each of our hands. "Oh no!" I look down at the torn paper and feel like I might cry. "We broke it!"

He sees how upset I am and puts his hand on my shoulder. "It's okay, don't worry." Another one of those funny ripples goes through my body. "But I have to take this back."

"Then why did you give it to me?" I ask, still clutching my half.

He thinks about this for a moment. "Because I wanted to, er, uh, . . . I thought maybe you might . . ." he stops, and I can see a red flush crawling up his neck. He shoves the other half of the paper at me. "You have to read it silently and commit the info to memory, then destroy it."

I laugh. "Are you joking?"

He shakes his head, and I realize that he's very serious.

"Okay," I tell him. I smooth the halves on the countertop and fit them back together so I can read the words again. Then I pull out my Gizmo to give Astrid the info, but Basil reaches out and lays his hand on mine.

"No," he says. "Don't. You have to remember. It's the only way."

"Nobody can remember that much info."

"People used to memorize entire books, whole maps, important dates, phone numbers for all their friends and family, all kinds of stuff," he insists.

"When?"

"When they had to."

I stare at the paper, rereading the lines over and over, trying to get them to stick inside my brain.

"You got it?"

"I think so."

"If it's important, you'll remember," he tells me.

I read it one more time. "Okay," I tell him uncertainly.

He picks up both pieces of paper and rips them into pieces.

"Hey!" I yell.

"It's the only way." He tears and tears until only tiny shreds are left, then he opens the lid on a bucket of murky water and drops the pieces in. "Don't worry," he says. "I'll make a new piece later out of this."

"You can do that?" I ask astonished.

"That was the original recycling." He leads me out of the room, turning off the light as we go.

When we get into the first room, my Gizmo pings with another message from my mom demanding to know where I am. "Sorry," I say. "I better go or my mother will have my Smaurto looking for me." I head for the door, but then I turn around and look at Basil. "You'll be there, right? At the meeting?"

He nods. "See you there?"

My cheeks grow warm and I have to take a deep breath. "Yes, see you there!" Then I turn and run outside into the night air.

✤ ✤ ✤

I run blindly for a minute or two, turning corners and zipping up empty streets. I have no idea why I'm running. It's not like I'm in danger or in a hurry. But meeting Basil and learning about other people like me makes me feel so good I have to move. It's as if every muscle in my body is elated and about to explode, shooting me up into the air until I'm flying over the entire city, looking down at everyone far below me. *Hello! Hello!* I would call. *Look at meeeeee!* while I do loop-de-loops in the sky. My feet pound against the pavement as my heart pounds in my chest. The giddy, throbbing excitement propels me forward until I'm out of breath and panting while leaning against the side of an old building. I catch my breath and look for something familiar, but I'm lost and even that feels good because no matter how turned around I get out here, I know that I'm not alone.

I imagine wandering around this maze of streets until I bump into Basil again. His face floats up in my mind and my heart revs. I laugh out loud, sending my voice bouncing around the walls. Will Basil hear? Will he know it's me? Thinking all these crazy thoughts makes my face grow hot, so I press my cheek against the cool metal wall behind me.

My Gizmo pings and I jump. Just another message from my mom demanding that I come right home because she can see that my heart rate has skyrocketed and I'm using too much CO2. I breathe deeply, trying to calm down. There's no way I'm calling her. The last thing I want to deal with are her questions. I turn on my locator, reconnect Astrid to my car, then send a quick text telling my mom that I'm heading home soon.

I feel like a different person retracing my steps back toward the PlugIn. Will Mom be able to see this shift on my face or hear it in my voice or read it in my vitals? How obvious is it that something interesting has happened? That I met someone, in person, who is so different from everyone else I know that he's like me? And that I loved talking to him. It wasn't awkward or weird. Even though we spent almost an hour together, there's so much more to say! I can think of so many questions I wish I'd asked Basil. Like where he's from and how old he is and if he's in an ICM and whether he's ever read a book that's not about food and why he doesn't have a Gizmo and a thousand more about the Analogs and the meeting. I can't stop thinking about how he looked. How his eyes flashed when he was angry and how they glimmered when he was happy. How his mouth changed from a hard straight line to a soft lopsided curve when he smiled. It's as if his image has been downloaded to my brain and is now a screensaver on the backs of my eyelids. Every time I blink, I see him in my mind.

I wonder if this is what it feels like when people find a dynamic interpersonal connection in the Procreation Pool. Except I'm only 17. Finding a person to love outside the Pool, without the help of algorithms and avatars, only happens in fiction when two people are so compatible that their desire to be together busts through the hormone barriers meant to save us from ourselves and keep the population in check. They have a word for this kind of thing in the movies. It's called *romance*, and until today I thought it was a total crock of crap.

Now I'm not so sure. Maybe it was fate that I stumbled into Flav-O-Rite on a night when Basil was mixing scents. And maybe it was kismet that allowed us to sit next to one another, look each other in the eye, and let our fingers graze one another's skin. Maybe somewhere he is thinking all the same things about me. And if he is, could this be what the Procreation Pool system is meant to re-create with its algorithmic meet-ups and synthetic hormone boosters? That thing Grandma talks about when she talks about *love*. My skin tingles at the thought.

No, that's not tingling. It's my Gizmo buzzing in my hand, pulling me out of my reverie. Who needs a virtual life when you can have this heady feeling in reality? But the feeling is fleeting. It's already skittered away into the night sky, leaving me staring down at the directions to my Smaurto that Astrid is showing me. I sigh then shoot a quick text to Yaz, telling her that my mother wants me home and I'll see her tomorrow at our ICM.

I focus my attention on the map, which leads me back past vacant buildings I vaguely recognize and retraces my steps up the alleyway I remember. Everything around me is beginning to seem familiar, but I feel different. Like I've walked through a time warp, only I'm not sure I want to go back to my life. Part of me wants to stay in this old part of town, caught in the past while searching for my future. That's silly, though. The future is unknown until you get there. But I won't leave it to something as false as fate to ensure that mine includes Basil.

Basil? Could that really be his name? It dawns on me just then how little we really know about each other. I close my eyes and silently say the words he had written on the paper.

Analogs . . . Friday . . . 6:00 p.m. . . . 1601 South Halsted

⚜ ⚜ ⚜

The minute I walk in the door to our house, my mom is all over me. She's standing, Gizmo in hand, firing questions before I even have my shoes off.

"Where were you? I couldn't locate you! And what on Earth were you doing? Your vitals were all over the place. Heart rate up and down, your metabolism swinging, and your calorie burn skyrocketed!" She shoves her Gizmo in my face as if the graphs and numbers on the screen mean anything to me.

"God, Mom. I just walked in the door." I push her Gizmo away and head into the living room, where Dad is engrossed in a 3-D historical docudrama about the invention of some old thing called an iPhone. "I was out with Yaz. We went to a new PlugIn. I was probably playing a game or something that got my heart rate up. Then I got bored and took a walk." I feel a little bad for leaving out some of the truth, but not bad enough to tell her what really happened. I plop down on the sofa beside Dad. "How do you know that stupid patch is accurate, anyway?"

Mom stands in front of us, hands on hips. "Of course it's accurate!" she says. "I invented it and your father made it." My dad shifts so that he can see around my mom.

"If this is how you're going to treat me . . ." I lift my shirt and try to rip the patch off my back. "Ouch!" I yell when it won't come off.

"You have to wear it for the full twenty-four hours before it will release," she says.

I slump back on the couch and mutter, "You might as well put a chip in my head."

At this my dad perks up. "Actually . . ."

Mom shoots him a look, and he stops short of launching into his diatribe about singularity—his favorite topic.

"What?" I look from Mom to Dad and back to Mom. "Do I already have a chip in my head?"

"Not yet," Dad says with a smile.

"Max," Mom says, exasperation in her voice. "Could we talk about that another time?"

He shrugs and goes back to the docudrama.

Mom takes a deep breath and tries to reason with me. "I'm collecting this data for your own good. Your Synthamil formula has been precisely calculated, and any little shift—"

"You said you wouldn't look at the data until tomorrow," I point out.

"I wouldn't have except there are built-in warning signals if a patient's vitals suddenly go haywire."

At this I feel myself turn pink. When did my signals go bonkers? When I met Basil? When we were using his device to smell roasted chicken and chocolate brownies? When I ran through the streets? I certainly don't want my mother knowing any of that. I should have hacked the dumb patch. "I shouldn't be made to feel abnormal," I say, reciting Basil's argument, but somehow it sounds ridiculous when I say it to my mother.

"I didn't say you were abnormal." She screws up her face like I'm babbling nonsense. "I think your metabolism is out of whack for some reason, so we might need to tweak your Synthamil formula."

"Well," I huff at her, "I'm not your test subject."

"First of all, I'm not experimenting on you. Secondly, it's a privilege to have a personal optimized formula. Not everyone gets that."

"So I should be grateful?" I snipe.

She draws a long breath in through her nose, trying to stay calm. "Thalia, I only want to make sure that you're okay."

"I'm sitting here, aren't I? Obviously, I'm all right."

Dad looks over. "She's got a point, Lil."

Mom sighs and rubs her forehead. Finally she says, "Data doesn't lie."

"But daughters do?"

"I didn't say that," Mom says with her teeth gritted. We stare at one another for a few seconds until she says, "I just want to know that you're safe and healthy."

"I wasn't doing anything wrong," I tell her as I haul myself off the couch and stomp toward my room.

As I'm leaving, I hear her say to my dad, "She has no appreciation for the work I've done in my life. No appreciation at all!"

I can't help but roll my eyes. How many times have I heard her speech? How if it weren't for her and One World, all humankind would be dead. How her breakthrough in the lab helped refine the inocs so no one experiences hunger anymore or procreates without permission or gets horrible fatal diseases. And how without nutritional beverages like Synthamil, humans would still be starving and fighting. The thing is, I do appreciate it. Of course I do. I wouldn't want to watch the people I love starve or kill each other for meager scraps of food. But I don't like having it shoved down my throat all the time. Like I have to agree with everything she says just because she was instrumental in saving humanity. She's still my mom and she can still be annoying.

⚘ ⚘ ⚘

The next night, Mom, Papa Peter, and Grandma Grace gather around the main screen in our living room to discuss my vitals, which Mom uploaded from the patch.

"Her insulin level is definitely spiking." Grandma Grace points to a sharp line. "It should stabilize between her morning and evening ingestion of Synthamil."

"And her glucose is falling too rapidly," Papa Peter adds. "Which would explain the headaches and fatigue. But her hydration level is fine, so she's getting enough water."

"Look at her ketone level here," Mom says. "It shouldn't be that high."

I sit on the couch, hugging a pillow, while they discuss me like I'm some sort of chemistry project.

"When was her last inoculation?" Grandma asks my mom.

"Three months ago," Mom says. "So she's not due for another three months."

They flip through screen after screen showing how my body operated on an hourly basis for the past two days.

"That's odd," says Grandma Grace. "Her dopamine level shot up here. When was that? Zoom in." Mom commands the chart to enlarge. "Friday night around eight p.m."

They both turn to me. "What were you doing then?" Mom asks.

My heart begins to race and my palms sweat. I know from bio-chem that dopamine is a neurotransmitter that's released in the brain when something unexpected and good happens. I remember sitting next to Basil that night. How close my thigh was to his while we were smelling roasted chicken and chocolate. I almost get dizzy thinking about it. I bet my dopamine level's sky-high about now.

"I don't know," I say, trying to act nonchalant. "Maybe playing some game at the PlugIn."

"The time-released benzodiazepines in her inocs should suppress spikes like that," says Grandma Grace.

"Unless she's not getting the right dose," Mom says.

Grandma turns to me. "How much do you weigh now?"

"I don't know," I say.

She frowns. "Why not?"

When I was little, Grandma Grace's frown scared me. And now with a bold stripe of gray down the front of her jet black hair, she looks even more fierce, like she could face down an angry mob loot-ing a hospital pharmacy, which according to Papa Peter, she did once during the wars.

"I never weigh myself," I tell her, annoyed.

She doesn't budge. Doesn't change her face. Doesn't say any-thing. She just stares at me until I hoist myself off the couch and slink into the little vestibule in the back of our house. Between the water tap (which is connected to the Whisson Windmill on the roof) and the closet with our urinal is the cabinet holding our monthly supply of Synthamil—our personal cocktails designed to optimize each per-son's brain and bodily functions. Small bottles of blue for me. Red for Mom. Green for Dad. And orange for Grandma Apple. Each one is wrapped in a gold embossed label bearing our names. Technically, you're supposed to weigh yourself once a week, and do an at-home spit test, urine sample, finger prick, and hair follicle analysis to make sure all your nutritional needs are being met, but almost no one does it. Except for little kids who are still growing. Their doses need recalibrating all the time. Although I bet Grandma Grace and my mother do it, since they do everything by the book they helped write in the first place. I step on the scale and wait for the number to appear. One hundred twenty-two pounds.

By the time I walk back into the living room, they've pulled up my weight on the screen.

"Three pounds less," Mom says. "A little odd, but nothing to be alarmed about."

"No," Grandma says. "But it could be an indication that her metabolism shifted slightly."

Mom and Grandma Grace both whip out their Gizmos and start calculating.

Papa Peter rolls his eyes at them then drops down on the couch beside me. He leans in close so I can smell his aftershave, which reminds me of the pine trees programmed in December. When I was little, I loved rubbing his cheeks so I could get his scent on my fingers. "In the old days," he tells me, "I would've told your mama to fatten you up on some hamburgers and french fries."

I can't help but grin. There's something about Papa Peter that just makes people comfortable and happy. "What are french fries?"

"What are french fries?" He shakes his head. "Hm-mm-mm. Only the best thing there ever was. First you took a potato—that was a tuber that grew underground. Then you sliced it up and dropped those slices down in a deep-fat fryer full of bubbling oil. They came out all crispy on the outside but soft and fluffy on the inside. You'd sprinkle them with a little salt, which tasted like tears of joy. Then finally, we'd dip them in something sweet and tangy called ketchup that was made from tomatoes."

I try to mix all those descriptions together, but my mind gets blurry. "My friend has this little machine," I start to say, excited to tell Papa Peter about Basil's gadget, but then I stop.

"And what's this machine do?"

"Nothing. Never mind."

"You can tell me." Papa leans back and crosses his hands lazily over his belly like he's got nowhere to be and nothing better to do than listen to me.

I wish I could tell Papa Peter. And Grandma Apple. They would probably love Basil's scent device because they could relive all their favorite foods. But if I tell him, then my mom will have a zillion questions about how and when I met him and who his family is and where they live and what they do. So I change my tack. "Do you ever wish you could see and smell food again?"

"Thalia!" My mom whips around and blinks at me. "What did you just say?"

"I asked if Papa Peter ever wished he could see and smell food."

Mom and Grandma Grace exchange looks. "You know perfectly well that we don't do that," Mom tells me.

I think about this for a second then ask, "Why don't we?"

Mom is at a loss for words but Grandma Grace says, "Because it's unnecessary, not to mention illegal."

"Illegal?" Papa Peter's eyebrows lift up, causing a line of wrinkles to march across his forehead. "You sure?"

"Of course it is," snaps Grandma Grace.

"Under the Universal Nutrition Protection Act," Mom adds.

"The young people call it forno," Grandma Grace says, and Papa Peter laughs.

"Forno?" I ask.

"Food porno," Grandma Grace says.

"Mother," Mom protests, embarrassed.

"She's seventeen. She should know," says Grandma, ever the pragmatist. "But him?" She nods at Papa, who's giggling like a little kid. "He's hopeless."

I wonder if Basil and I were actually breaking some stupid law. Did he know it was illegal? I swallow a giggle. He must have been freaking out when I told him he should turn his device into the newest form of entertainment. "But how is that illegal?" I ask.

"Breach of contract," says Mom, which clarifies nothing.

Papa Peter interrupts. "Well then, I must be breaking the law in my mind right now because I'm sure thinking about french fries!"

"Peter!" Grandma admonishes him, but I laugh.

He closes his eyes. "Now I'm thinking of a chocolate shake. Thick, cold, creamy, chocolaty."

I remember the smell of chocolate. Deep and heavy, slightly bitter but sweet.

"Watch out, here comes a doozy," Papa says. "Call security. I'm picturing a banana split with whipped cream and a cherry on top."

Suddenly my stomach groans and gurgles. Papa's eyes open wide and he laughs. "Well I'll be darned. Did you hear that? I just made this child's stomach growl." He looks at me. "Let's try that again." He leans down close to my belly, lifts the bottom of my hoodie and T-shirt like I'm a little kid and he's going to give me a belly blow. I try to protest, but it's hard not to laugh when Papa Peter is being such a goofball. "Hello in there!" he calls. "How about a big plate of flaky, buttery biscuits and nice thick sausage gravy? Or a pepperoni pizza with lots of melted mozzarella cheese?"

"Peter Alan Pike!" Grandma snaps at him.

He sits up. "Yes, my dear?"

"What nonsense are you telling our granddaughter?"

He grins at me and lowers my shirt, then pats my belly sweetly. "Nothing you need to worry about."

"I should hope not," Grandma Grace says, turning back to the screen and her calculations.

"I must be doing this wrong," my mom says with the same frown Grandma wore earlier. "I keep getting the exact calibration for her Synthamil formula even though obviously it's not working correctly for her."

"Me, too," Grandma admits. "So either we're making the same error or there's something we're overlooking."

"She's hungry," Papa Peter says. Mom and Grandma Grace exchange a quick worried glance.

"But that would mean..." Mom starts to say, then she trails off, bewildered. For half a second I think about telling her I'm not the only one, but I keep my mouth shut. "Do you think I should take her to a specialist?" she asks Grandma Grace.

"No way," I say from the couch.

Grandma and Mom both turn, put one hand on a hip, and stare at me. "And why not?" they ask me at the same time.

I think of what Basil said about the others who tried to get help. "Because they'll probably say it's all in my mind and drug me up...."

"So you're a doctor now?" Grandma asks me.

"She's probably right," Papa Peter says. Grandma gives him a look that could wilt hologram daisies, but he's not deterred. "If I were her, I wouldn't want some stranger poking around me either. Especially when she's got two of the smartest medical minds in the world right here in the living room." He grins at both of them and I know what he's doing. Papa Peter's favorite saying is "you can catch more flies with honey," which I think means that you get farther with people if you're nice, although I have no idea what flies and honey have to do with it. And it seems an odd choice for Grandma Grace, since she uses the exact opposite approach. She only believes in bossing people around. Maybe that's why they work well together. Opposites attract after all.

"Just give her some extra Synthamil, a little at a time, until her tummy's not growling anymore," Papa Peter suggests. I look to my mom hopefully as she considers Papa Peter's advice. "Sometimes trial and error works just fine," he adds.

"I suppose we could try it for a few days," Mom says, but she doesn't seem convinced.

I sit back, relieved and mouth "Thanks" to Papa Peter.

"But," Mom adds, "if that doesn't work, then we have to see someone."

⚘   ⚘   ⚘

The next morning, I head off to One World, Happy World for my monthly Interpersonal Communication Meeting. As I walk into the enclosed glass atrium (where all the toy and game design is done), a hologram of a giant pink, banjo-playing animal that has spines all over its back and a little snout sings, "Happy time. Fun time. One World loves us all! Welcome to our happy home. Welcome to our mall!" I stop and stare at it. Not out of amazement or adoration, but out of sheer loathing. *Really?* Do people really feel inspired to buy toys and games if a giant pink, banjo-playing extinct spiny, piglike creature sings some inane song? Most people push right on by and head straight for the shops, but a few slow down or stop, especially the little kids.

A girl, probably five or six, stands across from me, looking up with her mouth hanging open. She's dressed head to toe in purple Silkese and Cottynelle with ruffles and sequins. She watches in awe as an animated Synthamil bottle with big eyes and chubby hands floats down. "Remember, always drink your Synthamil!" it says, then giggles when the pink animal grabs it, pops off its lid, and chugs its contents. Creepy, if you ask me.

"Can we get one, Mommy, please?" the little girl begs the woman who's busy snapping pix with her Gizmo because the spiny pink creature has floated down and positioned itself right beside the kid. When the weird animal and the bottle begin to dance and sing around her, the girl squeals with delight.

Someone smacks me on the arm and says, "Can we get one, too, Mommy?" I turn to see Yaz, grinning stupidly at me. Today she's wearing navy blue trousers and a three-button jacket. Her hair is parted neatly to the side and tucked behind her ear. Yaz always looks the part she's playing, which today is Good Student. Unlike me who refuses. I'm in a bright blue fleece hoodie and a pair of real denim jeans, so soft and worn from my grandma's farm days that the knees and butt have patches.

"What's that thing supposed to be, anyway?" I ask, staring at the pink monstrosity dancing toward another kid who's come to stare.

Yaz shakes her head like she can't believe the things I don't know. "New game launch. That's the mascot—Hedgy." She starts digging in her bag. "I should put this on my PRC. Didn't you read your ICM dox?"

"Didn't even download them," I tell her.

"Of course not," she mutters as she launches her HoverCam. "And you'll still score higher than the rest of us on the final."

"Tests are stupid," I say, then wonder if this Hedgy thing is what AnonyGal is hoping to hack. Even though I've vowed to never mess with a product launch because it would upset my dad too much, I wouldn't mind watching the Dynasaurs take this one down.

I step back and watch Yaz film a quick duet with the pink creature. Even I have to admit it's kind of hilarious, especially when she blows it a kiss as it floats away.

"You know," I say when the photo op is done, "you're really good at engaging others, even animated others."

She stashes her camera in her bag and shrugs like it's no big deal.

"You should do something with that talent," I say as we head into the atrium.

"I'm trying to," she says. "That's what the PRC is for."

"I mean something that makes people think and question the status quo instead of perpetuating it."

Yaz stops and puts a hand on her hip. "We don't all have that luxury in our lives, Thalia."

"It's not a luxury," I argue.

"Not if you're you, but it is if you're me. You can be so judgmental sometimes," she says.

Jilly starts yapping step-by-step instructions about how to get to our dreaded Interpersonal Classroom Meeting as if we're likely to walk into a wall without her help.

"Sorry . . ." I say. "I don't mean to be judgy. I just think you could be doing something more interesting with your PRC."

"Interesting to who?" she asks. "You?"

She's got me there, so I drop it.

We pass more Hedgy projections on the windows of every real-time toy store, where kids can pick up and play with the merchandise, since they're the one group that won't fall for pure VirtuShops. Then we step onto an escalator that bisects the center of the atrium.

"My dad told me once that everything in a mall is thought out and has a purpose," I say. "And do you know what that purpose is?"

Yaz looks at me with a blank face. "The real question is, do I care?"

"It's to get people to spend more money."

"Duh," she says.

"I mean, look at this. The escalator forces you to pass by every floor. And since this building is circular and there are no solid walls in here, just windows and glass beams, you can see inside every shop." I point to the store for dolls, the one for toy cars and trucks, the one for dress-ups.

Yaz sighs. "I loved coming here when I was a kid."

"You know they're watching you, right?" I ask.

"Who?"

"One World marketeers!"

"Again I say, *duh*. How else are they going to know how consumers react? I mean take Hedgy there." She points to yet another projection of the pink beast, this one in flowered bell-bottom pants boogying beneath an ancient disco ball. "If everyone was walking right past, or worse, scared and running away, they'd need to know that."

"What kind of animal is it supposed to be, anyway?"

"I think it's called a hedgehog or something. Apparently cats and monkeys are so last year."

"A giant singing and dancing pink hedgehog?" I ask. "That's idiotic."

"Speaking of which, look what I got." She slips her jacket off her shoulder so I can see a new temp-i-tat of that stupid hedgehog on her arm.

"You have got to be kidding! Why would you put that dumb thing on your skin?"

"It's a new kind! Nobody else has it yet. Watch this." She twitches her muscle and the hedgehog begins to dance. "Fiyo, at that little Spalon outside the East Loop, created it."

"But how did he make it move like that?" I ask, looking more closely at her arm, trying to understand the technology.

"He designed some itty-bitty projection thingie that he slipped right under my skin. It activates when my muscles twitch." She moves her arm again so the hedgehog boogies. "You should come with me next time. Fiyo mixes all his own serums. You'd love it. Spend some cash, fight the system. Isn't that what you like to crap on and on about?" She waves her arm, which makes the hedgehog dance wildly.

"My god, you've practically gone rogue!" I say.

"Pretty soon I'll become a Dynasaur," she teases.

"As if!" I say in mock horror. "But I'd watch your PRC then."

She laughs. "You and twelve other weirdos."

We round the corner and step onto the last escalator that will carry us to the fifth floor. Something catches my eye. I see a guy with soft brown hair, dressed in green, looking in the window of a model-building shop. My stomach does a flip-flop and my heart races. "Oh my god! That's him!"

"Who?" Yaz asks.

I hurry to the escalator and head down, going against the flow of people. "Excuse me. Sorry. Pardon me," I say pushing past as everyone shoots me dirty looks. I half lean over the railing, trying to get a better look.

"What are you doing?" Yaz calls from up above.

I ignore her because I'm trying to figure out what I'm going to do when I get to Basil. Will he remember me? Of course he will. But what if he doesn't? That would be mortifying. Just as I'm about to step off the escalator and hurry over to him, he turns and I see that it's not him at all. In fact, he doesn't look a thing like Basil. This guy is way younger, probably only fourteen, and he doesn't have Basil's dark, beautiful eyes. Embarrassed, I stop and ride the escalator up backward.

Yaz is waiting for me on the fifth floor. "What was that all about?" she asks when I step off.

"I thought I knew that guy, but I didn't," I mumble.

"A guy?" Yaz asks. "From where?"

"It was nothing," I snap, because I feel really silly for getting so worked up.

"But where would you meet a guy? At the PlugIn the other night? Were you holding out on me?" She pesters me as we walk to our classroom.

"Let's drop it."

"No way. I want details!"

When we get to our classroom, the door whooshes open, and I say, "I'll tell you later. Promise," so that she'll stop pestering me.

I managed to get Yaz and me assigned to the same class without even hacking. It isn't hard when you understand the system. No matter what my mother and One World want to call it, most ICMs are just elaborate focus groups. For three months before we got our class assignments, I let Yaz do half of all her purchasing through Astrid, that way our consumer profiles were nearly identical. Then we made sure to put in the right balance of likes and dislikes on our placement questionnaires. And, since we're both girls, the same age, who live in the same Loop, the algorithm ended up assigning us to the same group. As for the other eight kids in our class, they're lame.

I slouch down into a seat and prepare to be bored for the next four hours of blatant product placements and faux debates. We all sit in a circle with our Gizmos facedown on the table and our PCAs on mute. We're not allowed to touch them until break. That way, everyone has to practice making eye contact when they speak. Having their Gizmos so close yet so far away nearly kills most people.

Mika, our instructor, sits in the circle, too, because we're all just one big human family, as the One World slogan goes. To her left are two OW human resource workers, who'll be picking our brains then writing up their assessments of our interpersonal communication skills, which go in our reference files along with our test scores to be considered by future employers. Which is why I have to at least play along a little bit, even if it does annoy me.

Mika clears her throat and smiles at everyone. She has the same warm brown skin tone as most people and dark wavy hair. She's tall and has bright blue eyes that look natural, which makes her appear striking and is probably the reason she got the job. As she welcomes us and models small talk by asking personal questions, I wonder if this is what she wanted out of life or if it's just the job some optimal employment algorithm assigned her.

"Yaz," Mika says, "what a wonderful pantsuit. That color is great on you. Is that visquinylon or an acetate-acrylic blend?"

Yaz runs her hand over her sleeve and says perfectly pleasantly, "It's a new fabric, Mika, called NylonDex, developed at One World Fashion. I love it. Would you like to feel it?"

I see the One World folks jotting notes, surely giving Yaz points for using someone's name, plugging a product, and offering body contact in a socially appropriate way.

After stroking Yaz's arm, Mika turns the conversation to Jadari. "I saw on your status bar that last night you played New Vegas Zombie Busters, the latest in the New Vegas series. How'd you like it?"

"Good," Jadari says, remembering to sit up straight and look at Mika, but he loses points for a one-word answer with no return question.

I know my turn is coming soon, but when Mika gets to me, she fumbles for something to say. "Uh, um, Thalia." She glances down at her Gizmo desperately searching for some piece of data about me from the last month. But since I haven't bought anything, played anything, or participated in anything under my own account, she's dumbstruck. I decide to bail her out and start the conversation, which should win me a few points anyway.

"Mika, last night my grandmother taught me a traditional craft called knitting back from the days when human beings used to create things." I pull out the Gizmo holder Grandma and I made together and launch into an explanation of how people used to make clothes out of animal by-products like hair and skin. Of course, I know I'm losing points by talking about a socially inappropriate topic and not mentioning any One World products, but watching Mika panic at the thought of me derailing the class to talk about knitting makes it worth it.

Before Mika can figure out how to rein me in, one of the HR reps interrupts me. "Humans still create things," he says. "Who do you think came up with our latest mascot, Hedgy?" He smiles to himself, as if he's so very clever.

I blink at him. "Probably a computer program that calculated the optimal animal within recent human memory for selling more products."

"Well, uh, sure, but," he sputters, "someone had to write that program."

"Someone like my dad," I say, which shuts him up for a moment as he checks his Gizmo to figure out who my father is. "And that's different. I'm talking about when people used to create things that weren't meant to be bought and sold. Sometimes they just made gifts with no thought about profit."

"And what's wrong with profit?" the other rep, the woman, wants to know.

"'Profit makes the world go around,'" I quote, using another One World slogan, as if I'm daring them not to give me points. "But what's wrong with art for art's sake, too?"

"Art?" the woman rep snorts. "So go create something. Nobody's stopping you." She sounds hostile, which makes me nearly laugh and Mika squirm.

"Thank you. I will!" I tell her with a perfectly pleasant smile on my face.

Yaz shakes her head at me, but I can tell she's trying not to giggle.

"Let's try to get back on topic, shall we?" Mika manages to say, her voice tight.

"Yes, let's," I say, sarcasm dripping.

❧   ❧   ❧

I tune out for the next hour of new-product vids, which we're sup-posed to watch and then debate. I can't muster any interest in another game or movie or device to make my life more fulfilling unless it were the scent generator Basil invented. I think back to the other night, but I can't quite remember his face. I try harder to remember how his dark hair curled across his forehead. Was it black or dark brown? I do remember that his eyes lit up when he smiled, but I can't remember if they were blue or green or maybe hazel. I wish I could see him so I could burn his image into my mind again. I wonder what he's doing. And why I thought I saw him earlier today. For a moment I imagine that I walked into my ICM today and he was here. What would I do? What would I say? Would he acknowledge that we know each other? I wonder if we both answered our placement questionnaires honestly whether we could be in the same group? Probably not, because the data collected are not the right ones. If someone really wanted to know about me, they'd have to find out more than what three products I most recently purchased using VirtuShop coupons or whether I prefer dance games over war games. Plus, I have no idea if we live in the same Loop.

Silently, I repeat the info from the piece of paper: *Analogs . . . Friday . . . 6:00 p.m. . . . 1601 South Halsted*

He said it would be a meeting, but it must be more interesting than this. I wonder if they use his device there? My cheeks grow warm as I think of the tantalizing smell of roasted chicken and the heaven that was chocolate. I wonder if that machine could reproduce the smell of an apple. Grandma says the good ones were sweet and tart. That they crunched in your teeth then filled your mouth with juice. My mouth gets watery when I try to imagine what that might feel like. As I'm considering this, that weird gnawing in the pit of my stomach starts up. I feel empty again, as if someone has hollowed me out.

I'm only half listening when Mika starts in on a discussion of what everyone just watched, but I'm too distracted by the sensation in my belly to add anything to the conversation. Mika glances my way. "Thalia?" she asks.

"Um, yes?" I say.

"What's your opinion?"

I shift in my seat, trying to sit up straight as if I've been paying attention. "About what?"

I notice the edges of Mika's mouth pull a little tighter. "How could we improve large-platform social games such as the new Big Battle Cyborg Defenders to better serve society?"

"Well . . ." I say, then just as I'm about to launch into a tirade about how those types of large platforms undermine the very fabric of our society by endlessly invading our personal privacy, it happens. That yawning in my stomach grows. The gnawing gets more intense. I feel it bubbling up, and I clamp my mouth closed to make it stop, but I have no power over it, and suddenly the loudest, most obnoxious, primordial growl escapes from me. Everyone glances around.

"What was that?" one of the One World reps asks. He looks up at the ceiling.

"Was that someone's Gizmo?" Mika asks. She looks straight at Jadari, who shakes his head furiously.

Under the lip of the table, I clutch my stomach and implore my body to stop. I've never been so embarrassed. In front of all these people, including OW HR reps. Such a nightmare! Papa Peter said a little extra Synthamil would quell the groaning inside of me, but he was wrong. I can feel another one creeping up, and I start to panic. Yaz stares at me. She can see that something's wrong.

"Mika!" she says loudly, jumping in. "Can you tell us about the new Fun-Time Hedgehog Dance Party launch? That giant Hedgy hologram downstairs is just so adorable! I can't wait to hear more about it!"

"Yes," says Mika, looking relieved that something has put a cork in me before I could get started. "Great timing, Yaz. We were just about to get to that."

✢   ✢   ✢

Somehow I get through the last hour of class without another howl coming from my insides. By the time we leave, I'm sweaty and exhausted from worrying that it would happen again. I'm so relieved that when Yaz asks me to go to the EntertainArena with her, I say yes. She's shocked that she hasn't had to cajole me into going, but I'd rather go to the EA with Yaz than go home and have Mom ask me about my stomach.

As usual, the EntertainArena is a madhouse. The second our Smaurtos drop us at the entrance then go in search of parking in the underground garage, Jilly starts yapping, only adding to the chaos.

"Hey Yaz! It's so awesome to be back here," she says in an overly perky voice that marketeers must think all girls our age use. "We haven't been here in, like, forever. There's so much to do! How are we ever going to decide?"

"Aren't you sick of her yet?" I ask Yaz as we make our way through hundreds of people milling around the portico with its faux fountains and giant spinning holograms advertising the newest games and latest movies.

"I barely hear her anymore," Yaz admits as we avoid racers from the hottest simulators zipping past us and hologram soldiers from some historical-war game running around, hiding behind columns and benches. Overhead, a trailer for a 3-D movie tour of *The World's Lost Treasures Part 45* takes up an entire two-story screen. When that's over a thirty-second newsfeed starts up just as we enter the building.

All the way down the crowded corridor, Jilly tries to cajole us into the entrance of each different cyberworld. "Oh!" she squeals at a sleek black-and-white facade with tidy awnings covered in retro designer logos like Chanel and Prada. "'Fashion-Forward Fashion Fun' is fun for everyone!"

"No way," I say.

When we pass a faux-stone arch entryway guarded by hologram sentries in togas, Jilly says, "Hey, Yaz, your friend Miyuki Shapiro is inside playing Rugged Racers of Ancient Rome: Chariots on Fire, a fast-paced thriller from a bygone era!"

"Lame," Yaz mutters. Then she stops in front of a closed entrance to a new cyberworld, and Jilly launches into her spiel.

"Coming soon, Hedgy's World! Tunnel through an English hedge-row just like the little hedgehogs of yore."

"'Hedgehogs of yore'? Who writes this crap?"

"Sounds kind of fun to me," says Yaz. "The whole world was cre-ated to be ten times bigger than you are with super-lifelike plants and giant automaton animals so you feel like a little creature running around in nature. I'll probably camp out the night before it opens so I can be one of the first people inside."

"Why on earth would you do that?" I feel woozy and empty again, and everything is beginning to annoy me.

"I might get a full sponsorship out of it if enough people hit my PRC feed. And today Mika told me that if I can get enough sponsor-ships and product placements, I could have a shot at a spokesperson internship with One World Fashion."

I lean against the wall on wobbly legs. "Is that really what you want to do with your life?"

"Obviously, I should be a fashion designer." Yaz lifts her arms as if to say, ta-da! "My employment algorithm proves that. But there are only a few positions open, so I have to get my foot in the door, and Mika says—"

"What does Mika know?" I grouch.

"More than you give her credit for," Yaz says. "Besides, I could use her help. Not everybody can post the best grades and have a mom and dad like yours and call the OW CEO Auntie Ahimsa. I need all the connections I can get."

I frown at her. "I don't use my parents' connections to get special treatment."

"I know you don't, but you don't need to. And I know you think it's all fun and games how the Dynasaurs try to mess with One World all the time, but most of us can't afford to do that."

"That's why we stay anonymous," I tell her.

"That's not the point," she says. "You'll be able to have any job you want because you're crazy smart and talented and, like it or not, well-connected, but people like me can't bite the hand that feeds us." I start to protest, but Yaz shakes her head and says, "That's just the way the world works."

I cross my arms like a petulant child. "Well, it shouldn't work that way!"

"No kidding," Yaz says with a laugh. "And humans should still eat food and have unlimited numbers of babies. But the world doesn't work that way anymore either."

"If you ask me, the whole thing is stupid!" I press my fingertips into my temples to try to stop the pounding inside my head.

"Are you okay?" Yaz asks me. "You look weird."

"You mean weirder than usual," I snap. I meant it to come out funny, but I sounded mean. "Sorry," I mumble.

"No for real." Yaz studies my face. "What's wrong?"

"Isn't there anyplace less crowded and noisy in here?"

"You're at an EntertainArena."

"I realize that," I say with a tired sigh.

"I know what you need." Yaz grabs my arm and tugs. She looks right then left, and when she's sure no one is watching, she slides along the wall between the entrances to Hedgy's World and Rugged Racers to slip through an unmarked door camouflaged between the two cyberworlds. I stand there like an idiot with my mouth hanging open until she reaches out and yanks me through the door, too.

✤   ✤   ✤

"What is this?" I whisper when we're on the other side in a pristine and nearly silent white hall.

"Shortcut," she whispers excitedly. "You hack. I sneak." She winks and hurries down the hallway with me following closely behind.

Again, I stand and stare at her, amazed by secret Yaz who's come out to play. "How come you never showed me this before?"

"You never come to the EA with me."

"If I'd known about this . . . wow, look!" I stop and point to the data-access panels positioned by the back entrances for each cyberworld we pass. "Dynasaurs would flip out if they knew about these. You should put this on your PRC!"

She rolls her eyes and yanks me past the panels. "Do you know how much trouble that would cause?"

"Yeah," I say with a huge grin.

We traipse down some stairs and through another hall then pop out a hidden back door into an empty cyberworld. "Guess where we are?" Yaz says, almost triumphant.

I look at a huge open pit painted black, which looks vaguely familiar, but in my addled state, I can't quite place it. Even Jilly seems befuddled because she's got nothing to say.

Then an automated voice with an old-world southern accent starts up. "Welcome back, ya'll! Haven't seen ya in a long spell. Come on in and make yerself at home."

"No way!" I half groan and half laugh. "Is this Pesky Petey?"

Yaz cracks up. "This is the only place in the entire EntertainArena that's quiet because nobody comes here anymore. I heard they're going to tear it down and put in something new."

A hologram possum in an old-fashioned bowler hat and bow tie appears at the edge of the pit and dances his little jig, singing, "Catch-catch-catch me if you can. I'm a little ol' possum dressed like a man. I hide in trees. I hang by my tail. Bonk me with a hammer or you fail!"

"I haven't played this since I was ten," I say. Bright lights flood the all-black terrain inside the pit. The surface rises and falls in a series of hills and valleys with tall spires poking up, as if we've stumbled on the burned-out remains of an old forest fire. After a second or two, the animators blink on and transform the pit into a virtual field with grassy rolling hills, leafy trees, and a clear babbling brook under a dusky pink sky.

I laugh. "It looks so . . . so . . . so . . ."

"Retro? I know! And look at that." She points to the ugly pointy-faced hologranimal zipping across the field in front of us singing, "Catch-catch-catch me if you can!" over the twangy music. "Might as well be two-D."

I remember running myself to exhaustion with all my social-time buddies, chasing Petey who seemed so real to me back then. It was the newest thing when we were little, and we loved it. I almost hate seeing it again because now it seems so rinky-dink.

From a rack by the pit, Yaz grabs two comically oversize hammers that light up and buzz as if they are thrilled that someone is here to play with them. "Let's go sit by the pond," Yaz says.

I follow her on heavy legs up a hill, past some shimmering shrubs, and down to the edge of the water that never splashes. Out of the corner of my eye, I see the opossum zip by us, taunting us to try to catch him, but neither of us can be bothered to give chase.

I cradle my head in my hands then lie back on the grass that isn't there, which makes me think of the video I uploaded at the PlugIn the other day. "This would be better if there was some kind of animal grazing," I say to Yaz. "And if they used smell generators to re-create the scent of fresh grass. Or, I know!" I sit up too quickly and my head spins. "Someone should make a game where you could hunt or farm your own virtual food!"

Yaz wrinkles her nose. "That doesn't sound fun at all."

"But you could harvest everything and cook it and smell it!" I wonder if Basil's device could generate the aroma of roasted lamb or fresh vegetables just dug from the ground. As I'm trying to imagine the smell of roasting meat, my stomach shrieks. I double over, hugging my knees to my chest.

"Oh my god!" says Yaz. "What the hell is wrong with you?"

I stay curled in a ball, avoiding her eyes, wishing the whole thing would go away.

"No, really," Yaz says softly. "Are you okay?"

I peer up at her. "It keeps happening," I whisper while clutching my belly. My heart races because I'm afraid Yaz will scoot away, but she does the opposite. She moves closer. "Mom tried giving me more Synthamil the past couple of days, but it's not helping." I sigh because it's almost a relief to admit the truth. "But I can't tell her because if she finds out, she says I have to see a specialist."

Yaz blinks at me, then she says quietly, "My cousin Enid had to see a specialist."

I stare at her. "Why?"

"She got all obsessed with food. That's all she'd talk about. Then it got so bad she started eating weird things like dirt and lint." She shudders. "My aunt and uncle took her from one specialist to another, but nothing worked. She ended up on so many different drugs, she was like a zombie."

Yaz must see the look of horror on my face because she quickly adds, "But Enid had a lot of other problems. . . ."

"Like what?"

"Mental problems, I guess. She's older than me and this was a few years ago, so I don't remember that much about it. My mom told me she would make up stories about how One World is really evil and how no one knew the truth but her."

"What happened?" I ask.

Yaz chews on her bottom lip as if she's reluctant to tell me, but then says, "She disappeared. Vanished. They heard from her a few times. Last they knew she was in the Outer Loop. Then she stopped using her Gizmo. They think she joined some kind of cult or resistance group and just sort of fell off the face of the planet. It broke my aunt's heart. But that's not going to happen to you! Your mom will figure out what's wrong. She's the smartest person in the world."

"She certainly thinks so," I mutter.

"I don't think you should worry," says Yaz, then she chuckles and points at Petey rowing by us in a boat. "Look at that stupid possum."

I draw in a breath and sit up straight. "You know, if you wait long enough, the program sends him closer and closer to you," I tell her as he slinks around the edge of the pond toward us. I figured that out by standing back and watching the game over and over when I was a kid. I memorized Petey's patterns and found the weaknesses in his programming then talked to my dad about ways to improve the game. *If he was more unpredictable, the game would be more fun*, I remember saying. My dad said, *There's a word for that*. Verisimilitude. *The more a game feels like real life, the more intense it is to play.* "The thing is, he's programmed to get clobbered. Like it's in his DNA."

"Poor Petey," says Yaz, bouncing her hammer off the ground. "Never stood a chance."

"Do you ever think it's the same for people?" I ask.

"What? That your DNA decides your future?"

"No," I say. "Because DNA isn't deterministic. There are so many other things, like epigenetics, that come into play. I was thinking more esoteric. Like whether our fate is written in some cosmic code that we have no control over."

"You mean like your death has already been decided and there's nothing you can do about it?"

"I guess so." I stare up at the fake pink sky. "But other things, too. Like, were you and I destined to be friends or . . ." I stop, not sure how to phrase what I want to say.

"Or what?" she asks.

"I don't know. Do you think two people could be destined to meet and fall in love?" As soon as I say it, we both laugh out loud.

"Sounds like a movie!"

My body tingles as thoughts of Basil crowd my mind. "You don't think that can happen in real life, though?"

Yaz starts to answer, but then she stops and studies me. She's always had what our personality testers call Above Average Empathy. It's like she can read your mind sometimes just by looking at you and really listening to what you say or how you say it. "Did something happen?" She leans closer. "Did you meet someone? Is this about the guy you thought you saw earlier?"

Slowly, I nod. Then a smile spreads over my face, and before I know it, words are pouring out of me as I tell her every detail of how I met Basil at Flav-O-Rite, his scent machine, everything we talked about, and how he invited me to a meeting. Finally I say, "I can't explain why, but I think about him all the time, and I have this feeling. . . ." I sit up and press my hand over my breastbone.

"What feeling?" Yaz looks leery.

"This kind of dull, heavy ache in my chest. It doesn't hurt. Almost feels good. And my stomach gets all loopy. And my heart races and my palms sweat, and I think I see him everywhere. And I can't stop thinking about him."

Yaz stares at me perplexed and slightly amused. "You should tell your mom about that! Maybe that's why your stomach's making all those weird noises."

"The growling started before I met him, but do you want to hear the weirdest part?"

"It gets weirder?"

I hesitate.

"Tell me," she demands.

"Okay," I say, "but you have to promise not to freak out."

"What?" she leans in closer.

"The same thing happens to him."

Yaz pulls back and shakes her head. "That is not normal."

Disappointment crawls over me like a shadow, and I fling myself backward to the ground. "I don't care!" I holler to the phony heavens above me. "Maybe we were destined to meet."

"Ha!" Yaz laughs and snatches up her hammer. Out of the corner of my eye, I see Petey creeping toward us. She crouches, then in one quick motion she lunges and bonks Petey on the head. "Just like my hammer was destined to meet his skull!"

I laugh as we watch poor Petey spin in circles, lurching from foot to foot while little hologram blue jays orbit his head. "Ah, ya got me!" he exclaims and falls to the grass where he disappears, replaced by a bouquet of wilting yellow flowers.

"Let's just hope my destiny ends better than that," I say.

⚘   ⚘   ⚘

After the EntertainArena, I chug another blue Synthamil so my stomach will stay quiet while I'm around my mother. When I walk into the living room, I find my entire family gathered with my parents' best friend, Ahimsa DuBoise.

"Finally!" my dad shouts. "We've been waiting for you."

"Why, what's going on?" I ask, half afraid they know what I've been up to. But Dad is beaming, and then it hits me. "Is your product launching?"

My dad never looks happier than when he's got some new invention to share. I swear his green eyes are brighter and his sandy curls bouncier, like they're buoyed on top of his head by all his brainpower. Ahimsa, on the other hand, absorbs every kilowatt of his excitement into her deep calm like a black hole soaking up light. As always, she is poised and elegant, with long graceful arms, a beaky nose, and huge gray-green eyes edged in kohl that take in every detail of her surroundings. Ever since I can remember, her thick black hair has been cut in the same short, swept-back style that looks as if she's flying. Grandma Apple calls her the Bird Woman. Like my parents, she started out in science. They all studied at university together, but she quickly moved up the ranks of One World, pulling my parents along with her, until she was named CEO two years ago and she made my parents project leaders in their fields.

"I had to see our first test group," Ahimsa says as she gives me a cool, dry peck on the cheek. "How are your classes?" she asks, standing back and surveying me with arms crossed.

"Fine," I tell her with a shrug.

"And your ICM?"

I roll my eyes, which makes her laugh.

"Yes, I know," she says. "A necessary evil for the least common denominator among us. We really should have an exception for gifted children like Thalia," she says to my mom.

"It's good for her to interact with kids her age," Mom says glancing from me to Grandma Apple.

"Enough chitter-chatter!" Dad is like an eager kid dying to show off his new favorite toy. "Come see what I have."

We all gather around the low table in the living room. I feel like we're at a birthday party, watching a little kid open a present as my dad pulls out a small gray box and cradles it on his lap. "This," he says ceremonially lifting the lid, "is the latest generation One World Gizmo."

He reaches in and takes out a small black device about the size of his palm and the thickness of his finger. I glance at Ahimsa. Her dark eyes shine with pride.

"Looks just like the last generation," says Grandma Grace.

"Yes, it does," my dad says. "But this one can do something no other Gizmo has ever done."

"It can do something that no other working device on Earth has ever been able to do outside of a lab," Ahimsa adds.

"Cure male-pattern baldness?" Papa Peter jokes, patting his shiny scalp. We all laugh, even Grandma Grace.

"Nope, still can't do that," Dad admits, but his enthusiasm isn't the least bit diminished by our teasing. He turns the new Gizmo over and over in his fingers.

"What's the most annoying thing about your Gizmo?" Dad asks.

"We only get to name one?" I say. Papa, Grandma Apple, and I look at each other and laugh with our eyes.

"Yes!" Dad eggs me on. "The thing that most burns your butt!"

I think for a few seconds then say, "That I have to have one at all."

"Exactly!" says Dad. "That's why you, my darling, were the inspiration for this." He holds the Gizmo flat on his palm for us to see, then he rubs his hand over the surface and it disappears. Everyone stares, flabbergasted.

"What? Where'd it go? Where is it?" we ask each other.

Dad laughs. "Still right here." He rubs his hand back over the surface and the Gizmo reappears.

We ooh and aah. Ahimsa claps her hands, delighted by our reaction. I lean forward to get a closer look because even I'm impressed.

Dad smiles big at me. "We finally mastered the nanotechnology of invisibility cloaking!"

"And it works the same, whether you can see it or not?" Mom takes it from Dad and practices making it disappear and reappear in her hand.

"All the same functions," Ahimsa says.

"Does the cloaking mode scramble the locator?" I ask.

"Excellent question!" says Dad, clearly proud. "Most of the work in cloaking up until now was to scramble radar signals so objects couldn't be detected by other machines, but we did something different. We embedded tiny crystal molecules like hinged shingles across the surface. On one side they absorb light and microwaves so you see the object, but when you flip them those nanoparticles cancel the electron scattering. In other words, it bends the light around the object so your brain thinks it's not there."

"Say what now?" Papa asks with a laugh. Then he waves his hands and admits, "Aw forget it. I'll never understand, but it sure is amazing." He takes the Gizmo from Mom and plays with it before giving it to Grandma Grace, who is equally impressed.

"And the best part," Dad says, reaching into his bag, "is that you'll have plenty of time to figure it out, because you each get one." He pulls out five more gray boxes. "But first, we have to recycle your old Gizmos." Papa, Mom, and both of my grandmothers happily pull out their old Gizmos and lay them on the table.

"Of course, we need to fix any bugs before we launch to the public," Ahimsa explains as Dad hands the devices around. "So, we'll be collecting data while you use yours."

"Nothing out of the ordinary," Dad says. "Just a log of functions and malfunctions that occur."

Ahimsa turns to me. "Obviously we want you to show yours off to all your friends."

Obviously, I think, *you don't know me well if you think I have a lot of friends or that I like to show off devices.*

"We want to get some buzz going in your demographic," Ahimsa says, "because that will create demand, and you know what demand creates. . . ." She waits for me to fill in the rest.

"Profit," I mumble.

"And . . . ?" she asks. When I don't answer, she looks at my mom and dad, who both chime in. "Profit makes the world go around."

"I'll go throw these in the compactor, so we can get your cyber assistants uploaded," Dad says, gathering up the old devices, then he realizes he only has four in his hands. He looks up at me. "Where's yours, Thal?"

"Mine?" I ask nervously. "Um, uh, I'm sure it's in my room somewhere. I'll take care of it later."

He shakes his head. "We have to crash your old one."

"Can't I keep it?" I ask.

Ahimsa scowls. "Keep a piece of obsolete technology? Why?"

I can't answer since the truth would incriminate me as a hacker to the CEO of One World.

"Don't worry," Dad says, cheerily. "Astrid will operate on your new phone, too."

Lucky me, I think, but what I say is, "I'll go get it," and trudge off to my room. All the time I've spent over the past year reconfiguring my Gizmo will soon be smashed into a million tiny Recyclabits. At least I know how I'll be entertaining myself for the next few weeks while I reconfigure the new one.

I find the Gizmo nestled in my bed beneath a wad of blankets. "Sorry, old girl," I tell it as I carry it off to its death. "You've become obsolete."

✳   ✳   ✳

Sitting in front of my room screen the next night is a worthless endeavor because I can't focus on my assignment. I've tried every possible position—lying across my messy bed, sitting up at my desk, curling around a big pillow on the floor. But no matter what, my head aches, my stomach rumbles, and my mind keeps wandering to Basil.

I've tried a dozen times to find more info about him or the Analogs, but every search comes up as empty as I feel. It's as if there is no group called the Analogs and no one with the name Basil (first or last) has ever logged on to a OW site. No record at any EntertainArenas, PlugIns, TopiClubs, or ICMs. No purchase history. No birth records with that name from fifteen to twenty years ago, and there are no Basils in the Dynasaur chat logs. Either he's more of a virtual ghost than I am, which sends a shiver of delight down my spine, or he lied to me about everything, which makes my grumbling stomach queasy.

To take my mind off Basil and my belly, I pull out my new Gizmo and try again to hack into the operating system. So far, everything I've tried has failed. In addition to cloaking this sucker, Dad's team must have upgraded the firmware so none of the old Dynasaur programs I used before work this time. I've tried tweaking the old programs and even written half a dozen new ones since Dad handed me the device last night, all to no avail. After another half hour of failing to install my own operating system that will allow me to turn off my locator and make Astrid sleep on command, I throw the Gizmo across the room out of sheer frustration. It skids across the floor and slips into invisibility. I never thought I'd think this, but I miss my old Gizmo.

From her hiding place, Astrid shouts, "Your family genome map is due in an hour!"

"Oh, shush," I shout back, but I glance at the clock on my main screen and see that she's right, so I try to refocus on my assignment.

A's, T's, G's, and C's swim in front of me as the program I wrote cranks through lines of code, looking for traits I share with my parents and grandparents. I've found all the easy physical features. The OCA2 SNiP that gives Grandma Apple and me our green eyes. My earlobe attachment from Mom and Grandma Grace. My inability to roll my tongue just like Papa Peter. And the more complicated multigene soups for personality traits where I can pinpoint my family's propensity for intelligence and shyness and why none of us have perfect pitch. I've accounted for all the disease mutations that have been carried by my grandparents, treated in my parents, and altered in me. But, no matter how many times I run the data, I come up with a mutation on my chromosome 16 FTO gene that doesn't make sense.

Someone knocks softly on my door. "Come in," I call, assuming it's Grandma Apple, but when the door slides open, my mom stands there.

She's still in her lab coat and has her hair pulled back in a tight low bun, but she's slipped off her shoes and pads into my room barefoot.

"You're home early," I say. "It's only seven."

"Easy day in the lab." Mom drops down on the bed beside me. She reaches back to loosen her hair, letting it spill over her shoulders. She looks younger that way. And pretty. I try to imagine my parents falling in love. Did their hearts race when they thought about each other after they first met? I almost laugh out loud at the thought of my mother feeling as out of control as I do.

"Remember when we used to play spalon when you were little?" she says, lifting a lock of thick hair from her shoulder and examining it for split ends. "I'd look like a crazy person when you were done with me."

"I can't believe you'd sit there for that long and let me put braids and clips and ponytails all over your head."

"I wasn't very playful when you were little, was I?" Mom says with a sigh.

"I had Grandma Apple."

"What are you working on?" She points to my screen.

I stiffen because I don't want her to see my mistake. Chromosome 16 and its FTO gene were her first babies. The thing she loved more than anything until she had me. Her breakthrough in the lab tweaking this gene to create an ongoing satiety response in humans meant no one would ever feel the sensation of hunger again. Once no one felt the urge to eat anymore, Synthamil finally caught on. That made her a superstar scientist at One World.

"It's our family's comparative human genome map," I tell her. "I'm almost done." I start to close my screen, but I'm too late.

"Wait." She stands up to get a better look at the line of code I've puzzled over for the past hour. "That's odd." She points to the questionable letter sequences. "Did you check the public genome databases for this mutation?"

"Of course, but I didn't find anything. Maybe there was a glitch in the program I wrote."

"I doubt it." Mom stares at the code and shakes her head, bewildered. "Could be a spontaneous mutation." She gathers her hair in her hands and twists it back into a bun.

"Can that still happen? I mean with the inocs continually fine-tuning DNA?"

She thinks this over, then she says, "It would explain a lot. . . ."

I'm not quite listening to her puzzle through the implications of what she's seeing while I attach a footnote about the possibility of spontaneous mutation. "All I know is that I'm glad to have this done!" I hit send and submit my assignment. When I look up, Mom's still deep in thought. "What's wrong?" I say. "You're looking at me weird."

"Is your stomach still growling?"

I shrug, unwilling to admit the truth.

"Because if your FTO gene is flawed that could cause all the symptoms of hunger. And if you have it . . ." She paces around my room. "It could be present in a larger population. But what would be causing it?" She stares at the screen while biting the side of her mouth. "There must be a specialist I can take you to—"

"No way," I say. "Leave me out of it."

She whips her head around. "I can't leave you out of it." She jabs her finger at the screen. "You *are* it and I'm trying to help you."

"By dragging me off to some *specialist* who wants to patent some new procedure?" I say. "I'm not going to be someone's lab cat."

"Lab cat?" Mom asks.

"Isn't that what they used to experiment on?"

"Rats," Mom says. "Lab rats."

"Well, I don't want to be one of those either."

"Science is constantly evolving, Thalia. We have to be open to new advances. What if no one allowed me to do my work when I first started? Where would we be then?"

"Your work was for the greater good," I argue. "Not for personal gain."

She crosses her arms and raises her chin. "I've been paid well for my discovery."

"But that's not why you did it. The money came later. Right?"

She nods but then admits, "When I started out, there was still public money, from the government, for researchers, so I could at least get started on my work before I had corporate sponsorship. It's harder now. Researchers have to find revenue streams however they can. I'm lucky to have One World behind my work, but there are still reputable people out there who put science over profit. I would only take you to someone who has your best interests at heart." She cocks her head to the side and searches my face as if I've become temporarily unrecognizable. "Surely you know that I want what's best for you."

"There's nothing wrong with me," I say, but even I'm not totally convinced anymore.

Mom looks over her shoulder at my screwy genome. "No," she says looking back at me with pity. "Something's not right here, and we have to find someone to fix it."

✤   ✤   ✤

It doesn't take Mom long to find the specialist who might have the answer. In less than twenty-four hours, we're sitting across from Dr.

Darius Demeter who leans back in his sleek office chair and stares at us over his expansive faux-wood desk. He's listened to Mom talk non-stop for fifteen minutes about my "symptoms." My ketone, dopamine, and insuline levels. My height, weight, and metabolism. The optimal formula for my Synthamil. The hollow feeling I've described. My growling stomach. My irritability. I sit there, barely breathing, afraid that all the talk of hunger will trigger some crazy banshee screech from my insides.

Of course, she also marches out my messed-up genome sequence as further proof that something must be deeply wrong with me. Dr. Demeter nods, occasionally grunts, and jots down notes on his Gizmo as my mother yammers on. Now he pauses, gathers his thoughts, and finally launches into his interpretation of her data.

"Unfortunately, we're seeing more and more of this." He leans on one elbow and taps the side of his head with his finely manicured index finger. Everything about him appears too well-kempt from his precisely trimmed steel-colored hair and close-cropped beard down to his pointy brown wing-tip shoes so polished they nearly gleam. There's not a wrinkle on him. Not a hair out of place. Not a speck of stray lint to be found. It's as if no variation from perfection will be tolerated by this man. He gives me the willies.

"Obviously I don't have to tell you, Dr. Nguyen," he continues, "that we know she's receiving the proper amount of nutrition. More than anybody, you understand how Synthamil is calibrated, so I won't waste your time convincing you that her feelings of hunger are not physical."

I slump back in my seat and cross my arms. "Here we go...." I mutter.

"Thalia!" Mom gives me the eyebrow. "Hear the doctor out. He's an expert in this field."

Dr. Demeter is not deterred by my skepticism. He leans forward and folds his hands on top of his desk then gives me a weak smile. "It's a very honest and natural response to believe you need more nutrition when you feel this way. During the obesity epidemic in the early twenty-first century . . ."

"I didn't say that I needed more nutrition," I protest.

He sits back and fires off a round of questions. "Do you ever dream of food or imagine what it would be like to eat? Do you find yourself searching for an elusive scent or sensory experience, but no matter how hard you try, can't pinpoint exactly what you're looking for?" I feel color rising to my cheeks. "Have you used forno to try to quell the desire to consume?" I flush and squirm in my chair, willing my insides to stay quiet.

He plows ahead, not needing to wait for my answers. "There's a pattern in these cases. It starts with a vague sense of malaise, an unnamed desire, a hollow, empty feeling that can't be assuaged. The body may respond. In some people it can express itself as a sexual desire even when there's no hormone surge initiation. In others, it mimics what humans used to experience as hunger. The stomach growls, energy levels dip, moods swing and yet, as we can see from the data, you are receiving enough nutrition. Which can lead us to only one conclusion."

"Let me guess," I say, my sarcasm barely contained. "It's all in my mind?"

He lifts his hands as if to say, *Who knows?*

My mom has little patience for this. "What's your research show?"

He crosses his legs and taps the side of his head again. "As best as we can surmise, some people, especially those who might be at risk for obsessive-compulsive disorders, may not be able to handle the stress of not eating. Afterall, we are hardwired to eat. Because our inocs and daily Synthamil cocktail now regulate nearly everything, including the serotonin production in our brains, we rarely see the kinds of OCD behaviors that would have been present in the past. Ritualistic behaviors such as repeated hand washing or door locking or a heightened sexual response have largely been eradicated. But this question of not eating seems to be trickier than we thought. No disrespect, of course," he quickly adds when my mom blanches.

"None taken," she says, but I sense she's miffed.

He hefts himself from his chair and walks toward the window behind his desk. "The problem is that eventually the thought cycles about food and eating become actions." He turns, hands clasped behind his back, eyes locked above our heads as he lectures. "The desire to fill the perceived emptiness becomes a physical imperative." His pace quickens. "Patients begin to seek experiences that they believe will alleviate their overwhelming urges. They may turn to forno or engage in pica."

"Pica?" Mom asks.

He props himself against the front edge of his desk, arms and ankles crossed, and levels his gaze at her. "Consuming nonfood items. Dirt, lint, fabric." He shakes his head. "I've seen patients eat all kinds of things."

Mom makes a sick face.

"It's very sad," says Dr. Demeter. "And the worst untreated cases often end up in jail, because as we know, engaging in such activities can lead to illegal behavior."

Before I can ask why eating dirt could possibly be illegal, Dr. Demeter spins around and heads to the window, booming, "But luckily we caught this early!" He turns and smiles. "I have no doubt that with some cognitive behavior therapy, perhaps an added dash of serotonin to Thalia's Synthamil, and constant monitoring, we'll get this under control in no time."

"Do you think the mutation on her FTO gene has anything to do with it?" Mom asks.

"I doubt it." He waves away her concern. "I'd say a month in our rehab facility, and she'll be well on the road to total recovery."

My stomach drops. "Rehab facility? A month?"

Dr. Demeter has settled himself in his chair again. "Yes, I run an inpatient treatment program."

I shake my head. "No. No way. I am not going to be locked up for an entire month!"

"We find that having a controlled environment for several weeks facilitates the process," says Dr. Demeter.

"Mom?" I catch her eye. My breath quickens and sweat prickles my armpits. "You can't do that to me. I won't let you." I press my hands into the chair, wanting to push off and flee.

"Well, um, Thalia, if that's . . ." Mom stutters.

"Dad would never go for it," I say. "And Grandma Apple wouldn't either. They won't let you lock me away just because my stomach sometimes growls."

"Thalia," Dr. Demeter says in a calm, even voice. "The thing you need to understand is that this will get much worse. If we take care of it now, you will save yourself from lengthier, more intrusive therapies down the road. And I assure you both, my facility is state of the art with a very comfortable, homey feel. Our care is excellent. And seeing as you're Dr. Nguyen's daughter, I would personally oversee your case from start to finish."

"That's very kind of you," Mom says, clearly flattered.

"I've been such a fan of your work for years," Dr. Demeter goes on, buttering up my mother. "And not to be too presumptuous, but I believe you would find our research very interesting. You would be welcome to visit anytime and see the exciting discoveries we're making."

Mom leans forward eagerly as he talks. This is too much for me. I slam my hands on his desk and shout, "We're talking about my life, not your research!"

Mom jumps. We stare at each other for a few seconds before she says, "Honey, we're talking about both."

Tears press hot against my eyes. The thought of being locked in a lab for a month is almost unbearable. I won't be able to see Basil again or talk to Yaz or be with Grandma Apple. "You can't do this to me." I fumble for the knit holder Grandma made me and pull out my new Gizmo. "I'm calling Dad."

"Put that down. You're being ridiculous!" Mom says sternly. "And embarrassing. We're trying to help you."

Dr. Demeter folds his hands and presses his long index fingers against his top lip. "I can't force anyone to come here. Unless there's been an arrest and a court order."

Mom huffs. "Well I can. She's only seventeen so I have jurisdiction over her."

My jaw drops.

"We have a higher success rate with willing participants," he tells her.

Mom narrows her eyes and thinks for a moment. Then she turns to me. "So what's it going to take, Thalia? What would make you willing to give this a try?"

I'm so surprised that my mother is seeking my opinion that at first I'm speechless. But then I squeak, "No drugs. I don't want to end up like some brain-dead zombie."

"We only make minor tweaks to your personal Synthamil cocktail designed to make you feel better, not worse," says Dr. Demeter.

"And second," I add, before my mom can butt in. "I don't want to be locked up. I didn't do anything wrong."

"You shouldn't think of it as being locked up. . . ." Dr. Demeter tells me.

"So I can come and go as I please?" I ask.

"Well no, but . . ."

"Then I'm not doing it." I turn to my mom. "It's like you want to get rid of me, the minute I'm not perfect Thalia anymore. Ship me off to a lab and let them fix me. If you're such an expert, why don't you take care of me?" A few tears escape and roll down my cheeks. I swat at them angrily.

"I'm trying to," Mom says through gritted teeth.

We sit quietly for a moment at an impasse. I think of my alternatives. I could leave. Hide out for a while. Go stay with Yaz on the sly or live out of Flav-O-Rite—if I could find it again.

Mom stares at her hands in her lap and takes a long, deep breath as if she senses my determination. "Would you agree to come as an outpatient?" she asks me.

Dr. Demeter frowns. Deep lines from the sides of his nose to his chin appear, and he shakes his head.

"You said she needs a controlled environment, right?" she asks him.

"Well, yes, but . . ."

"What if I can provide that for her at home, but she comes here daily for treatment?" Mom offers.

I figure this is the best deal I'm going to get so before she can change her mind or he can talk her out of it, I say, "Fine. I'll do it."

Mom looks Dr. Demeter square in the eye. "I think that would be most beneficial to us all. If I can follow your research firsthand in my own home, I might find that it would parlay nicely with a future One World project I'm considering for funding."

At this Dr. Demeter perks up. "Given your esteemed position, I suppose we could make an exception this one time."

"Excellent," Mom says, straightening her jacket.

"But," Dr. Demeter adds, "only on the condition that if she's not making enough progress after two weeks, we reconsider inpatient treatment."

"That's reasonable." Mom gives him a tight smile. "We'll start Monday morning then." She stands and extends her hand.

Dr. Demeter pushes awkwardly out of his chair and reaches for her. "But Dr. Nguyen," he says when they clasp hands. "I should warn you, this condition can change or progress quickly. You'll need to be vigilant in your observations. If you notice anything out of the ordinary—say, personality shifts, mood swings, or erratic behavior—you must alert me right away."

"Of course," Mom says, withdrawing her hand. "We'll see you Monday."

⚘   ⚘   ⚘

During the ride home from Dr. Demeter's office, Mom craps on and on about how much she's sacrificing for me to have outpatient treatment. How her integrity is on the line. How I better take this seriously. When her Smaurto pulls into the driveway, I can't take it anymore, so I slam out of the car and into the house, but she's right on my heels, shouting, "You should be grateful!"

Dad and Grandma Apple look up startled from where they sit side by side on the couch.

I turn on my mother and clench my teeth. "You should want to take care of me, not hold it over my head."

"Of course I want to take care of you. . . ."

"Could have fooled me!" I yell.

My dad looks from Mom to me and back to Mom. "Did I miss something here?"

"Dr. Demeter . . ." Mom starts to explain.

"She tried to lock me in his lab for a month!" I say. Grandma looks appropriately horrified.

Mom throws up her hands. "Stop being so dramatic!"

"You're the one who's dramatic. Acting like you're some kind of martyr for making me one of your research projects. I'm not some petri dish of chromosomes in your lab!"

"I practically offered to make that man my protégé so he would take you as an outpatient!" Mom shouts. "Do you have any idea how coveted my help is for someone like him?"

I shake my head, fighting back tears of frustration. "I would hope," I say quietly, "you'd believe in his work that much if you're going to send me there."

Mom looks stunned. Then she stutters, "Thalia, that's not . . . you misunderstood . . . I do . . ."

But I'm not listening, because I stomp off to my room, fuming.

⚜   ⚜   ⚜

For the next hour, I lie on my bed with an empty feeling tugging at my belly while I search for any information about other people who feel the way I do. Astrid finds nothing. Like Basil and the Analogs, it's as if they don't exist online. Sometimes I feel like I must have conjured up the whole thing. It's possible they could have an underground presence, I suppose, but since I haven't been able to crack my OS on the new Gizmo, I can't snoop around without giving myself away. I've never seen anything about this on the Dynasaur chats. I know they must be out there, though. Dr. Demeter claims to have a whole rehab facility dedicated to freaks like me. The only conclusion I can draw is that they've all been locked up or drugged up—a fate I'm going to do everything in my power to avoid.

The next time I glance at the clock it's nearly five, and for the first time today, my life doesn't seem so bad. Silently, I recite the info one more time: "Analogs, Friday, six p.m., 1601 South Halsted."

In less than an hour, I will see Basil again! This thought fills me up and makes my stomach buzz with anticipation.

"Good, you're back!" Grandma says when I come into the living room where she's sitting in front of the main screen with my parents. "I thought we could all play Scrabble tonight."

"I have plans," I tell her and immediately feel bad.

"But, but, but . . ." Grandma sputters.

"It's family night," Dad says, finishing her sentence. "We're all here finally. It was on the schedule."

"I have my parents' old board with real tiles," says Grandma.

"Sorry." I bend down to give her a quick hug. "You'll have to do it without me this time."

"Where are you going?" Mom asks.

"Just out," I say.

"I don't think so," Mom says, but no one pays attention to her.

"Are you meeting up with friends?" Grandma asks, forcing a smile.

I nod, even though I know that's not how they would categorize Basil.

"Well, okay then," Grandma says, and this time she does smile at me, genuine and true.

"No," says Mom. "It's not okay. Dr. Demeter said . . ."

"I'm not his patient until Monday morning," I remind her.

She starts to argue with me, but Dad squeezes her thigh and says, "It's okay, honey. You should go."

"Max!" Mom shouts. "You're completely undermining me."

"I think you both need some space from one another," Dad says calmly. He turns back to me. "Don't stay out too late."

"I won't," I say then I hesitate. Part of me feels like I should tell them what I'm doing. I'm sure they're imagining me at the EA with Yaz. But, I know my mom would never allow me to leave if she knew where I'm heading. I decide to keep the details to myself and get out before she harangues my dad into changing his mind. "See you later," I say, heading for the front vestibule.

"She can be so impossible, and you two let her get away with it!" my mom huffs.

"Oh now, Lily," Grandma Apple says in a rare moment of standing up to my mother. I pause in the vestibule to listen. "She's seventeen. She's supposed to be impossible. And she's not supposed to want to be with us. It's good that she's going out with friends."

"Hmph," says Mom. "My next research project is going to be further altering teens' Synthamil formula so they're less of a pain in the butt."

After hearing that, I'm happy to walk out the door.

✢   ✢   ✢

In my Smaurto, I tell Astrid the address Basil made me memorize. If it weren't for the fact that I have no idea where I'm going or how long it will take me to get there, I'd leave my stupid Gizmo behind. The only thing I've figured out is how to completely block the network signal so at least I can stop Astrid from constantly yapping at me. The problem is, if I want to use any of her features, like her GPS, I have to accept the signal again, which makes everything I do online trackable and traceable.

As I wait for Astrid to calculate directions, I realize that I could have the address wrong. The numbers could have transposed themselves in my mind over the past few days. The name could have morphed into some other street rattling around inside my brain. Memory is a tricky thing and without a cloud keeping track of hard data, the edges of information become fuzzy. It takes Astrid longer than it should to find the address, which makes me worry that I'm wrong. If I am, I could end up anywhere. But then she says, "Got it!" and we pull out of the drive.

I'm nervous and I second-guess myself as my Smaurto carries me west. What if my parents find out where I'm going? They never told me I couldn't go to an Analog meeting. Then again I never asked. Do they even know about the Analogs? I'm in that murky territory of not exactly lying but definitely evading the truth. That's something I don't mind doing as HectorProtector, but real-time Thalia doesn't like to disappoint her parents. Then I have a worse thought. *What if Basil isn't there?*

Then again, what if he is there? Will he be excited to see me? My pulse quickens and my stomach gets all jumpy when I think of him. Has he been thinking about me this week? Will there be a chance for us to talk? Could we find a quiet place to sit, facing each other, our knees nearly touching, so I can ask him all the questions that have been circling around inside my head since I first met him? While I run through possible scenarios, my Smaurto goes farther and farther west, until after almost twenty minutes it slows down and idles at a tollgate on the western edge of the Inner Loop.

"Would you like to proceed?" Astrid asks, which snaps me out of my daydream, sweaty and a little embarrassed for getting lost in thoughts about Basil. Again. At least the patch is off my back so Mom can't spy on my emotions while I sneak around.

"1601 South Halsted is in the Outer Loops," Astrid tells me. A map appears on the Smaurto's screen with a red star flashing a few blocks on the other side of the wall. Usually when I've left the Inner Loops it's been in my family's helicopter on the way to a vacation center, but I've never crossed over alone.

During the wars, the mega-highways lying like belts around the city were easy to convert into these reinforced steel-and-concrete walls during the worst of the fighting when each population center was fending for itself. Of course, being inland and to the north, our city lasted longer than those on the coasts, which were battered by decades of superstorms then eventually swallowed up by the encroaching seas. Since we were surrounded by farmland, our food supply lasted longer. And the fresh water on one side of us still has enough algae to keep oxygen in our air. Geography, my dad has pointed out, was more than half of the equation when it came to who survived into this century and who didn't. Of course, having One World headquartered in our population center didn't hurt either. Once governments failed, the world's largest corporation cleaned up the mess, starting in their own backyard, which is why our population center recovered more quickly than others.

The walls remain today, but they're no longer sealed. Automated tollbooths every few miles segregate the Inner Loops from the Outer. The most privileged from the less so. When I question this, my parents shrug and say it's not really any different than how it always was, just more clearly defined. My mother likes to point out that anyone can come in, to which I always add, as long as they can pay. And her retort: *We foot the bill for automated roads, security, and a constant network connection in the Inner Loops, so why shouldn't everyone pay for services they use?*

"Do you want to proceed?" Astrid asks me again.

I hesitate. I could turn around and go home to play Scrabble or go find Yaz. The gate stays down, waiting for me to make up my mind. Then my belly speaks for me. It rumbles the answer: *Go find other people who feel like this.* I suck in a deep breath. "Proceed," I say, trying to sound confident.

⚘   ⚘   ⚘

My Smaurto turns onto Halsted Street. The whole area is run down and dingy. Nothing much has happened here since this part of the city was abandoned. Other places in the Outer Loops, like the South, are starting to come back to life but this one looks beyond resuscitation with its crumbling buildings and rough roads. There are no solar panels and no Whisson Windmills. I think about heading back, sure that I've remembered the address wrong, or worse, that Basil gave me false info, but then I see a group of people clothed in shades of green and brown chatting happily as they file into a low brick building with 1601 above the door. Relief washes over me.

I study the crowd. For a moment every boy looks like Basil, except that when I look more closely, none of them are. As the Smaurto pulls up to the curb, I see men and women, old and young, even a few little kids. How will I ever find him? Of course, if he had a Gizmo I could ping him. While I agonize over whether I should get out or give up and leave, someone taps my window. I jump when I turn and see Basil. I command the window down with a shaky voice.

"Apple?" he says, peering at me.

Hearing him call me Apple immediately takes me back to Flav-O-Rite, and I start to smile. He grins as if we're sharing a private joke. He's even more beautiful than I remember, and for a moment I can't talk because he looks at me with the kind of yearning I feel deep in my gut every day. Then he shoves his hands in the pockets of his brown pants and shakes the hair out of his eyes, looking uncertain while I sit like a moron on mute. I force myself to squeak, "I made it," and cringe at the tremor in my voice. What the hell is wrong with me? I swallow hard and try to pull myself together.

"I was afraid I might have scared you away the other night," he says, his voice serious and concerned.

"No!" I blurt out. "Not at all. I've been looking forward to this all week." My skin flushes with embarrassment for admitting it, but Basil's face lights up like the sun coming out from behind dark clouds, and I feel better.

"Me, too," he says and waits. We stare at each other, smiling awkwardly. "So, are you going to get out of your car?"

"That'd be a good idea!" I say like an idiot. I command the door open then tell the Smaurto to go park, but when I look around, I notice that no one else who is going into the building is coming out of a Smaurto. "Where are all the other cars?"

Basil looks at me out of the corner of his eye and sort of smirks. "Not everybody has their own automated transportation device, Apple. There are other ways of getting around." Before I can ask what that might be, he touches my elbow. Tiny bumps flash across my skin, and a ripple goes through my belly, which for a moment quells the gnawing hunger inside me. "Let's go inside."

We head for the door where people have formed two lines to pass between a man and a woman carefully scrutinizing each person before allowing them inside.

"What's that all about?" I ask.

"Security," he says.

I almost laugh. "Against what?"

"The wrong element."

"Titanium? Helium? Or the dreaded sodium?"

He barks a surprised laugh. "Was that a chemistry joke?"

"Yes!" I say and my heart soars. "Hardly anyone ever gets my nerdy sense of humor."

"Sounds like you've been hanging around with the wrong crowd," he tells me.

"Understatement," I say, and he laughs.

We step up to the door. The woman nods to Basil, but the man holds out his arm, blocking my path. "She's with me," says Basil. The man glances at the woman, who gives a slight nod. The man lifts his arm for me to pass, and I follow Basil through the door.

⚡ ⚡ ⚡

The space inside the building is empty and crude. The floor is hard gray concrete and the walls are real brick. Actual wooden beams hang overhead. Weirder still, the room is lit only by the late afternoon sun streaming through a large bank of windows. There's not a screen in sight or the low-level drone of tiny motors, and yet the place seems more alive and interesting than any PlugIn or EA I've ever been to. "Wow," I say. "This place is beautiful."

"I love it here," Basil says. "We used to meet in a dark basement below a machine shop in the North Loop like we were hiding, but then Ana found this."

"Who's Ana?"

"You'll see," Basils says.

We walk around the perimeter of the room, and I put my finger on what's so strange but compelling about this place. "Look," I say, pointing at a group of people. "Everybody's talking to one another. If we were any place else they'd all be murmuring to their screens."

"That's why we don't allow Gizmos here."

I stop myself from gaping at this information and blurting out, *You mean no one here has a Gizmo!* Instead, I slip my hand inside my pouch and cloak mine.

Basil presses his hand into the small of my back. I want to lean into his touch. "Let's find a place to sit."

There must be over a hundred seats and most of them are already filled, but we find a couple of rickety metal chairs, probably from my grandma's era. I turn to Basil and whisper, "Is everybody here, you know . . . ?"

"Are they what?" he whispers back.

"Like us?" I ask. "You know, hungry."

"There are many kinds of hunger," he says slyly. A hush falls over the room. He points to the front. "It's about to start."

A woman in a billowy flower-print dress walks to the front. "Hello and welcome, Analogs!" she says cheerfully.

"Hello," everyone says together, which startles me.

Basil puts his hand on my knee and swallows a laugh. "You okay?" he whispers.

I nod, slightly embarrassed. "Is that Ana?"

He shakes his head then leans close to my ear. His breath tickles my neck. "First there'll be some entertainment, then she'll come out."

"What a wonderful program we have planned," the woman says. "So many exciting offerings from our pool of talented Analogs. First up, we have our beautiful Radish."

A small and spritely woman wrapped in fluttery green clothes skips to the front of the room. She looks out on the crowd and announces, "This is called *Full Moon Planting*. It's an interpretive dance about when farmers would sow their seeds beneath the light of a full moon."

Everyone politely applauds but me because I'm too busy wondering what the hell an "interpretive dance" is. Radish bows her head and closes her eyes for a moment. Then she looks up and lifts her arms in a circle. She twirls, the edges of her clothes fluttering to the sides. She glides across the floor, pretending to pluck something small from an imaginary basket under her arm and drops it lightly to the ground. It's as if she's playing a dancing game, but there's no animated 3-D world around her or hologram creatures to avoid. Then she stops and curls into a ball. She rolls to the ground, slowly snaking her arm upward into a shaft of sunlight speckled with dust.

I have no idea what she's actually doing. Part of me is embarrassed for her but another part is mesmerized. I want to laugh because it's like watching a little kid who still plays make-believe, only she's a grown woman. On the other hand, her movements are lovely and fluid. And when I stop questioning why she's doing what she's doing and I simply watch her, I find myself thinking of my grandfather Hector coaxing his green shoots from the ground. Or of my grandmother picking vegetables from her garden. When Radish stands with her arms above her head, reaching for the sky, beaming with happiness, I feel her joy. She bows and everyone, including me, claps.

"Thank you, Radish!" the woman in the flower-print dress shouts over our applause. "Thank you for sharing such beauty of the human body with us. You are an inspiration."

Next, the woman brings up a man named Kumquat who strums an antique wooden guitar and sings, "There once was a tree. A pretty little tree. The prettiest little tree that you ever did see. Oh, the tree in a hole, and the hole in the ground." Then everyone joins in, "And the green grass grew all around, all around, and the green grass grew all around!"

I feel silly, like I'm at toddler social time when we'd sit in a circle singing songs together. I used to love how our voices blended and everybody was happy. But that was when I was three years old. I can't believe all of these adults are willfully joining in. I glance at Basil who unself-consciously sings along. On the next round, I figure what the heck, and I join in, too, singing as I haven't since I was tiny. "And the green grass grew all around, all around. And the green grass grew all around!"

I laugh wildly at the freedom of acting like this in public. I hope no one is streaming this. I can just imagine the snarky comments about us on some PRC chat board. Then I remember—no Gizmos. Which means no cameras. Which means that only the people who are really here will ever experience this. It's just us. Here. In the moment, as Grandma Apple would say. And when we leave, there will be no permanent record. What a wonderful feeling.

Another woman, my grandmothers' age, recites a poem about birds. A guy, not much older than Basil and me, plays a fiddle while a little girl with curly hair dances what she calls a jig. When the entertainment is over, everyone applauds for a long time. Even I clap until my hands hurt. I'm excited about what I've seen and experienced with these people, and I didn't need an algorithm to tell me that I'd like it.

Now the woman in the flowery dress stands in front of us again.

She bows her head for a moment and clasps her hands, which seems to signal everyone to quiet down. She takes a deep breath and everyone breathes with her. She exhales and everyone lets their breath go. Then, as if on cue, everyone rises. I stumble to my feet, looking around, wondering how they all knew what to do. The woman beams at us and says, "And now, please join me in welcoming our beautiful and amazing Ana."

↯   ↯   ↯

Everyone remains absolutely still and silent as a tall woman with flowing brown hair enters the room from a side door. The sun has sunk lower in the sky, bathing the room in golden light. The woman appears gossamer in her emerald green garment embroidered with intricate designs of extinct life-forms—both animals and plants. She radiates a broad smile toward her admirers, some of whom seem nearly overwhelmed. As she walks by the chairs, she squeezes people's hands and stares into their faces but never speaks, then she moves on. It takes several minutes for her to get through all the people who want to touch her, and in all that time, no one makes a sound.

I want to ask Basil a million questions. Who is she? Why won't she talk? What's with the staring? And why is everyone so reverent? Basil stands placidly at my side, hands folded behind his back, watching calmly. When I look at him with my eyebrows raised, he smiles gently then turns toward the front of the room again. I do the same and see that someone has placed a small platform in the center. Ana lifts the edge of her robe and climbs the steps then positions herself so that she's facing the crowd.

I wait but nothing happens. Ana simply stands on the platform looking out at all the people who stand and gaze back at her. She turns her head, imperceptibly slowly from the right to the left, as if she's scanning the room in super slo-mo. Like everyone else in the room, I can't take my eyes off her. I'm not even sure why. Am I afraid I'm going to miss something? Like she'll suddenly disappear or burst into flames? Or is it simply the novelty of standing quietly with other human beings while we really look at one another? No screens between us. No devices to distract us.

After several minutes she faces forward again, and her arms seem to float gently and effortlessly up from her sides. People begin to sniffle. Others moan or whimper quietly. Some have closed their eyes and bowed their heads while tears stream down their cheeks. Basil stands exactly as before until slowly Ana's arms begin to descend. I feel a twinge of disappointment as her gaze softens, like I'm not ready for this to end. When her eyes are half closed and her hands hang loosely at her sides, she draws in a deep breath. Everyone around me does the same. Then, by some invisible cue, they all exhale simultaneously like before, breaking the spell in the room.

Soft murmurs travel through the crowd as people start engaging in all kinds of interpersonal touching. They hug one another, shake hands, and pat each other on the back.

"Amazing," someone near me says.

"So much love and light," a woman answers.

"My heart is full again."

I jump when a man lays his hand on my shoulder. "Namaste," he says.

"Uh, yeah..." I mutter, wriggling away, uncomfortable beneath his grip. "Same to you."

"What'd you think?" Basil asks me quietly.

"Honestly," I tell him, "I'm not sure what to think."

He leans close and says out of the side of his mouth, "A little weird, huh?"

I snort a surprised giggle. "Just a little."

"But powerful anyway," he adds and reaches for my hand. When he intertwines his fingers with mine, a thrill zips through my muscles like protons on waves of light. That is a touch I'll happily accept. Then he nods toward the front. "Show's not over yet."

We settle into our seats, hands clasped together, as Ana climbs down from the platform, which is wheeled off by the man and woman who had been guarding the door. Ana beams proudly at her followers and says, "Welcome Analogs, you beautiful perfect human beings." Her voice is strong, but she sounds tired, as if all that staring took something out of her. "Here we are again," she says with a little shrug as if she's not surprised. "Unplugged, unimpeded, uninhibited."

People in the audience are so excited, they begin to shout.

"Here we are!"

"They cannot keep us apart!"

"We are drawn together by energy." Ana draws her hands together at her chest. "Forever united by the ingenuity of the greatest invention ever made." She stops and I almost groan.

Here it comes, I think, feeling like a dupe when I hear the word "invention." Now it all makes sense. Is this an elaborate setup for some product or method or way of thinking that she wants us to buy into? I've heard of this kind of thing. She probably has her own PRC. I should have known.

Ana holds the silence for another beat, then she steps forward. "Ladies and gentlemen," she says, "I give you"—she sweeps her arms wide—"the human being!"

The crowd goes crazy. People whistle and clap and yell.

"Huh?" I ask Basil over the noise of the energized crowd. "What's she talking about?"

He squeezes my hand. "Us."

"Me and you?" I motion from him to me.

"No." He motions around the room. "All of us. Together."

Ana seems to gain momentum from the energy of the people and begins to pace, stopping in front of a little girl. "Come here, my love," she says, holding her hand out to the child. The girl stands up and follows Ana to the front. Ana kneels beside her. I have to crane my neck to see. "What's your name, sweetie," Ana asks.

"Marjoram," the girl says.

"And what do you have here?" Ana takes a sheet from the girl's hands.

"A drawing I made," the girl tells her.

Ana stands and holds the drawing above her head. It's a picture of animals on what appears to be real paper. "It's beautiful," says Ana, stroking the child's hair. "Can I borrow it for a minute?"

Marjoram nods, wide-eyed, then scurries back to her father's arms. Ana stares at the drawing for a few seconds and looks deeply troubled before she asks, "Where has all the beauty gone?" Her face clouds over. "This was called an apple." She points to a round red blob with small green leaves.

Basil jabs me in the ribs and grins.

"I'm famous," I whisper.

"This was an ear of corn," Ana continues, pointing to other parts of the picture. "And here is a sunflower, and this looks like a chicken," she says, laying her finger on a red-and-white bird the kid painted. "And this was called a fish." She touches a pucker-lipped creature. "I bet some of your old-timers remember these. Fish once swam in the sea. And so did we. In the actual ocean." She walks to an old man and says, "I bet you went to the beach as a boy, didn't you, Spinach?" He nods happily.

"So where did it all go?" Ana paces now, picking up speed, waving the paper in front of her.

"Tell us!" someone shouts.

"All that beauty? Gone! Vanquished from the face of the Earth. Not by a meteor strike."

"No, no!"

"Not by an act of God."

"Not God!"

At the word "god" I wince and wonder if this whole thing is going to get weirder. Did I unwittingly stumble into one of those religious zealot groups still hanging on by their last shreds of faith?

"Where did they go?" she asks again. Even the youngest kids know the story. Is she a doubter? One of those hard-core skeptics who doesn't believe there was truly climate damage perpetrated by the selfish, uninformed humans from generations ago, who then fought over the few remaining resources until most of the world's population was decimated? Is she going to stand here and tell us that near-total global destruction was all a conspiracy by One World to get complete market domination? I'm not One World's biggest fan, but even I'm not that cynical.

"The fish, the fowl, the four-footed furry beasts," Ana continues, "have been eradicated from our midst, and we are left with what? Holograms?" Her laughter is bitter and harsh. "As if that is any kind of replacement? But it's not just the fauna. The flora has gone, too. The self-replicating lush green landscape that made Earth the most amazing planet in our solar system. Animals and plants of the Earth evolved as one. There was a symbiotic relationship." She laces her fingers together. "A give and take." She sways. "Our carbon dioxide for their oxygen. Our oxygen for their carbon dioxide. We fed one another with our very inhale and exhale." She stops, closes her eyes, and breathes deeply.

"And we felt things. Deep in our bodies. Hunger." She presses her hand over her stomach. "And desire." She moves her hand lower, just beneath her belly button and I squirm. "And in our hearts." Now she places both hands over her sternum. "Because the heart, my friends, is more than a muscle. We used to understand this when we were one with the Earth. When our energies were combined. We had empathy. We had love. We had anger and jealousy. And what's more, we relished the unpredictability of it all. We could experience a whole range of emotions that weren't tamped down by some chemical cocktail scientists create in a lab and tell us is for our own good."

The crowd jeers, and I sink in my seat, hoping no one realizes she's talking about my mother.

"We are supposed to be filled with yearning and compassion. If we will only allow ourselves to feel it again."

"I feel it, Ana!" someone shouts.

"You unchained my heart," another person yells.

"Those emotions made us human. They distinguished us from the machines we built. And no matter what they say, becoming one with machines is not the answer."

I wince, because this time the "they" she's talking about is my dad.

She clutches her robe tightly. "We humans are at our greatest when we work in tandem with the universe, not when we fight against it!" Ana stops and lowers her voice. "There are consequences when we distance ourselves from the natural order of things and go mucking around with the very fabric of our beings. We must recognize ourselves as part of the macrocosm rather than fool ourselves into believing we can exert control over it. But"—she shakes her head sadly then gives a little laugh—"we humans are not as wise as animals."

This kind of talk would drive both my parents crazy. They have no use for the idea that if we let nature take its course, everything will be fine. As my mother says, *Fine for whom? The cockroaches?*

Now Ana becomes coy. A little smile plays at the corners of her mouth, and she looks up and to the left as if imagining another time and place. "You know, when the first few fish grew legs, they didn't think to themselves, *Wow I should really chop off these legs.* No, they started roaming the Earth." She prowls through the crowd.

"And when that creature later sprouted wings, she didn't think to herself, *Wow I should really get rid of these wings*. No, she soared into the sky." Ana spreads her arms wide and spins. "We must accept the slow and subtle shifts nature confers on the lucky few so that they can find ways for all of us to soar!" She steadies herself but keeps her arms open. "Because my friends, we're standing on the edge of a precipice"—she teeters on her tiptoes—"ready to plummet toward our demise if we don't embrace the changes in our midst."

Now I'm sure this lady has lost it. Fish cutting off their own feet? Flying humans falling to their deaths? I have no idea what she's talking about. It all sounds crazy to me. And then, all of a sudden, she's very serious again. "Some of our brothers and sisters, like Tulip and Lettuce and Gardenia, have had their wings clipped. They've been locked away."

Gasps and protests rise up from the crowd. I look at Basil, who doesn't seem surprised by this news.

"Oh, yes," says Ana. "It's true. For what, you ask?" She stares at everyone, absorbing the energy buzzing through the room. "For being undeniably human. For participating in the most basic of human behaviors. For acting on the most fundamental of all human impulses. The thing we're meant to do from the moment we are born, which has been stripped away from us in the name of greater good."

A hush falls over the room as we wait for her to reveal their crime to us. I run possibilities through my mind. Acts of aggression? Theft? Breach of contract? I can't imagine someone named Gardenia doing anything so vile.

Ana lowers her arms. She lets her shoulders slump. She stands before us like a broken soul. "They were hungry," she says quietly. "Hungry for the give and take between the human being and the earth we are meant to have. Hungry for the life source meant to sustain us. This is not a bad thing, my friends. It is a human thing. It is this very desire that will carry us forward if only we have . . ." She points to the child's drawing again. Everyone claps and whistles. "And I'll tell you what's more," she shouts over the crowd. "It's out there, if only we will allow ourselves to find it."

People go crazy, but I let go of Basil's hand and lean far back in my chair, shaking my head because she's gone off the deep end.

Basil sees my reaction. "You okay?"

I raise an eyebrow at him. Surely he can't buy into her nonsense. "All the food is gone, remember?" I tell him as if he's an alien who hasn't heard the latest news about Earth. That it was my mom's discovery about controlling the hunger impulse by altering the FTO gene on chromosome 16 that led to the end of the wars. Foodless nutrition had been in the works for twenty years and was the only thing keeping humanity from joining all those plants and animals that were vanishing at an astonishing rate. The last piece of the puzzle, controlling insatiable appetites hardwired in humans, had to be conquered if the fighting was going to stop, especially if One World wanted control.

I've always thought the Dynasaurs were the only legacy of the Svalbard seed vault rebellion, but now I wonder if the Analogs could be a sister branch of skeptics. I gaze around, wondering if anyone here is sporting a Svalbard tattoo of a sprouting seed over the word *Remember*. Then again maybe not. Unlike the Dynasaurs, these people believe there's food all around us. Yeah, right. Maybe it's been cloaked just like my new Gizmo.

Ana draws something out of a pocket in her dress. "Behold," she says lifting it for everyone to see. It's a metal tin that fits in her palm. It doesn't appear to have a screen. She unscrews a lid. People in the audience stand to get a better look as she opens it. A subtle aroma fills the room. It is not a bad odor or a good one, but it's strangely compelling. Everyone sits up straighter and strains to take in more of the scent. As I draw in my breath, my stomach growls quietly.

"How'd she do that?" I ask Basil. "Is it another kind of scent device?"

This time, he seems as surprised as I am. "I don't know," he admits.

Then Ana does the strangest thing I've ever witnessed. She reaches into the tin with her fingers, brings out a small flat piece of something light brown, holds it up for us to see, then pops it in her mouth! She closes her eyes and works her jaw. A smile spreads over her face as she swallows. "Ahhh," she says and opens her eyes again. "Food."

⚘　　⚘　　⚘

While Ana stands before us, relishing the morsel she put onto her tongue, a hush falls over the room. Everyone seems to be asking themselves the same questions: *Where, how, what . . . ?*

The old man, Spinach, stands up. "Ana Louisa Gignot," he announces loudly and clearly. "You are under arrest on suspicion of breaching your contract with One World Nutrition, harboring illegal foodstuffs, and promoting fornography." As he speaks, five other people from the crowd stand up and advance on Ana, who stays perfectly still, smiling nearly beatifically at the front of the room, as if she expected this all along.

The woman in the flowery dress gets to her feet and shouts, "Infiltrators!" Then everyone is up, shouting, jostling, knocking over chairs, trying to get to Ana.

I clutch Basil's arm. "What's happening?"

"I don't know," he says, but I see panic in his eyes. "They must be security agents."

Several people, including the man and woman who had been stationed at the door, form a protective circle around Ana, but the agents easily push them aside to handcuff her. Spinach pulls out a Gizmo and addresses the mob through an amplifier. "You must remain here for further questioning," he instructs. "Agents will begin processing you shortly. Please remain calm."

Basil wriggles out of my grip. "They'll arrest me," he hisses. "I'm already on their watch list. I have to get out of here!" He pushes into the jeering crowd, advancing on the agents who are leading Ana away.

"Basil!" I shout and run after him, weaving in and out of angry bodies. I fumble in the pouch slung around my body and pull out my cloaked Gizmo. Cupping it in my hand, I hold it next to my mouth. "Astrid, bring the Smaurto!" I command quietly. Then I grab the back of Basil's shirt. He turns, ready to shove me away, but I shout, "My car!" I pull him out from the scrum. In the chaos no one seems to notice us as we skirt around the edge of the room. I point to a stern-faced woman stationed by the door where we're heading. Basil and I both stop short, bumping together like electrons.

He grabs my hand. "This way!" We scurry into a dimly lit corridor off the side of the main room. "There's an exit to the alley."

"Astrid, locate!" I command as we run.

When we burst through the side door, my Smaurto is there, waiting patiently like only a machine can. "Open!" I command the doors, then shout, "Home! Home! Home!" as I push Basil inside ahead of me.

The door shuts and locks, the car buckles us in, and Astrid begins her usual routine, "What would you like to do?"

"Shut up!" I cry. "Nothing. Just go home."

"Home located," she announces. The car starts down the pock-marked street between dark buildings. "Please sit back and relax and enjoy the ride."

Basil looks around to make sure no one is following us.

"Do you see anyone?" I ask. My heart is in my throat, and my stomach squeezes like my insides want to crawl out of my mouth.

"No," he says. "No one."

We pull up to the tollgate, and I yell, "Go through! Go! Go!"

The toll is processed, a green light appears, and we slip through the gate and onto the highway.

"Oh my god!" I shout. I lie back against my seat, panting with relief. "What the hell was that? What was going on in there?"

Basil shakes his head, clearly confused. "I don't know. Nothing like that ever happened before."

As we put some distance between ourselves and the chaos in the Outer Loop, I feel almost giddy and have to fight an urge to laugh or cry. "That's the craziest thing that ever happened to me."

"Me, too!" says Basil. "That old guy, Spinach? He's been in Ana's most trusted inner circle since I started going to meetings a few years ago."

I point and yell, "Infiltrator!" just like the woman in the flowery dress, which sends us both into a fit of nervous giggles.

Then Basil stops, suddenly serious. "You're not one of them, are you?"

This cracks me up. "How could I be? I don't even know who they are or what they want. Or who you are for that matter." I toss up my hands and laugh harder. Then I get serious. "No really," I say. "Who are you?"

Basil doesn't answer. Instead, he looks over his shoulder again at the clear highway behind us. "They must have been planning this for a long time. Just waiting for her to slip up so they could swoop in and arrest her."

"For what?" I ask. "All she did was stare at us and make a crazy speech then nibble on something she claimed was food. How illegal can that be? And why didn't more people leave? It's not illegal to go to a meeting. Were they just going to stay there and let those One World goons question them?"

"They're afraid!" Basil says.

"Of what?" I ask with a snort.

"You have no idea how strict the no-food laws are, do you?"

"No-food laws?"

"Ever heard of the Universal Nutrition Protection Act?"

"That law about forno?"

"That's only part of it," Basil tells me. "But it's not why security was there. They know Ana is an agent of change. She's waking people up, and One World will use any excuse to stop her. Even if it means starving her followers." His voice turns bitter and cold.

"Wait, whoa, hold up." I wrench around in my seat to face him. "What do you mean? Agent of change? Waking people up? Starving her followers? Aren't you being a bit dramatic?"

"She unlocks something inside people." He jabs his chest. "She connects people and fills them with hope."

"Do you feel that way?"

He stares at me. "Didn't you feel something while you were there?"

"No," I tell him, although that's not exactly true.

"Nothing at all? Not even a little twinge of something?" He squints at me through a half-inch space between his thumb and forefinger.

"Well," I say slowly. "It was interesting being with all those people. I felt . . ." I pause, searching for the word.

"Connected," he says.

"So what? People feel connected at a PlugIn or an EA. That's why they go."

"But the connection Ana provides makes people believe in a better life."

"Except she's wrong."

"What's that supposed to mean?" he asks, indignant at my skepticism.

"Look, the dancing and the singing and the staring were all very nice, but her whole notion that animals were smarter than we are is complete crap. They're all dead, remember? And we can't all just stop drinking Synthamil and refuse our innocs. The population would get out of control, we'd have more wars, and everyone would starve! You must realize that."

He looks around as if he's making sure no one else is listening. His hair has fallen over his left eye. I want to reach out and brush it away, but I keep my hand in my lap, hoping that he's not about to tell me something weird, like he buys into Ana's kooky brand of optimism.

He lowers his voice and leans closer. "But what if she's right?"

"Basil." I lay my hand on his shoulder. "She's not."

"You don't know that."

"Yes, I do. Look outside."

He shakes his head. "There's more to the world than you see." As I'm pulling away, Basil sits up and says, "But let's say she's wrong, for argument's sake. And that her whole gazing thing is a little hokey."

"Just a little?"

"Okay, super-hokey. But that's not the point. People need hope. Ana gives them that. And if they have hope, then maybe we can create change in the world."

"What would you change?" I ask, but Basil has become distracted by what's outside the window as my Smaurto exits the highway.

"Is this where you live?" he asks, eyebrows knitted together.

"Yeah. What Loop do you live in?"

"Nowhere near here. You can let me off anywhere."

The thought of parting with him makes my chest tight. "Really? But . . . I want to know more. Could we go somewhere and talk?"

"Where?"

"I don't know." I'm afraid I might not see him again, so I say, "Why don't you come to my house? We'll see if we can find out what's happing with Ana, and you can tell me more about the Analogs. Then I'll have my Smaurto take you anywhere you want."

He shakes the hair out of his eyes, and for a moment he looks like a shy little kid searching for a buddy at toddler time. "You sure your family wouldn't mind if I came unannounced?"

"Why would they?" I say, but I know the answer. If my mom finds out I've been in the Outer Loops, she'll be mad at me, but she can't blame him. It was my choice. Besides, it'll be better if I introduce Basil to my family now. That way I won't feel like I'm sneaking around the next time I want to see him. Because I hope there will be a next time.

A small smile tugs at the corners of Basil's mouth. "Okay," he says quietly. "If you're sure it's alright."

"Positive," I tell him.

$$\text{\Large ⚘ \quad ⚘ \quad ⚘}$$

When we walk into the house, my mom and Grandma Apple are so engrossed in a news stream on our main screen that they don't notice us. A reporter stands in front of a brick building with the number 1601 above its door. "This evening in a dilapidated area of the Outer Loops," she says, "One World security agents arrested Ana Gignon, leader of a resistance group who call themselves Analogs."

"Oh my god, we were just there," I blurt out. So much for keeping that part of my night under my hat. Clearly I'm better at being sneaky online.

Grandma looks up. "You're back," she says with a smile. "And you brought a friend."

Mom whips around. Confusion washes over her when she sees Basil. "Who's this?" she asks, but before I can answer she adds, "And what do you mean, you were just there?"

On the screen we see footage of Ana putting the food into her mouth and chewing. Basil and I both gasp.

"Someone was filming," he says.

I decide I better put the best possible spin on the situation so I say, "That woman, Ana, was giving a very interesting and educational speech...." I point to the stream of Spinach leading Ana, hands cuffed behind her back, through giant portable floodlights that have been erected outside the building. The camera zooms in close as Spinach gently pushes her head down so she can climb inside a One World security van. Before she gets in, she looks into the camera and smiles, which sends a little ripple through my stomach. It's as if she's looking directly at Basil and me, letting us know that she's alright. Then, as she turns away, before her hair slips across her shoulder, I catch a glimpse of a small green tattoo with the word *Remember* on her neck just below her ear. "Svalbard," I whisper.

Basil grabs my wrist. "Uh, Apple," he says urgently.

Mom rises off the couch. "Why were you there? And how do you know *him*?" Her eyes narrow into the Nguyen stare.

"We met the other night when I went out with Yaz," I say, stumbling over my words a little.

"How nice." Grandma stands up. "I'm Thalia's grandmother, Rebecca."

"Thalia?" Basil asks, caught off guard. "Thalia *Apple*?" I nod and Basil cringes.

Grandma walks toward us with her hand extended. "It's very nice to meet you."

Awkwardly, Basil shakes her hand, mumbling, "Very nice to meet you, ma'am."

"So polite," Grandma coos.

"But I really should be going." He backs away.

"No," says Mom sternly. "You should stay right there." Basil stops moving. Mom stands with her arms crossed and her science face on, as if she's working through a set of calculations. "Now let me get this straight. You and this boy, who you met, what, three or four nights ago, went to a meeting in the Outer Loop?"

"God, Mom," I snap at her. "Don't be such an Inner Loop snob. It was just a meeting."

"Of the Analogs," she says.

"Yes," I tell her, matching her pissy tone. "And it was amazing. People danced, we sang, there was poetry and not a screen in sight. People actually had conversations." I conveniently leave out the kookier parts. "Ana talked about things that are important. It was like family night to the power of ten. You would love it, Grandma!"

Mom snorts a mean little laugh. "Thalia, you were at a resistance meeting!"

I roll my eyes at her. "Resistance to what? Everything lame and annoying?"

"This isn't a joke!" Mom says. "Those people are corporate resisters." She points at the screen, where everyone at the meeting, including Radish, Kumquat, Strawberry, and the little girl with the painting, sit in quiet orderly rows.

"Security agents are still questioning the nearly one hundred people in attendance," the reporter says.

"You're wanted for questioning, young man," Mom says to Basil.

He shifts from foot to foot.

"Mom! You know that's ridiculous. It's not illegal to attend a meeting. All of those people could walk out of there this minute if they understood their rights."

"She's got a point," says Grandma. "People are allowed to freely gather."

Mom whips around to my grandmother. "Whose side are you on?"

"I'm not taking sides," Grandma tells her. "I'm trying to understand what's happening."

"I'll tell you what's happening," Mom says. "This kid, whoever he is, is part of the resistance against everything Max and I have worked so hard for, and he's dragging in my daughter, who has no idea what's she's gotten into!"

"Max?" Basil blurts. "Max Apple? Is that your father?"

"Yes," I tell him. He shuts his eyes tight as if he suddenly has a terrible headache.

Mom steps toward Basil and me. "How did you find her? Are you targeting the children of One World execs? What were you hoping to do? Brainwash her? Kidnap her for ransom?"

"No, that's not..." Basil is flustered and scared and can't get his words to come out straight.

"I finally bring a friend home...." I say to my mom.

"This is not the kind of friend you want," Mom snaps. "I'm calling security."

"Mom, no!" I look to Grandma. "Where's Dad?"

"He went back to work," she tells me, her eyes wide.

Mom slips her Gizmo out of her pocket.

"Stop it!" I scream. "What are you going to do? Have them arrest me? I was at that meeting, too." Mom scoffs so I grab Basil's hand and pull him close to me. "If he goes, I go!"

Mom's mouth drops open. She stands perfectly still for a moment then mumbles to herself as if she's puzzling through a set of data. "It's like you've got Arousatrol in your system...the spikes in your dopamine, your mood swings, this sudden passionate response to a boy...." Her eyes open wide like something's just hit her. She looks at me carefully. "Listen, Thalia. These things you might be feeling—the hunger and these new emotions for this boy—they're not real."

"How do you know?" I bark at her. She has no idea what I felt when I saw him looking in my car window tonight. Or what happens every time his fingers brush against my skin.

Mom takes a step toward us. "Do you remember that mutation on chromosome 16, the one on your FTO gene that you found? I did some research that I'm going to share with Dr. Demeter and ..."

Basil tenses at my side. He squeezes my hand and we lock eyes.

"I think that mutation might be inhibiting your inocs and your Synthamil formula from working correctly," Mom goes on. "Your hunger response isn't being suppressed the way it should, and your neurotransmitters and hormones seem out of whack, so you're having urges and emotions that shouldn't be there. These things you think you're feeling are just chemicals in your brain. Dopamine and serotonin flooding your circuits and shutting down your prefrontal cortex so a more primitive part of your mind that has the biological urge to eat and, uh, well, procreate is all fired up. And this makes you act impulsively."

For a split second I think she might be right, but then I think back to what Ana said. How the emotions we used to feel before all the inocs and Synthamil cocktails were what made us human and distinguished us from machines. "What could be more real than that?" I yell. I grip Basil's hand tighter. "You might be able to stop hunger and keep the world's population under your thumb, but you can't control my emotions. Those are mine. They're a part of me no matter what you say!"

"And you think he feels the same way?" Mom asks, the cynicism clear in her tone. "He doesn't. He's using you, Thalia. You're a pawn in his movement."

I look at Basil. "Is that true?"

He drops my hand and searches for words.

"You're going straight to Dr. Demeter," Mom says, stepping toward us with her Gizmo poised. "And him? He's going to jail."

Basil moves so fast that I hear the door wheesh before I realize he's gone. I turn and gape at the late evening sun spilling across the threshold. I run after him, but by the time I get to the open doorway, he's nowhere to be seen. The driveway, the walkway, the sidewalk, and the street are empty and quiet as if he's disappeared. "Basil!" I yell and start to run outside, but Mom catches my wrist.

"No!" she shouts and drags me back into the house. "You're going to rehab!" I struggle against her, but she's surprisingly strong. She gives me one more yank then commands the door to close and lock.

✤   ✤   ✤

Ahimsa glowers at us from the main screen in the living room. "What the hell was she doing there? How long has she been a part of that group?" she bellows at my mother. "Don't you have any control over her for god's sake!"

Mom paces the room, trying to assure Ahimsa that she's just as surprised as anyone by my deplorable behavior. I hug a pillow on the couch, fighting back tears while Grandma strokes my arm and assures me that everything is going to be okay. But I know it's not, because I'll never see Basil again. Even if I could find him, he won't want anything to do with me after what my mother said.

"She's right there in the footage," Ahimsa complains. "We've gone through the images one by one, and there she is plain as day, running out with some boy we can't identify. There's no way we can deny it. I looked at her location data. It puts here there at the time of the arrests."

"Last time I checked, it's still legal to go to a meeting!" I snap.

Mom spins around horrified while Ahimsa leans so close to her camera that her beaky face looms large in our living room. "You have no idea what you've gotten yourself into, Thalia. Those people are a danger to society. And your involvement could cause all kinds of problems for your family. For me. For One World." She leans back and shakes her head in disgust. "Top execs' kid at a resistance meeting." She looks at my mom. "You have to take her in and let security question her." She turns to me. "And you," she says jabbing her finger at the camera. "You have to tell them everything you know about that boy."

"No." I hug the pillow tighter. "I won't tell them anything." Of course, the truth is, I know nearly nothing about him. He was gone so fast that I wonder if he were just a hologram in some game I was playing.

"Now, Thalia," Grandma says, nervously patting my leg. "You need to cooperate so we can straighten out this mess. I'm sure you didn't mean to do any harm. You were at the wrong place at the wrong time." She looks at Ahimsa. "She only met him a few days ago. She didn't know what she was doing."

Mom balls up her fists and squeezes her eyes shut as if she's trying to stop herself from exploding, then she shouts, "It's the genetic mutation! And her Synthamil formula isn't working right. It's all tied together. Impulsive, erratic behavior. Strong emotions. Poor judgment. Being drawn into the nonsense of the Analogs and that boy. This . . . this . . . this *attitude*!" she shouts, waving her arms at me. "She needs to go to Dr. Demeter's rehab facility right this minute so we can get her straightened out."

"We had a deal!" I shout at her.

"You broke our deal the minute you stepped foot in that meeting," Mom says.

"That might work, actually." Ahimsa sits back with her arms crossed and thinks for a moment. "If you commit her tonight, we can avoid involving security just yet. We'll say she was targeted by Analog operatives because she's mentally ill and vulnerable. Then we find that kid. What's his name? Brazil?"

Mom takes a deep breath and nods. "It's a good plan."

"I'm not mentally ill!" I shout, but they ignore me. "Grandma?"

"I'll call Dr. Demeter to make arrangements," Mom tells Ahimsa. "You work on finding the boy."

"Where's Dad?" I shout. "You can't drag me away without talking to him first!"

"He's in a meeting," Ahimsa says coolly. "I'll fill him in when it's over."

Grandma throws her arm protectively around my shoulder. "You really should speak to Max first," she says to my mother.

"Max will agree with me," Mom says as she stomps down the hall to my room. "I'm going to pack a bag for Thalia."

"Don't let her do this to me, Grandma," I beg.

Grandma holds my shoulders. I see tears glistening on the edges of her eyes. "Listen, honey, it's going to be okay. It's probably for the best right now. We'll get you out of harm's way. Just go to Dr. Demeter's and sit tight while we work out all the kinks."

"But Basil . . ."

"Oh honey," Grandma says and pulls me into a hug. "I don't think he's the kind of boy you want to get mixed up with."

"She's right," Ahimsa says smugly from the screen. "He's trouble. They're all trouble. And you're just lucky we got you out in time."

⚘   ⚘   ⚘

"I know you're angry," my mother says after she locks us in her Smaurto. My grandmother stands on our stoop, sweater wrapped tightly around her body, waving sadly to me as we pull away. Before we left, I begged her to get a hold of Dad, which she promised to do.

"I know you think I'm punishing you, but I'm not, Thalia," Mom tries to explain. "I'm trying to help you. If your body was ailing, I would do everything I could to make you get better. This is no different."

"Of course it's different," I insist. "I'm not sick!"

"Your mind is sick," Mom says gently as if I'm a child with a fever who wants to go outside to play.

"No. I'm making choices you and your boss don't agree with."

Mom shakes her head, refusing to believe me. "You're not behaving this way on purpose. Your brain is misfiring."

"The only misfire my brain made was to trust you."

Mom winces. "Thalia, honey, your brain chemistry is not optimized right now. That's all I'm saying. We just need to tweak your inocs and Synthamil formula to get you optimized again so all those desires you're feeling to eat and well, um, the emotions you have for that boy, are turned down to a safe level. Don't you agree?"

"No," I snap, arms crossed and jaw set.

She gives me a pitying look. "I know you can't understand this now, but this is the hardest thing I've ever had to do. I hope someday you'll believe me and you'll know that I did this to protect you."

"You're covering your own ass," I mumble, then I get quiet. I won't look at her again or talk to her because she's made up her mind, and nothing I can do will change it.

I stare out the window as we travel via surface streets toward what used to be the heart of the city before it was destroyed. The ribbon of elevated highway that goes from my house to the EntertainArena surrounds this area. When I was little, it was filled with mountains of twisted steel and shattered glass from fallen skyscrapers. Most of the wreckage has been removed, but a few shells remain standing. Giant green letters, HOLE FOO ARK, hang loosely from the hull of an abandoned building curved like the prow of ghost ship floating nowhere. W, D, and a smattering of other fallen letters litter the ground. We zip past an old bike shop, a cleaner, a bank, and a hardware store. Lights out. Most of the inventory looted long ago. Will I be left and forgotten like all this? The Smaurto turns onto a street that cuts through an area of new construction. The reminders of the crumbled past have been razed and replaced by signs that read THE FUTURE BEGINS NOW WITH ONE WORLD CONSTRUCTION CORP!

"Look," Mom says gently. "We aren't even that far from home. As soon as Dr. Demeter says it's okay, we'll come visit you every day."

"Don't bother," I tell her. "Dad will get me out."

"No, Thalia. This time Dad will be on my side."

We approach a low-slung, dome-shaped building glowing in the pinks and purples of the fading evening sky. Windows encircling the top reflect the gaudy glare of the EA, which can't be more than two miles away on the other side of the highway, but it might as well be in outer space once they lock me up. The building itself sits on a flat expanse of land surrounded by hologram shrubs blooming with pink and yellow flowers, probably programmed to last all year long, as if the seasons never change and time never passes here. I wonder who is behind those curved walls and how long they've been in there.

My mind skips to Basil. I remember his face contorting when he learned my name, the panic in his eyes when my mom threatened to turn him in. I know I should be happy that he escaped, but all I can think is, *Why didn't he take me with him?* For a moment, I wonder if my mom is right. Was he using me? I wish I knew how to get in touch with him so I could apologize and tell him that had I known my mother would act like this, I would have never brought him to my house. I press my forehead against the window. For his sake, I hope we never see each other again.

That realization makes my body ache with sadness.

The Smaurto stops in front of the walkway leading to Dr. Demeter's facility. Mom looks up, chin held high. She has pulled herself together but I'm falling apart. My hands shake. My legs are weak. I fight the urge to cry. "Please," I whimper. "Please don't do this."

She stares ahead at two men dressed in identical pale green pants and shirts who walk to meet the Smaurto. They position themselves by my door. Mom hands me my bag.

My stomach contracts like someone just punched me in the gut. "You're not coming in with me?"

She shakes her head. "Dr. Demeter asked me not to."

One of the men peers in and nods at my mother, who commands my door open.

"I love you," she says and reaches for my shoulder.

I push her hand away. "I hate you." I climb out and the men escort me to the entrance.

⚓ ⚓ ⚓

Deep red carpet inside the dome muffles the sound of our footsteps once the men accompany me inside. On either side of the entryway are identical waiting areas with low ceilings, ash gray walls, and dark overstuffed furniture, where I imagine nervous families wait for news about their flawed loved ones. I turn to see if my mother has driven off yet, happy to be rid of me, but the floor-to-ceiling windows are covered by heavy dark curtains. The only natural light comes through the door, a small portal to the world outside, which is closing fast. It shuts with a decisive clunk, then I hear automated dead bolts grind into place.

Dr. Demeter waits in a straight-backed chair, impatiently jiggling his shiny wing tip shoe. He rises and extends his hand as we approach. "Welcome, Thalia. Glad you made it," he says, as if I've come for a weekend getaway. "I hear you had an exciting evening."

I drop his hand and stare at him. "Are you being sarcastic?"

He shakes his head. "Oh no! Not at all. I'm sincere when I say your adventure in the Outer Loop sounds quite interesting. I'd like to hear more about it." He smiles at the men flanking me. "Thank you, Ravi. Thank you, Sar. I'll take it from here."

They nod and push through the double doors ahead of us where one takes a staircase up and the other down. Dr. Demeter leads me to the left, into a tunnel-like hallway. I notice an identical hall to the right. I imagine you could walk endlessly in circles here.

"On this floor we have patient rooms and treatment rooms." Dr. Demeter motions to closed doors on either side of the curved hall. "And upstairs we have our labs."

"Do you give everyone a personal tour?" I ask him sarcastically.

"No," he says with a small laugh. "As I told you in my office, I've taken a personal interest in your case."

"I don't expect special treatment because of who my mother is," I snap at him.

"And I'll expect the same things out of you as I do of all my patients," he says. Then he stops and studies me for a moment. "I do hope you'll learn to trust me, Thalia. The better our relationship, the more quickly you'll recover."

"The only thing wrong with me is that I'm here," I tell him.

"Aha!" he says with a grin. "I'll be sure to note that on your chart. But for now we'll just drop your bag in your room, then I'll take you to join some other guests."

"Guests?" I say. "That's quite a euphemism."

Dr. Demeter actually laughs at my smart-ass comment. "What would you have me call them?" he asks. "Inmates?"

"Well . . . I . . . uh," I stutter, surprised by his sense of humor.

"Here we are." He opens a door on the right then flicks on the light to a sparsely furnished room with a single bed, a squat dresser with four drawers, and a small square sink beside a door marked URINAL.

"Are there cameras here?" I ask, peering into the corners.

He shakes his head. "No, we don't wish to invade your personal privacy. If someone is deemed a threat to herself or others, she might go into an observation room, but otherwise, we'd like you to feel at home."

"Home?" I say as I drop my bag on the bed. "I have no intention of being here that long."

Again Dr. Demeter surprises me by smiling and says, "I hope you're right." Then he turns. "Come, I believe there's an art-therapy group meeting now that you might enjoy."

I follow him with my head cocked to the side, trying to imagine what he means.

He sees my confusion. "We've found that expressing emotions through art or conversation can help break the cycle of compulsive feelings. So we encourage our guests to do something creative every day."

"Sounds like an Analog meeting," I say half to myself as we walk the circle.

He glances at me sideways. "I hear Ms. Gignon had a bite to eat."

This catches me off guard, and I nearly laugh. "Maybe she needs to be your *guest*."

"You know," he says almost absentmindedly, "she may be on to something. Humans are meant to eat after all."

"Too bad there's no food," I say.

He turns his head sharply. "And what if there were? Would you eat it?"

"Wouldn't that make me crazy?" I counter. "What did you call it? OCD?"

He thinks on this for a second, then he says, "Historically mental illness has been the name for anything science couldn't explain about human behavior. The more we learn about the brain, the less we categorize as crazy."

"Just as long as you can optimize that brain chemistry, huh?" I quip, mocking my mother.

"Yes," he says with a smile. "Very well put!"

I can't help but roll my eyes.

"Shall we?" he says, pointing to a closed door.

✤   ✤   ✤

Inside the brightly lit room, people sit around circular tables covered with colorful scraps of what might be paper. There are girls younger than me. Guys who are probably in their twenties. A few men and women most likely pushing thirty, but the only person my parents' age is an orderly helping someone on the other side of the room.

"What are they doing?" I ask.

"Making collages, I believe," Dr. Demeter tells me.

I watch the people in the room, but nobody seems to be creating anything. Most of them stare blankly at the wall or rock back and forth, humming or muttering to themselves. One guy punches himself in the forehead over and over.

"Why are they all so out of it?" I ask as my stomach tightens with fear.

"First we have to suppress that urge to eat using psychotropic drugs," Dr. Demeter explains. "This breaks the cycle, then we can start rebuilding the personality through alternative therapies such as this." He glances at me and sees that I am utterly horrified. "Oh, but don't worry," he says clapping me on the shoulder. "This will not be your experience. Most of these people are late in the stages of their illness. They've been through so much. Their families have turned them out. Many of them have been in jail. These are some of the hardest cases, but we caught yours early and will only have to tweak your Synthamil cocktail to . . . how did you put it—optimize your brain chemistry.

"Would you like to meet one of my most successful guests?" Dr. Demeter asks.

I don't answer because the idea that anyone in this room is a success story makes my stomach churn.

"Haza," Dr. Demeter calls. A short, round girl a little older than I am looks up and beams when she hears Dr. Demeter's voice. "Oh, Dr. D!" she says and rushes to greet him. He opens his arms so she can wrap him in a hug and lay her cheek against his chest. Her frizzy gold hair looks like a ratty rug against his neatly ironed shirt. I can't believe he's allowing her to touch him like that. She's not a child. "Is it time?"

"Soon, soon." He pats her on the back. "I have to prepare the lab. While you're waiting, I'd like you to meet our newest guest, Thalia."

Haza looks me up and down like a frightened child clinging to her father.

"It's okay," Dr. Demeter assures her. "She's here to get better, just like you. Why don't you take her to your table and introduce her to your friends?" He pries her arms away from his body and gives her a little push in my direction. She stumbles toward me on stiff legs.

ψ   ψ   ψ

I pull up a chair between Haza and a girl called Zara who has spiky dark hair, the ends of which are fading magenta. At first I think she's younger than I am, but when I look at her eyes, I see the worry lines of someone much older. Across from us a skinny, shifty-eyed boy huddles in his chair, avoiding eye contact. The orderly, who introduces herself as Shira, hands me a large blank sheet of slick paperlike material and a little tube of something sticky, then she goes to tend another "guest" who's gotten the sticky stuff in her hair.

"Did you hear what he said?" Haza asks, reaching into the jumble of scraps in the center of the table. "I'm going up to the lab tonight."

"Who gives a crap?" Zara says, ripping purple scraps into ragged strips. I'm relieved to hear someone else talk, even if she is incredibly hostile. She smears the sticky stuff on the back of the scraps then smacks them down on her piece of paper, which is nearly covered corner to corner with jagged shapes.

"You do, Zara," Haza says. "You wish *you* got to go."

Across the table, the nervous boy carefully tears a long thin strip of paper then rolls it into a tiny precise ball, which he lines up next to other tiny precise white balls he's made.

"Only the most special people get invited," Haza continues. "The ones he trusts the most."

"He's probably going to try to screw you," Zara says, slamming her fist onto her collage.

My mouth drops open. I look at the boy to see if he's surprised by this, but he's too busy popping the small wads of paper in his mouth to notice what's happening across the table. He looks side to side as he chews.

"You're crass. And foul. And disgusting," Haza snarls at Zara. "What happens up there is a secret. A wonderful, beautiful secret."

"Sounds like screwing to me," Zara says and pounds a slab of black on top of her palimpsest.

"Shut up!" Haza hisses. "You're just jealous because I'm getting out of here soon. Dr. D. says so."

As their argument escalates, the boy rolls bigger and bigger wads of paper that he shoves into his mouth and chews nervously. I look around to see if Shira notices what's going on, but she's busy trying to stop the head puncher from knocking himself into a coma.

"Where are you going to go?" Zara asks Haza with a snort. "Your parents won't take you back. They kicked you out after you tried to eat their curtains."

"That's not true!" Haza says. "And Dr. Demeter says he has a place for me. A place where only the most special guests get to go. Soon, I'll be a part of the harvest."

This catches my attention. "Harvest?"

Zara looks at me and rolls her eyes. "Don't listen to her. She's deluded."

"I am not!" Haza almost yells. "My eggs are ripe. He told me so."

Zara bursts out laughing. "Your *eggs* are *ripe*? You really are insane."

This sends Haza over the edge. "Shut up!" she screams. "Shut up, you horrible girl!" She stands up so quickly, she tips her chair and shoves the table into the boy's gut. He doubles over and gags.

"What's going on? What's the matter now?" Shira rushes across the room.

I slip out of my chair as Zara and Haza scream and point at one another while the boy vomits soggy wads of paper onto the floor.

Shira pushes a button on the wall and shouts, "Ravi, Sar! I need your help."

Within seconds Sar runs in and grabs Zara in a bear hug from behind. She thrashes and kicks and continues to scream taunts at Haza who sobs, "You're wrong! You're wrong!"

"Where's Ravi? Lev, no!" Shira yells as she tries to stop the boy from shoving more paper in his mouth.

"Don't know," Sar says.

I press myself against a wall to stay out of the way, but none of the other patients seem to notice or care about what's happening. They just continue staring and rocking and punching themselves as Sar drags Zara out the door howling, "I'm getting the hell out of here! You can't keep me! You can't make me stay!"

"What a mess," Shira mutters. She digs the last bit of paper mush from Lev's mouth then stands up and claps her hands. "Okay, everybody, art is over for today." One by one, she gets the other patients to their feet. They shuffle toward the door. "Time to go back to your rooms," Shira tells them. "We'll try again tomorrow."

As I leave, Haza looks at me. "I'm getting out," she insists.

"You and me both," I mutter as I walk by.

⚲　　⚲　　⚲

As soon as I'm in my room, I reach for my Gizmo. I've been surprised that no one confiscated it yet, but when I uncloak it, I see why. There's no signal. I drop down to the bed to think. No signal means I can't call my dad, which means I'm stuck here until Grandma talks sense into him, which will be tough as long as my mom insists she's right, which will be until the end of time.

But there is no way in hell I'm staying here. This place is a nuthouse. Face punchers, paper eaters, egg harvesting, sex! These freaks could never be in the Procreation Pool. Nobody is going to let their hormones surge. I have to find a way to get a message to Dad. It's the only chance I have of leaving before I become as crazy as the others.

I open the settings on my Gizmo and move around the room to see if I can pick up even the faintest hint of the network or a private hot spot. Nothing. But somewhere in this building a signal has to be accessible, even if it's encrypted. All I have to do is find it so I can start hacking my way out of this prison.

I peek out my door to make sure the hallway is empty and quiet, then I slip out. My heart pounds as I trail my fingers against the soft, smooth surface of the curved wall. I figure my best bet is to get upstairs near the windows so I can pick up the general Inner Loop network signal that's probably been blocked down here. I make my way back toward the waiting area, praying that Dr. Demeter wasn't lying and there are no security cameras. When I get there, I press my back against the wall and make sure no one is nearby. The waiting room is empty, so I scurry to the double doors where Ravi and Sar disappeared earlier. I run up every other step to the second floor. I press my ear against the door, then slowly open it.

Instead of the sound-absorbing carpet, dark walls, and low ceilings of the first floor, everything up here is gleaming white and silver. I take out my Gizmo and point it toward the dome of windows overhead. The first few stars bright enough to compete with the Inner Loop lights dot the night sky, but my screen remains black because there's still no signal. I tiptoe down the hall, searching for a hot spot. Then I hear voices and clunking heels echo from the left. I panic, my heart in my throat, as I dart away. I round the curve in the opposite direction, but a door swings open and someone in pale green steps out. I skitter backward, desperate for a place to hide and grapple with a door handle behind me. I fall inside a room and someone gasps.

I turn to see Haza on an exam table in a hospital gown with her knees pulled up to her chest. I press my fingers to my lips and plead with my eyes for her to be quiet. She's so surprised that at first she can't speak. Outside, the footsteps and voices fade.

Then Haza snaps out of her shock and whispers, "Is it your turn, too?"

"Yes," I answer, thinking fast. "But don't tell anyone. They'll be jealous."

"I know," she whispers eagerly. "We're special."

I steal a glance through the door and see that the door catty-corner from me is still slightly ajar. "I have to go," I whisper to Haza and bolt across the hall.

The other room is empty and dark, but my screen faintly glows, which turns my fear into elation. As soon as I pick up this signal, I can send a message to my dad and hurry back to my room before anyone misses me. Then all I have to do is wait for him to come. I open my settings and skirt the edges of the room, trying to find a signal strong enough to send my message, but I hit a wall. Literally. My screen has gotten brighter, so I know I'm heading in the right direction, but I'm going to have to go out in the hall to get into the next room, where the signal must be stronger. As I grope my way forward, I bump against a table. What sounds like hundreds of tiny glass dishes tinkle and rattle. I grip the table, willing the noise to stop and use the light of my Gizmo screen to see what I've set in motion.

Rows and rows of small shallow glass dishes bump together, sloshing a thin pinkish film growing in a clear solution. I back away, not sure what I've seen, but it turns my stomach. I tiptoe to the door.

The hall is quiet so I step out slowly, then just as I'm darting toward the next room, someone comes around the curve. I fumble for the handle but not before an orderly grabs my elbow.

I try to wriggle away while talking fast, "Dr. Demeter told me to . . ."

"Shhhh," the man in the pale green uniform hisses and tightens his grip as he shoves me in front of him down the hall. "This way."

Again, I work to wiggle free, thinking I might be able to run for the stairs and get back to my room before he can identify me, but he digs his fingers into my skin and growls, "Apple, stop."

I whip around and come face-to-face with Basil. Before I can shriek, he clamps his hand over my mouth. "Shhhhhh," he says, his eyes wide with worry. "We have to hurry."

I follow blindly, gripping Basil's hand, looking again and again to make sure it's really him. We burst through the exit door and careen down the staircase toward the first landing, but he pulls me down another flight. "We can get out this way."

"But how, but who, but, but . . ." I stammer as I stagger after him.

"Keep going," he tells me.

We flee into a utility room where Basil leads me through a maze of meters, water tanks, and washing machines until we come to a large, windowless steel door sealed tight. He takes a Gizmo out of his baggy pale green pants, points it at the door, and commands it to open. Automated locks whirl as the door does what he says, and we step outside onto a small concrete pad under the weak light of the stars.

"Ravi," Basil whispers hoarsely. "Ravi!"

A guy in boxer shorts and a T-shirt steps out from behind a pillar. "Man, took you long enough. I'm freezing my balls off out here."

Basil quickly strips off the pale green uniform to reveal his regular clothes underneath. He shoves the shirt and pants at Ravi. "She wasn't where you said she'd be."

"But how? But what?" I continue to splutter.

Ravi puts the uniform on. "Where was she?"

Basil half grins. "Snooping around on the second floor."

Ravi looks at me and laughs. "What were you looking for?"

"A signal," I say.

"It's a dead zone out here," Ravi tells me. "The only signal is Demeter's VPN and for that you need a password."

"Yeah, I figured, but . . ." I stamp my foot because this is not the conversation I want to have. "Would one of you tell me what's happening?"

Basil hands Ravi the Gizmo. "Thanks," he says. "I owe you."

"Nah," Ravi tells him. "Now we're even." They grab hands and bump shoulders before Ravi steps inside the building. "Be safe," he says, then he looks over his shoulder at me. "And Apple." I stare at him. "Thank you for getting him out of the meeting safely. He's important." He smiles kindly then disappears behind the closing door.

Basil reaches for me. "You ready?"

I stand mutely, trying to process everything that just happened.

"Unless you want to stay here?" he says withdrawing his hand a little.

A small breeze carrying the scent of faux roses rouses me from my stupefied state. I look up and see the lights of Smaurtos circling the elevated highway and, just beyond that, the gaudy glare of the EA. On the other side of this place is my home. I don't know which way we're going, but I grab Basil's hand and say, "Get me out of here."

⚘   ⚘   ⚘

Basil and I run across the craggy lot toward a shell of new construction. I look over my shoulder at the glowing dome receding behind us, expecting to see orderlies with flashlights burst through the back door, yelling my name, but everything stays eerily calm and quiet. Soon someone will notice that I'm missing, though, and they'll know I couldn't have gotten far.

"Where are we going?" I pant.

"This way." Basil leads me inside the skeleton of a building. "I have a vehicle."

Giant robotic construction machines loom like replicas of dinosaurs in the darkness around us. "You going to fire up one of these?" I ask.

"That'd be inconspicuous," he says, as he disappears behind a half wall and returns pushing some contraption that looks half a bicycle. Instead of a front wheel, there's a big metal cage thing on casters.

I step closer and blink, trying to find more light. "What is that?" I stick my fingers through the spindly metal bars of the cage.

"It's the vehicle," he says.

"But, what is it?" I persist.

"It's a bike and a shopping cart. A bike-cart."

"What's a shopping cart?"

He huffs, impatient. "A thing people used to push through stores where they bought food."

"Why?" I ask.

"How should I know? And why is that important?"

"But what are we going to do with it?"

"You ride in here." He points to the cage. "And I'll be back here." He points to the seat.

"Where's the motor?"

"For god's sake, Apple!" he says, indignantly. "It doesn't have a flippin' motor. I'm going to pedal it!"

I'm too flabbergasted to say anything. My mouth just hangs open stupidly for several seconds. "What good is that?" I finally blurt out.

Basil balls one fist on his hip. "It's good enough to get us the hell out of here if you'd stop yapping!"

"Sorry," I say quickly. "I mean, thank you? It's just, I never thought I would see you again and . . ."

"Didn't you want to?" he asks, frowning.

"Yes! Of course, but . . ." I slump back against one of the hulking machines. My head spins and my ears ring. "I don't understand what's going on."

"Ok, look." Basil takes a deep breath, probably realizing that I'm not going anywhere until he explains a few things. He leans against the vehicle next to me with the bike-cart propped at his side. "After your mom threatened to call security, I hid outside your house. I heard her say she was taking you to rehab at Dr. Demeter's, so after she put you in the Smaurto, I made my way down here and figured we'd need a way to get out again. I found some old abandoned shops and made this thing, which apparently is very stupid."

"No," I say. "It's not stupid at all. It's amazing. And you're amazing. But how did you get inside Dr. Demeter's? How do you know Ravi? Why did he help you? What did he mean that you're important?"

"Ravi's an Analog," Basil tells me. "There are lots of us. We help each other. A while back Ravi had some trouble with security. I let him hang with me until things died down so he owed me a favor. We're all working for the cause."

"What cause? I don't get it." I run my fingers through my hair. "I need to understand more about the Analogs and . . ."

"I know." Basil lays his hand on my arm. "And I'll tell you everything you want to know, but right now, we should really get out of here, because they'll be looking for you very soon. Ravi can only cover for so long." He grabs the bike-cart contraption.

"Wait," I tell him. "I have to know one thing." He stops and looks at me like he wants to pick me up and shove me inside the cart. "Did you know who I was before we went to my house tonight?"

"No," he says. "I just thought you were some really cute girl named Apple that I was trying to impress."

My stomach zings when he says this. Blood rushes to my cheeks and despite everything, I smile.

"And to be honest, if I had known who your parents are, I would have never invited you to an Analog meeting." He looks up and laughs as if he can't believe all that's happened. "The whole idea of a privy at a resistance meeting is absurd."

"Privy?" I ask.

"That's what people like me call privileged people like you," Basil says, a note of apology in his voice.

"Then why did you come here for me?"

"I owed you one," he says, but then he drops his eyes. In the murky light I can't make out his face. "And," he says quietly, "you're still a cute girl I'm trying to impress."

I can't help but laugh out of surprise and embarrassment. "Well, I'm pretty impressed."

He looks up with a little grin on his face. "It's the bike-cart thing, isn't it?"

"It's definitely the bike-cart thing," I tell him.

ψ   ψ   ψ

I climb inside the cart as Basil balances the bike. It takes a few tries before he can pedal without nearly toppling over, but soon we're bumping across the empty lots away from my house and Dr. Demeter's and toward the lights of the EA on the other side of the highway.

"Where are we going?" I ask.

"That depends," he says.

"On what?"

"On you."

"Me?" While I'm trying to figure out where we should go, Astrid suddenly comes to life. "Yaz is calling! Yaz is calling!" she shouts happily.

"What the . . . !" Basil is so startled that he loses control of the bike. We wobble violently side to side.

"It's just my Gizmo!" I shout at him, gripping the cart so I won't fly out. But it's no use. He careens sideways. The cart pops off the front of the bike and topples over, dumping me to the ground. I roll and land several feet away from where he's tangled in the fallen bike.

I scramble to get the Gizmo out of my pouch. "Accept," I tell Astrid and Yaz comes on the screen.

"Hey, I've been looking for you!" she shouts over the raucous noise of an EntertainArena crowd. "The new Hedgy's World is open and . . ."

"Yaz! Yaz!" I shout urgently. "I need your help."

"Turn that off, for crap sake!" Basil yells. He tries to get free from the bike, but his pant leg is caught in the chain.

"What's going on?" Yaz yells. "Are you okay?" She squints. "I can barely see you."

Basil scuttles over, dragging the bike along with him. "They're going to find us in ten minutes unless you get rid of that!" He tries to grab the Gizmo from me, but I swat at his hand.

"Who's that with you?" Yaz asks as Basil wrestles me for the Gizmo, but I push him away.

"We're in trouble. I need your help," I plead.

"Is he hurting you?" Yaz screams. "Tell me where you are. I'll call security!"

"No don't!" I yell at her. "He's with me."

"What's going on?" she demands.

Out of the corner of my eye, I see Basil's hand coming toward me. "Meet me out front of the EA in ten minutes," I yell right as he slaps the Gizmo from my hand, sending it clattering to the ground.

He runs toward it and lifts his foot then hops in a circle trying to find it, shouting, "Where did it go?"

"Stop!" I dive toward the spot it landed, sweeping my hands from side to side. "Are you crazy?" My hand brushes against something solid, and I realize that my Gizmo has gone into cloaking mode. With my back to Basil, I scoop up the invisible Gizmo and whisper to Astrid to kill the signal receptor so the whole thing powers down.

Basil stomps toward the bike shouting, "Now we're screwed. They'll have our location in no time."

"Yaz will help us!" I tell him.

"I can't trust a privy." Basil jerks the bike up from the ground and drags it toward the cart, which lies on its side, one caster still spinning. "People like you are the enemy of people like me."

"I'm not your enemy!" I shout.

He stops what he's doing long enough to scowl at me. "Not you. Your friend. Your family."

"You're wrong about Yaz!" I run toward him while slipping the silent, invisible Gizmo in my pouch. "She'll help us. I know she will."

"She'll help you. Not me." He struggles to put his contraption back together, seething like that enraged boy I accidentally cornered a few nights ago. "And even if she can't help you, you'll be fine because your family has the money and the connections to stick you in a fancy rehab center or pay your restitution so you stay out of prison if you get caught," he says. "But I don't have that. Nobody will bail me out of this. I will rot in prison, working off my restitution until I'm thirty years old if they get a hold of me." He swings his leg over the bike. "Maybe we're better off apart."

"How can you say that?" I yell at him. We stare at each other. "I feel something when I'm with you." I press one hand against my chest where it aches at the thought of being separated from him again. "It's something I've never felt. No matter what my mother says, this is real to me." I reach out and press my other hand onto the same place on his chest, and my pulse dances when I feel his heart beating fiercely. "You can't tell me you don't feel it, too." I wait. Watching him. Feeling his heart beat beneath my palm. Wondering if my mother was right.

Basil sucks in a deep and ragged breath. "Of course I feel it," he nearly whispers. "From the moment you stumbled into Flav-O-Rite."

For a split second, the world becomes a small, perfect place. It's just me and Basil alone in the middle of this rocky field under a few diligent stars. He leans forward and tilts his head to the right. I do the same. My eyes close. Then our lips touch. I pull back and press my fingers against my tingling mouth. Suddenly nothing seems quite as bad as it did a few seconds before.

But Basil shakes his head. "I can't afford to get caught."

"And I don't want to go back to rehab," I tell him.

"Then we have to get out of the Inner Loops."

"My friend will help us," I tell him. "She's just across that highway." I point to the lights. "She has a Smaurto, and she can take us to the border and get us through the toll."

"I can get us through the toll," he says.

"Yeah, right. On this thing?"

"That's not the issue. . . ." he says, but I cut him off.

"Do you know how long it will take us to get there without a Smaurto?" I look over my shoulder at the lights from the dome. "We don't have that much time."

He turns his face to the sky and groans out of frustration.

"Basil," I say, grabbing his arm. "Trust me. She will help us."

He shakes his head as if he can't believe what's happening. But then he sighs and says, "Let's go."

⚶   ⚶   ⚶

We ditch the bike-cart at the edge of the EA entrance pavilion and head for the doors. Basil stares at all the hologram ads and virtual fountains. "Have you been to one of these before?" I ask as we quickly weave through all the people milling about.

"Nothing as fancy as this," he says. "Things in my area are a little less . . ." he searches for the word.

"Obnoxious?" I say, pointing to the giant two-story screen over the entrance that's playing a trailer for the new 3-D *Hedgy Adventure* movie.

"I was going for interactive, but obnoxious would work, too."

"There's Yaz." I wave to my best friend in her sleeveless orange minidress and bouncy blue trainers. I start to run toward her but suddenly I stop short. "Oh, no," I say when the massive screen above her head changes.

"What's wrong?" Basil asks, but he follows my finger pointing up and sees our faces looming large above everything with the words: MISSING PERSON ALERT. Thalia Apple. Age 17. My photo is a portrait my dad took a few months ago on a family trip. Basil's is a blurry image probably caught on tape at the Analog meeting.

I spin around. To our left a small group of men and women in matching burgundy shirts march toward us, talking into their Gizmos. I spin the other way. Behind us, more adults in matching shirts walk quickly through the parking lot, heading straight toward us. "Oh god," I say. "This is bad." I grab Basil's hand and pull to the right.

"No!" He motions toward a cadre coming from that direction, too. "Security agents."

"What now?"

"Get lost in the crowd!" he shouts and pulls me through the front doors.

As we pass Yaz, I grab her arm. "What the . . . ?" she shouts, but when she sees my face on every screen, she shouts "Holy crapoly!" and follows us into the crush of humanity.

Yaz trips along beside me as we thread our way through the bodies moving en masse in the main hall. Smell blasters assault us with the fragrance of meadows, oceans, and the acrid smoke of simulated war. Anything and everything to stimulate the senses and entice people inside the game rooms to frolick, or surf, or fight in the virtual worlds created solely for our pleasure.

"You better start talking fast, Thalia Apple," Yaz says, her grip tight on my forearm. "Who is that guy and why are we running from those people?"

"That's Basil," I say pointing ahead of us. "And those are security agents." I look over my shoulder at a burly bald-headed guy leading the guards. "Basil and I went to a corporate resistance meeting that got raided. My mom went ballistic and committed me to rehab, but Basil busted me out."

"Dang!" Yaz says. "I thought you were home text chatting with Dynasaurs."

"Not this time!" I look back at the blockhead gaining on us. We skirt around a gaggle of tween girls who've stopped to ogle themselves with virtual celebrities on a giant Smarty Party Fun Pants screen. "If we don't get out of here, we'll be in deep trouble." My words are lost under the high-pitched shrieks of the tweenies in a frenzy over the appearance of the Jiminy Jim Jam Twins. The girls jostle and push to get on camera and see themselves onstage, bopping along with the computer-generated twosome tricked out with green hair, yellow eyes, and nearly alabaster skin covered with bright swirling tattoos under their fake-fur bikinis.

"Please help me, Yaz," I beg as we continue to snake our way toward Basil.

Every personality test Yaz has ever taken revealed loyalty as her strongest characteristic. Of course, One World likes this because she'll stay true to a brand she loves, but since Yaz's second strongest trait is empathy, it also means she'll do anything for the people she loves. And so Yaz, my friend since we were tiny, takes my hand. While the big guy is tangled in the girl frenzy, she yells, "Grab Basil!"

I catch Basil's wrist as Yaz yanks us hard to the left.

"What are you doing?" Basil yells. "We have to get lost in the crowd!"

"Trust her!" I say as she pulls us through the entrance of Hedgy's World.

We round a corner and are suddenly inside the gargantuan animated world of the dancing pink hedgehog. I feel like a tiny mouse inside the pages of a children's novel as we dash behind a giant red-and-white polka-dotted mushroom to hide. All around us flowers soar, green grass glimmers, and the air smells fresh and clean. Within seconds, the bald-headed goon bursts through the entrance. He is red-faced and panting, staring down at his Gizmo screen.

"They must be following your Gizmo signal," I whisper at Yaz. I snatch her Gizmo and command the locator off, making us virtually invisible crouching behind the mushroom.

"Huh?" says the bald guy as three more agents run through the entrance. "Where'd they go? They disappeared off my screen right there!" He jabs at his screen

"Go! Go! Go!" Basil yells, pushing us from behind.

The agents look up just as we scurry beneath the lush leaves and twisting brown vines of the hedgerow. We tear through the thicket, ducking branches, skirting bugs and other critters ambling along the path. Yaz scrambles over a rock the size of my Smaurto, and we pop through a hole onto the main path, where a group of kids our age chase after a giant automaton mouse. But the bald guy has a bead on us. He pushes past everything in his path, determination on his face.

"Blackberries!" Basil yells and shoves me hard to the right. I grab for Yaz and pull her with me. We stumble off the path into a tangle of thorny stems hanging heavy with globular purple fruit. My shirt snags on one of the pointy spines, spinning me around. Basil unleashes me and we keep running. I remember my grandmother telling me something about blackberries. How she'd pick them warm off the vine and pop them juicy in her mouth. My stomach rumbles, and I feel an almost visceral urge to stop and gorge myself on those berries. Then Basil stops and grabs a stem as thick around as my upper arm.

"What are you doing?" I scream, thinking he's lost his mind with hunger. "It's not real! You can't eat it!"

"Keep going!" Basil shouts as he runs, still holding the barbed branch which bends so far I think it will break. Over my shoulder, I see the bald guy crash through the sticks and sprint toward us, then Basil lets go of the stem. It whips forward. The man raises his arms to protect his face as the giant thorns career toward him. The branch catches him across the chest and sends him reeling backward as we slip on through the brambles.

"Over here," Yaz shouts. We round the corner and race beneath a huge hologram rose-covered trellis into Hedgy's Fun Time Dance Party, where a long line of kids snakes through the arena. "Get on-stage!" Yaz yells.

"They'll see us!" Basil hisses.

"It's the only way out." She points to four burgundy shirted guards positioned near the exits, scanning the crowd. "We have to go now!" We sprint toward the steps, plowing past the people waiting patiently for their turns.

Basil follows us onto the stage, where a throbbing beat and syn-thesizer riff has started. The Hedgy hologram, decked out like a Klub Kid in a padded iridescent jumpsuit with little wings across the back, descends from the ceiling to a platform front and center. "Are you ready to dance?" Hedgy shouts in her booming squeaky voice. All the contestants scramble to bright pulsating flowers on the stage floor as music fills the room. The guards storm up the steps, two on each side. The bald brute hurdles himself over the front end, taking out a couple of little kids as he rolls then scrambles to his feet again. He's tattered and scratched from the brambles, his face nearly as purple as the berries, he's so enraged. Then Hedgy begins to dance.

All around us arms and legs fly as contestants bust their moves, following Hedgy's complicated choreography. I see a guard's head snap back as a girl does a roundhouse kick into a lunge. One of the women trips and gets tangled with a dancer. When we hit the back corner of the stage with no place else to go, Yaz screams, "Get on a flower!" She pushes a kid off a purple spot on the floor and pulls me next to her. "Dance!" she shouts in my ear.

"What? Why?" I scream back, but as soon as I flail my arms and legs, the floor beneath my feet opens and I plunge through a gaping hole, screaming, "Basil!" as I slide away.

I scream his name over and over, clawing at the stainless steel chute, trying to stop myself from sliding down three stories into the underbelly of the arena, but the surface is too slick and I'm moving too fast, my legs entangled with Yaz as we hurtle down, down, down. I look up, hoping I'll see Basil cascading above us, but the chute is empty except for the echoes of my voice.

Yaz and I land in a heap on a giant pillowy surface, our bodies twisted together like the vines of the hedgerow up above. I thrash around the soft folds of the mat, still trying to find a way back up the chute to Basil. All around us, bodies thwump on landing mats, as kids scramble up, laughing, calling to one another, "Let's go again!" They run for the glass elevators that will whisk them back upstairs.

"Come on," Yaz says, pulling me free from the deep pocket of the mat. "We have to get out of here."

I resist, digging my feet into the ground. "We have to find Basil. We have to go back up."

"It's too late," she says. "The slides under the flowers go all over the place. He could be anywhere."

"No!" I whimper. I feel like I'm caught in one of my dreams where

I've finally found that elusive thing that will fill the hole in my gut, but it's fallen through me, and once again I'm hollow inside.

"Come," Yaz says gently, but she tugs firmly on my arm. "We have to go."

Just as we turn to leave, there is a loud thwump beside us. Basil. I run to him, sinking into the embrace of the landing pad. "I thought I lost you!" I scan his face, making sure it's really him. "I thought I'd never see you again!"

Yaz grabs my ankle. "Let him up," she commands. "We have to get out of here."

Another thwump. This time a burgundy shirt hits the mat beside us. The bald man thrashes and Basil shoves me onto the floor. Then he scoops his hands beneath our mat and yells, "Push!" I shove as hard as I can. We lift the edge of the mat and throw it onto the guard, whose arms and legs wriggle from between the puffy layers.

"Come on!" Yaz runs away from the elevators and pushes us through a silver door. As it slams behind us, lights sweep down a ramp ahead, and I realize that we're deep inside the bowels of the parking garage.

"Now what?" I shout.

"Run!" Yaz yells as she skitters between sleeping Smaurtos.

Behind me, faint footsteps echo toward the door. I turn and leap in front of the Smaurto coming down the ramp and wave my arms at its anticollision sensor. The car turns sharply and rams sideways into the door, jamming it shut. The car's airbags deploy while the security goons yell from the other side.

As I'm running away, I hear a human voice come over the speakers inside the car. "Is anyone injured?"

The automated Smaurto voice answers, "No persons are on board."

The human voice commands, "Power off," and the Smaurto complies.

In the distance we hear the low whine of a siren as we run willy-nilly through the lot.

"Hide!" I whisper hoarsely and duck behind a line of parked Smaurtos. We press ourselves between the cold concrete wall and the rubber of the tires.

"They know we're here," Basil whispers.

A red light flashes across the walls and we all duck, but I get a glimpse of the vehicle reflected in the side mirror of a blue car in front of me. "It's okay," I say. "It's just an auto-tow. There's no one in it."

"We have to keep moving!" Basil insists.

"I'll call my Smuarto." Yaz reaches for her Gizmo.

"No!" Basil and I both bark at her.

"Jeez," she says. "I'm only trying to help."

"See?" says Basil. "We can't trust her."

"Hey," says Yaz. "Who just got you out of there?"

"Shut up, both of you," I snap. Basil and Yaz glare at one another. "Let me think." I stare down at Yaz's Gizmo. "We can use this to our advantage."

"How?" they ask at the same time.

"We'll send Yaz's Smaurto to a different exit," I explain as I access her Smaurto and tell it to head for the south side of the parking garage.

"Like the decoys in Revenge of the Trojans: Horses from Hades," Yaz says.

"Something like that," I say. "Hopefully security will think we're inside of it."

From the distance, we hear the slow whining siren again. We all crouch down as traces of a red light flash across the walls of the garage. Then we see the automated tow truck slowly round the corner dragging the smashed-up Smaurto I sent into the door.

"That's our way out," says Basil. He runs hunched over between the wall and the cars toward the auto-tow. Yaz and I hesitate, but when he swings open the passenger-side door of the Smaurto, I grab Yaz's hand and pull her after him. We all three scramble inside and cover ourselves with the deflated airbags.

When we get to the top of the parking garage, the tow truck stops and the door swings open. We gasp. A man in blue coveralls jumps back and shouts, "What the . . . !"

Not missing a beat, Yaz climbs out of the car, huffing. "Are you with car recovery services?" she demands of the startled man, then she motions for us to follow her. Basil and I climb out slowly, not sure what to do.

"Uh, yeah," he says. "But my report said there was no one on board. Who are you?"

"Didn't you hear us calling you?" she asks, hands on hips as if she's super annoyed. "We've been stuck down there for five minutes!"

"Sorry about that, miss . . . uh . . . uh . . . Sauconiss," the man mutters as he looks over the info on his Gizmo. "But the system said . . ."

She grabs his Gizmo from him. "That's not even me!" she shouts, poking her finger at the photo of a different girl on the screen. "You better tell your supervisor to get that system checked! What are we paying you for? We could have been stuck down there for hours!"

"I don't understand this," the man says. "I apologize. I'll call you a medical transport."

"No!" we all three say at the same time.

Just then, a commotion begins as burgundy shirts converge on a Yaz's green Smaurto leaving the parking garage a few exits over.

"What's going on over there?" the man says.

Yaz flinches when she sees the bald guard disable her car's door and dive in.

"We better go find your mom," I say to Yaz. "She'll be worried sick." I turn to the man. "Thank you for your help."

"Sure thing," he mumbles as he continues to watch swarms of

guards tear apart Yaz's Smaurto looking for us, while Basil, Yaz, and I slip away in the opposite direction.

✤   ✤   ✤

"My poor baby!" Yaz moans after we hide in the dimly lit edge of the parking garage. We press ourselves against the side of the concrete structure so no external cameras will be able to see us. "How am I going to get around?"

"I'm so sorry," I tell her. "I promise when this is over I'll make sure you get a new Smaurto. You can have mine. I swear."

"God forbid you don't have your own personal transportation device," Basil mutters only half under his breath.

I turn on him. "That was supposed to be our ticket out," I remind him. "Now we're stuck. Our faces are on every screen in the Loops by now. We'll be picked up in three seconds flat."

"She's right," says Yaz. "Everybody will be looking for you." We're all quiet for a moment then Yaz says, "Wait!" She wrenches around so we can see the fading temp-i-tat of Hedgy dancing on her skin. "If we could get to my Spalon guy . . ."

"Now is not the time for a touch up!" I snap at her.

"No! Fiyo can change how you look. Your hair, your eyes, your skin color. Then nobody would know who you are."

"They can do that?" Basil asks, eyes wide with surprise.

"Of course," says Yaz.

"Let's go then. Where is this guy?" he asks.

"Somewhere in the Outer Loop," she says.

"Where exactly?"

Yaz and I look at each other blankly. "How should we know?" says Yaz.

"Can't you use that thing," he flicks his fingers toward Yaz's Gizmo, "and look it up?"

"He's sort of underground," Yaz says. "Doesn't locate. I programmed his address in my Smaurto, and it just takes me there but now . . ."

"Oh no," Basil says sarcastically. "You mean, technology can't solve every problem?"

"We can figure this out," I say. "There's an old building near his place."

"That's helpful," Basil says drily.

"Give me a second," I tell him and close my eyes, trying to picture it, but it's been so long since I let Yaz drag me there that the images are murky. "The old building has a sign on top. Maybe blue and yellow?"

"Oh yeah," says Yaz. "A factory or something."

"Right." I try to drag the picture from the recesses of my mind. "Something about . . ." My eyes pop open. "Sugar! I remember because after you took me there for the first time I asked my grandma what sugar was, and she said it was the sweetest taste you'd ever know, but my mother said it was poison. It's like Do Re Mi Sugar or Don and Mo Sugar or something."

"Domino Sugar?" Basil asks.

"That's it! How did you know?" I ask.

"I've seen that building before," he says.

"So you know where it is?" Yaz asks.

Basil grimaces and shakes his head.

"Guess this might come in handy then, huh?" Yaz waves her Gizmo in Basil's face.

"Even if we look up the Domino Sugar factory, we still don't have a way to get out there," I point out.

"There has to be some worker transport around here somewhere," Basil says, scanning the area.

Again, Yaz and I look at him blankly.

"How do you think people from the Outer Loops who can't afford Smaurtos and highway fees get to work?" he asks.

"There's a fee to drive on the highway?" Yaz asks.

"Who do you think pays for it?" Basil asks. "The government?"

"Oh my god," I say to Yaz. "We are privies."

"What's a privy, exactly?" Yaz asks, hands on hips.

"It's okay," says Basil. "I didn't know what a spelunk was."

"Spalon," Yaz corrects him.

"Right," he says. "The transports will be around the back, away from where all the consumers come in, because god forbid you ever see workers outside of their jobs."

"But won't One World know when we get on the transport? Can't they see our transaction when we pay? Or what about cameras?" I ask.

Basil looks at me with one eyebrow up. "One World doesn't run these transports."

"Who does?" I ask.

"People."

⚘   ⚘   ⚘

Once we get to the backside of the garage, we see another lot, this one cracked and dusty with a line of large, strange, beat-up vehicles waiting in the dusk.

"Are those the transports?" Yaz asks, wrinkling her nose.

Basil shakes his hair out of his eyes and says, "Follow me."

The transports are old, big boxy looking things with dented metal bodies. Nothing like our sleek Smaurtos.

"Who are those people?" I whisper to Basil while trying not to make eye contact with the men and women leaning against their machines watching us.

"The drivers," he says. Yaz and I can't help but gawk.

When we get nearer, they start calling to us.

"Where you going?"

"Best price here."

"I got air-conditioning."

"Smoothest ride, cheapest fare."

Basil walks past the first few drivers then stops in front of a short, squat woman with choppy orange hair. He looks momentarily surprised to see her but quickly recomposes his aloof demeanor. She, on the other hand, smiles a patchwork of wrinkles and laughs until she coughs. "Haven't seen you for a while, kiddo," she grumbles. "Where you been?"

Basil cocks his head to the side almost shyly. "Just around. How are you?"

"On top of the freakin' world," she says too loudly, looking at the other drivers, who laugh along with her. But then she looks at him and asks more gently, "You okay?"

"I need to get to the Outer Loop."

"You got any money?"

"We can transact," Yaz says, showing the woman her Gizmo.

The woman exhales sharply as if she's been insulted. "Where'd you pick up these two privies?" she asks Basil.

"They're friends of Ana's," he says.

Yaz looks at me and whispers, "Who's Ana?"

"Tell you later," I whisper back.

"Well la-de-da," the woman says loudly. "Ms. Ana has friends in high places."

"Not high enough," another driver says, but no one laughs.

"I've got cash," says Basil.

"In that case . . ." The woman steps back, sweeping her arm to the side. "Your chariot awaits." The other drivers cackle meanly as the woman grabs the silver handle on the rear door of her vehicle and yanks. The door screeches in protest when she jerks it open.

Yaz shows Basil and the driver the location of the Domino Sugar plant on her Gizmo screen, then we climb in the backseat. The woman slams our door and climbs in the front.

Yaz can't help herself. She leans forward and asks, "What is this thing?" but then the vehicle roars to life, sputtering and shuttering beneath us, and we grab onto each other. "What's happening!" Yaz squeals.

Basil and the woman laugh. "It's okay," Basil tells us. "These run on combustible fuel so they're a little bit loud."

"And bumpy!" the woman yells over the sound of the engine as we take off, bouncing and clattering across the lot.

"Where do you get fuel?" I ask. "My dad would find this amazing."

Basil rolls down the window and leans back against the seat. The wind ruffles his hair. "They ferment kudzu."

"They do what to who-zu?" Yaz asks.

"Kudzu," he says. "It's a plant."

My mouth drops open, but Yaz cracks up. "Hello, did we just enter another time dimension?"

Instead of being annoyed by this, Basil laughs right along with her. "Yeah, welcome to the past!"

"But where would they get a plant?" I ask looking out of the car window at the hologram trees and virtual grass zipping by. I think of the hard compacted beige dirt in abandoned lots between buildings and the synthetic smells pumped into the oxygenated air.

"Past all the Loops," says Basil.

"But that's a wasteland," I say.

"Not anymore," he says, and a shiver runs down my back.

I brace myself as we bump along the worn-out interior road that leads us away from the EntertainArena. In the distance, I can see a line of lights along the highway, punctuated by large colorful screens. Beyond that are more clusters of twinkling lights branching off the highway. "What is that?" I ask, pointing.

"Your world," Basil says. I look at him, confused. "When you're on the highway, the light from the screens is too bright to see the landscape beyond your car. But this is what we see from our roads."

"It's almost pretty, isn't it?" Yaz says quietly. "Like jewels on a necklace."

"That's one way to look at it," says Basil.

While we roar along the dark rutted roads other vehicles occasionally whoosh past us. I slump back, and Basil drapes his arm lightly across my shoulders. It feels good to snuggle into his side and inhale the scent of him—soap and sweat and something deeper that I can't name, but it makes me feel safe. "God, I'm tired," I admit and close my eyes as the familiar lethargy of hunger rolls over me now that all the adrenaline of the past few hours has worn off. My mouth is dry, and I can feel an ache wrapping around my head from behind my ears. The rhythmic rocking of the vehicle lulls me into a quick half-waking dream. I'm balanced precariously on the thorny stem of the berry bush. My mother is below me violently shaking the stem, trying to knock me off while I grope for that glistening purple fruit. My stomach gurgles loudly, waking me with a start. "Sorry," I mumble and wrap my arm around my belly.

Yaz snickers and I elbow her in the side. "Shut up," I say.

Basil studies me for a second. I smile weakly at him. "You're hungry," he says.

"I was dreaming about berries."

He pushes himself forward and climbs over the front seat of the car so he's sitting next to the driver. "No passengers up here," she grumbles, but she doesn't make him leave.

They talk in hushed whispers for a few moments. I catch Basil say, "How much?" and "You're gouging me." At which she cackles. Finally after lots of back and forth, she unlatches a compartment between her arm and Basil's. He reaches in and pulls out a bottle of light yellow liquid then climbs back over the seat.

"Drink this," he says, handing it to me.

"I'm not going to drink her Synthamil! What would she drink then?"

"It's not hers," says Basil.

I look at the label. Instead of someone's name embossed in gold, it just says, SYNTHAMIL (BASELINE FORMULA) in black and white. "Where'd she get this?" I ask, knowing full well it's a breach of contract to exchange Synthamil for money.

The woman looks back at me in the little mirror above her head. "Oh baby, there's a market for anything if you know where to look and have money in your pocket."

"But it's not even calibrated for an individual," I say.

The woman locks eyes with Basil. "First time princess came down from her golden tower?"

"Hey," I protest. "I'm not a princess, and anyway I can't pay for this without my Gizmo."

At this the woman guffaws. "I don't take that electronic currency. It's cash only in my ride."

I push the bottle toward her, but Basil says, "I can pay."

Yaz leans forward again. "Do you have actual real money?"

"Yes," he tells her. "Actual real hold-it-in-your-hand money."

"Whoa," she says. "This is like one of those history re-enactment villages at the Relics."

Basil twists the cap and pushes the bottle to me.

"What if it's not calibrated right?" I ask.

The woman shakes her head and mutters something I can't quite make out, but I'm pretty sure it's not a compliment.

"It's okay. It's has all the basic nutrients One World uses for everyone," he tells me. "Yours starts like this then gets personalized because your parents pay for it."

"Oh," I say, feeling stupid. I had no idea how it worked.

"Just drink it," he insists.

"But what about you? When's the last time you had nutrition?"

He looks at the bottle and gnaws on his bottom lip.

"We'll share," I say and lift it to my lips.

"*Bon* freaking *appétit*," the woman rasps.

I down half the liquid then hand him the bottle to polish off as the woman pulls up to the tollgates. He gulps the Synthamil and tosses the bottle to the floor, then he pulls something out of his jacket pocket. At first I think it's his scent machine, but he hands it over the back of the seat to the driver, and I see that it's a smaller device that looks cobbled together from various other gadgets. She points it at the toll. The green light flashes and the gate opens.

"I gotta get me one of these," she says.

I look at Basil.

"Don't ask," he tells me and takes it back from her.

I sit back and brace myself for my second trip out of the Inner Loop in one night.

PART 2
OUTER LOOP

"When the apple is ripe it will fall."
—*Irish proverb*

Once we're through the border, it only takes a few minutes for the driver to find Fiyo's street. She pulls up to a crumbling curb under the burned-out DOMINO SUGAR sign and announces, "You have arrived."

Yaz and I get out of the rackety old car. Over my shoulder I watch Basil hand the woman a wad of folded bills, but she pushes his hand away. Then she grabs him and pulls him close to her chest in a fierce embrace. Basil stiffens and pats the woman's back awkwardly as she clings to him. Then she lets him go and swats away a few tears before she climbs back into her car and roars off into the dark night.

"What's that all about?" Yaz whispers to me.

"I have no idea," I admit.

Basil joins us. "You *actually* come here regularly?" he asks.

"Sure," says Yaz. "Why not?"

"I didn't think privies ventured this far," he says.

"Anything for a good haircut!" Yaz says, only half joking.

The three of us jog across the street to Fiyo's Spalon, a small lonely house with an older model Whisson Windmill and sagging solar panels among dark buildings. Yaz tries the front door. "Crap," she says when it won't open. "Come on, Fiyo," she begs. "You can't be closed. Not now." She cups her hands around her eyes and peers inside the front window. "There's a light on in the back."

We creep around the house, staying in the shadows of the eaves to a rear door which butts up against an empty lot. Suddenly I'm wary out here where everything seems to be asleep. There are no big venues nearby. We have no car. Which means there's no place for us to run and no way to get there if Fiyo won't let us in. I'm sure we've made a huge mistake and I feel woozy.

Basil seems to be having the same misgivings. "What if this guy turns us in?" he asks, hanging back. "I bet your parents are offering a bounty by now."

Yaz shakes her head. "He wouldn't. You'll see." She bangs on the door.

We hear rustling on the other side, then two slats of the blinds are lifted apart. "Who is it and what do you want?" a deep voice calls.

"Fiyo, it's Yaz. I need your help."

"Yaz? Don't you own a clock?" The voice has changed to a higher lilt. "I'm cleaning up now."

"It's an emergency," Yaz pleads, rattling the door handle.

"An emergency, huh? Somebody desperate for highlights? Hang on, don't get your panties in a twist!" We hear locks turn then the door swings open. Fiyo stands in a halo of warm yellow light, one arm up the side of the door, the other hand on his, or should I say, *her* hip. The last time I saw Fiyo he was a short trim man in a white lab coat with a blue goatee and long red hair pulled back into a sleek braid. This person is a petite woman in work boots and a white Tyvek jumpsuit with pert breasts and curvy hips. Like lots of Spalon workers, she's tricked out in all the latest fads. Purple eyes that contrast with her white-blonde crew cut and warm brown skin that is as smooth as a baby's butt, as my grandma likes to say. "Ever heard of calling ahead for an appointment?" she asks. The three of us look at each other dumbly. Why didn't we think of that? But then she smiles. "No worries. You're here, might as well come in."

❧   ❧   ❧

Basil and I sit side by side on a little couch in Fiyo's waiting area while Yaz talks to her in another room.

"You sure about this?" Basil asks me.

"Yaz trusts him, er um, her," I say.

"That's not what I mean." Basil looks at his hands, folded between his knees. "I mean, maybe you want to go back home now. Since we're even. You saved me, I saved you, your friend saved us both." He peers up at me with those beautiful dark eyes. "I wouldn't blame you."

I shake my head. "I have too many questions to go home just yet," I tell him, not mentioning that he's more than half the reason I want to stay.

"Like what?" he asks.

I turn and sit cross-legged to face him on the couch. Like the night we first met, I feel as if I could get lost in a conversation with him and talk for hours without ever getting bored. "Like what are the no-food laws? And who is Ana, really? And how long have the Analogs been around? And what do corporate resisters want? And . . ."

"Slow down." Basil grips my knee. "One thing at a time."

My inner thigh quivers beneath his touch, and I lose my train of thought. Part of me wants to stop talking altogether and climb into his lap. Run my fingers through his hair and press my lips against his like we did earlier tonight. These thoughts make me squirm, and thinking that I'm uncomfortable, he pulls his hand away. I draw in a breath and move back, self-conscious and embarrassed by the visceral reaction I have to his touch.

"Do you . . . ?" I start to ask if he feels the same way about me, but then I worry that he doesn't.

"Do I what?"

I look down to hide my embarrassment and mutter, "Do you understand the Universal Nutrition Protection Act?" Then I cringe. What a stupid question!

"That's a doozy," he says. "First you have to understand the Population Stability Act."

He seems almost excited to talk about this so I go along. "You mean the one that says everybody gets nutrition and inoculations for free from the government?"

"Not exactly," he tells me. "The Population Stability Act originally said that every person, regardless of birth circumstance, would receive inocs and nutrition from the government. But after One World cornered the market on synthetic nutrition and became the government's sole provider of nutritional beverages, they pushed a resolution through the government called the Universal Nutrition Protection Act, which does two things. First, it says free nutrition is only available to the first, legally born child of a family."

"Right," I say. "That helps keep the population in check. That's why if parents want a second, they have to prove they can afford it before they can procreate. Makes sense, don't you think?"

Basil blanches. "But what about seconds who are born illegally? What happens to them if their parents can't pay?"

I scoff. I've never heard of such a thing. "Who would go to all the trouble of having a second if they couldn't afford it?"

"What if it's an accident?"

"But the inocs and Synthamil take care of that, right? They suppress more than the urge to eat." I blush a little when I say this.

Basil's quiet for a moment, then he says, "Maybe it doesn't always work that way for everybody."

"But that would mean . . ." I try to work out what would happen to babies born without families to support them, only Basil's already moved on.

"The other thing UNPA did," he says, "was make it so that every individual has to sign a contract in order to receive free nutrition from the government."

"I've never signed a contract," I point out.

"Until you're 18, your parents do on your behalf."

"What's the contract say?"

"That you won't engage in any agricultural practices as long as you're accepting free nutrition. Since One World is the only corporation producing nutrition anymore if you breach your contract, you're out of luck."

"So they're afraid we're all becoming farmers? With what?" I motion out the window. "Depleted soil and imaginary seeds?"

"Their interpretation of agricultural practices is broad," Basil says with a sneer. "UNPA states, 'Upon acceptance of your allotted synthetic nutritional beverages, you hereby agree that the growing, harvesting, selling, reproducing images of, and/or consuming food from other sources is strictly prohibited under penalty of law and will be considered a breach of contract.'"

"But that's not protecting universal nutrition!" I say.

"That's why we call it the no-food law. And now you understand why all the people at the Analog meeting cooperated when security agents told them to stay. Better to do what they say and be put on a watch list then run away and get caught later because then you might lose your supply of Synthamil."

"That's ridiculous," I say. "If people get cut off, they'll starve."

"First you'd have a chance to pay restitution to One World for breaching your contract. Which probably means paying them market value for every bottle of Synthamil you've ever received up to that point. Most of those people at that meeting are just workers from the Outer Loop. They don't have that kind of money."

"So then what happens?"

"Same thing that happens whenever someone can't pay restitution after they commit a crime. They end up in jail, working off their debt. Except that the debt they owe is to the very entity that is threatening not to feed them."

"But . . . that's unfair!" I say in what may be the biggest understatement in history.

"Your choice becomes to either accept the status quo out of fear or organize to make change."

"You mean like a rebellion? Like Svalbard?"

Basil flinches. "How do you know about the Svalbard Rebellion?"

"From my dad and the Dynasaurs," I tell him.

"Dynasaurs?" He looks puzzled.

"They're an underground hacking group that formed after One World suppressed the protests. I thought maybe the Analogs and Dynsaurs might be related. I saw a Svalbard tattoo on Ana's neck."

"Never heard of the Dynasaurs," Basil says. "What do they do?"

"Nothing much," I admit. "They're just a bunch of people who resent how much power One World has, so they mess with them. Hack into games and product launches when they can find a weak spot in the code. They try to be a constant unreachable itch on One World's back."

Basil rolls his eyes, clearly unimpressed. "Analogs want real change. We believe people should have the freedom to seek nourishment from any source without punishment. We want universal food rights with multiple providers."

"But Basil," I say, and this time I'm the one who reaches out to touch him. "There is no other food."

"You really believe that?" he asks.

"Don't you?"

"I don't know. Maybe not."

"Then where is it?"

"Ana says that beyond the Loops, in the Hinterlands, we'll find it." I withdraw my hand. "What if she's wrong?"

Before Basil can answer, Fiyo strides into the room and stands over us, legs wide, hands on hips. "Yaz told me all about your predicament, and I just want to say that I am a friend and my services are at your disposal."

"Wait," I say, feeling suddenly uncomfortable. "Do you actually know who I am?"

"You're Thalia Apple," Fiyo says.

"And you know who my parents are?"

"Of course."

"You'd be taking a big risk," I tell her.

"I'm not a fan of corporate control," Fiyo tells me. "One World this and One World that. As if any of the rest of us have a chance to make a buck. Anytime anyone is sticking it to them, I'm happy to lend a hand."

Yaz grins at us from the doorway. "She's a genius, I'm telling you! An absolute genius!"

"We'll let my work speak for itself." Fiyo steps forward and runs her fingers through my hair. She grabs my chin and lifts my face to the light. "But I can promise that nobody will recognize you two when I'm done." She flips my hair over my shoulder, gives Basil a once-over, then nods. "Come with me."

We push through a heavy blue curtain that leads into her treatment room. Movie trailers, product launches, and celebrity interviews pass by silently on a large wall screen across from a black reclining chair.

"Who's first?" Fiyo asks.

Basil and I look at one another. We look to Yaz and back at each other. "I'll go," Basil says and steps forward.

"A true gentleman." Fiyo leads Basil to a recliner. Yaz pulls up two little stools so we can watch.

"What are you going to do?" Yaz asks. "Eyes? Hair? Skin tone?"

"All of the above!" Fiyo says as she studies Basil. Then she pulls on a pair of gloves and considers her options. "You have excellent bone structure," she tells him. "And great coloring. Speaking professionally, I would say you are a beautiful human creature." She winks a purple eye.

Basil squirms but Yaz and I both giggle because it's true.

"Now tell me," Fiyo asks as she pushes up Basil's sleeve and swabs his skin with some antiseptic. "How has Ana been? I haven't seen her in a long time."

"She's okay," Basil says. "Except for the whole being in custody thing."

Fiyo prepares the first syringe. "Well, the next time you see her, tell her to come to my Spalon. Some highlights around her face would really make her green eyes pop. She'd look better on camera the next time she gets arrested." Another wink. She pushes a tiny bubble of serum from the top of the needle.

"How do you know Ana?" I ask Fiyo.

"Just because you're only now getting wise to the ways of the *not* One World, doesn't mean it hasn't existed for a long time," Fiyo says as she massages the injection point on Basil's arm. "I might look young, but I've been around for a while and so has Ana."

"What are you giving me?" Basil asks, staring nervously at his arm.

"Just a little genetic material to change your eyes," Fiyo says casually as she prepares his next syringe. "We're going light! Iceberg blue."

"What's an iceberg?" Basil asks.

"Who knows," says Fiyo. "But the color is divine! Now blink for me."

Basil blinks and blinks again. Each time he opens his eyes the brown of his irises fades as the melanin recedes, taking him from the phosphorescent yellowish green of algae to the grayish blue of a true daytime sky. I imagine his eye color alleles doing the do-si-do. G's, T's, C's, and A's temporarily changing positions. Fiyo watches the whole thing carefully. "Hmmm," she says. "I think we'll go just a touch lighter. Take away your smoldering stare." She injects Basil again. And within a few moments, his eyes are the brightest blue I've ever seen.

Basil looks at me. "Do I look really weird?"

I nod, captivated by how different he seems already.

"Hair time!" Fiyo announces as she holds up the next syringe.

I nudge Yaz. "Can I talk to you?" I cut my eyes toward the waiting room. "Out there?"

"We're going to step out for a sec," she announces.

"Mmm-hmm," Fiyo says knowingly. "Girl talk, huh?"

"Yes," says Yaz. "Be back in a minute."

In the waiting area I ask to use Yaz's Gizmo. "What are you going to do?" she asks as she hands it over.

"I want to talk to my dad, but I can't turn mine on or they'll know where we are. I blocked your locator at the EA."

"They must be freaking out!" says Yaz. "They think you've been kidnapped."

"Please," I scoff. "A million dollars says that's just a story my mom and Ahimsa concocted so they can arrest Basil and cover up that I busted out of rehab."

✤   ✤   ✤

I take Yaz's Gizmo outside to talk in private. In the darkness of the empty lot, illuminated by the faint glow of the small screen in my hand and the distant stars overhead, I command Jilly to call my father.

He answers immediately. "Yaz? Is Thalia with you?"

Tears sting my eyes when I see his face on the Gizmo screen. I know he must be worried and disappointed. "No, Dad," I say, swallowing the lump in my throat. "It's me. Thalia."

"Thalia! Oh thank god!" he shouts. "Lily! Mom! Everybody. It's Thalia!"

"Dad, wait!" I say. "I only want to talk to you." But it's too late. Over his shoulder I see Mom, Grandma Apple, Papa Peter, and Grandma Grace rush into the living room.

He turns back to the screen. "Are you okay? Where did they take you? What do they want? Did they hurt you?"

"I'm fine," I tell him, crunching loose pebbles and clods of dirt as I pace. "Nobody wants anything. I left rehab on my own. I ran away."

His face contorts. "But that boy you were with? They saw you at the EA."

"Yaz and I got separated from him," I say and realize this is the first time I've lied to my father. "I'm pretty sure they arrested him."

"Not as far as I know," he says and glances at my mom who bullies her way into the camera eye.

"Where are you?" she demands. "How dare you leave! Do you know what kind of trouble you've caused?"

"Lily, stop," Dad snaps at her. "The most important thing is she's safe." He looks at me. "I'm not picking up your location. Tell me where you are so that we can come get you."

I stop pacing. "I need to ask you some questions first."

"Look, Thalia," Dad says, hunching close to the camera eye so my mother can't interrupt. "I don't care what you did. I don't care that you ran away. Just tell me where you are, and I'll come get you, no questions asked. Maybe we can find a different rehab facility if you didn't like that one. We'll work it all out. I promise."

"Honey," Grandma Apple peeks over Dad's shoulder. "Honey, please. Just tell us where you are."

"Thal baby," Papa Peter calls. I can make out only the top of his head behind Dad and Grandma. "I know there seems like a lot of hoo-ha going on and you might feel angry or scared or confused, and maybe the adults around you haven't handled things correctly, but it's time to come home now. You hear me?"

"First, I need to understand some things," I tell them all. I look up into the night sky. It's so dark out here away from the Inner Loops that I can see patterns in the stars. I try to connect the dots and form a picture as I talk. "I want to know more about the Universal Nutrition Protection Act and why One World arrested Ana and what happened to all the people at that meeting...."

Mom shoves her way into the camera eye again. "Why is that any of your concern?"

"Because it affects people," I say. "Because it affects me!"

"It doesn't have to affect you!" she says. "If you would come back here and let us get you straightened out..."

"I don't need straightening out," I shout at her, then I try to calm down because I'm tired of fighting with my mother. I take a deep breath. "I don't want to come home and go through rehab to *optimize my brain* so that I can go to more stupid ICMs and more stupid PlugIns and more stupid EntertainArenas. That's just mindless fluff meant to keep the masses busy and happy."

My dad presses his hand across his mouth and nods thoughtfully when I say this. I feel buoyed by his response and start pacing again as I talk. "If I come back now, then for the rest of my life I'll have this feeling inside of me, gnawing away, never satisfied because I'll know there's a whole other part of the world that's hidden from me." I stop at the far end of the lot. "I need answers."

"You're right," says Dad, which stops me. "There's so much more to this world than you likely know. We've probably sheltered you too much. But we did it because the truths are ugly and none of us wants to relive them. Your grandparents and your mother and I worked very hard to make a world we wish we had when we were your age. A place that's safe from war and starvation and all the other horrible things human beings are capable of when resources are scarce."

"You can say what you want about One World," Mom says, pushing Dad aside. "But at the end of the day, we're keeping everybody alive. And as a privileged person on this Earth, you have an obligation to contribute to that system."

"Not if I don't agree with it," I tell her.

Grandma Apple squishes in front of my mother and father. "You don't have to agree with everything, but you can work for change from the inside."

"Let me talk to her," another voice commands. My family parts and I see Ahimsa march across our living room. She leans down to the camera, her black eyes fierce with anger. "I don't know what kind of lies that boy you've taken up with has been feeding you, but you have no idea who these corporate resisters are and what they're capable of. Ana Gignot is a lunatic. She's endangering the lives of others with her delusions. The longer you stay out there, the deeper your trouble. But it's not just you. Eventually your behavior could have a negative impact on your parents' position at One World. There's only so long I can protect all of you." She stands up and backs slowly away from the camera, never taking her eyes off my face.

Her words feel like a kick to my chest. I watch as my mom and dad and my grandparents swarm around the camera eye again. Of course I don't want to hurt them, but the thought of going back to Dr. Demeter's dome or Basil winding up in prison makes my blood run cold. "Will you promise not to send me back to rehab if I come home?"

My dad starts to nod but my mom says, "We can discuss what kind of treatment you'll get."

"And what about Ba—I mean the boy?" I ask.

Ahimsa steps forward again. "We cannot and will not protect a corporate resister."

Across the parking lot, Fiyo's door swings open. "She's ready for you!" Yaz calls into the night.

"Who is that?" Dad squints at the screen. "Where are you?"

"I have to go," I tell my family.

"Don't hang up. . . ." Dad says.

"Good-bye," I say.

Before I disconnect, I hear my mother roar, "Find her, Max!"

"I can't," Dad says. I kill the video but keep the audio connection and press my ear against the speaker again. "She figured out how to block the locator."

"For god's sake! You're the head of One World programming and the chief security officer. Find a way in," my mother insists.

"Search the video feed," Ahimsa tells him. "There's bound to be a landmark or a clue."

Quickly I end the call and run for Fiyo's door, knowing it's only a matter of time before we're traced.

✢   ✢   ✢

Fiyo steps back from Basil. "Now we wait," she says.

As far as I can tell, Basil doesn't look all that different yet.

"It takes more time for the skin and hair serums to work." She studies Basil for another moment. "Unless of course, you really want to change it up. Add a little of this." She caresses herself from breasts to hips. "It's my latest endeavor. Temporary estrogen. Lasts five weeks."

Basil shrinks in his chair. "No thanks."

"Don't worry." Fiyo winks and laughs. "I've still got the other equipment, too."

Basil comes close and blinks at me with his newly blue eyes. "Everything okay?" he asks. When I hear his voice, that cold, kicked-in-the-gut feeling I had in the parking lot subsides. For a moment I feel warm and safe, like I've curled up beneath one of my grandmother's hand-knit blankets. "Do I look weird?" he asks.

"No," I whisper and take his hand.

"Good," he says as he intertwines his fingers in mine like he did at the Analog meeting. I feel like I never want to let go. "I was afraid . . ." He stops.

"Of what?"

"Nothing," he says and brings my knuckles to his lips then kisses them gently.

Fiyo turns to me. "You ready?"

I take a deep breath and square my shoulders. "Yes, I am."

⚘   ⚘   ⚘

Fiyo moves Basil to a small recovery room with a bed and soft music. Within seconds we hear loud snores, which makes Fiyo chuckle. "Poor guy, he's exhausted." She leads me to the black reclining chair. "Then again, it's hard work running from the Man."

"You should know," says Yaz.

Fiyo gives her a sidelong glance then grins.

"Really?" I ask. "Are they after you, too?"

"One World can't stand true competition." Fiyo flips through a rotating caddy of different serums then holds up a little vial, squints at me, and puts it back. "They try to claim I'm poaching from them, but I make all my own juice. I even hold a few patents. They're the ones always snooping around here. Sending in their *researchers* posing as customers, trying to see what I'm doing. But I can spot those nanobrains a mile away with their cruddy One World dewrinklers and slightly off skin tones. Ugh." She shakes her head in disgust. "If anything I should be suing their asses for making people look so damn fugly." She looks from Yaz to me and grins. "But who has that kind of money?" She goes back to her search then holds a vial up to the light and smiles. "Ah, perfect."

"Thalia, Thalia, wake up. Hey, wakey wakey." Yaz shakes me gently. I blink a few times and open my eyes, confused for a moment about where I am. Then I recognize Fiyo's treatment room, even though the lights are turned low.

"Oh, sorry," I say through a yawn and rustle under the soft blanket someone has put over me. "Did I fall asleep?"

Yaz stares at me and smiles. "For, like, an hour."

"An hour! Oh, no. We need to go," I say, sitting up so quickly my head spins.

"It's okay," Yaz says, putting a hand on my shoulder, and staring at me. "We're done."

"Why are you looking at me like that?"

"Is Sleeping Beauty up?" Fiyo calls from the other room.

"Yes," Yaz calls back, but she doesn't take her eyes off me.

"What?" I demand.

"You are not going to believe it." She laughs.

Fiyo strides into the room and raises the lights. "Hmm," she says circling me. "Color's even." She runs her fingers through my hair. "Skin looks natural," she touches my cheek. "Eyes are balanced." She stands back and nods. "You may now officially call me a genius!"

"What? Let me see," I insist anxiously.

Fiyo helps me from the chair and leads me to the center of the room. "Stand here while I get Romeo. Cover her eyes," she tells Yaz.

"Oh, come on," I protest when Yaz wraps her hands around my face. "This is silly!" But I have to admit it's kind of exciting. I have no idea what to expect. "Do I look totally bizarre?"

"Amazing," is all Yaz says.

I hear Fiyo in the other room waking Basil and leading him toward me.

"Is this necessary?" Basil asks.

"No, only possible. Now, on the count of three," says Fiyo. "One . . . two . . . three!"

Yaz pulls her hand away.

The person across from me and I stare at one another, our mouths agape. If it weren't for the clothing, I would have no idea who that blonde-haired, blue-eyed, pale boy is.

"Do I look ridiculous?" the boy with Basil's voice asks.

"Do I?" I ask him back because of the way he's staring at me.

"Mirrors!" Fiyo shouts happily, and the screen behind Basil shifts from its continuous channel surfing to our reflection.

Basil turns. We stand side by side, staring at the mirror, trying to find ourselves in the strange boy and the girl in my clothes but with darker skin, short pink hair, and emerald green irises, who stares back.

"You look like a Klub Kid," Yaz says with a laugh.

"And he looks like a Scando boy," Fiyo says. "I might have to go for that look soon."

Basil and I glance shyly at one another, but suddenly I'm filled with doubt. Is this the same person who captivated me that first night at Flav-O-Rite when we sat with our thighs nearly pressed together, inhaling the scents of food? The one who held my hand at the Analog meeting and kissed me under the stars? I close my eyes because I can't look at that boy beside me without apprehension filling my belly, but then Basil begins to talk. I keep my eyes closed and I listen.

"How bizarre," he says. "To walk in here one person and walk out another." His voice sends a little chill of recognition up my spine. With my eyes still closed, I inch closer to him and breathe deeply, trying to pull in his smell. "It's like starting over." He grabs my hand. "But with you."

His skin on my skin sends a warm rush over me. I open my eyes and see Basil staring at me through that other boy's eyes. Then he shakes his hair away from his face and smiles that familiar smile, which starts my heart pounding. My mother says my feelings aren't real. Nothing more than chemicals surging through my brain. She sees it all as a giant chemistry equation meant to regulate some primal urge that physically attracts one person to another. But she doesn't understand that I don't need to be in the Procreation Pool to fall in love. What's clear to me tonight is that what I feel for Basil is something so much stronger and deeper than her inocs can control.

ψ   ψ   ψ

To make sure we're completely disguised, Basil and I decide to change our clothes. Yaz and I trade my soft denim jeans and worn-in boots for her slick orange minidress and clunky trainers with their springy soles. Fiyo lends me a pair of silver Teflon leggings and a fuzzy green sweater to keep me warm. The only thing of mine that's left on me is the red knit pouch on my hip holding my cloaked Gizmo. Fiyo has leant Basil a pair of black trousers and a red padded jacket from her closet of men's clothing.

When we emerge from the changing areas, we find Fiyo busily cleaning up empty vials, spent syringes, and clippings of our hair as the screen continues to flip through channels. PRCs, historical docudramas, archived nature shows, and fifteen-second comedy blasts blip past. A newsfeed with the headline "Breaking News!" catches my eye. Just before it switches to a personal transformation story, I think I see my parents.

"Go back!" I command.

On the screen, my parents and Ahimsa stand beneath hologram magnolia blossoms in front of our house. Mom and Dad look worn and worried with their arms wrapped around each other's waists. Then my picture, pre-Fiyo, fills the wall with the words, "$10,000 Reward for any Information Leading to the Return of Thalia Apple" scrolling across the bottom.

"Sound on!" I command.

"...she was targeted by corporate resisters in retaliation for the arrest of Ana Gignot," Ahimsa says.

"Liar!" I mutter.

Next, a blurry photo of Basil, taken either from the footage at the Analog meeting or the EA comes on-screen. "The man who abducted her is a leader in the underground corporate-resistance movement and could be armed and is definitely dangerous," she adds.

"We just want our daughter back," my mother says. "Please, if you have any information..." She trails off and wipes a nonexistent tear from her eye.

The picture switches to old footage of Spinach putting Ana in the One World security van as the reporter explains, "Ms. Gignon and nearly one hundred of her followers are being held at a South Loop security facility." A shot of a prison fills the screen.

I turn to Basil. Despite his light eyes and pale skin, he still smolders when he's furious. "Those bastards!" he spits. "They arrested every single one of them."

I look back to the screen, but the two minutes of news has been replaced by a Hedgy promo with the words "Escape into Another World" floating over images of automatonic animals hopping through a verdant hedgerow. "Well, that's ironic," Yaz mumbles.

"What are we going do?" I ask Basil.

He's too furious to talk.

"We have to do something," I say. "One World is lying about me, and they're holding innocent people. I can't believe they'd go to this much trouble just to shut Ana up!"

Basil slumps. "They'll want to make a deal," he says. "You come back, I turn myself in, they'll keep Ana and let the others go."

"No!" I say. "We can't let One World get away with that. People would protest if they understood what's really going on."

"Who's going to care?" Basil asks.

"Dynasaurs and other Analogs," I tell him. "You said yourself that they're out there. We just have to find them and tell them the truth. How do Analogs communicate?"

"Through non-network channels like word of mouth or paper sometimes or . . ." Basil says.

"You don't have anything more sophisticated than that?" I throw my hands in the air and look at Yaz. "This is why we need a good counter-corporate PRC! To spread the word . . ."

She rolls her eyes. "Not this again."

"One World controls the media," says Basil.

"Not everything," I say.

He shakes his head at me. "You are so naive."

"No, you are!" I say like a three-year-old. Then I turn to Yaz. "Give me your Gizmo." She hands it over.

"You have to stop using that!" Basil says. "You're going to get us caught."

"No," I say. "I'm going to get us organized."

I drop down on the couch and search for a private network signal. Surely there must be a few Dynasaurs out this far. Immediately, I find a strong one. I glance up at Fiyo. "Is this your VPN?"

She shrugs and raises one eyebrow. "Depends on who's asking," she says. Then she turns her head slightly to the right and lifts her chin so I can see the smooth skin just below her left ear. I gasp when I recognize a tattoo just like Ana's.

I grin. "I never saw a thing," I tell her as I log on to the Dynasaur boards. I'm so excited to be with another Dynasaur and to be back online. My fingers fly as I zip around the recent posts. First I search for AnonyGal because she's the kind of person who can rally the troops, but she's not online, so I post a "Call to Action" as a general message.

To: All Dynasaurs

From: HectorProtector

Calling all Dynasaurs! One World has gone too far. The arrest and subsequent imprisonment of Ana Gignot and her followers, the Analogs, is an affront to personal liberty. I was at the Analog meeting in the Outer Loops when Ana was abducted by OW security. Her crime: speaking out about emotional freedom, human connection, and a vision for a better future. One World is hiding behind the Universal Nutrition Protection Act, aka No-Food Law, to muzzle Ana and her followers. They are also propagating lies. I know from a very reliable source that Thalia Apple was not kidnapped in retaliation for Ana's arrest. She willingly fled a rehab facility her family placed her in. One World is using Thalia Apple as a pawn to manipulate public opinion against the Analog movement, whose people are the kindred spirits of Dynasaurs. They, like us, believe One World has too much power and seek ways to create a different future. If you find the arrest of Ana and her followers despicable, speak up! Spread the word. Protest the arrest!!!

And then I sign my post in a way I never have before, with the image of a sprouting seed and the word *Remember.*

The last thing I do before I sign out of the Dynasaur network is send a direct message to AnonyGal, hoping that she'll lend her skills to our cause once she's back online.

AnonyGal: I need your help. Please read my general post and rally the troops. This is serious. If ever there was a time for the Dynasaurs to act, it is now. Due to

my involvement in the Analog cause, I must go off-line
for a while. I hope I can count on your support in my
absence to create a groundswell of opposition to the
unjust imprisonment of Ana and her followers.

I log off and hand the Gizmo back to Yaz. Then we all look at one
another. Yaz is the first to break the awkward silence. "Now what?" she
asks.

"We should split up," says Basil. A pain jabs me in the chest when
he says this, but then he adds, "Thalia and I should leave first. Then
you. You'll have a better chance of getting home that way."

Yaz looks to me. "What do you think?"

"I think he's right," I tell her. "You've already risked enough."

She looks uncertain.

"Besides," I tell her. "We're going to need someone to look out for
us from the other side."

She nods. "I'm your girl."

"I know you are," I tell her.

"But where are you going?" she asks.

"We have to get the Analogs organized then head to the prison
where Ana is, I guess." I look to Basil, but he doesn't respond.

"I wish I could help you more," says Fiyo.

"You've done so much already," I burst out. "We have to repay you!"

Fiyo waves me away. "This one's on the house. Anything to stick it
to those corporate jerks."

"Thank you," I say. "Thank you so much.

"What about you?" I ask Yaz. "How will you get back?"

"Don't worry about her," Fiyo says. "I'll give her a couple of touch-ups
to make her visit seem legit, then I'll get her home safe," he promises.

I throw my arms around Yaz. "I love you!" I say, squeezing her tight.

Yaz stiffens. "Wow, that's a lot of interpersonal touching, Thal," she says as she clutches me just as tight. "Be careful," she whispers in my ear.

"You, too," I say then I turn to Basil.

"Ready?" he asks.

I look into his artificially blue eyes, and although I have no idea where we're going or what exactly we're going to do, I nod. "Let's go."

↯   ↯   ↯

Basil and I leave through the back door, the same way we came in. But I feel even less sure of myself when we step into the night, which seems darker and stiller since we got here. Basil stands in the empty lot, looking around, as if he has some kind of internal GPS connecting to the satellites circling overhead.

"Do you think we can get another transport if we head back toward the tollgates?" I point past the DOMINO SUGAR sign glowing faintly under the yellow moon.

Basil takes my hand and pulls me in the opposite direction. "We can't take another transport," he says quietly as we slip into the alleyway behind Fiyo's place.

I follow closely. "Why not?"

"Eventually one of them will turn us in for the bounty," he explains as he slows by an old garage to peer inside the dirty windows.

"How did you know that woman driver wouldn't?"

"Just did," he says without looking at me and moves on.

I slow down. Maybe it's because he looks different, or because this place is so unfamiliar, but for a moment I feel cautious about following him. "There's so much about you that I don't know."

Basil turns and walks back to me. When he reaches me, his eyebrows flex as he studies my face again. "It's hard to get used to you like that."

I touch my pink hair self-consciously. "You, too." I look down at the crumbling asphalt beneath my feet. "Do you feel differently about me now?"

He thinks this over for a second. "When I first saw you, I did, but then I realized that it's still you in there."

I glance up. "You smell the same."

He laughs. "I bet I stink by now."

"I like it," I tell him shyly, feeling the warmth of my emotion for him come back.

He puts his hand on my shoulder and gently squeezes. "The driver was someone I knew when I was a little kid."

"Was she a friend of your family?"

He hesitates. "Sort of. More like a neighbor who looked out for me when my parents weren't around."

"Where were they?"

"Usually in some kind of trouble. For my mom, it's drugs. And my dad's been in and out of prison for years. As soon as he pays off one restitution, he does something stupid and goes right back in." He looks up at the night sky. "I'd like to find him. Help him out if I could. He's not a bad guy. Just frustrated. Like a lot of people." He puts his hands inside the pockets of the borrowed jacket and kicks at loose rocks on the ground.

"Frustrated by what?" I ask, trying to understand this life he's describing that's nothing like my own.

"All our lives we're told to be grateful to One World for their generosity and compassion. The high and mighty benevolent overlord keeping us all alive! But One World figured out a long time ago that you have to feed the masses so they can buy a lot of useless junk. The whole Universal Nutrition Protection Act is part of a profit model. We feed you, you buy more stuff. But the thing is, giving people just enough sustenance to keep them alive without letting them have real opportunities isn't enough. There's this myth that ingenuity and diligence are all you need to move up in the ranks, but it's total crap. Unless you're already in the ranks, you're invisible to the machine. People like my mom lost hope a long time ago and started looking for ways to escape. And people like my dad end up being eaten alive by the system they've been told to be grateful for."

"And people like you?" I ask.

"We get mad," he says. "And we look for ways to circumvent the system."

"What about people like me?"

Basil chuckles into the quiet night. "I don't even know what to make of you, Apple. You're not like anyone I've ever met. A privy, but it seems like you might get it."

"Get what?" I ask.

"That what you have has been built on the backs of others."

I feel fire rising in my cheeks as I admit, "I didn't know that before I met you."

"But you're willing to listen. And you think about what you hear."

"My mother would say I didn't know how good I had it."

"That's just a different way of saying you didn't know how bad it was for everybody else," Basil tells me. Then he steps forward and wraps me in an embrace. I slide my arms around his waist and settle against his chest inside the warmth of his hug.

"I'm so glad I found you," I whisper. All of my hesitation about going with him has vanished. "All my life everyone has claimed humans are more interconnected than ever, but I've always felt left out." I squeeze him tighter. "Until now."

"I feel the same way," he says, and then for the second time beneath this same night sky, we kiss.

✤   ✤   ✤

It takes almost an hour of creeping through the sparsely lit back alleys of this Outer Loop neighborhood and peering inside garages until

Basil finds what he's looking for in a rickety old shed behind a ram-shackle house. When he finds it, he waves me inside and smiles broadly. "Jackpot!" he whispers, whisking away a black tarp.

"What is it?" I ask, staring at the strange two-wheeled vehicle in the dim light of the moon.

"A motorbike," he explains as he roots around in the dark corners of the shed.

"From a bike-cart to this! We're moving up in the world," I say, which makes him snicker.

He brings over a metal container with a long spout and hands me a thin little wire to hold while he unscrews a cap on the back end of the bike.

"What's that?"

"Biofuel."

"And this?" I hold up the wire.

"A wire."

"Thanks, genius."

"You're the one who asked."

"I meant, what are we going to do with it?" I watch him for a few seconds, then it hits me. "Wait, are we stealing this?"

Basil looks up while the fuel glugs into the tank. "You've never stolen anything before, have you?"

I shift, uncomfortably. "Only from One World," I say, which makes him laugh.

"Like what?" He screws the cap back on the tank and puts the canister where he found it.

"Stupid stuff. I hack into their system so they can't track me or charge me when I play games or chat."

He stops what he's doing and stares at me for a moment. "You can do that?"

"When your dad is the one who designs Gizmos, you learn some things that might come in handy," I tell him.

He shakes his head and I can see that he's smiling. "That is so subversive."

"Guess you're not the only criminal, huh?"

"You're only a criminal if you get caught." He smirks and points to the bike. "Shall we?"

I hesitate. "I don't know. Stealing from One World is one thing, but what if somebody comes out here tomorrow who needs to get to work?"

Basil sucks in his cheeks. "I don't think this person is going to work, Thalia."

"How do you know?"

He points to a table in the back of the shed, where I can just make out rows of glass bottles and beakers, burners and tubes.

"What is it?"

"Drug lab," he says. "Just another local entrepreneur."

I gasp. "How'd you know that?"

Basil raises an eyebrow at me.

"Oh right, your mom," I say quietly, then I eye the bike. "What if we get caught?"

Basil steps away from the bike. "I guess we could walk all night."

My knees go wobbly at the thought.

"Or . . ." He slings one leg over the seat.

While I'm hemming and hawing, a light flicks on in the house in front of the shed.

I scurry toward Basil. "What should we do?"

He reaches down into the bowels of the bike and yanks free some thin cables, then he breaks a flimsy casing that holds them together. "Give me that wire!" he says.

I fumble the little wire toward his hands, but when I hear voices, I flinch and drop it on the ground.

"Find it!" Basil whispers harshly. "Quick."

I drop to my knees, whisking my shaking hands over the dirty floor. "Oh no, oh no," I chant, straining my eyes to find that little sliver. A door creaks open somewhere.

"Hurry," he hisses.

The wire pokes the side of my hand. I grab it and shove it toward Basil, who bends it into the shape of a U then shoves each end inside two tiny ports of the connector. "Get on!" he says, as he pushes a switch and the bike roars to life. I scramble to throw my leg over the seat and cling to him as we go screaming backward, spitting dirt and rocks from beneath the tires.

The back door of the house flies open. A tall woman runs down the steps, yelling and waving her arms.

Basil jams the bike forward and cuts the front wheel hard to the right, which sends me flying sideways. My butt careens off the seat as I claw at Basil's jacket to regain my balance, my legs flying out to either side. He cuts hard the other way, which pops me upright again. Then we go forward, straight toward the woman who's running at us full force, red in the face and screeching.

"Watch out!" I scream, terrified we'll hit her.

Basil swerves, but she catches hold of the handlebar, knocking us off balance and her to the ground. We teeter left then right, Basil grunts as he tries to regain control, but the bike tips, spilling us in the dirt. I look over my shoulder to see the woman hauling herself up and sprinting toward us again. I jump up, grab the handlebars, and yank the idling bike upright.

"Come on, come on!" I scream at Basil.

He half crawls, half runs toward me. Behind us, another person bursts out of the house. He stands on the top step and raises something long and skinny to his shoulder. For a moment I'm bewildered and feel like I've been transported inside a virtual game, until I realize that what he's holding isn't a virtual gun. It's real.

I know then that I can't wait for Basil to drive this thing so I throw my leg over the seat and scream, "Get on!" over the sound of the first shot. As soon as I feel Basil's weight behind me and his arms around my waist, I pull back on the right handle as I'd seen him do. The engine revs and the bike flies forward, sending us both backward, but we hold on tight. More shots echo off the houses. Basil gasps and grunts in pain. Although I have no idea what I'm doing, I keep the handle back as far as it will go. We veer wildly from side to side, but I don't lose control. I hunch forward, keeping my eyes on the road and my legs wrapped tight around the seat, driving as fast as I can, to put as much distance between us and them as possible.

When we're around a corner and on the interior road, I yell, "Are you alright? Did they hit you? Are you bleeding?"

He slumps against my back and pants into my ear. "Just keep going," he says. "Get us out of here."

⚝   ⚝   ⚝

Within ten minutes of twisting and turning through alleyways and dirt yards, we're back on a crumbling, dusty road heading toward the tollgates with nobody behind us. Every once in a while, we pass the remains of decrepit strip malls and old hotels looming in the moonlight like memories lurking in the shadows of my grandparents' minds. The landscape here is so burned out and bald that it looks like the playing field for Pesky Petey before the virtual effects kick in. In the distance, beyond the toll wall, I see the highways circling the city Loops like tiny twinkling strings of gemstones. I keep blinking, half expecting this world to light up with virtual trees and grass and flowers, but the other part of my brain is slowly coming to terms with the fact that this is the reality behind every facade One World has created.

Once I believe we're safe, I gather my courage and slow down to check on Basil. "Hey," I call. "What happened? Are you okay?"

"He got my arm," he tells me through gritted teeth.

"Are you bleeding badly?" I ask.

"I don't know," he says.

I cruise to the side of the road and kill the motor. "We have to take a look," I tell him.

"It's fine," he says as I slide off the seat. "We should just keep going."

I shake my head and come around to his right side where his arm hangs limp. "You've been shot, Basil," I tell him because I think he might be in shock and not realize the seriousness of the situation. In the dim light, I gently press my fingers against a warm, sticky splotch on the back of his coat sleeve. Basil moans and slumps forward a bit as if he's going to be sick.

I crouch beside him and lay my hand on the back of his head. "We have to stop the bleeding," I tell him.

When I was little, I loved to play a game with Papa Peter. It was always the same. We were doctors in a war with few supplies. I'm sure it was my childish way of making sense of the stories I overheard. Sometimes we'd rip up old bedsheets and dress each other's wounds. He usually ended up looking like a mummy by the time I was done with him. Now I try to remember how he did it when he tended to my imaginary injuries. "First we need to make a bandage," I say, looking around for something to use. "Then we'll get you to a doctor."

"No doctor," he says.

I choose not to argue with him even though he's wrong. "Are you wearing a T-shirt under there?"

He nods.

"I'm going to need it." I take a deep breath and grab the cuff of his jacket. "I'm going to take this off you slowly. It might hurt, but you'll be okay. Why don't you talk to me while I do this?" This is a trick Papa Peter used on me when it was time for my inocs. He'd get me so caught up in telling him a story that I'd forget all about the injections, which I hated. "Have you ever been hurt before?" I ask as I slowly thread his arms out of the coat.

"One time, when I was six or seven," he says in a calm, almost monotone voice.

"What happened?" I ask in an effort to keep him talking.

"I was running through an abandoned hotel." He gasps as the jacket peels away from his wound.

"And?" I ask and crane my head around to get a better look at the back of his arm. It's too dark to make out anything but mangled skin.

He takes a breath. "I wasn't supposed to be in there, of course, but what kid can resist jumping on all those beds or throwing old TVs inside an empty pool?"

"We need to take off the long-sleeve shirt, too." I move around to the front and begin undoing the buttons, which makes me blush furiously. As Yaz says, this is a lot of interpersonal touching. I breathe deeply to keep my hands steady and focus on the task, rather than thinking about being so close to Basil's body. "What happened next?"

Basil seems to relax just a bit as he digs back into his memory. "I was tearing down a hallway, and my foot went right through a rotten floorboard," he tells me. "Whump! Down I went. One minute I was zooming around, the next, my leg had been swallowed up."

I lean forward to shimmy the green shirt over his shoulders and down his arms. Heat rises off his skin. He winces. "Sorry," I say.

"It's okay," he tells me and turns his face away.

"Now . . ." I stand back and try to figure out how to get the T-shirt off without killing him. "I wish I had some scissors," I mumble.

"Here." Basil uses his good arm to reach inside his pants pocket and remove a small compact red utensil.

"What is this?" I turn it over in my hand.

"Swiss Army knife."

I open up different blades, some kind of screwdriver and several pointy things. "This is amazing!" Then I get to the tiny scissors. "Whoa! So cool." I pull his shirt away from his body and slowly cut a straight line up from his belly to his neck. "So what happened to your leg?"

"I had a big gash all the way up my shin."

"What did you do?"

"I was with my brother. . . ."

"Wait. What?" I stop cutting. "You have a brother?"

"He was older. His name was Arol."

"Was?" I ask. Basil doesn't answer so I refocus on slicing his shirt open. His newly pale skin faintly glimmers. I can see that he is lean and muscular and gorgeous in the hazy light, like something from a dream that disappears the moment you wake. With my eyes, I trace a path of hair that marches from his belly button into the waistband of his pants. Then I notice just above his right hip bone a smudge of ink. I lean closer and squint until I can see a sprouted seed and the word *Remember* tattooed on his skin. I reach out to touch it and feel the warmth of his skin beneath my fingers. I have so many questions, but I realize that now is not the time to ask. Instead, I stand up and carefully slip the shirt over his arms.

"So, um," I ask, my voice a little shaky as I try to stay on track. "When you hurt your leg, what did the doctor do?"

Basil half laughs. "There were no doctors where we lived. This was before the free clinic came to town. And my parents didn't have the money to pay someone in the Inner Loop, let alone get me through the tolls."

"Didn't your family have insurance?"

Basil frowns at me. "Uh, no."

"Wow," I say, unable to hide my surprise. "My grandfather used to go to the Outer Loop to treat people without insurance." I cut the T-shirt into long, wide strips that I lay over my shoulder. "It infuriated my grandmother that he'd work for nothing. She'd call him a socialist, which made him laugh and say, 'I've been called worse.'"

"Why did he stop?"

I shake my head because I don't know the answer. "I guess he got too old."

"He sounds like a good person," Basil says.

I stop cutting and stare at Basil sitting shirtless on the bike. "He is," I tell him. "He would like you."

Basil looks down, uncertain or embarrassed. I can't tell.

"I'm going to have to touch your arm now." I step closer and gather up my confidence. "It might hurt, but you're going to be okay." I place one hand firmly on his shoulder and hold him steady in my gaze.

"Okay," he says quietly. "I'm ready."

"Actually, it's not as bad as I thought it would be," I tell him and it's true. "I think the bullet just grazed your skin. Good thing you had on that jacket. It took most of the hit." I quickly wrap the strips of fabric from his elbow up to his shoulder, keeping it tight enough to stop the bleeding but not too tight that it will cut off his circulation. "Want me to sing to you?" I ask. "That's what Papa Peter used to do while he'd give me the inocs." I try to remember the song. "'Don't worry about a thing. . . .'" I sing, but I can't quite recall the words. I hum, but I can't get the melody right. "Something about three little birds."

"Never heard it," he says and breathes deep.

I step away and check out my handiwork. It's not half bad. Papa Peter might even be proud. "This should slow the bleeding until we get you to a doctor."

Basil pulls away and winces in pain. "Thalia, I can't go to a doctor!

One bit of genetic material, and we'll immediately get picked up by security agents."

"We'll go to my grandfather," I tell him. "He'll help us."

"I thought you said it wasn't so bad."

"I just meant, you're not going to bleed to death, but you're going to need more than a dirty shirt wrapped around it to heal properly." I help him back into his long-sleeve shirt and jacket. He tucks his mangled arm against his body and sighs with relief.

"What happened with your leg?" I ask.

"A neighbor stitched me up."

"Stitched?"

"Needle and thread."

I grimace and look down at his legs. "And you were okay?"

With his good arm he lifts the cuff of his pants. "Good as new." In the dusky light, I can barely make out the jagged white scar snaking up his leg, but still it makes me flinch. "I didn't need a doctor when that happened." He pulls his pant leg down. "So I won't need one now."

"No. You *couldn't* see one. That's different." I climb onto the bike in front of him and kick-start the bike like he did earlier. "Now let's get to the tollgate so we can find my grandfather," I say and pull onto the road again.

✣　　✣　　✣

Just as the sun begins to come up rosy through the dust that hangs thick in the air out here, we reach a tollgate. Across the road a small cement building sits on an island of fractured concrete beneath a brightly blinking sign that reads, BIOFUEL AND KUDZARS. The haze makes everything appear ethereal, as if we are dreaming the pink-tinged, fuzzy-edged structures. With his good arm, Basil reaches in his pants pocket and pulls out the little device he handed the driver last night.

"What is this?" I ask.

"A transponder I built." He points it at the scanner above the tollgate, but nothing happens. "Move closer," he says. I shuffle the bike forward, and he points the device again, but the light remains red and the gate firmly closed. "That's weird." He shakes the device and tries a third time.

I look over my shoulder at him. "Is your account low on money?"

He gives me one of his sideways smirks, and I realize what a dumb question I just asked. I reach for the machine and study it. "How's it work?"

"First I made a radio-frequency ID device so I could borrow account info off some Gizmos."

"*Borrow?*" I ask. "Like how we borrowed this motorbike?"

"Something like that," he says with a little grin. "Then I uploaded all the account info." He turns the device over, looking for the source of the malfunction, but finds nothing. "Not all of the accounts could be empty at the same time. Maybe it got damaged when I fell off the bike. I'll have to take it apart later and figure out what happened." He looks over his shoulder at the biofuel and kudzar place. "We can probably get a black-market toll pass in there."

"Is that what a kudzar is? A black-market pass?"

He chuckles. "No. A kudzar is a thing you smoke. It's made of dried kudzu leaves and it gives you a buzz."

"Where do people get all this kudzu?"

"The Hinterlands, I think. At least that's what I hear."

"God." I shake my head and nearly laugh. "It's pathetic how much I don't know."

"You'll learn," he says.

I pull into the parking lot next to the dumpy building. "You think it's safe?"

Basil looks up and down the empty road. "I don't think anybody's following us if that's what you mean."

"What makes you think we can get a pass here?"

"Anything's for sale out here if you have enough money," he says as he dismounts the bike.

     

"Well good morning! You two sure are early birds today," a woman chirps at us. She's tall and concave like a human question mark hunched over the counter across from a large screen playing the end of a game show where people compete against virtual versions of themselves for better jobs. She stubs out what I assume is her kudzar and straightens herself up as we approach. "What can I get for you?"

The smoke from her kudzar makes me dizzy. I walk to the back where the air is more clear and check out the racks of kudzar packs next to a darkened doorway, while Basils heads up to the counter.

"I want to get through the toll," Basil tells her. "But my mom must have forgotten to replenish our autopay. Can I buy a pass from you?"

She narrows her eyes at him. Her skin has a grayish pallor like the ashes in the little bowl by her elbow. "You see that sign out there?" she points to BIOFUEL AND KUDZARS blinking through the dawn. "Doesn't say anything about toll passes, now does it?"

Basil shoves his good hand in his pocket and pulls out a few bills. "Yeah, I just thought maybe . . ." He lays the bills on the counter.

On the screen, a newsfeed starts up. The sound is low, but I see a reporter surrounded by people standing in front of the prison where the Analogs are being held. "Hey look," I say. Basil turns. "Do you mind if we listen?"

The woman shrugs and commands the sound up.

". . . hundreds of people outside the South Loop prison where Ana Gignot and her followers are being held," the reporter says. The camera pans over men and women, old and young, many with signs that say, FREE ANA! More people stream down the road toward the gathering crowd. I beam at Basil, amazed by what I'm seeing, but his face betrays no emotion. Behind me, a short barrel-chested man lurks in the darkened doorway.

The woman leans against the counter again and studies Basil over folded fingers. "Why you going in the Loops?" she asks. "You joining that protest?"

"Don't know anything about it," says Basil. Then he peers at her. "Do you?"

"I know they're a bunch of idiots," she says, shaking her head. "Gonna get themselves arrested."

Basil fumes silently, then he takes out another bill. "Do you have a pass or not?"

From where I'm standing, I can see that the man in the doorway is holding an old clunky Gizmo. The blue light from the screen illuminates his hardened face so that he looks as if he's made of stone.

"What happened to your arm?" the woman asks Basil.

Without missing a beat, he says, "Spilled my bike and tore it up on some gravel."

"Looks bad," she says. "You need a doctor?"

"That's where we're headed right now," I say. "So we really need to get through the toll."

"An Inner Loop doc, huh?" The woman straightens up. "You got insurance?"

"Of course . . ." I start to say, but Basil flashes me a look.

"Can you help us or not?" Basil asks, his patience wearing thin.

"For the right price." The woman lights up another kudzar, lazily waving the match until the fire goes out. "Pico? You come out here a minute?" The man steps through the door and I shrink back.

Basil looks wary. "How much?" he asks the man.

Instead of answering, the man says, "That your bike out there?" Then he crosses his arms. He's still holding the Gizmo but now the screen faces me. I see a picture of a motorbike with the word STOLEN stamped across the bottom in red.

My chest tightens and my stomach drops. "Um, Basil." I hurry toward the front. "Let's just get the pass and go, okay?"

"What kind of bike is it?" the man asks, jerking his thumb toward the front window. In the parking lot, a beat-up yellow car, a lot like the transport we took last night, pulls up to a fuel pump next to the bike.

"Let's just go, okay," I hiss, bullying Basil backward.

"Where'd you get that bike, huh?" Pico walks toward the door. Through the glass, I see that someone has gotten out of the car and tethered it to a pump with a long hose.

"What are you on to, Pico?" the woman asks.

He hands her his ancient Gizmo. "Look-a here, Iris. Somebody stole this bike. Insurance company sent out a bulletin."

The woman rummages through a drawer beneath the counter and pulls out a pair of cock-eyed glasses. "There a reward?"

Basil squeezes my arm tightly and we shuffle toward the exit. "That's my bike," he says. "Had it since I was fifteen."

"You got your ownership certificate?" She looks at us over the top of her glasses with a little smirk playing at the corners of her mouth.

"We don't have to show you anything," says Basil.

The man steps around the big metal display racks of kudzars and blocks the door. His face cracks into a crooked smile, like a fault line after an earthquake. "You hear that, Iris. He thinks we got no jurisdiction."

The woman guffaws then coughs and wheezes. "Oh dear, did we forget to add our side business to our sign?" Iris feigns regret. "It should read, 'Biofuel, Kudzars, Toll Passes, and Insurance Investigators.'"

"'Less you got a certificate of ownership from an insurance company, you'll have to stay here while we make a call," Pico says.

Basil gets close to the man's face. They're about the same height, but Pico is twice as wide, all bulk and muscle. "You can't hold us here against our will."

"Sure I can," Pico says without the slightest flinch. "That bike matches the description on the insurance company bulletin, and you can't prove you own it. Then as a private security agent for the insurance company, I got jurisdiction to detain you until the proper authorities arrive to sort things out."

Basil rests one fist on his hip and keeps his gaze locked on Pico. "How much they pay you?"

At this, Pico chuckles deep in his throat. "Well, there's my commission from the insurance company if that turns out to be the stolen bike. And you'll probably need a lawyer. Then you're going to have to pay the rightful owner for loss of property if you're found guilty. If you can cover all that, then we might be able to work something out."

Basil's head droops forward.

Outside I see the person remove the hose from her car then walk toward the door, pulling bills out of her pocket. As she nears the building, I recognize her shock of choppy red hair. "Basil!" I say, pointing. Both he and Pico look through the window, and I see a chance. I drop my shoulder and run with all my might straight at Pico. I catch him by surprise and plow him back into the kudzar rack. He stumbles and flails into the collapsing shelves as I scream, "Run!"

Pico reaches up and catches a hold of my wrist. Basil charges up beside me and wallops him square across the jaw with his good arm, but Pico doesn't let go of me so I squirm around and kick him between the legs as hard as I can. He goes down like a fallen statue, and Basil and I flee out the door while Iris shrieks behind us.

"Betta! Betta!" Basil yells at the red-haired woman who turns and runs when we come screaming out at her. "Betta, help!"

I run after him as fast as I can but I step into a rut in the concrete and feel my ankle twist, right then left, sending a searing pain up my leg as I fall on all fours. Tiny pebbles of concrete lodge into my hands and knees. "She doesn't recognize us!" I scream at Basil as I struggle to get up, but my leg isn't working right.

Iris lurches outside, shouting obscenities at us.

"Betta, it's Eli!" Basil shouts and lunges for the back door of the car. He catches hold of the handle with his good arm just as Betta puts the car in gear. "Arol's brother, Eli!" Basil shouts as the car half drags him, but then it skids to a stop. Basil swings the door open and runs back for me. He scoops me up under the armpits and stuffs me in the backseat then slams the door behind us, screeching, "Go!" just as Pico limps into the parking lot. Betta jams the car in gear, leaving Pico and Iris howling and shaking their fists in the dust cloud we've left behind.

⚜   ⚜   ⚜

"How do you know my name?" Betta yells over the roar of the engine. "How do you know Arol and Eli?"

I writhe on the seat, clutching my ankle, which has quickly begun to swell. In the rearview mirror I see the trepidation in her eyes, but there's something else there, too. Something like hope.

Basil leans forward. "You picked us up outside the Inner Loop EA and dropped us at the Spalon last night. You gave us a bottle of Synthamil." He reaches in his pocket. "We used this to get us through the toll. Then I tried to pay you, but you wouldn't take it."

Betta's face softens. She looks over her shoulder. "But how . . ."

"We altered our appearance," he explains. "At the Spalon."

"I saw you on the news," she says. "But I didn't tell nobody. That the girl?"

"That's her." He motions to me, then he notices that I'm in pain. "You okay? Did you break it?"

I try to breath and stay calm but tears sting my eyes. "Probably just a sprain," I say, but I think I might pass out because it hurts so bad.

"Loosen your shoe and put your leg up." He gently lifts my foot onto the seat in front of me and tugs at the laces, which helps immediately.

In the front, Betta's shoulders shake and she begins to wheeze. "Holy hell!" she says and I realize that she's laughing. "You little bugger! You're really sticking it to those One World jerks, aren't you?"

Basil looks down, half embarrassed and half proud. "I didn't think it would get this crazy so fast," he admits.

She glances at me. "He really kidnap you?"

"No!" I say, breathing easier as the pain begins to subside. "Not at all. I wanted to go with him."

She nods, not needing any other explanation. "Yeah, that didn't make much sense the way you two were snuggling up in my backseat last night," she teases, and my cheeks grow warm.

Basil looks at me and grins.

"Eli, huh?" I say, as the waves of pain recede.

He laughs. "Not such an exciting name."

"It's a fine name," I tell him and pat his thigh. "But I think I'll just call you Basil."

"Ana gave me that name."

"Then it's good enough for me."

He leans toward Betta again. "We need to go back to the Inner Loops."

I look at him. "We do?"

"Now you need a doctor," he says, nodding at my throbbing ankle.

"No, you do," I say.

"You two are a sorry lot, aren't you?" Betta says with a sad laugh. "I'd like to help you, you know I would, but I can't."

We look at each other. "Why?"

"Haven't you seen a screen lately?" she asks.

"Only for a minute in the fuel stop," he tells her. "We don't have

Gizmos." Without thinking, I put my hand on my pouch to make sure my sleeping device is still cloaked and tucked away. It is.

"The tollgates aren't working," Betta tells us. "The news is all over the place. First time they shut them down since . . ." In the mirror I see her eyes flick to Basil. "Anyway, some kind of protest started at the prison where they're holding Ana and her followers."

"You know about Ana, too?" I ask, suddenly sitting up, which is a terrible idea because it sends a shooting pain through my leg. I settle back and take a few deep breaths.

"Of course I do!" she says. "I don't live under a rock. Every time you get on a screen, a message pops up that says, 'Free Ana!' and tells you to go to the prison if you care about personal liberty."

I squeeze Basil's arm. "This is amazing!" Then I pepper Betta with questions. "How many people are there? What's One World's response? Have the protesters made any demands?"

Betta looks over her shoulder, annoyed. "I don't know. See for yourself." She tosses over an old beat-up Gizmo, and I yelp with delight.

"What are you doing?" Basil asks, reaching for it.

"Just checking the news." I elbow him away and scan headlines to confirm everything Betta's saying, which is the only thing that could take my mind off my ankle.

While Betta and Basil hypothesize about how all of this is happening, I hunch over the screen and quickly crack the operating system, so I can turn off the locator and find a VPN. There are several out here so I can easily hop on the Dynasaur chat. I search the logs for AnonyGal, sure that she's the one who's taken charge, but I can't find her anywhere. I go back to the original call to action I posted yesterday, which seems like weeks ago. There is a huge response. Dynasaurs are riled up. They've honed a message and called on programmers to release bots so they can take over the most heavily trafficked One World sites.

"It's amazing!" I can't contain my smile. "We have to find a way back so we can join them!"

"Won't be easy," says Betta. "I think One World's afraid people are going to start flooding in from the Outer Loop to start a riot." She and Basil lock eyes, then both look away quickly. "I can drop you outside the tolls, but you'll have to find another way in. Things are shut tighter than Ahimsa DuBoise's butthole."

"Hah!" I crow from shock, then I giggle uncontrollably. "I've never heard anyone insult Ahimsa like that."

"People insult her all the time," says Basil.

"Not where I'm from." I try not to snort from laughing so hard, but I can't help it. "At least, not so accurately."

"You know her?" Basil asks.

"Unfortunately, I do," I admit, which kills my amusement. "And I'm sure she's furious." I remember how she scowled at me from the screen in my family's living room, telling my mother to commit me to rehab and demanding that I give up info about Basil. Serves her right that people are pushing back. She needs to know that she can't just lock up anybody she wants. I hunch over the Gizmo and post a message from HectorProtector, courtesy of Betta the driver.

> **Calling all Dynasaurs and Analogs! You've got One World running scared. The tolls are shut to keep the Inner Loop secure from the riffraff of the Outer Loop, but don't let that stop you! If you are in the Outer Loop go to the tolls. Bang on the gates. Demand to be let in! If you are in the Inner Loop, join the masses. Don't stop until Ana is free!**

I add the Svaldbard symbol at the end then reset the operating system and hand Betta back her Gizmo. I sit back and smile at the thought of Ahimsa having to admit that she's been wrong. In fact, I wish I could see that moment myself. I look out the window at the wall separating us from what's happening inside. "Maybe we could climb over," I suggest.

"I doubt it," Basil says, pointing to my leg and his arm.

"First, you both need a doctor," says Betta. "Even I can see that."

"What are we going to do?" I ask.

"Don't worry," she says. "I know where to go."

✢   ✢   ✢

Something gnaws at me from inside, creating a perfectly round opening from the bottom of my ribs to the top of my hip bones. When I bend over I can see straight through a gaping hole in my gut to the hard and dusty ground beneath my feet. I need to fill up this wormhole that was my belly to stop myself from draining away. I look around for something to put in there. Something solid. I pick up bloody, tattered clothing. A filthy knit bag the color of my grandmother's hair. A shoe. I try to stuff them inside that space, but everything falls through and lands behind me in a puff of dust. I find my Gizmo. I uncloak it. Then it begins to expand. I try to force it in the hole in my gut, but it's grown too big. Something bubbles up from the emptiness into my mouth. I catch it with my tongue. Hold it tight between my teeth. The taste is bitter and I moan.

"You alright?" someone says.

I open my eyes and find myself slumped back on a bed, my arms and legs akimbo as if I've fallen from the sky. To my left and right and across from me are rows of examination tables like the ones Papa Peter had in his office when I was little. They are filled with people, some bloody and bandaged, others laboring for breath, a few curled on their sides crying. IV bags drip, monitors beep. From somewhere far away a person screams in pain. My stomach churns and I feel faint. I've never seen this many people sick and hurt. I wonder if there was some kind of natural disaster.

"You were groaning," the man next to me says.

I shake my head and push up on my elbows, trying to focus on what he's saying. The side of his face is swollen and discolored, and he holds his ribs when he moves.

"What happened?" I ask, mostly to myself but the man answers.

"Don't know about you, but I got jumped. Goddamn geophags. Somebody's got to do something about them. Roaming the streets like wild animals." He winces as he shifts his weight.

A woman in a crisp blue uniform walks by whistling, but she stops when she sees me sitting up. "You're awake!" She's tall and solid with broad shoulders. Her hair is pulled back in hundreds of tiny braids gathered at the nape of her neck. She has skin as dark as Papa Peter's. Suddenly I miss him terribly.

"Where am I?" I ask, still cloudy-headed.

"Clinic," she says and waves her Gizmo slowly over me to check my vitals. "Hmmm." She studies her screen. "Not had any nutrition lately?" I stare at her dumbly because I can't clear the fog in my mind. She grabs a bottle of light yellow baseline Synthamil from a shelf behind me. "Drink this," she commands. Without hesitation, I gulp it greedily, not even stopping for a breath, which makes her laugh. "You want more?"

I nod.

She takes another bottle from the shelf, twists off the cap, and watches me guzzle that one, too. I catch my breath and say, "Thank you."

"How long's it been?" she asks while snapping on sterile gloves.

"Don't know," I mumble.

"That's a long time then," she says. "I think the painkillers made you groggy. Let's have a look at that leg."

Slowly, the past few hours come back to me. Betta decided the safest place for us would be a medical clinic far from the Inner Loop, so she drove us another hour west to the settlement where Basil grew up, and she dropped us here. They whisked Basil away to clean his wound and graft Just-Like-Skin onto his arm while a doctor gave me pain medication then set to work on my ankle, after assuring us all medical treatment was confidential. At some point, I passed out from hunger, pain, and exhaustion.

"Where's Ba...um, my friend?" I ask. "With the hurt arm?"

"He was asking about you, too," she says. "You can find each other in the waiting area as soon as I'm done." She lifts my leg. The silver legging flaps where they've split it at the seam to make room for an inflatable brace that compresses and releases rhythmically against my ankle. "Any pain?"

I shake my head.

"Good," she says. "It's just a sprain. We injected the muscle fibers with corticosteroids, which should alleviate the swelling and begin rebuilding the tissue pretty quick." She stands back and cocks her head. "Now, you want to tell me what really happened to you two? Because you and your friend don't look like people who got into a car wreck. In fact, he looks like he's been shot."

"Those damn geophags got guns now?" the man beside me asks.

"What's a geophag?" I ask, imagining some horrible mutant creature roaming this desolate place so far from the Inner Loop.

"Dirt eaters," the man snarls. "Don't know why they had to come out here. We got to run them off."

The nurse sighs. "Garvy, you don't know it was them that beat you."

"Who else?" he huffs.

"Who you owe money to?" she asks, which shuts Garvy up. She looks at me and rolls her eyes a bit. "Anyway, those poor folks are too crazed with hunger to do much damage."

"They're hungry?" I ask, my eyes wide.

She shakes her head sadly. "They keep coming in here, bellies full of weird things. Dirt's the least of it. I don't know what to do other than give them some Synthamil and send them on their way." She sighs and looks at me. "You going to tell me what happened then?" I keep my mouth shut. "Fine," she says. "You'll need to come back tomorrow. . . ."

"But, I don't have any money," I blurt out, and for the first time in my life, I feel the shame of being at the mercy of someone else's generosity. For a quick second, I think about turning on my Gizmo to access my insurance info, but the price of being located is too high.

"No need," the nurse says with a smile. "It's a free and confidential clinic."

"How can it be free?" I ask, skeptical.

"We have a benefactor." She pulls off the sterile gloves and begins whistling a familiar tune.

Don't worry about a thing. 'Cause every little thing's gonna be alright. " 'Three Little Birds!' " I say.

She stops whistling and smiles. "That's right." She points to a sign above the door. Three chubby little bluebirds sing in a branch, the words EVERYTHING'S GOING TO BE ALRIGHT written in cursive below them.

"Papa Peter?" I start to say, but then I catch myself and stop.

"Who?" she asks.

"Nothing." I shrink back, but certain I know who's behind this place. "Never mind," I say quietly, full of homesickness. "I'm not thinking clearly yet."

"The medicine will wear off soon," she assures me. "I'll bring you some painkillers for when it does."

As she walks away, a woman from across the row removes an oxygen mask from her face and calls, "Hey, Garvy, you see that newsfeed?" She points at a screen taking up the far wall. The sound is too low for us to hear, but I see the repeat of my parents in front of our house and I cringe.

Garvy nods. "Been all over the screens today. Some privy girl got snatched up by corporate resisters. Her mommy and daddy are offering ten grand for her," he says with a snort.

I can't believe Basil was right. They've offered a bounty for me.

The woman pulls the mask away from her face again and laughs. "You'd think she'd be worth more. You see who her parents are?"

"I'd take their money," Garvy says. "They offering extra if you nab the guy who took her?"

"Another ten thou, but they say he's dangerous," the woman says and I nearly protest.

"You got to bring him in alive?" Garvy asks.

My stomach drops.

"I doubt it," says the woman. "Why would they care as long as they get their little privy back."

I groan again. Garvy squints at me from his good eye. "You hurting, honey?" He reaches out to pat my arm and I flinch. "The nurse will be back with your meds in just a sec." Then he leans in close. "But if that's not enough I got a line on some good stuff. Take you right to the moon, baby."

"No thanks," I mumble and scoot to the end of the exam table then try to slip my foot into Yaz's shoe, but it won't fit.

"Hey now!" the nurse comes back and hurries toward me. "What do you think you're doing?"

"I have to go," I tell her.

"Not without this, you don't." She holds up a patch. "This will release pain meds steadily for the next forty-eight hours." She starts to pull down the sleeve of my sweater.

I wriggle away. "Is there a location device in it?"

"No," she says, tugging at my sleeve again. "Why would there be?"

"You're sure?"

"Yes, positive. It's not connected to anything." She looks at me squarely. "This clinic is private, free, and confidential. Do you understand?"

I glance at the bluebirds on the branch again. "Okay," I tell her and lower my sleeve so she can affix the patch to my shoulder.

"You have to stay off your leg for a few days to give it time to heal." She grabs a pair of crutches leaning against the wall behind me. "And we should see you again tomorrow for another injection, okay?"

"I understand," I say, but I have no intention of returning. "Thank you for taking such good care of me."

"You're welcome," she says with a kind smile.

$$\psi \qquad \psi \qquad \psi$$

I manage to loosen Yaz's shoe enough to fit my swollen foot inside it then go find Basil in the lobby among more despairing people slumped in chairs, waiting for their chance to see the harried doctors and nurses. He looks even paler than I remember. "You okay?" I ask.

"No bullet in there. Didn't hit the bone. I'll be fine." He lifts his expertly wrapped arm.

"We should go." I hobble past on my crutches.

"I told you they'd offer a bounty." He nods toward the giant wall screen where my parents are looping through again.

"Let's just get out of here," I say, then I immediately regret it when we push through the double doors and walk outside into thick, acrid smog that smacks me in the face like a dirty wet sock. My eyes sting, my throat burns. I start to wheeze and cough. "Good god, what happened?" I wave my hand in front of my face, but the heavy orange air doesn't budge.

"The wind changed directions." Basil pulls a blue handkerchief from his pocket and rips it in two with his teeth. He hands me half, and I tie it around my face like he does. "Won't help much," he says through the cloth, "but it's better than nothing."

All around us the world seems in shambles. Along the street, entire fronts of buildings have collapsed into heaps of rubble, leaving the interiors exposed like giant dollhouses. Some resourceful folks have covered over the gaping holes with fading black plastic tarps, rust-speckled strips of corrugated metal, and half-rotted blankets flapping faintly in the breeze.

"What's that noise?" I ask about the grind of some machine that sounds as if it's on its last leg.

"Generators," says Basil. "One World Renewable Energy Labs hasn't made it out here quite yet, or ever, so we burn what we can salvage to power the place." He points at the wires crisscrossing overhead like tangles of hair. "When something nasty gets in the incinerator and the wind turns, it gets ugly."

People shamble past us, eyes down as they choke through the smog. A group of kids cough and chase one another over and under a huge curl of sun-bleached red metal lying on its side in the dirt. Between two half-collapsed buildings, a group of men and women pass around kudzars and bottles filled with liquid that's too clear to be Synthamil. They stare at us as we walk by. They're a scary-looking bunch with face tattoos and angry eyes.

"I take it strangers don't often come to town."

"Not a lot of tourism here," Basil mutters, while keeping an eye on the crowd watching us.

"Who are they?"

"Mercenaries," he says. The word sends a shiver down my spine.

We turn a corner onto a dirt road that runs alongside a trickle of muddy water carving its way around big mounds of dirt and trash and what looks to be an old bridge buckled with rot. On the opposite bank, a giant skeletal arm with gnarled fingers reaches for the sky.

"Oh my god." I stop and point. "Is that a . . . tree?"

"What's left of it," Basil says. "When I was really little and the river ran, it got leaves sometimes. But now the only time there's water is during a storm and then watch out, this trickle becomes a torrent. I've seen it carry away houses then dry up again within hours."

The wind shifts, taking the most caustic air with it and revealing, beyond the tree, a squalid huddle of makeshift houses taking up most of an open field. The shanties, which are cobbled together from odds and ends, reach all the way back to an enormous set of stairlike bleachers.

"What's that?" I ask.

Basil stares. "Huh?" he says as if confused. "Used to be a football field at an old school. We played there all the time when we were growing up."

"Looks like people moved in."

"But there's no electricity. And probably no running water." He turns away with a shrug.

After hobbling along on my crutches for another ten minutes, we come to a collection of houses along a curvy street that parallels the dried-up riverbed. Most of these places are in better shape than what we saw in town with all four walls intact, but Basil heads for the strangest home on the block. The roof has slumped in on one side of the top floor, and most of the windows are broken or boarded over. All sorts of discarded objects that have been fused into bizarre statues fill the apron of dirt surrounding the front. A stack of old screens, 2-D TVs, and computer monitors form a stairway going nowhere. The slight breeze makes brightly colored circular saws and disembodied fan blades attached to metal poles whirl as old eating utensils—forks, knives, spoons, and cups—dance and chime from the brittle branches of another dead tree. Everywhere I look, I see human faces and animals staring back at me through flashlight eyes and smiling with wire lips. The saddest thing is that most of these creations are falling apart, littering the ground with objects from the past that I can't name. The only thing that looks like it might work is a tall windmill attached to a pipe sticking out of the ground.

"What's that?" I ask.

"Windmill pump," Basil tells me. "You like it?"

"How does it get the water out of the air?" I ask.

He shakes his head. "It's not a Whisson Windmill, it's a pump. See the pipe goes down to the water table underground and pulls the water up. Then I ran a line from that into a holding tank in the house."

"Wait," I say. "Did you build it?"

He nods.

"Did you build all of this stuff?" I point to the weird sculptures.

"No," he tells me, seeming a bit embarrassed. "That's my dad's handiwork."

"Oh," I say. "What about that?" I point to a rusted-out blue car with mismatched wheels sitting near the front door of the house.

"That would be my mother's car," Basil says, even more embarrassed now.

"So, this is where you grew up?" I ask.

"Yep," he says. "Pretty gruesome, huh?"

"Oh Basil," I say, feeling slightly sick. "I've always known my family is privileged because of the work my parents do, but I had no idea people live like this. I thought the differences were in what kinds of Smaurtos we all drove and what percentage of our houses were voice command, but this . . ." I can't finish my sentence because I'm about to cry.

"Now you see why Ana is so important to people like me?"

In that very moment, I am smacked with a realization as horrifying as the thick orange air that hit me a half hour ago. This whole thing isn't about me proving Ahimsa and my mother wrong. And it isn't about One World allowing people like Ana to talk about food. There is something deeply troubling going on in the world, and for the first time, I feel genuinely scared. More scared than when we were being shot at or fleeing from Pico and Iris, because the reality in the Outer Loop is not temporary. Nobody here can just run away. And the people who are flooding the Inner Loop to protest Ana's arrest want more than her release. They want their lives.

I feel like a small-minded idiot for not understanding this before. I feel like a privy. And even that is troubling, because for the first time, I get what justice for the people out here might mean for people like my family. "Basil, I . . ." I start to say, but I can't finish. How can I tell him I'm worried about my family now that they've put a price on his head?

"Listen." He squeezes my shoulder. "This is all overwhelming, I know. And we're both exhausted. We need to rest and give ourselves a few days to get better."

"Here?" I ask, looking around at the rubble and ruin. Then I back-pedal, trying to sound less appalled than I am. "I'm sorry. I'm sure it's not as bad as it seems."

"Nope." He pulls open the front door with his good arm. "It's worse."

❖   ❖   ❖

"Mom," calls Basil as we enter. "Mom, it's Eli." We walk slowly through the dark and cluttered rooms toward the sound of a personal transformation story coming from a screen in the back of the house. The air inside hangs heavy with stale kudzar smoke, making me want to flee outside for a breath of marginally fresher air.

"She won't recognize you," I whisper to Basil.

"Not sure she would recognize me even if I didn't look like this," he tells me.

"She can't be that bad."

"Want to bet?"

When we find his mother, she's sprawled across a dingy orange sofa, one arm slumped to the floor among empty Synthamil bottles.

Ashy skin pulls tight across her sunken cheeks. Dark hair, threaded with gray, spills across her eyes. The screen blares and flashes, but his mother doesn't stir.

"Is she . . . ?" I hold my breath.

"Alive?" Basil asks, matter of factly. He finds a remote device and manually mutes the sound of the screen. "Don't know until you check." He picks his way through the detritus then crouches down beside her, staring at her as if he's come across something only vaguely familiar. "Mom." He pokes her bony shoulder. "Mom, wake up." He pokes her harder. "Hey Mom. Hey Alice!" he says and shakes her.

"What the hell!" she spews as she jerks awake, arms and legs flailing. "Who are you? What do you want?" She reaches under a cushion, searching frantically for something.

"It's Eli," Basil shouts as he skitters backward. "It's your son."

"You don't look like Eli." The woman squints, uncertain, and slowly withdraws a gleaming knife from under the cushion. I stagger backward, not breathing.

"Well," he says, arms up. "It's me."

She furrows her brow. "Who's that then?" She motions to me with the point of the knife.

"A friend," he tells her. "We need a place to stay for a couple of nights."

"How do I know you're who you say you are?" she asks him.

He sighs, as if he's been through this many times before. "Elijah Robb Mintner. Born March twenty-ninth. Age seventeen. Son of Alice Jane McHill and Robert 'Buddy' Mintner. Younger brother of Arol James Mintner born July third, died twelve years ago on September eighteenth. I have a birthmark on my butt the shape of a sock and a scar on my shin from where I fell when I was six years old."

Without warning, the woman bursts into tears. She sobs as if she's just lost everything. Basil looks over his shoulder at me, rolls his eyes, and mouths, "Sorry." I'm too stunned to speak.

"You need a smoke, Ma? Want a kudzar?" He searches for a pack on the cluttered table beside the couch.

"Yeah," she says through her crying jag. "Give me a ciggie, honey. It'll calm my nerves." She holds out a shaking hand. Basil unearths a crumpled pack, removes a kudzar, lights it, and takes a long drag before he hands it to her. She sucks hard, pulling it down to mostly ash, then exhales loudly. As if he knows the drill, he lights another one. "How about you put the knife away?" he asks, then hands her the second kudzar as she smashes the butt of the first underfoot on the rug.

"You don't know what it's like out here," she says, her voice still quivering. "I have to protect myself. Especially now that all those blasted geophags are living in the football field."

Basil frowns at her. "Who are they?"

"Who knows!" She wipes the back of her hand across her eyes and sits up a little straighter. "Why are you here?" she asks him, sniffling. "And what are you doing with this girl? Doesn't look like she's from around here."

"Just passing through. Wanted to check on you."

She smirks as if she doesn't believe him. "Well," she says, sucking on the kudzar like it's a lifeline. She shoves the knife back under the couch cushion. "Ribald's not going to like it."

"Ribald?" Basil asks, eyebrows up.

His mother chews on the inside of her cheek, a habit I've seen in Basil when he's nervous. "My friend."

"Where's Dad?"

"How am I supposed to know?" his mother explodes. "In the joint again, I reckon. Man couldn't stay out of trouble inside a bag." She looks at me. "Where you from? What's wrong with your leg?" She looks at Basil. "And your arm? You get beat up or something?"

"We met at a meeting," I tell her. "And we had a little motorcycle accident on the way here."

"A meeting, huh? So you're all political like this one? Fighting the big fight?" She punches at the air with one gangly arm. "Going to bring down the system? It's not enough that I lost one son for the cause?" She spits the last word then laughs bitterly. "You're both idiots! Gonna wind up in jail or worse. Just like your old man!" she shouts at Basil. "Can't hold down a job. Gotta rabble-rouse and make everybody around you miserable! You saw what happened to your poor brother, trying to be just like your father! And for what? For what?" She smacks the cushion. "You keep this up and you'll be just like him. A loser."

Basil stands stiff, staring over her head as she berates him. I step forward on my good leg and say, "He's not . . ." but Basil grabs hold of my wrist and shakes his head.

"Not worth it," he whispers.

I breathe deeply and swallow all the words I'd like to use to defend Basil.

She rolls her head against the back of the couch. "My head is killing me. You got anything?"

"You know I don't," he says.

She narrows her eyes at him like she's about to explode again, but then her face clears and she laughs. "Guess that proves you're my boy. You never give me nothing."

He ignores her dig and kicks at an empty bottle. "You had any nourishment lately?"

She shrugs. "Probably."

"Got any more?" he asks, cautiously.

She scowls at him. "Get your own."

My breath catches in my throat, but Basil seems unfazed by her unkindness.

"Why?" he asks with a chuckle. "So you can sell it like you used to?"

"Don't you start on that again," she says with a fresh kudzar dangling from the side of her mouth. "If your father had . . ."

"Let's not do this," he tells her, holding up his good hand. "We'll be here a couple days, then we'll be out of your way." He glances at me and jerks his head toward the door. I follow him out of the room.

"I'll have to check with Ribald," she calls after us. "He's the one who pays the bills around here."

Basil stops and stiffens, then looks over his shoulder at her. "Is it money you want?"

His mother picks flakes of dried kudzu from her tongue. "Ever since your father got arrested again, it's been tough to make ends meet."

"Fine," he says and marches back. He hands her several bills from his pocket. "That should cover it. Make sure no one knows we're here."

She sucks on the kudzar, squinting one eye against a curlicue of smoke. "You in trouble?"

He pulls out one more bill and dangles it in front of her then says, emphatically, "No."

She snatches it from him. "Nice to have you home, son."

⚘ ⚘ ⚘

Basil takes me through a warren of dreary disorganized rooms to the other end of the house. Through the back door, I see more disintegrating sculptures and junk littering the dirt. Beyond that is the dry riverbed. Around us, three-legged chairs, mattress springs, crooked lamps, and all kinds of artifacts from another time are piled high. Tangles of clothing cascade from the open drawers of tall metal cabinets. There are at least three washing machines and a dozen ancient gutted computers stacked up in a corner.

"What do they do with all of this stuff?" I ask.

"Mostly nothing." He runs his finger through the dust on an old piano that reminds me of my second-grade network photo when I was missing most of my teeth. "My dad fancies himself an artist, but in reality, he's just a hoarder, and the only thing he makes is trouble."

"I can picture you when you were little," I say with a half laugh at the thought of a cute curly-haired kid digging through all this junk. "I bet you created all the things you couldn't buy."

"The noble savage," he sneers.

"You should be an engineer!" I tell him.

He scowls at me. "God, you really are clueless, aren't you?"

I stumble backward as if his words shoved me. "What? I just meant you'd be good at it. You're really brilliant. The smell scanner, the transponder, the bicycle cart, that windmill pump . . ."

"Don't you get it yet? I'm not like you," he says with a cold glare. "But I suppose from your perch up there on the ladder to success, you can't see down this far."

I blink away my surprise. "What's that supposed to mean?"

He stomps his foot. "ICMs, the right Virtu-Schools, internships, and family connections are all part of a big machine churning out the status quo and protecting the exalted few who'll never let someone like me elbow my way in. I can't be an engineer no matter how brilliant I am because there is no ladder for me to climb, but you got halfway to the top just by being born!"

I try to get a word in so he'll know that for the first time in my life I understand how unfair the world is, but Basil bulldozes right over me.

"When One World gobbled up the entire nutrition market then one by one snatched every other enterprise and bought off all the politicians, they killed any chance that someone like me could ever make it out of this mess. The best I can hope for is a menial job fixing what's broken in a system that couldn't care less whether I live or die. A loser! Just like my dad."

"You're not a loser," I argue, but I'm angry at him for screaming at me, so I add, "And don't get mad at me about the system. I didn't make it, but at least..."

"You profit from it!" he snaps. "What was I thinking, getting involved with a privy!"

"Why are you screaming at me?" I shout at him. "I don't deserve this."

"Then go back home!" he shouts.

His words sting. "You don't mean that."

"Yes, I do," he says calmly and clearly.

I search his face, trying to find that boy who filled me with so much emotion that I grabbed his hand and ran away, but he looks at me blankly with unfamiliar icy blue eyes as if he doesn't know me.

"Basil..." I take a step toward him, but he turns, throws open a door, and stomps up a sagging staircase to the second floor. "Fine!" I yell after him, wondering if I every really knew him before this moment. "Maybe I will go back!"

"Fine!" he yells down at me. "Then go."

I stand among the wreckage of this house, crutches chafing the underside of my arms, wishing I could storm out rather than limp away. I can't believe I let him drag me all the way out here to treat me like this!

I hop on one leg to a decrepit love seat half hidden among the shadows and plop down exhausted. Stuffing spills out of the cushions like guts from an open wound. I'm tired. I'm dirty. And my leg hurts. At the moment I want nothing more than a bath, a drink of water, and some clean clothes. Then maybe I could think straight.

From another part of the house, I hear Basil's mom shuffling around, muttering to herself. My mom might be self-absorbed and difficult to deal with, but at least she feeds me. And no matter how angry I've been with her, I know that she loves me. My parents would pay my restitution if I had to go to jail, not charge me to stay a night or two in my own home. And they would never speak to me the way she spoke to Basil. I had no idea a parent could be so awful to her child. If I weren't so pissed off at Basil right now, I might feel sorry for him, but he had no reason to be mean to me, especially when I've thrown everything away to be with him.

Obviously I can't stay here. I glare at the stairway, wondering how he could flip on me the minute that we're safe. Grandma told me Basil isn't the boy I thought he was. I should have listened while I had the chance.

I see another door beside the stairs. It's half open, revealing a sink, a tub, and an old-fashioned big-bowled urinal. It occurs to me that I could clean myself up, "borrow" some clothes from the piles lying around, and be on my way. The thought of accepting this whole ordeal as a mistake makes my chest hurt, but the thought of staying here with Basil so suddenly hostile makes me feel worse. So I haul myself up and rake through the shirts and skirts and pants in the metal drawers. Most of the clothing is threadbare or totally the wrong size, but with enough digging, I find some things that might work. Then I hobble to the bathing room, shut the door, and start to clean up.

While I'm washing and changing, I hear the front door open then feel the house shake when it slams shut. Overhead, I hear Basil run across the floor and barrel down the creaking stairs. The front door slams again. I hear shouting as Basil and his mother argue, then a car starts and roars away. The house becomes very still.

I realize then that Basil isn't going to come back inside and apologize to me like I've been hoping. He's left with his mother and I'm alone. Despite my bravado about walking away, suddenly my predicament feels much more dire. I have no money, no friends, nobody to turn to for help out here. Worst of all, Basil's mother, that awful hateful woman, is probably right. The puny little protest by the Dynasaurs and Analogs and their sympathizers won't put a dent in the gigantic machine running society. Basil's right, too. I'm nothing but a privy who finally figured out the world sucks and thought she could change it. Tears creep into my eyes. This time, I'm too worn-out to stop them.

I pull a sky blue Cottynelle shirt over my head then hike up black Velvelore pants over my inflatable brace and cinch them with a belt so they won't fall down. I slip on Yaz's shoes and grab my pouch from the pile where I've discarded Yaz's orange dress, the tattered silver leggings, and filthy green sweater. Inside the pouch I can feel my cloaked Gizmo. My family must be worried sick. If they know even a fraction of what goes on in the Outer Loop, they're probably freaking out. I could head back to the clinic and call home. That way Basil and his mother wouldn't be involved. No matter how disappointed I am, I don't want him to go to prison because of me. It will probably take less than an hour for my parents to find me, which seems totally unfair compared to how far I've had to go to get here. Not just in miles since I left my house, but in how much I've learned about the tightly circumscribed life One World has created for privies like me.

I grab my crutches and head for the back door. Outside, in the bitter air, I round the corner of the house but stop and press myself against the wall when I see Basil sitting in the dead tree by the windmill pump. My heart pounds. Part of me wants to go to him and ask again if he really meant what he said, but then I think about his eyes, how he looked at me with such hatred. He made it very clear that getting involved with me was a mistake. What hurts the most is that in my heart I don't feel the same.

I know I have to leave, but I don't want him to see me on the road, so I turn and head toward the riverbed that leads to the town. *All this for nothing*, I think as I hobble past crumbling sculptures. *What a waste.*

✤   ✤   ✤

Even though the clinic isn't that far away, it takes me nearly half an hour to get back on my stupid crutches. I'm so tired and pissed off that I'm almost happy to walk through the double doors and claim a small corner of the floor in the overcrowded waiting room, where hordes of people stare blankly at the screen playing thirty-second clips from the most popular PRCs. I turn to face the wall and uncloak my Gizmo so nobody will see it. From the way Garvy and Basil's mom talked, you'd think everyone around here is waiting to rob me. I hesitate before I turn it on. I assume my dad will know the minute my locator connects to the network, so it's no use trying to call Yaz or Grandma Apple first. Better that I call home and ask my parents to come get me so they don't send security agents screaming my way. I rack my brain for any other alternative, but without money or someone to help me, I have no choice except to give in.

It takes several seconds for Astrid to wake up and orient herself. I turn her volume down as low as it will go, but the big screen is so loud that I doubt anyone would hear her anyway. "Ignore, ignore, ignore," I command as she flashes through dozens of messages from the past day and a half, most of them unimportant—assignments from school, topix for my next ICM, a barrage of vids from my family after Basil and I disappeared, a text from Yaz with the subject line "Don't Believe It!" then another text pops up that catches me by surprise.

It's from AnonyGal directly to my Gizmo. I check the time and see it arrived late last night. I stare at the screen, puzzling through how this could be without really taking in the content of the message. How does she know who I am? I've always used private networks and have never revealed my true identity on the Dynasaur chats, but she has directly messaged Thalia Apple. My heart races. If she knows who I am, then who else knows HectorProtector is me? I concentrate on what she's sent, and then I'm really flabbergasted.

Use this link to crack your Gizmo OS.

My shaking finger hovers over the link she's sent, half fearing I'll open malware, but I have little left to lose, so I take the chance and click. It only takes a few seconds for the program to install and open a back door to all my Gizmo settings. I gasp. She did it. AnonyGal, whoever she is, cracked the code. Quickly, I shut off my locator and press the Gizmo to my chest. Now I have options other than calling my parents.

Just as I'm getting ready to ping Yaz to ask if she could find a transport to come get me, I hear "Thalia Apple" and bolt upright, sucking in a deep breath. I turn slowly to see who's recognized me, but no one is looking my way. Then I see my photo, pre-Fiyo, on the big screen. Relieved, I sigh. Just another newsfeed about the missing privy girl, I suppose. Out of curiosity, I pay attention, wondering if they're saying anything new.

My photo is replaced by a reporter, standing in a sea of people outside the prison. "We go now to footage of Ahimsa DuBoise at a press conference earlier this afternoon," the reporter says.

Ahimsa stands proudly behind a podium in front of One World headquarters. My parents are nowhere to be seen. "This morning," Ahimsa says, "One World security was able to confirm the identity of the hacker HectorProtector, who has incited civil unrest over the detainment of resistance leader Ana Gignot."

"Oh no," I whisper, my voice gone. The room spins. My head feels as if it's detaching from my body.

"Thalia Apple, the daughter of our most respected One World executives, who've worked tirelessly for the improvement of our society through foodless nutrition and network communication, is a leader in the underground hacking group calling for protests over the legal detainment of Ms. Gignon," she says.

A leader? Hardly. I bend over and put my head between my knees, trying to stop myself from hyperventilating.

The reporter comes back. "Despite earlier assumptions that Ms.

Apple had been kidnapped, it appears she willingly joined forces with the Analog resistance leader seen here." I snap upright to see the same blurry photo of Basil they've been using since we went missing. "The two have brought together followers of Ana Gignot known as the Analogs with an underground anticorporate hacking group known as the Dynasaurs and have been terrorizing the area since she disappeared from a rehabilitation center in the Inner Loop two nights ago. We have obtained exclusive footage and spoken to victims of their crime spree."

Crime spree?

They cut to security footage of Basil and me pushing through the chaos of the EA then to an enhanced shot of Basil releasing the blackberry branch into the bald guard's chest. Then the guard, standing in front of the EA. The camera zooms in on his banged-up face as the reporter explains, "Mr. Lauder received multiple lacerations and a broken rib while pursuing the assailants."

"They were violent," he says. "These aren't just a couple of innocent kids out for a joyride, but a couple anticorporate terrorists set on crumbling our social stability."

Terrorists? The word makes my mouth go dry.

Next, the reporter talks over footage of the girl I've never seen walking slowly around a smashed-up red car, shaking her head and crying. "The assailants impersonated Ali Sauconiss in order to steal her Smaurto and escape from the West Loop EntertainArena after assaulting Mr. Lauder."

That's not even true, I think. *We didn't steal it, just took a ride in it after it had already been wrecked.*

The next time I look up, the reporter is saying, "Ms. Apple and her cohort kidnapped this student." Yaz's face fills the screen. She looks tired and scared. The reporter goes on to say, "They eluded captors by heading to an Outer Loop Spalon."

"She was my best friend," Yaz explains. "But she's a hacker. She does it for fun. She can break into anything." Her language is clipped and choppy. She moves erratically, twitching as if she can't sit still in her chair. "She cracked my Gizmo's operating system. And communicates secretly with other resisters. They used some kind of device to get through the tolls so they couldn't be traced. It was terrifying. I never knew she was capable of this kind of thing. Who knows what they'll do next."

I sit, dumbfounded. What have they done to Yaz to make her turn on me like that?

Then the scene switches to footage of security agents milling outside Fiyo's house. "It is believed the wayward youths forced this unlicensed Spalon worker to alter their appearance in order to evade authorities," the reporter says.

Fiyo comes on, looking shaken, inside her treatment room. "They wanted me to make them look completely different so no one would recognize them." Someone asks her a question from off camera that I can't hear. She shakes her head and scoffs, "No, they didn't pay me."

Next, a scraggly, greasy couple fills the screen. "They drove it right out of here!" the woman says angrily, pointing to shed doors hanging off their hinges. "Stole our motorbike in the middle of the night." The camera zooms in, and I see that the shed is oddly empty, not a trace of drug paraphernalia to be seen. "Now how are we going to get to work?" the man asks, shaking his head sadly.

The couple is replaced by Pico and Iris who stand in front of a fuel pump. "He came in looking for a black-market toll pass," Iris explains. "But I don't trade in those."

Pico winces through a puffy black eye. "So they stole fuel, hijacked a transport, and drove off."

They cut to three seconds of blurry footage of us running out the front door while Pico writhes on the floor. I scrunch down to hide my pink hair, but at least I'm no longer wearing the orange dress so visible in the video. I brace myself, wondering if Betta ratted on us too, but they make no mention of her.

Ahimsa comes back on-screen. "What's particularly disturbing is that unlike the people she has hurt, Thalia Apple is a highly educated, privileged person with every advantage," she says. "Rather than help create a better world, she defaces One World sites and encourages hardworking individuals to unlawfully protest the detainment of Ana Gignot and her followers, who were clearly in violation of the Universal Nutrition Protection Act. This type of reckless behavior puts all of us at risk as it jeopardizes our food supply."

This last bit confuses me. I try to puzzle through what she's implying, but then the screen returns to the reporter who stands next to a guy about my age, holding a FREE ANA! sign in the midst of the prison protesters. "Does knowing that the leader of this movement is actually the daughter of One World execs change your opinion of what's going on here?" she asks him.

"Yes, of course!" he says into the mic. "If I had known she's just some privy rebelling against Mommy and Daddy, I wouldn't have come. She can afford to get arrested, but I can't and she's not even out here!" He rips his sign in half and tosses it to the ground.

A still frame of us running from the biofuel building fills the screen. "Anyone with information leading to the arrest of these two armed and dangerous individuals should contact proper authorities immediately," the reporters says.

When did we become armed?

Finally, Ahimsa comes back on-screen. "Naturally," she says, "anyone who aids in their capture will be compensated for cooperation."

Her words send a sickening chill down my spine. Now everyone will be looking for us, but only one person knows where we are. Slowly, I stand up and make my way shakily through the waiting room with my head down. Everyone discusses the sensational story about the privy causing trouble. I try to stay calm and focus by thinking logically and systematically about what needs to be done so I don't panic.

First, I have to get out of here because by now someone in the Inner Loop has zeroed in on the locator signal I sent out into the world while my Gizmo was linked to the network signal. It's no longer a matter of asking my parents to come get me. I've been accused of serious crimes. Soon, security agents and vigilantes will descend on this place, and no matter what anyone might think, once I'm arrested I doubt my parents will be able to buy my freedom—even if they wanted to. Next, I have to warn Basil. Despite how crappy he was to me, I owe him a chance to get out of here before his mother turns him in. After that, I have no idea what I'll do since all the people that I thought were on my side, including Yaz and Fiyo, have turned their backs on me.

Once outside, I toss the crutches because they'll only slow me down. I don't know if it's the brace or the adrenaline coursing through me or if the medication from the patch has kicked in, but I feel no pain as I limp down the road. Or maybe I can't feel anything because the agony of being abandoned by so many people I love is too great.

ψ   ψ   ψ

I keep my head down on the way through town. Fearing Basil's mom is nearby, I cross the road when I see the rusted-out blue car with mismatched wheels parked in front of the broken-down buildings. It's not until I turn the corner and reach the anemic river and skeletal tree that I start to feel less conspicuous, but I still hurry because whoever's living in the football field could be just as dangerous or more so than the people back in town. From the distance, I hear sirens, but I see no flashing lights on the dirt road. I imagine security agents are swarming the clinic by now, pulling patients off of gurneys, overturning beds, and smashing equipment while demanding that the startled doctors and nurses find me. On the road ahead, I see a figure running.

Probably a thrill seeker wanting to know what the sirens are all about. I step aside to let him pass, but then he stops, turns around, and runs toward me.

Startled, I break left, heading away from the river, but my leg won't move that fast. I look over my shoulder to see a man with a hat pulled low on his head gaining on me. I fear it might be Ribald sent by Basil's mother to find me. I try to go fast but I trip and fall. Sprawled on the shoulder of the road, I scramble backward to find the man nearly on top of me. I start to scream and kick, but then Basil offers me his hand. He's changed out of the jacket and pants Fiyo gave him into dirt-colored coveralls and a dark gray mechanic's cap.

"Thank god I found you," he yells and pulls me into his arms. He holds me so tight that I can barely breathe. "I thought I lost you. I thought you were gone," he says into my hair then kisses the top of my head over and over.

"Basil," I struggle to get free from his grip. "Let go. Let go of me."

"I'm so sorry," he says, his voice husky. "I didn't mean what I said."

I smack his shoulders and push him away, shouting, "You have to get out of here! They know who we are."

He hugs me tighter. "I know, I saw the whole thing on my mom's screen."

I stop fighting and let myself go limp against his body. I hate how good it feels to be in his embrace and that's when the tears finally come. "Everyone abandoned me!" I wail.

With his good arm, he grips my shoulder and holds me away so he can look into my face. "It was a setup. They either paid those people or coerced them to say those things or took their words out of context. Yaz. Fiyo. That idiot with the sign. It's not true, Apple. None of it is true."

"How do you know?"

"Because they do it all the time. They act like the media is independent, but it's not. They manipulate people. Twist their words and doctor images when it suits them." He lifts my chin. "And because Yaz would never do that to you. She just wouldn't and you know it."

I suck in a ragged breath and will myself to stop crying. "Are you sure?"

"Positive," he says.

"But what about you? What about all those things you said . . . ?"

"I was wrong," he says and hugs me tighter. Over his shoulder, I see a cloud of dust moving down the road from town. "I came to find you because when I stopped being an idiot and went back into the house to apologize, you were gone."

"I saw you in the tree." The dust cloud gets closer, and I hear an engine coughing.

"I thought I had made you so mad that you took off. But when I saw the newsfeed, I knew I had to find you and make sure that you were safe."

I pull him closer. "Me, too."

The dust cloud zooms past us on the road. We turn our faces away and cover our eyes, but then we hear the car skid to a stop. We look up and see Basil's mom jabbing her finger at us through the back window. The driver throws the car in reverse. Rocks and dirt spit out from under the spinning wheels.

"We have to get out of here!" Basil yells. I head away from the river, but he grabs my hand and pulls me back across the road behind the car.

"What are you doing?" I do my best to keep up with him as he half drags me down into the river ditch and up the other side of the embankment toward the football field. "We can't go in there!"

"There's no other choice!" he shouts.

The blue car spins around and careens off the road, bumping and bouncing over the hardscrabble ground straight for us. It hits the ditch with a loud thud and scrape. Just as we make it to the jumble of shanties, two men explode from the stalled car and charge up the riverbank. I look over my shoulder one more time to see Basil's mom standing next to the car with her arms crossed, waiting for the men to drag us back.

⚘   ⚘   ⚘

Quickly and quietly, we lope through the labyrinth of paths between rows and rows of rickety shacks, catching glimpses of the inhabitants' most intimate lives through flimsy walls and makeshift windows. Someone washing from a bucket, another sleeping, two women fighting, a couple caught in an embrace. The people are thin and haggard. A few snarl or babble nonsense when we elbow past them in the passages but most seem to take no notice of us. At every corner, we turn, trying to put as much disorienting distance between us and the two men who got out of the car, until we come to an opening: a kind of courtyard in the center of the jumbled houses, where some people gather in small groups. Others sit alone on the outskirts, scratching at the dirt. I see a man gather a handful of earth and shove it in his mouth.

"Basil," I pant. "I can't go much farther." I can barely put weight on my leg.

He slides my arm over his shoulder to bolster me.

"Be careful of your arm," I say.

"It's okay," he says. "If we get to the other side, I know a place we can go."

We slow down and stick close to the edge of the courtyard, ready to dart back into the maze if needed. I catch snippets of conversation as we pass the huddles of people.

"Said she died of malnutrition."

". . . no, some kind of allergic reaction."

"He takes their eggs."

"You know they killed her."

"...said it's a farm."

"What about the others?"

"They were stupid for ever trying."

Then I see a familiar woman with magenta-tipped hair. I try to place her. "Zara?" I call uncertainly. She swivels around and frowns at me. "Uh, um, hi," I stammer awkwardly. Basil tries to get me to move along, but I shake my head at him. "We met at rehab," I tell her, knowing she won't recognize me, but hoping she might be able to help us anyway.

"Which time?" she says with a snort.

"Just recently at Dr. Demeter's."

"Sorry," she says. "I don't remember."

"That's okay," I tell her. "What are you doing here?"

She shrugs. "Long story short is I slipped away when all hell broke loose one night. Met up with this geophag." She elbows a guy beside her, who chuckles nervously. "He told me about this place where nobody would harass us. Decided it was better to take my chances out here instead of sticking with that creep Dr. Demeter. What about you? How'd you get out?"

While I'm trying to come up with a plausible answer, a man lurches into the courtyard. He squints at us then points and yells, "There!" and it hits me. He's Garvy from the clinic. Another man rushes out from a different path. He's big and ugly with a tattoo wrapped halfway around his face. "Ribald!" Garvy yells. "That's them!"

Everyone turns to look. Basil wastes no time. He scoops me up and dashes away. We can't outrun them this time, but Basil is smart. He rounds a corner and ducks inside an open door to a shack. Luckily, no one's home. We press ourselves against the wall, holding our breath until we hear Ribald and Garvy run past. Basil waits until their footsteps fade, then he peeks out and we head back the other way. Quickly, we cross the courtyard, back past Zara and the others who seem unfazed by the chase. Basil sticks his head inside every open door as we get ourselves lost in the maze.

"What do you want?" people yell. "Get out!"

"Sorry!" he calls.

Finally we come to an empty dwelling. It's bigger than the others, a giant blue box made of ridged metal with MAERSK painted in faded white letters on the side. The crude windows cut in the walls are covered with flimsy plastic sheeting.

"You said there was another place we could go," I say.

"We'll never make it."

"But what happens when the owner comes back?" I protest, pulling away from the door.

"We'll deal with that then, but for now we need to hide." We step inside the box. There's not much there except a nest of blankets in the corner and some improvised chairs and storage containers made from junk.

I follow him to the back and slump down against the wall. My leg is throbbing and my heart is pounding.

"How's the ankle?" he asks.

"I'm okay," I lie, and he must know it because with his good arm, he drags over a small metal box with a funny little door and a number pad with "Start," "Reheat," and "Popcorn" buttons along the side. Through the window, we see it's filled with shoes. "Here," he says and lifts my foot gently. "Prop up." Then he settles himself beside me.

We're both quiet for several minutes, listening for footsteps and shouts, but none come and my heart slows down again. Finally, Basil breaks the silence by saying, "Apple, I'm sorry I was such a raging jerkface at my mom's."

"Look, you don't have to stay with me after we get out of here," I say. "I get it. You don't think a privy like me could actually ..."

"No, you don't get it at all," he says. "I didn't mean anything I said.

It's just that, when I'm around my mom, she makes me feel like such a loser and..."

"You're not a loser!"

"But being back at my house with her brings out the worst in me," Basil says. "I think I was pushing you away before you had a chance to bail on me, like everyone else in my life. No one's ever stuck by me like you have the past few days. Except my brother before he died."

"Oh, Basil. I'm so sorry." I start to lean against his shoulder, but I sit upright quickly, afraid I'll hurt him.

"It's okay," he says. "Nothing a little Just-Like-Skin couldn't fix. What about you?" He points to my ankle.

"Hurts a little," I tell him. "But it'll be alright soon."

We hear people walking by. Their words float through the door.

"I can't believe it."

"I don't believe it. They're lying."

"...just saying that so people will go home."

"Who are they talking about?" I say, but Basil is lost in his own thoughts.

"Back at the house," he says. "When you saw me in the tree, I was trying to picture you. How you were the first time we met. Do you remember? When you came through the door at Flav-O-Rite?"

"Of course I remember."

"The light hit you and it just bowled me over. Literally!" Basil says. "Remember? I fell off my stool. You must have thought I was pretty awesome."

I laugh.

"You were so..." He stops and breathes deeply. "Beautiful," he says on an exhale.

A blush wraps around my body as if someone has tossed a coat over my shoulders. A clear picture of that night forms in my mind. Basil scrambling to his feet. Fists at his sides, jaw clenched, brown hair flopping over his dark eyes, and then that moment of hesitation as he sized me up.

"I never told you this," Basil says. "But after you left that night, I wandered around the West Loop for over an hour, just hoping I might run into you again. I even went into some PlugIn looking for you." He laughs a little. "Which was stupid. Even if you had been there, what was I going to do? Pretend I just happened to stumble in without a Gizmo?"

I think back to that night, running like a lunatic through the abandoned streets. I felt like a switch had been flipped inside of me and I couldn't stand still until I found him again.

He looks down at his hands clenched together in his lap.

"I'm sorry," he says quietly. "If I hadn't met you then, I would have never put you through all this."

"You didn't put me through anything."

"Yes, I did!"

"No, I willingly came along. That's different."

"But you didn't really know what you were getting into."

I nod. "That's true, but now . . ."

He won't let me finish. "It's all my fault and . . ."

I press my hand over his mouth to shut him up. He holds my wrist and kisses my palm. In the quiet of this place where we're finally alone, I wish we could stay forever. No Inner Loop and Outer Loop. No privies and workers. No One World and corporate resisters. Just me and Basil—alone. Maybe that's why people like Zara and the others wind up in a place like this. Maybe it's the only place nobody will bother them anymore.

He leans in. We bow our heads together, foreheads touching, arms around one another's shoulders. "I'll get us out of this," he says.

"No," I tell him. "We'll get out of it together." Then I kiss him. "I love how you taste," I whisper.

"Better than Synthamil?" he asks with a laugh.

"Way better," I tell him, and we kiss again.

Outside, more and more people file past, talking urgently.

"Do you think it's true?"

"... they could be lying."

"But if they aren't?"

"... we should get there before they close it."

Basil and I look at each other. "Something's up," he says.

"Should we find out?"

"You stay here, I'll go." He gets up.

"No," I try to stand. "We should stay together."

"I won't go far," he tells me. "And you need to rest that leg as long as possible because once we leave ..."

"But what if someone comes in?"

"I'll stay close. Just yell and I'll be back in a flash."

I nod and sit down again as he heads for the door.

⚘   ⚘   ⚘

As soon as Basil's gone, I pull out my Gizmo and search for a signal. Now that my locator is off, I can find out what new lies Ahimsa is spreading about us. Maybe even check in to see what the Dynasaurs are saying. As I'm searching for a connection to the Dynasaur network, another text from Yaz pops up. My stomach immediately rolls over when I think back to what she said about me, but then I realize it's very strange for Yaz to text me. She hates texting. The subject line says "Don't Believe It!" same as the earlier text I skipped over. This time I open it.

> Not sure how to reach U so trying text. I hope U know I'm
> not against U. OW twisted my words. Interrogated us for
> hours. Threatened us then doctored the footage. I M w/ U!

I hug the Gizmo to my chest. Basil was right. Yaz would never forsake me. I hate to think what security has done to her. The threats they might have made against her and her family. The opportunities they could have stripped from her. And for what—being my friend?

As I sit and stare at my screen, trying to find the words to text back to Yaz about how sorry I am that she had to get involved, a headline pops up and punches me hard in the gut: *Ana Gignot, leader of the Analog movement, is dead.*

I scramble to my feet, calling, "Basil! Basil!" but he's back through the door before the words are out of my mouth.

"Ana!" he says. He looks stricken and can't say the rest.

"Oh, Basil!" I hold open my arms. "Is it true? Is she really dead?" His face twists with agony. I hold him tight. "What happened? How?" I ask, but he can't talk. I get him back to the floor and cradle his head in my lap while I look for a newsfeed. I find one from the prison warden at a press conference half an hour ago.

"At five forty-seven p.m. today, Ana Louisa Gignot, leader of the corporate-resistance group the Analogs, died in custody at detention center number forty-eight in the South Loop," the warden says. "As a result of not properly imbibing synthetic nutritional beverages over the past several weeks, Ms. Gignot was weak, dehydrated, and malnourished when she entered our facility a few days ago."

"That's not true!" Basil nearly shouts.

"After refusing synthetic nutritional beverages in our care, doctors prescribed an intravenous solution to correct her health issues," the warden says. "Unfortunately, Ms. Gignot suffered an allergic reaction to this solution and entered cardiac arrest at five thirty-four p.m. Doctors were unable to revive her."

"Liars! They killed her," Basil growls at my Gizmo. Then he blinks at it and looks up at me. "Where did you get that thing?"

"I . . . I . . ." The truth is too complicated to explain so I say, "I *borrowed* it."

"Get rid of it," he tells me. "It'll only bring us trouble."

"No wait, let's find out more." I surf for news and come across an archive of another press conference with Ahimsa from earlier.

"Unfortunately, the situation has gotten rather out of hand," she says coldly from behind her massive desk. "If people don't come to their senses soon, we may be forced to halt the distribution of Synthamil to certain areas. I can't send my workers into civil unrest." She looks straight at the camera. I feel her eyes on me. "As I said before, until the unlawful protest against One World is stopped, our ability to uphold the Universal Nutrition Protection Act could be jeopardized."

"What does she mean?" I ask.

"She'll make sure the government cuts off the supply of Synthamil."

I shake my head. "She can't do that. It's the law that everyone receives it."

Basil sits up, weary and brokenhearted. "No, Apple. It's the law that legally born citizens have the right to free nutrition from their government, but nowhere does it say One World has to provide it. They could break their contract with the government anytime they wanted, and what could anybody do about it? They've put every other provider out of business over the years and they've got the no-food laws in place. Privies will have the money to pay for private One World Synthamil distribution while the government pretends to scramble to find another provider for everybody else, but there is none and we all know it. Ana always feared this would happen if we moved too fast. That's why she wanted us to find a place where we could feed ourselves someday."

As I'm trying to process all of this, Basil says, "And you want to know the worst part?"

"What could be worse?"

"That everyone would still receive their inocs so they wouldn't even know that they're hungry."

I feel the blood drain from my face. "They'd just starve?"

He nods. "That's what happens to seconds whose families can't afford to feed them."

"No." I shake my head, horrified by the thought.

"Yes."

"But you . . ."

"I'm different," says Basil. "Like you. I feel it when I'm hungry. I always thought there was something wrong with me. I tried to hide it. Until I met Ana. She was the first person who pointed out to me that feeling hunger is a good thing. It's what kept me alive."

"Oh, Basil," I say, swooning and nauseous.

Outside, an endless stream of people pass, their voices mixed into a cacophony of fear.

"Where do you think they're all going?" I ask.

"Probably the distribution point before Ahimsa tells the government to shut it down." He pulls himself up. "And we should, too. We'll need to stock up before there's no more available."

"What about Garvy and Ribald?"

He shakes his head. "Just have to take our chances." He holds his hand out to me. "What happened to your crutches?"

"They were slowing me down," I tell him. "I wish I had them now."

"Wait." He rummages around the room until he finds some weird stick kind of thing with a big brush on the end.

"What's that?"

"A broom."

I look at him blankly.

"It's a manual sweeper." He shows me how it moves dirt around the floor. Then he unzips his coveralls part way and pulls out a knife.

I gasp. "Where'd you get that?"

"*Borrowed* it from my mom," he says with a smirk as he cuts off the bristles of the broom. He lowers the hinged metal door of a large boxy thing with dials and buttons. Inside on sturdy wire racks, he finds neatly folded clothing. He pulls out a pair of pants and cuts off one leg which he wraps around the brushless head of the broom. I stand on one foot so he can measure the stick against the side of my body. He hacks at the tapered end then flips it over and slides the padded part under my arm. It fits perfectly. I lean on the pad and take a step. "Brilliant!" I tell him. "Someday, in a better world, you will design amazing things."

"Thank you," he says and slides the knife inside his coveralls. "Ready?"

I nod.

"Get rid of that Gizmo," he tells me.

"Okay," I say and set it on the floor, but when he turns his back, I snatch it up, cloak it, and slide it back inside my pouch.

⚘ ⚘ ⚘

We stay in the center of the flow of people heading out the far side of the camp, figuring Garvy and Ribald will be less likely to spot us that way. With the pain medication kicking in and Basil's crutch at my side, I'm moving well now. Plus, the distribution center is close by, just inside the old school beyond the football field, but by the time we get there, we're too late. The worker in a burgundy sweater vest with the One World logo across the chest is already pulling down the gates and locking up the doors.

"One World orders," he shouts at the restless crowd. "You know I'd give it to you if I could."

People jeer at him and beg, but they keep their distance and the guy doesn't budge.

"I could lose my job," he says. "And if we don't do what they say, they might not let me reopen. Then what? I have a family, too, you know!"

I look at the drawn and fearful faces around me. I see Zara in the crowd. Women and men my parents' age. Little kids straggling on the edges. I've never had to go without, but I've known the same hunger that they feel. If these are the geophags, they seem more downtrodden than violent, and the truth is, I am one of them. My mother thinks there's a flaw in me, but that blip in my genetic material has allowed me to see the world differently now. I realize that what we need is not charity from some corporation lording their benevolence over us but a voice and a say in our most basic human rights. That's what Ana was trying to do before they shut her up. Ahimsa accused me of many things, but she's totally wrong on one account. I can use my privilege to change things.

As loud as I can, I shout, "It's our constitutional right to receive free Synthamil!" People around me crane their necks to see who's yelling. "We demand our Synthamil! They are not yours to distribute!"

"Yeah!" someone else shouts.

"She's right!"

"Hand them over!"

I start to chant, "Synthamil! Synthamil! Synthamil!"

Slowly, the crowd joins in.

"Settle down!" the worker yells, but he's barely heard over the growing dissonance of our voices. "You're only going to make it worse," he shouts. "I'll have to call security if you don't stop harassing me."

Some people shrink back, but I know we can't stop. I see an old Dumpster against the wall of the building. "Help me up," I say to Basil.

"No, it's too risky."

"We have nothing if we don't have this," I tell him. "It's the one guarantee our society makes, and I won't stand by and watch it held hostage. Now help me up!"

"I'll help you," a guy behind me says.

"Me, too," says the woman beside him.

"Apple!" Basil hisses and tries to grab my arm. "Don't! They'll see you!"

But it's too late. I don't care anymore. Ahimsa can arrest me. She can throw me in jail until I rot, but now I'm pissed. After what I saw on the screen back at the hospital, I realize that I can't go back to my old life. And not just because they want to arrest me. Too much has happened. I see the world differently. One World may have been the hand that fed me, but they're the same entity that will let other children starve.

I hold out my arms so the man and woman can lift me to the top of the Dumpster. Then I take out my Gizmo, uncloak it, and turn on the amplifier mode.

"Nourishment is a human right, not a corporate commodity," I tell the people. "The Universal Nutrition Protection Act is a sham meant to protect One World and should be struck down as inhumane. No corporation has the right to starve human beings. This is our Synthamil as provided by our government! And if they won't give it to us, we must take what's ours!"

A rallying cry erupts as the crowd surges forward.

"Get down!" Basil shouts at me. "We have to get out of here!"

But I won't listen. I open a direct video feed to the Dynasaur network and begin filming the geophags overtaking the distribution site. I narrate what's happening as they push aside the lone worker, take his keys, and unlock the gates. "Citizens of this Outer Loop Synthamil distribution center will not be denied the human right to nutrition!" I say as the group of people closest to the store pass crates of bottles brigade style, to the rest of the crowd. Then I turn the camera onto me. All the times I badgered Yaz about speaking out on her PRC, I should have taken my own advice. "This is Thalia Apple," I say into the camera.

"Apple, no!" Basil yells and rushes toward the Dumpster, but the man and woman who lifted me up hold him back.

"Aka HectorProtector. Do not let Ana die in vain. Do not fear prison. As long as One World controls the only source of nutrition we are all in prison! Take what's rightfully yours!"

I hear the sirens before I see the security cars arrive. The crowd scatters as guards flood the scene, swinging blunt clubs and bashing their way toward the store to stop the looting.

The man and woman holding Basil let go and run. He sprints toward the Dumpster and grabs my good ankle. But I still won't budge. I try to train my camera on the violence in front of me, but my hands shake and my voice quivers with hate as I describe the scene.

Then, above the din of the chaos a man screams, "That's her! That's Thalia Apple!"

People spin around, evading the security agents while trying to get a look at the fugitive. Ribald runs through the middle of the scrum toward the Dumpster, pointing and shouting at me.

"Basil!" I scream as Ribald lunges. Basil spins around. I see the knife flash. Ribald jumps back. Basil brandishes it at him while I scramble down from my perch.

"Come on," Ribald yells, egging Basil on. "Try to stick me, boy. You don't have the guts."

Garvy runs up behind Ribald but immediately backs off when he sees the knife in Basil's hands. I press myself close to Basil's back. He holds on to me with one hand while jabbing at Ribald, sending him dancing backward through the pandemonium.

"You good-for-nothing piece of crap," Ribald growls. "They're going to lock you up and throw away the key, just like they did your daddy."

Basil keeps pushing forward, away from the building where the security guards battle the geophags for control of the Synthamil. We inch closer to the police cars on the perimeter. "Get ready," Basil says to me. "One..." I don't know what I'm supposed to be ready for. "Two..." He swipes at Ribald, ripping the fabric of his jacket and drawing a thin line of blood across his chest. Ribald looks down flummoxed, then Basil shouts, "Three!" He throws the knife aside and lands a hard punch to Ribald's gut that sends him reeling into Garvy, knocking them both to the ground.

"Go!" Basil screams and pulls me past the two men trying to disentangle themselves from each other.

We dive into a car. I pop up behind the steering wheel as Basil slams the door.

"Go! Go! Go!" he yells, but I stare stupidly at the screen on the dashboard. "You have to drive it!" he shouts.

"How?" I yell back just as Ribald throws himself across the hood of the car. He snarls and spits with rage.

"Push the pedal!" Basil screams and jams his foot on top of mine. The combustion engine roars, but we don't move.

Suddenly Ribald's sliding across the hood of the car away from us. We look out the windshield to find Zara, her magenta hair flashing as she and her geophag friend yank Ribald off the car by the ankles. I jab my finger against the touch screen in front of me. Lights go on and off. Wipers swish. Air blasts in our face, then we lurch forward, heading straight for Garvy. His mouth drops in terror, and I yank the wheel to the right, sending the vehicle in a big arc through the crowd that scatters as we race toward the building, the engine bellowing.

"Turn, turn, turn!" Basil yells at me with his foot jammed on top of mine. "Now straighten it out."

I pull the wheel and swerve around Zara who's too busy kicking Ribald in the ribs to hear me shouting, "Thank you!" through the open window. My voice trails after us as we hit the road and zoom through town.

"There has to be a location device in here," I yell over the engine.

"Can you dismantle it?" Basils asks.

"Not while I'm driving," I tell him as I clutch the steering wheel so tight my knuckles go white. This is nothing like steering a bicycle or motorbike, and I'm petrified that we'll crash as we pass the decrepit buildings and the clinic, surrounded by flashing red-lighted vehicles. Everything whizzes by in a blur.

"Climb over me," Basil says. He grabs the wheel then slides across the seat toward me.

"We'll wreck!" I'm too afraid to let go.

"It's okay," he assures me. "We can do it." I pry my fingers from the wheel and slide across his lap so that we change places. Then I jab at the screen, trying to work my way into the operating system, but nothing makes sense to me.

"I can't figure it out," I spit, sure that security won't be far behind. "Stupid thing!" I lift the crutch Basil made and smash it into the dashboard, over and over. The screen shorts out with a loud pop, a puff of smoke, and a sad little whinge. Every light inside and out of the car dies. We continue barreling down a rutted road toward the setting sun. We don't stop. We don't slow down. We don't even talk. We buckle ourselves in and we fly.

⚘   ⚘   ⚘

For the next half hour we drive in silence with the wail of sirens not far behind. I continually scan the road and the air for red lights, but we seem to have gotten enough of a head start. Each time there's a fork, a curve, or another road away from the town, Basil takes it until after nearly an hour we're zipping along an unlit dirt path alone and the sirens have faded into the night. But Basil keeps pushing the car forward, bearing down on the pedal, so that our heads scrape the ceiling with every bump. A few times I gasp when I think I see something lurch in front of us, but it's just the shadows of clouds moving across the moon.

"Maybe we should stop now," I say.

"Maybe we could if you hadn't announced to the world who we are!" he snaps at me and keeps his eyes locked forward and his foot on the pedal like a man possessed.

"Sometimes you have to do the right thing!" I yell.

"Not at the expense of your safety."

"But if you're not willing to take a risk, how will anything ever change?"

"I take risks," Basil argues. "But I'm smart about it. I stay under the radar. Until now!"

"I did the right thing," I tell him defiantly. "Maybe we should go back and be a part of what we started."

"No," is all he says.

Before I can argue with him anymore, the car tilts sharply, and we head up a steep uneven incline. As we reach the crest, the moon slips behind a large cloud. He guns the engine and the wheels leave the ground. My body lifts, airborne between the seat and ceiling. Basil floats beside me. I hear myself screaming as we soar like a meteor rushing through deep dark space. In that time, which can only be a second or two, my mind slows enough for me to have one clear thought: If I'm going to die, then I'm glad I'm beside this boy.

But we land quickly then bounce and bang down an equally steep decline, screaming and flailing into the air bags, which have burst from the dashboard and doors to cushion our blow. Then, just like that, the bags deflate and we're motionless. We sit in stunned silence as fine powder from the air bag explosions sprinkles over us like simulated snow.

"You okay?" Basil asks quietly as if he's afraid his voice could send the car rolling over another precipice. We've landed at a tilt and I'm pressed against the door. I brush the powder from my skin and clothes and grope my limbs to make sure everything is still intact.

"I think so. You?"

"I guess I am." Then he laughs. A weak, uncertain burble of bewilderment. He unbuckles his seat belt and carefully slides down toward me.

"We shouldn't be." I wrap my arms around his shoulders to stop myself from shaking. "We should be smashed to pieces."

He hugs me tight. We rock back and forth, breathing together, perfectly synchronized, like two parts of a machine made to fit. We linger in our embrace, each of us reluctant to let go.

"Maybe we're dead," he jokes.

I snicker, equally uncertain, then nuzzle my face against his neck. I smell the musk of his fear and press my lips against his skin, which tastes salty like tears. "That would make this the afterlife."

"Do you think One World owns that, too?"

I laugh a little harder. "They bought it from god."

"Sell out," he says, and we both crack up, but then Basil turns serious and asks me, "Do you believe in all that? The afterlife and god and stuff?"

"Not really," I admit. "Do you?"

"I'd like to think there could be something better. Like a place where everybody has enough, you know? Not too much, not too little. Just enough, and we could all be happy with that."

"I think you hit your head," I say.

He sighs long and loud as if letting go of everything that's happened to us in the past few hours. "It was Ana's vision."

"It's a lovely vision," I say, even though I'm not sure I believe it could ever happen.

He looks out the front window, searching the dark. "I can't believe she's gone. I can't believe I'm never going to see her again."

I'm not sure how to console him, so instead I point through the windshield and say, "Look, stars!" The clouds have trundled past, leaving an open swath of black sky dotted with thousands of tiny pinpricks of light, but the moon stays hidden. "Come on. Let's get out."

I jiggle the handle on my smashed-up door, but it won't budge so

Basil shoulders the driver-side door until it swings open with a sad groan. He climbs out and drops to the ground. I follow him and he helps me down gingerly.

"Wow," I whisper as I look up. "I've never seen a real sky like this with no giant lights in the way. It's even more beautiful than the planetarium."

Despite the starlight, it's still too dark to make out much of what's around us because we seem to have fallen into a shallow chasm. The air is moist, not dry like usual, and the smell is a bit musty, as if we've walked into a bathing room that hasn't been aired out. Even weirder, the ground beneath our feet is soft, almost spongy, as if we're stand-ing on a wet rug. We grope along until we find something solid and smooth and cool to the touch, a large flat rock maybe, and we both sit down. I lean over and rest my head on Basil's shoulder to contem-plate what's above us.

"Did you know that all the elements on Earth came from ancient exploding stars?" I tell him.

"For real?" He lies back and cradles his head in his hands so he's looking straight up into the night sky.

"Yeah. The dust swirled around and around for millions of years. Then heat from a supernova and the force of gravity gradually pulled all that dust together, spinning it into bigger and bigger spheres, which became the planets."

I blink up at the stars, some long dead, but their light just now reaching my eyes. "Think about it," I say. "Millions of years went by while the Earth twirled out here in the expanding universe. Bacteria wriggled around. Genes mutated and new stuff started popping up. Amoebas, algae, plants, little critters. And then one day, there were my great-grandparents standing in the middle of their farm, which could have been around here somewhere." I imagine Grandma Apple's mom and dad digging their hands into the soil, rich with nutrients left over from the primordial stew of early Earth before humans bled it dry. "They looked up at this same sky."

"Do you ever wish you'd been alive back then?" Basil asks.

"Kind of." I lie down with my head on his chest. "I'd like to know what food and animals and plants were like. But then I'd have to live through the wars and from what my Grandma Apple says, it was horrible."

We both gaze above us again. "Doesn't it make you feel small?" Basil asks.

"We're just specks of stardust in the cosmos," I say with a laugh. "But, you know, that also makes me feel good, like I'm part of something bigger than myself, and just maybe all the people who came before me, like my great-grandparents and my grandpa Hector are still here in a way."

Basil takes a long slow breath. I listen to his heartbeat. "I think the same thing about my brother sometimes. Like maybe he's watching over me. Keeping me safe. I know it's silly but . . ."

"I don't think it's silly at all," I tell him. Then I gather my courage and ask, "How did he die?"

Basil's quiet for a while, then out of the silence he says, "In the Svalbard Rebellion."

"Svalbard!" I pop upright. "Were you there?" I reach out and touch his hip, where the tattoo of the seed sits beneath his shirt.

"I was only five."

"But Arol?"

He nods.

"Was he killed in the riots?"

"That's what One World would like everyone to believe, but it's not true." Basil sits up and hugs his knees. "It all started out peaceful, you know? At first, everyone who wanted answers about the seed vault just sat outside the OW headquarters for weeks, trying to peace-fully force the execs into a dialogue. People like Ana understood what OW's ownership meant in the long run, especially if they had de-stroyed all the seeds, because that would mean the only food source left on Earth would be Synthamil."

"Do you think they destroyed the vault?"

He shrugs. "What's it matter? One World has complete control over the food supply whether the vault is there or not."

"And Ana and your brother were both part of the protest?"

He nods. "She was one of the organizers. She believed in nonvio-lent confrontation because she knew they'd lose a battle of force. But One World wouldn't talk. They just dismissed what was going on. Walked right past the protesters like they didn't exist. Some of the pro-testers got more serious. People went on hunger strikes and stopped drinking Synthamil."

"Is that what Arol did?"

Basil shakes his head. "Arol never did anything but sit there, oc-cupying One World land, making some noise. It wasn't really about the seed vault for him."

"What was it then?" I ask.

He works his mouth as if gathering words that won't come out. Finally, he says, "It was me. He wanted things to change so that One World would have to feed kids like me."

I don't know what to say, so I reach out and wrap one arm around his shoulders while he continues.

"He was a cog in a machine trying to get One World to take notice of how screwed up their policies were. Only what did they care? Every-one out there was expendable. Just another mouth to feed. Then one day, one of the execs, a guy named Walter Bennigan, got sick of walk-ing through the crowds of people, some of them chained to the lampposts, starving themselves. So he goes up to an office, opens the window, and starts chucking out cases of Synthamil at the crowd. One of the cases hit Arol. Got him right on the temple. He died instantly.

"That's all it took to spark the riots. People went nuts. They'd been waiting for a moment, an excuse, something to light the fire, and they found it when Bennigan killed my brother. They stormed One World. And One World retaliated. Sent out security agents full force. Dozens of people died."

"That's awful! I can't believe I never knew the whole story. Why hadn't I heard about Arol before?"

"Because it's a footnote," Basil spits with a bitter laugh. "A tiny part of the story that most people have forgotten. But not Ana. She always remembered Arol. After he died, she helped look out for me. Like Betta, she was a guardian angel. She told me to look at my hunger as a blessing."

I think back to Ana spreading her arms in the meeting and telling us to embrace the changes in our midst and soar. Was she talking about a genetic mutation that makes people like Basil and me and all the other freaks in rehab and the geophag campers feel hunger? I wrap my arms tighter around his shoulders. "I'm so sorry," I whisper. "And now you've lost her, too."

"Yeah. So you'll forgive me if I don't see One World as the provider of good things," he says sarcastically.

I sigh with frustration. "What ever happened to Walter Bennigan?"

"Nothing much," Basil tells me. "The security agents who killed the other protesters weren't even arrested. The court said they were acting in self-defense, even though they were the only ones with guns, so nobody was prosecuted. My family sued, of course. But the judge was in the pocket of One World. The company paid Bennigan's fine, confiscated all video footage, and let him retire quietly. The protests stopped. Everybody went home. It was all for nothing."

We sit quietly. He's caught in memories while I try to make sense of a world in which reality has shifted once again.

Then out of the silence, Basil says, "That's when my family fell apart. Not that it was ever all that good in the first place, but at least before Arol died, my parents tried to feed me. After it happened, my mom started with the drugs and my dad was so angry he got arrested and thrown in jail, so I was pretty much on my own."

I shake my head in disbelief as I imagine that curly-haired little-boy version of Basil learning to fend for himself in the Outer Loop while I was playing Pesky Petey with my social-time buddies at the EntertainArena "I wish I knew what else to say . . ."

Basil pulls away from me. "There's nothing to say." He stands up and stretches. "We should probably rest here for the night." He heads toward the car. "In the morning we can get our bearings." It's clear he's done talking about the past.

I try to pull myself together and focus on what's happening now. "Do you think it's safe?"

"I don't think anyone knows where we are."

"Including us?" I ask, but he doesn't answer. I get up and hobble behind him. He helps me climb into the car. We shut the door and get into the backseat, where we can lie on our sides, nestled together like the spoons I once saw in a drawer at the Relics. He drapes one hand across my hip, and within seconds he's snoring but I can't fall asleep.

There's too much to think about. Mostly I wonder what my parents know about life beyond the Inner Loop. They say that everything they've done has been to give me a better life, but would they feel their work had been worth it if they knew what Basil's family has gone through as a result? Can any one person's life be truly good if it's at another person's expense?

I poke Basil gently. When he doesn't stir, I slowly move his hand off my body and lean into the front seat where I take out my Gizmo. I mute the sound and hunch over the screen, making sure the light won't disturb him.

I'm surprised that I can still get a weak signal out this far, but those waves must travel well over fallow land. The first thing I do is look for newsfeeds about the protests, but the only new footage I can find is what's been added to our "crime spree" montage. In addition to running from the authorities at the Analog meeting, busting out of rehab, wreaking havoc at the EA and wrecking a car, kidnapping Yaz and stiffing Fiyo, stealing a motorbike, and running off with biofuel after beating up the station owners, we're now accused of not paying for services at a private medical clinic, beating up ordinary citizens (Ribald and Garvy), and single-handedly looting an Outer Loop Synthamil distribution point before stealing a security vehicle. Even without the sound, I have no trouble understanding the story Ahimsa's PR team is spinning.

Obviously, I'm not going to get any real information from the usual channels, so I head over to the Dynasaur chats to see what I can learn. I'm half afraid to log on. What if everyone believes the smear campaign against me? Or worse, what if knowing my real identity—that I'm Max Apple and Lily Nguyen's privy daughter who's run off with an Outer Loop boy—is even more damning than Ahimsa's lies? I decide I'd rather know what I'm up against than keep my head in the sand. Now that my identity as HectorProtector has been revealed, I don't have to worry about finding a VPN, so I log on using some network signal that's found it's way out this far and start perusing the chats. What I find brings tears to my eyes.

My video of the geophags looting the Synthamil supply has not only been uploaded to the site, but it has thousands of hits. Even better, the best Dynasaur programmers are working nonstop to hack One World security so my video is the first thing people will see when they enter ordinary One World sites in the morning. Every time One

World patches a hole in the security, the Dynasaurs look for a new way in. I find messages from Dynasaurs organizing other Synthamil distribution takeovers, inspired by the geophags. And more and more people have gathered at the prison, demanding the release of the other imprisoned Analogs. The only person missing from all the chatter is AnonyGal. This makes no sense to me. She's exactly the kind of person who would be involved, but she's nowhere on the chats. However, someone new has showed up and strangely, he or she is going by the name YAZ.

Can't be, I think. But just in case, I ping her to ask. She doesn't answer. So I send a quick, quiet vid to her message center, but it immediately bounces back. My heart sinks. One World probably knocked her off-line and confiscated her Gizmo when they arrested her. I read through some of YAZ's comments on the threads, and I have to admit, it sounds like my Yaz, so I direct message her through the Dynasaur chat.

> YAZ is that you?

Within seconds, I have an answer.

> Can u believe it? Me, a Dynasaur!

I press my hand over my mouth to stop from laughing out loud.

> How?

> Long story, deets later, but short version is, yr dad got me out of OW custody then set me up with a jalopy (sp?) some crazy thing he built & showed me how to get online without being traced—seriously awesome. still got my hovercam tho :)

> My dad?

> Yep. Yr dad=amazing. Yr fam is soooo worried ab U.

Really?

YES!!!! We all R. Where R U

I hesitate. The truth is I don't know where I am, but also I can't be sure this is really Yaz or if it is that I can trust her. Behind me, Basil stirs. "Apple?" he says.

"I'm here," I whisper then quickly send off one last text.

I'm ok more soon.

I cloak the Gizmo before I pocket it and climb over the seat to nestle up against Basil again. He hugs me close and presses his nose into my hair. "I thought you were gone," he says sleepily.

"I wouldn't leave," I tell him.

We lie twisted up together, our breath synchronized, as I gaze out the window at the stars above me again. When I was little, if I woke up from a bad dream, Grandma Apple would take me outside, and we'd look at the one lone star bright enough to shine through the haze that covers the Loops. *Make a wish,* she'd say. Now I wish I knew who to trust, who's really on my side. But it seems childish to expect help from some cosmic light, a mere projection of the past onto the present. I close my eyes and drift into a heavy sleep with Basil's arms wrapped snugly around me.

PART 3

THE HINTERLANDS

*"The revolution is not an apple that falls
when it is ripe. You have to make it fall."*
—Che Guevara

All night, I dream of war—flashes of artillery, earthshaking explosions from bombs, the rat-a-tat-tat of gunfire overhead, but I'm too exhausted to wake myself up fully, until a familiar gnawing in my belly rouses me. I struggle to open my eyes and see shimmering patterns on the ceiling above me. Basil's at my side. We bob and spin. The growling in my stomach turns into the roar of rushing water, and I force myself to sit up.

"What the hell?" I shout when I put my feet into a cold puddle on the floorboards.

Basil jerks awake. "Where are we? What's happening?" He presses himself against the window. Water swirls, frothy and brown, on all sides of us as the world rushes by, but I can't make sense of what I see. We're in a car, but we're not driving. We're in the water, but this isn't a boat. Then Basil shouts, "Flash flood!" He bashes his shoulder against the door but the pressure from the water outside is too strong. "Give me your crutch!"

I scramble to find it in the rising water, which has filled the wheel wells and reaches the seat. "Can you swim?" he asks as he smashes the crutch against the window until the glass shatters.

"Of course I can! Can you?" I yell back, but I don't hear his answer because water pours in through the opening, tilting the car hard to the left then back up to the right. The last thing I hear before getting a face full of water is Basil screaming, "Kick! Kick!"

I lift my head and take a final deep breath then push off the seat. Ahead of me, Basil slips through the window then he turns, hair swirling in the current, cheeks puffy with air, to look for me under-water. I fight against the torrent filling the car and grab the edge of the window to haul myself through. The car slips behind me like a lost shoe and sinks into the murky swirl, pulling me down with it. I swim as hard as I can but I'm disoriented. I somersault and twist, trying to find Basil, but I can't see anything. The roiling water bullies me forward. My lungs scream for air and I start to go limp. I feel as if I'm on a cloud, watching myself struggle in the water when a voice inside of me says, *Fight!* I see light above my head, so I kick as hard as I can and pop up above the surface, gasping and flailing.

Basil grabs me by my shirt. "Roll on your back," he splutters. "Point your feet downstream."

I do what he says and find myself swept into the current, but my head stays above the water.

"We have to get to land," he tells me with amazing calm. "Get ready." I nod and take a deep breath just as he shouts, "Go!"

We both roll to our stomachs and pump our arms and legs, furi-ously fighting the undercurrent trying to clear us away like flotsam, but we won't give up. I kick and claw and fight my way to the side until I'm scraping up handfuls of mud and rocks, then I put my feet down and stumble to the slippery shore. "Basil!" I shout. "Basil!" I look around frantically, fearing that he hasn't made it.

"Over here!" He's upstream from me, using old tree roots and rocks to climb up the muddy slope. I do the same, working my way toward him, until side by side we scramble over the top of the embankment and roll to our backs, panting and coughing.

"Oh my god. Oh my god. What just happened?" I sputter and half wonder if I'm stuck in a nightmare.

"Must've been in a riverbed," he says, breathing heavily. "Must've been a storm." That would explain my dream. Flashes of lightning. Explosions of thunder. Rain pounding the top of the car. "Those old riverbeds fill up fast when it pours, and once it starts, there's nothing anybody can do to stop it," he tells me.

I sit up and take stock. I've lost my shoes, my brace, and my pants, but I still have underwear. Luckily the shirt I took from Basil's mom is long enough to cover half of me. Somehow my pouch has gotten twisted tightly under my arm and miraculously my Gizmo is still inside. When I feel it, my first instinct is to make sure it still works and call for help, but then I remember, the people who would help us are the same ones who would throw us in jail.

"Goddamn it!" I yell in frustration. I grab a handful of rocks and dirt and fling them at the unrelenting water surging downstream. "How much more could we possibly go through? This is getting completely ridiculous!" I pound my fists into the ground and fling more rocks and dirt against the air. "I've been chased! I've been shot at! I've stolen a car! Everyone knows I'm HectorProtector and now this! A freakin' flash flood? You have got to be kidding me! I don't even have pants anymore!" I rant.

"But, Apple." Basil kneels barefoot beside me and holds my shoulders.

"What?" I seethe at him. I realize I'm acting like a toddler, but I can't help it; I'm just so fed up. "What is it now?"

"Look." He points behind us, away from the river.

Slowly I turn and see spread in front of us a thick tangle of green blanketing everything from the ground to strange foliage-covered figures reaching for the sky. "Oh my god!" I gasp as I try to take it all in, but my brain can't make sense of what I see. "What is it?"

"We made it."

"To what? Where are we?"

Basil stands and shakes himself, flinging droplets of water from his hair and clothes. They sparkle like tiny prisms in the sunlight. He reaches down and pulls me up beside him. We stand side by side, looking out onto the green horizon, then a smile spreads slowly over his face as he says, "The Hinterlands."

✤   ✤   ✤

I limp down the other side of the embankment behind Basil. Little green wisps tickle my ankles and my feet. "What is this stuff?" I point to the leaves creeping up the hill toward us, because honestly I'm scared that it'll swallow us up like it has everything else in its path.

"Probably kudzu," says Basil. "I've heard the stuff grows like a foot a day out here."

"But I thought . . . but everybody said . . . but . . . but . . . but . . ." I stammer and stutter because I cannot believe what I'm seeing. This is nothing like the desolate wasteland I've always heard was beyond the Loops. "This isn't supposed to be here," I finally spit out.

Basil looks at me and grins. "But it is here."

On tender feet, we step carefully through the thick tangle of vines with heart-shaped leaves. Gigantic shaggy green creatures populate the hillside like some long-forgotten zoo of extinct animals. Grandma and I used to play a game naming shapes in clouds. Now I try to imagine what these beasts could be. Dinosaurs or elephants or giraffes? Maybe a fairy-tale giant reaching for the sun.

I pull a leaf from one of the vines and rub it between my forefinger and thumb. It's as soft as worn denim and has a pleasant, almost sweet soaplike smell, only there is something deeper and more complex to the scent. I press it against my nose and inhale again. "This is amazing," I whisper reverently. "I had no idea anything could grow."

"Look up there." Basil points high on the hill where a giant, white stone face with a long green beard peers out of the leaves. I squint at the shape of a man towering toward the sky in a long robe. He holds out his arms. His hands are missing, but his eyes are kind and they seem to follow us as we explore. At the base of the hill is an arch between two pillars. Basil pulls back some vines to reveal the words BETHLEHEM—OUR HOPE inscribed in stone. A tumbledown staircase made from rocks leads up the terraced hill. White stucco parapets push through the vines. Black windows peek out of the foliage like hidden woodland creatures watching silently as we pass a flock of crumbling white stone animals, sheep maybe, grazing on the leaves. We wind around a ramshackle structure, half the walls collapsed to expose pairs of fallen animals impaled on posts. Horses? Hippos? Some kind of bears? Basils grabs the end of a vine and tugs. NOAH'S ARK CAROUSEL reads the sign in the dirt.

"What is this place?" I ask, half creeped out and half amazed as we pick our way through the rubble, avoiding the sharpest rocks.

"I don't know. Maybe some kind of religious park or something?"

We come to another archway decorated with more lacy shrubbery casting shadows across another sign. I pluck the vines away to reveal GARDEN OF EDEN carved above the arch.

Basil steps into the clearing, but I begin foraging around the edges, wondering what else might grow in the midst of all this kudzu.

Could there be flowers? Bugs? Small animals burrowing beneath the ground? I pull apart a snarl of leaves. At first all I see is green. Then, a tiny spot of red. And another. I kneel down to get a better look and am nearly bowled over when I come across a cluster of bright fruit.

"Look," I say with wonder, pointing at beautiful red globs among all the green. "I think these might be . . . could they be . . . ?" I reach cautiously through the brambles. Thorns scratch my hands but I don't care. I pluck a few from the vine and hold them up, dumbstruck. It's like if someone you thought was dead walks through a door and shakes your hand.

"What are they?" Basil asks, peering closely.

"Berries," I whisper.

"Are you sure?"

"Yes," I tell him, regaining my voice. "Grandma Apple told me about these." I marvel at their color, their texture, their utter perfection. "They're more beautiful than I ever imagined." I can't stop turning them over and over, exploring every facet that glistens in the sun. "They were one of her favorites. She told me so many stories about what they grew and what they gathered. Mushrooms, roots, ferns, and wild greens. We used to draw pictures of different kinds of fruit and vegetables or make them out of clay then pretend to cook. But I never thought . . ." I bring a berry close to my nose and inhale. The smell is subtle but sweet. A scent from my dreams.

"Be careful!" says Basil. "What if they're poisonous?"

"It's okay. See how it looks like lots of itty-bitty balls stuck together, but then it's hollow on the inside?" I turn one over to show him the concave white belly. I put five on my fingertips and make them dance. "The poisonous ones were smooth and not as bright, and they didn't grow on prickly vines like these." I stop and laugh. "Just think, all that time Grandma was playing with me, she was really teaching me what you could and couldn't eat." I hold one close to my mouth. "Should I?"

"I don't know," he says. "Are you sure it's safe?"

"Only one way to find out!" A little thrill zips through me as I pop a berry in my mouth. Basil stares. I roll it on my tongue. The texture is strange. Bumpy. Almost rubbery. I start to gag but then my mouth fills with spit. The taste is fleeting and too unfamiliar to name, but I like it and I want more. I move the berry to the side of my mouth, between my teeth and my cheek and I suck, drawing out small gulps of pleasure. When that's not enough, I cautiously bite down. A squish of sweet, tart juice is released. "Oh my god," I say as the amazing new flavor spreads across my tongue and up into my nose. "This is incredible. Delicious." The more I chew the stronger the taste becomes. Plus I love the satisfying crunch of tiny seeds grinding between my teeth. When I swallow the berry mush, I immediately reach for another one. "You have to try one!"

"You're sure?" he asks and I nod while I stuff myself with more. Carefully, Basil plucks a berry from the brambles and lays it on his tongue. When he chews his eyes get wide. "It's like my mouth and part of my brain are waking up," he says. "It's like . . . like . . ." He swallows and reaches for another. "It's like this is what we're meant to do!"

Basil and I laugh and chew berries one by one for several minutes. When he puts them on his fingers like I did before, I snatch them one by one with my teeth and growl, "More! Give me more!"

"You've become a monster!" He pelts me with fruit, yelling, "Back! Back, you beast!"

I roar at him then lunge and grab his waist. We spin around and fall to the ground with me on top of him demanding that he feed me.

He pokes me in the armpit, which makes me squirm and squeal. Soon we're wrestling, poking and jabbing one another, rolling across the soft ground, laughing until our noses are inches apart, and we're kissing under the warm morning sun. I love breathing him in. Feeling his skin next to mine. Tasting him.

"You are better than berries," I whisper.

When we come up for air a few minutes later, my lips sting and my whole body is warm. I roll away from him, unnerved by the yearning deep inside of me. Not just for berries but for him. I take a few shaky breaths.

"Do you think this is . . ." I trail off, searching for the word. "Normal? What we're doing?" I wag my finger from him to me. "I mean, we're not even in the Procreation Pool. Our hormones shouldn't be surging." My cheeks grow warm just talking about this stuff.

Basil props himself on one elbow and rests his hand where my shirt has come up over my hip. "Do you care? I mean would that stop you?"

I tug my shirt down. "My mom and Dr. Demeter would say that our brain chemistry isn't optimized. Or that we have some kind of mutation in our genes that makes us act this way."

"Guess that makes us mutants then," he says with a grin.

I look at his perfect face and can't help but smile, too. "Fish with feet, like Ana said."

He chuckles. "So we're the lucky ones?"

I shake my head and look around. "You call this lucky?"

"Maybe." He shrugs. "If it means we can go back to the way nature intended us to be." He puts his hand on my belly. "Like this." He leans down to kiss me again.

"It's a nice idea. . . ." I say and squirm away. "But do you think it's really possible?"

"Why not?" He sits up and motions to the greenery. "Look at all this!"

"It's just kudzu and berries. How much of this would you have to eat to equal one bottle of Synthamil?"

"Apple . . ." Basil looks at me intently. "If the soil can grow this"—he grabs a handful of vines—"then it's good enough to farm. If you clear away all the kudzu, which by the way we can eat and make fuel from and even smoke, then you could grow more crops, different crops."

"If you had seeds," I point out, but he ignores me.

"Plus, bees and butterflies have to pollinate this stuff, which means there have to be animals out here somewhere. Maybe even birds and small mammals. Ana always said, 'Life is powerful,'" Basil tells me. "This is proof that the earth is rejuvenating."

I gaze all around us, amazed and terrified. "Birds and bees are fine," I say. "But what else could be lurking out here? Or who? Aren't you even a little bit worried?"

"It's probably safer than where we came from." He falls back into the leafy bed, beaming up at the sky as if in ecstasy. "Do you know what this could mean, Apple?" he asks but doesn't wait for me to answer. "Never having to fight. To scrounge. Never having to ask for help. Not relying on anyone else. If I could find a way to make it work out here . . . if I could never go back . . ."

"Really?" I ask, my heart pounding in my ears. "You would never go back. Ever? But what about . . ."

He turns and looks at me sharply. "What do I have to go back to?"

I swallow hard. My mind is filled with images of my family. Grandma Apple standing in our doorway, her sweater held close. My father's face smiling at me from a screen. Papa Peter imploring me to come home. Even my mom and Grandma Grace searching my face with worried eyes. I can't tell Basil this. To him, my family is the enemy, so instead I say, "But the other Analogs. Don't you want them to know where you are? Wouldn't it be better if we were all together?"

Basil sighs. "I don't know anymore, Apple. I truly don't know."

I decide to change tactics. "Think about Ana then. What would she want you to do?"

"She always said it wasn't time yet." He considers this for a few seconds. "I don't know what she was waiting for."

"Maybe she didn't want to lead people into uncertainty but now you know," I say, getting to my knees. "We have to tell people about this. And not just the Analogs. Dynasaurs and people like Yaz and even my family because if they knew . . ."

He scoffs. "I guarantee your parents already know about this."

"They couldn't possibly know," I argue. "If they did . . ."

"Oh, they know, believe me." Basil sits up and angrily plucks leaves from the vines around us. "They just don't want anyone else to know. If everyone can go out and get their own food, it ruins One World's little business model to control the universe."

"Could you exaggerate any more?" I snap at him.

"I'm not exaggerating."

I shake my head. "Maybe someone at One World knows, like Ahimsa, but not my parents. No matter what you think of them, they're scientists first and foremost. And scientists believe in the truth. If my mom knew about this . . ." I hold up a berry like exhibit A in my argument for why my mother can't possibly know. "Things would be different."

"She's an employee of One World, first. A scientist, second. And the truth is relative. At least as far as One World is concerned. So don't delude yourself."

"I'm not deluding myself!" I argue. "I'm saying we have to go back and tell people about this because it changes everything."

Basil draws in a deep breath. "I don't know that it changes anything, Apple." He looks down between his knees. "And truthfully, I'm tired. Tired of living like a shadow for most of my life. And now, after all that's happened to you and me . . . I just don't know if I can fight a battle I'm not sure we can win anymore. As much as I admired Ana and as much as I've always wanted to avenge Arol's death, I don't want to end up in jail, or worse, die trying. Especially when I know this is here. We made it." He jabs his finger in the ground. "We got out and we found food. We could just . . . stay."

"Stay?" I say. "Here? In some creepy park eating berries while One World is back there making life miserable for everyone but the privies!"

Basil snorts. "Oh, so now all of the sudden you're a champion for the common people?"

"I meant what I said at the geophag camp. We are all in prison as long as One World has control."

Basil hops to his feet and marches angrily through the greenery. "You know, this is typical of someone like you!"

I scramble up behind him. "What's that supposed to mean?"

He spins around and shouts in my face, "You finally figure out that the world isn't this perfect little place with perfect little hologram flowers covering up the hard dry dirt beneath your feet and perfect smell-o-blasters masking the stench of rot and perfect Whisson Windmills sucking water out of thin air attached to every roof. No actually, it's a horrible, unfair place, where mothers would rather buy drugs than Synthamil for their kids and fathers go to jail because they can't stop raging over the hand they've been dealt. And, oh by the way, news flash! One World is a big fat megacorporate oppressor!"

"But . . ."

"So now you're freaking out and sure that you're the only one who can save the rest of us! Just because you finally figured it out, Apple, doesn't mean we have to go back and get our asses kicked. We got out. We don't have to save the world."

"But I thought that's what you wanted to do," I argue. "I thought righting the wrongs and saving the world was our plan."

"No, that was never *my* plan," he says. "*This* has been my plan all along. To walk away. And when I found you, I thought I had finally found someone to go with me."

I'm stunned. "Go where?"

"I don't know. Where the others have gone."

"What others?"

"Other people have walked away," he tells me.

"But what if they didn't make it? What if no one's out here?"

"We won't know unless we look for them. And the only thing I know for certain is that they are not in the Outer Loop or the Inner Loop or anywhere I've ever been before. If they made it, they're out here and I intend to find them."

"But Basil," I say, imploring him. "We know something now that others don't. Before we can truly walk away, we have to tell everyone back there about this so they have the option of leaving, too. That's the only way One World will be forced to change."

He puts his hands on his hips and hangs his head. "No," he says simply.

"But we have an obligation to use our knowledge to better the world!"

He looks up. "Do you even hear yourself?" he asks me. When I stare at him blankly he shouts, "You sound just like your mother!"

I'm so angry that I can't see. I can't hear. I feel like a train is driving through my skull. Without even thinking, I run toward him with my arms outstretched until I smack into his chest, pushing him backward while I scream, "Don't you dare say that about me!"

⚘   ⚘   ⚘

I storm away, limping and livid that he, of all people, would compare me to my mother. And that he, of all people, would fault me for trying to make the world a better place. So what if I'm a privy? I can't help where I was born! I can't help that I just found out the world sucks. And then to blame me for wanting to help? I don't know why I ever wanted to be with him. He's a hypocrite and a liar and an idiot. And my ankle hurts again.

I hobble along for several minutes, hopping and cursing each time something sharp pokes the soft soles of my feet. I come to what looks like the edge of the park. The exit is two more arches under a huge sign. I yank the vines away to reveal the words YOUR FUTURE IS IN YOUR HANDS: WHICH WILL YOU CHOOSE? I clear the foliage. The arch on the left says, HEAVEN. The one on the right says, HELL.

"Oh for god's sake," I huff. People have made up stories for thousands of years to explain what they couldn't understand. They'd say disease was caused by evil spells before they understood genetics. Or superstorms were the work of nasty genies. Or that a woman named Eve ate forbidden fruit and learned the truth about how hard life could be. But now that everything I've ever thought was true has been turned upside down, I understand why people grasp for answers. I only wish it was as easy as choosing path A or path B.

I choose neither. Instead, I find a different path that leads deeper into the kudzu jungle. It's calm and quiet out here and the ground is softer and smoother so it's easier to walk. Soon my head stops spinning. I feel myself relax a bit under the thick canopy of vines that let in only a smattering of sunshine here and there. My stomach unclenches as the pleasant smell of the leaves warming in the sun permeates the moist air. I take a few deep breaths and try to understand what just happened. One minute I was rolling around on the ground wanting to devour Basil. The next I was so mad at him that I couldn't see straight. I don't know what's wrong with me. Maybe my mom is right. Maybe we should control human hormones if this is how they make us feel.

I slow down and look around. At first, everything seems the same, but as I look more closely along the path, I begin to make out colors, shapes, and textures that I haven't noticed yet. Tall brown trunks—that were probably once trees—with soft green fur and brown stair-step disks growing around their bases. Another cluster of raspberries sparkles in the sun. I reach down and pluck a pink-and-white flower growing up from the earth. A real flower. Not a hologram or a synth plant. It is the most beautiful, amazing thing I've ever seen. So delicate and intricate. I want to tell others about this so they can decide for themselves whether to stay in the Loops or walk away. But, the thing that Basil doesn't understand is that we don't have to go back to spread the word. I reach inside my pouch and pull out my Gizmo, hoping that it still works.

Slowly, the screen comes to life with the animated One World globe spinning while the system searches for a signal. I can hardly believe it works, but I shouldn't be so skeptical. My father designed it after all. Astrid, still on mute, goes berserk, pinging me with dozens of messages, all of which I ignore because standing here, holding my father's invention in my hands, makes me miss him terribly. I have the urge to call him and let him know that I'm okay. But, first things first.

I log on to the Dynasaur chat, open a video feed, and film my surroundings. "This is HectorProtector. Since One World security forces attacked the Outer Loop Synthamil distribution point last night, I've made it to the Hinterlands. As you can see, the world is lush with kudzu out here." I pan the sea of green. Then I reach into the leaves and pick a few berries. I hold them close to the camera. "Ana Gignot thought arable land beyond the Loops was a possibility. I'm here to tell you that it's a reality."

Once my video has posted, I peruse the chats for AnonyGal. My heart leaps when I see a post from her, but it's just two short lines.

> Watch your step out there, Dynasaurs! Moles
> are everywhere and their holes are deep.

I puzzle over this. Why would she be warning people about the obvious? We all know One World trolls the chats—that's why we protect our identities. Except mine was leaked. Maybe hers was, too. One last time, I reach out to her through a direct private message:

Thnk U 4 the code. R U OK? I'm worried. Pls b n touch.

I wait for a few seconds, but nothing comes back and I worry that she's been arrested. Just as I'm about to log off, something entirely unexpected pops up—a vid of Yaz wearing a fuzzy purple jumpsuit standing in front of the green flashing 42. I sit, befuddled, wondering what's gotten into her and why she'd be doing her PRC through the Dynasaur network! I click the feed and watch.

> If you've logged onto my PRC before, you know that my name is Yaz, but this broadcast will be different than all the others. Thalia Apple, who some of you may know as HectorProtector, is my best friend. I was arrested for helping her escape One World security guards then they released a video of me slandering her, but that was a farce. One World has twisted the truth of Thalia's story into an indictment against her. But I am here to tell you, she is fighting the good fight for a more just world. Thalia Apple, aka HectorProtector, is on your side. Dynasaurs, Analogs, and Privies unite. Join us and tune in to my PRC for updates on the battle.

As she reaches toward her HoverCam to turn it off, I notice a new tattoo on her wrist. A tiny sprout unfurls from a seed as the word *Remember* flashes beneath. I should have never underestimated her. I leave her a comment below the vid telling her she's my hero for using her PRC to keep people informed, and I beg her to be careful. Then, knowing my time could be limited, I log off the Dynasaur site and I call home.

While Astrid pings my father, I see myself in the small subscreen. Pink hair. Green eyes. I look nothing like the Thalia my father knows and without my locator on, there's no way for him to know it's me. I worry that he won't pick up when this stranger from a strange place calls, but he does and as soon as his face fills the screen, I burst into tears. "Daddy, it's me. It's Thalia."

He looks gaunt and tired with deep lines across his forehead. "Thalia?" he says and I hear the skepticism in his voice. "Is that you?"

"Yes!" I pull myself together. "It's me. It's really me."

My mom jostles into the picture. Her skin is ashen and her jaw is tight. For the first time in years, I miss her like I used to when I was little and she'd go away on business. When she would walk in the door, dead tired, I'd throw myself at her, relieved to be in her arms again, even if her hugs were tepid. She scans my features, looking for some sign that it's really me. "Do you think it's her?" she asks my dad.

"It's me, you have to believe me," I implore them, "I know I look crazy but so much has happened and . . ."

"It certainly sounds like her," Dad says, still studying my face.

I rack my brain for something to convince them, some litany of facts like the ones Basil recited to his mother, but suddenly my screen goes black. "Dad!" I yell. "Mom?"

I can hear them in the background, but I can no longer see them. "Do you think it was her?" asks my mom.

"I don't know," Dad admits, choking up. "Where could she be?"

"I'm here!" I call to them desperately. "I'm right here."

Then the sound goes dead. Slowly an image appears. Fuzzy at first, but then it sharpens and I see Ahimsa staring at me. "Hello, Thalia," she says calmly.

I gasp and back up into the tree. "But . . . how . . . but . . ." I shake my Gizmo as if I'll be able to loosen her from my screen.

"I see you've changed your hair," she says. "I liked it better natural."

"What do you want?" I ask. "How did you get on here? Where are my parents?"

She raises an eyebrow at me. "Come on, a smart girl like you must be able to figure out how I did this. Especially with all those hacking skills, HectorProtector. Cute," she says. "But I'm not sure your grandfather would be flattered."

I ignore her dig. "You knew HP was me?"

She rolls her eyes. "Even before you announced it to the world. I had my best security agent working on it, after all."

This takes me a second to piece together, but then I inhale sharply and whisper, "My dad?"

She nods and leans back, letting his betrayal sink in as she slowly twists from side to side in her office chair. I remember twirling myself in circles many times in that chair when I was little. "I must admit," she tells me. "Even I was surprised. I never saw that one coming. You were such a good kid. I had high hopes for you at One World. Wonder where we went wrong?"

This makes me mad. I stand up and shout. "I wouldn't work for you if . . . if . . . if . . ."

"If what?" she asks. "Your life depended on it?" She laughs. "Funny, because it kind of does, doesn't it?"

"What's that supposed to mean?" I snarl.

She leans forward and gets her beaky face as close to the camera as she can. "I'm tired of playing this little game with you, Thalia. You're causing big problems for us. For our bottom line. For your family. You think you've uncovered some big secret . . ."

I grab a handful of leaves. "Like this!" I shout and shove the leaves in front of the camera. "You've been lying for years."

Ahimsa's face tightens. "It's just not that simple. Even if there is food out here, it's not enough to feed the world. You have no idea what it was like when the food supply diminished. The hoarding. The wars. The famine. Watching children die. Your parents and I promised ourselves that we would do everything we could to make sure that never happened again."

I toss the leaves in the air. "You're lying right now! I know about the children born illegally. How you don't feed them. You're not *saving* anyone!"

For a moment she falters but then she regains her composure. "The system might not be perfect, but it would be irresponsible to pretend that we can go back to the way life once was. If we did, war would break out again and only the richest would survive. We've found an acceptable solution for the greater good. Believing that is the most compassionate thing you can do."

"No," I say. "You've been hiding this so you could keep people under your thumb and make a profit."

She snorts. "Don't be so naive, little girl. Profit makes the world . . ."

"What do you want from me, Ahimsa?"

She cocks her head to the side. "Oh dear, I'm no longer Auntie Ahimsa to you?"

"You never were," I say. "Why did you hijack my call to my parents?"

She half smiles. "Anybody else who pulled the shenanigans you have, would be dead by now."

Her words send a sick ripple through my guts.

"But I've known you since you were born, and your parents are like siblings to me, so I'm trying to help you save yourself. Your restitution for all the crimes you've committed has been set extraordinarily high."

"You twist reality."

She shrugs and continues. "So high in fact, that your parents won't be able to meet it. They'll try of course, but they'll ruin themselves in the process. Not to mention lose their prominent positions at One World because of the stain on their reputations from your behavior."

My chest tightens and I find it hard to breathe. I've known this but haven't allowed myself to think about it until she puts it so bluntly. "What do you want from me?"

She folds her hands and stares hard. "Come back. Turn yourself in. Admit that you've been wrong. I'll get the restitution reduced and cover it. Then we'll lock you up in some chic rehab facility in another population center, where we'll treat you for your genetic flaw. I'll even let your mom work on your case. She'll find a cure; you'll come home. It'll be a sweet story. The public will eat it up."

"What about the others? The protesters? What about Basil?" I ask, breathless.

"They'll be treated fairly."

"I don't believe you," I tell her. This clearly makes her mad. She sets her jaw and looks to the side. "Now that you killed Ana, you need another scapegoat," I say.

She nearly hops out of her chair as she jabs her finger at the camera. "You better start cooperating right now. Don't think I can't find you. One snap of my fingers and we'll pluck you out of that forest so fast. . . ."

The screen goes black before she finishes her sentence.

"There!" I hear my dad say. "I think I fixed it." A new fuzzy image comes on my screen. "Thalia?" he yells. "Thalia, can you hear me?"

"Dad!" I yell back. "I'm here!" He and my mom stare at me again. "Ahimsa hijacked your call," I tell them.

"Ahimsa?" Dad asks, bewildered.

"She threatened me. Told me to turn myself in and . . ."

"Don't do that," my mom warns.

"What?" I sputter in disbelief.

"Listen to me," Mom says. "We don't have much time. Things have gotten bad here. You need to stay away. I've been doing a lot of research, and I think I'm beginning to understand what needs to happen, but One World's not going to like it. Promise me you'll go someplace safe until we can get to you."

"But I . . . I . . . I don't even know where I am," I admit. "And Ahimsa said . . ." From the distance I hear shouts. "Oh no!" I cry, fearing that my signal has somehow allowed Ahimsa to keep her promise.

"Thalia," Mom says to me.

"I have to go!"

"Wait!" she says. I look into the camera too afraid to move. "I want you to know, I don't think you're crazy, and I know you didn't do all those things Ahimsa has accused you of," she tells me. "I'm on your side," my mother says.

The shouting in the distance gets louder. I'm afraid they've gotten to Basil.

"We will help you!" my father calls as I throw my Gizmo to the ground and run.

⚘   ⚘   ⚘

I charge down the path toward the heaven and hell archways. I have to get to Basil. The entire area is probably crawling with security agents who've been looking for us all night. Somehow Ahimsa was able to zero in on my signal. At the end of the path, I skid to a stop on the moist ground when I hear loud voices.

I push into the kudzu curtained trees beside the path to hide. Tendrils from the vines wrap around me as if they too want to pull me down. I feel like I'm inside one of Grandma's knotted balls of yarn. I creep forward, carefully unraveling vines, so I don't snap a twig or rustle the leaves. Being barefoot makes it easier to tread softly, but my limp makes it hard not to stumble. I quickly realize that I have to stop moving or I'll give myself away. Instead, I peer through the lacy pattern in the undergrowth at the group of people surrounding the place where Basil and I wrestled for berries less than an hour ago.

Two men bend down, touching the ground where our bodies matted the green foliage. My heart pounds so loudly in my ears that I'm sure they will hear me. I count the people. Five, no six, half are women. Some carry huge curved blades on poles slung over their shoulders. Others carry coarsely woven bags on their backs. They are the strangest security agents I've ever seen, but I figure they are bounty hunters from the Outer Loop who've come to take us back, dead or alive.

"Please, please," I mutter, begging some invisible force to make sure Basil has seen them and hidden.

The men stand up. They talk in low voices, pointing in different directions. The discussion gets heated. They gesture at one another and grimace, but I can't make out what they're saying. One of the women steps between them and shouts, but her words are lost to the wind.

Not far from me, something crashes through the kudzu. I wrench around trying to find where it's coming from, then watch in horror as Basil rushes out from the brambles, squinting against the sun. "Apple!" he yells as he runs blindly toward the people. "What's happening? Are you okay?"

❖   ❖   ❖

In the time it takes the group to draw their weapons, surround Basil, throw him to the ground, and shout in his face, I have to make a decision. It must take no longer than a minute or two. They stand him up roughly, form a circle around him, curved blades on each side, so he can't run. I know in that time I have to choose. I can either turn myself in with the hope that Ahimsa will keep her word to go easy on me and treat Basil fairly or I can, for once, listen to my mother. The choice isn't easy. I'm not sure who I can trust, but my mind crystallizes around one single intention. I must, at all costs, protect Basil.

I stay hidden in the underbrush and follow the group as carefully and quietly as I can. They walk toward the heaven and hell archways and pass within a few feet of me. I'm confused about why they aren't going in the other direction, out of the park and toward the river.

Surely, there are no prisons out this far. Then they take the path through the woods that I abandoned, and I realize that they must be looking for me. I follow at a distance, but when they pass the place where I tossed my Gizmo, they walk by without slowing down or commenting.

Camouflaged in the twisted vines, I pursue them for what seems like miles. Sometimes I can hear them talking, but I'm too far away to know what they're saying. Anytime kudzu has grown close to the edge of the trail, one of them hacks it with a curved blade. Then, as suddenly as they slipped into the woods, they leave the trail. When they are all off the path, I sneak up close to the opening, which emerges into a clearing surrounded by a ring of strange low buildings with rough brown walls and woven roofs. This place certainly isn't a city, and it doesn't look like a prison or a settlement or even a geophag camp, yet clearly people live here.

Two men peel off from the group and shuffle Basil inside one of the buildings. I settle myself on the ground where I can lurk in the shadows of the vines. I'm exhausted from everything that's happened, and my feet are sore from tramping around barefoot and my ankle still hurts, so I'm grateful for the rest and a chance to make a plan. Hours pass. People come and go from the buildings and my eyes grow heavy. As the sun passes overhead and begins to descend, I let myself drift off, figuring it will be better to be well rested so when the opportunity presents itself, I can slip inside and find Basil.

⚮   ⚮   ⚮

A loud, fierce growl startles me awake. I flail in the kudzu, frantically trying to find the snarling beast that must be coming toward me. Images of angry giants and slithering snakes flash through my mind. I hear the growl again and realize that it's my own stomach making that terrible noise, but by then it's too late.

"It's in here!" someone shouts.

"What is it?"

Sharp claws slice through the vines where I've gotten myself tangled in a panic. A hand reaches in and grabs me by the back of the neck.

"I've got it!" someone yells.

"No!" I howl as I'm hauled from my hiding place onto the path. I look up into three faces bent over me. Their blades are raised. "Please don't!" I scream and cover my head.

The people gasp.

"It's her!" one says.

"You sure?"

"Who else could it be?"

"Gaia will be thrilled."

They haul me to my feet. I writhe around and try to break free from their grip, but they have me tight.

"Hey, calm down," one of them says.

I look into her face. She smiles cruelly.

"Let me go!" I yell.

"We won't hurt you," she says as they drag me toward the building. I hang my head in shame. I should have never fallen asleep because that blew my chance to save Basil and now we're both in custody.

When we get inside the building I hear him calling, "Apple! Apple, is it really you?"

"Basil!" I yell back.

He careens around a corner and rushes for me.

The people let me go and I run into Basil's arms. "I'm sorry," I wail. "It's my fault!"

"You're here! They found you!" He sounds relieved.

I look up at him. "I didn't mean for them to," I tell him through my tears. "I was going to rescue you. Get us both out of here." I cling to his shirt, which is brown and scratchy. "But I . . ."

Basil holds me at arm's length and laughs. This stops me cold. "No, don't you see?" he asks me. "This is it, Apple. This is truly it!"

"This is what?" I ask, looking around, angry at all the people who've gathered to watch our arrest.

Basil smiles. "The Farm!" Then he hugs me tight. "We're home. We made it."

Just as I'm trying to wrap my mind around what he's saying, the crowd parts and in walks a woman wearing a pristine white jumpsuit cinched at the waist with a bright green belt under a long flowing blue robe the color of the sky. "Is this the girl?" she asks with her arms wide open.

"Yes!" one of the women who found me says eagerly.

Basil wraps his arm around my shoulder and presents me. "Gaia," he says proudly, "this is Apple, er um, Thalia. This is Thalia."

"Oh my dear!" She glides toward me then wraps me in her embrace. She is soft and smells strongly of lavender, like the soap my grandmother uses. She takes my hands and steps back to get a good look at me. After studying me for a moment while I blink and blink, trying to understand what's going on, she says in nearly a whisper, "You are beautiful." I think I see a few tears glistening on her eyelashes. "Just lovely exactly as Basil said." She pulls my hands to her mouth and kisses my knuckles. I feel myself blushing from all the attention, but still, I'm so bewildered that my head begins to throb.

"We've been waiting for you and are so happy that you're here," she tells me. Then she hugs me tight again and says, "Welcome, darling. Welcome home!"

PART 4

THE FARM

"A man bears beliefs as a tree bears apples."
—Ralph Waldo Emerson

I shower in an outdoor stall with an open roof looking up into kudzu-covered trees. There's a hand pump that draws icy water up from the ground into a bucket. I hesitate, wishing there was a way to warm it up, but I can't be too picky. This is the first time in my life I've been dirty enough to actually need a shower, and to be honest, I kind of like the feeling. I go ahead and douse half the bracing-cold water over me then scrub with a thick cake of soap the same color as the kudzu leaves. When I'm clean, I find my underwear, damp but freshly washed, hanging on a peg in a little curtained area outside the shower. The shirt I took from Basil's mom's house is missing. In its place is a shapeless dress made of scratchy brown fabric that all the women except Gaia wear, plus woven sandals that feel good on my tender feet and help support my sore ankle, which is still a bit swollen and discolored.

I've never cared much about what I wear, but I find it slightly embarrassing to leave the stall dressed in a sack. Yaz would die if she had to wear this. I think of the video she made from PlugIn 42 in her fuzzy purple jumpsuit, declaring herself the chronicler of the revolution. I wonder if she's broadcast any more political PRCs?

I search for my pouch but can't find it anywhere. Hesitantly, I peek out from behind the curtain. The girl who's been assigned to take care of me is about my age and hugely pregnant. She sits on a bench, swinging her feet, waiting.

"Hi, um, do you know what happened to my stuff?" I ask her.

"The shirt?"

"Actually,"—I step out fully—"I'm looking for a little bag." She blinks at me. "It's red. Knit. About this big." She shakes her head. "It's really important to me."

"Was there something in it?"

"No," I admit, since I tossed my Gizmo into the never-ending kudzu. "It's just that my grandmother made it for me and . . ."

"Oh," she says, completely unsympathetic. "All fabric gets recycled."

"But it was mine," I say. She cocks her head as if that word is foreign and I get it. I'm acting like a privy. There is no *mine* here.

Basil saunters up, looking like an old-fashioned mountain man in his earthy brown shirt and pants.

"We match," I say, pointing from my clothes to his.

He smiles. "It's great, isn't it? No fashion slaves around here!"

I can't tell whether he's being serious or sarcastic.

"Ready?" the girl stands, seeming impatient to get on with her day.

"For what?" I ask, but she doesn't answer. Basil offers me his elbow since I'm still limping, but I hesitate. "Is that your good arm?"

"It's fine now," he tells me. "How about you?"

I roll my foot around slowly. "Still stiff and sore," I admit. "But better than it was." I take his arm to steady myself so we can follow the girl through the bustling clearing.

Everyone we pass hauls big baskets of kudzu vines out of the woods or carries the stuff into the strange brown buildings that encircle the open area. Each building is an identical rectangle made of big blocks of dried vines, what my grandmother might call bales, that are stacked eight feet high under peaked roofs made of tightly woven mats. Even the kids, and there are a lot of them, are occupied in small groups. The littlest ones strip leaves from long vines, others sort the vines by size for the oldest kids, who smooth them with small knives then throw them into tubs of water to soak. Looking around, I'm beginning to suspect that everything here is made out of kudzu, including my itchy, ugly dress.

"Over there are the fields where the farmers grow the crops," the girl says, motioning vaguely toward the kudzu that grows fifty feet to our left beyond the buildings. "And on the other side is where the gatherers go out into the woods to catalogue and collect what's already growing naturally." She tosses her hand in the general direction of the kudzu growing beyond the other side of the encampment. From the air this place must look like a bald patch with brown tufts in the midst of endless green.

"Which are you?" I ask. "A farmer or a gatherer?"

"Neither." She steals a sideways glance at me. "I do domestic work for Gaia. Cook. Clean. Whatever she needs. Over there is the pump house and the latrines." She points to three long narrow buildings along the edge of the clearing.

"What's a latrine?" I ask.

"For when you have to relieve yourself," she says.

"You mean pee?"

"Yes," she says slowly, "and for when you start to, you know . . . defecate."

"Defecate?" I wrack my brain for the meaning of this word. "Ohhhh," I say when it finally dawns on me. "Really?"

Basil cracks up. He laughs so hard his cheeks get flushed.

"Yes, really," is all the girl says. She keeps walking, pointing at more identical buildings every ten feet. "That's where the builders work. The seamstresses are in there. Weavers work in here."

"What's that?" I hesitate near a larger, airier structure with big open windows beneath the roof.

"Dining hall!" Basil grins at me. "It's where everyone eats together."

"You mean meals?" I try to imagine sitting at a table passing food like Grandma Apple has described so many times. Basil nods. "And where's the school?" I ask eagerly.

The girl shakes her head. "Gaia says, 'We learn through working.'"

"What about the kids?" I ask. "How do they learn to read?"

She half glances over her shoulder at me. "You ask a lot of questions."

"Well," I tell her, "there's a lot to learn, don't you think?"

She looks straight ahead again. "Gaia says, 'Learn by doing not by asking.'"

Her words sting and I get the point so I stop pestering her.

When we come to a fork where two paths lead out of the clearing, I look back over my shoulder. The whole encampment—from the communal housing on the far end to the work buildings in the center and the dining hall at this end—is no more than a hundred feet wide and a half mile long. "It's amazing how much is packed into this little area," I say.

"There's more," the girl says. "Down there are the harvest house and hospital." She points to the right.

"That's an interesting combination," I whisper to Basil.

"Maybe they'll have something for your leg," he says.

"And this way?" I point left.

"That's where Gaia lives," she says. "Come."

She leads us to a building that's different than all the others. This place looks like something from the photos of my grandparent's farm, a proper old-fashioned house made of brick with real glass windows.

"Does Gaia have a large family?" I ask since this place is bigger than every building but the dining hall.

The girl considers this then says, "We are her family."

"But she gets this whole place to herself?" I get an unfamiliar twinge in my gut. Jealousy perhaps?

"The dear doctor stays here when he visits."

"Who?"

She hesitates with her hand on the front doorknob, but she doesn't answer and I get the hint. I'm asking too many questions again.

Inside, I stare wide-eyed and open-mouthed as we pass through a living room with high ceilings and plush furniture into a sunny room. "You can sit there." She points to a long wooden table with benches on either side and one large, puffy chair covered in soft yellow fabric. Nothing here is made of kudzu. The girl pushes through swinging double doors at the far end. A puff of warm scented air escapes. The smell makes my stomach growl. I hunch over and cross my arms over my gut.

Basil reaches out and massages my shoulder. "You don't have to be embarrassed about that here." He pulls out the bench for us. "You're going to like this."

I wish I could be as relaxed as he is, but for some reason that I can't pinpoint, I feel cagey.

The girl comes through the doors again, this time carrying a tray with two steaming bowls. As she sets a bowl and spoon in front of each of us, I catch her staring sideways at me, but she quickly walks away before I can thank her.

Just as I'm about to ask what's in my bowl, Gaia bursts through the swinging doors, her long blue robe swirling behind. "Your first meal ever!" she announces and drapes herself across the puffy yellow chair. "Can you believe it?"

I stare at the cloudy liquid, unsure what to say.

"It's a lovely kudzu broth," Gaia tells me. "We have to start you with something simple. Let your digestive track learn to work with solid food. Plus, your palate isn't very sophisticated because your whole life you've only known the sweet and slightly salty taste of synthetic nutrition." She makes a face. "Ugh, horrid stuff, really. The world holds so many more flavors." She beams at us. "And now that you're here with me, I will give them to you! Dig in, before it gets cold."

I dunk my spoon in the bowl then slurp some of the broth.

"What do you think?" Gaia asks.

"Delicious!" says Basil, spooning more into his mouth.

It doesn't have much flavor as far as I can tell. Mostly like slurping warmer, saltier Synthamil, but I suppose if I had to fight for everything I'd ever eaten like Basil has, then having someone hand me a bowl of this stuff might seem amazing.

"You're taking to this life quite quickly," Gaia says, watching us eat. "Many people who come here are scared at first. Most of them have been punished severely for ingesting anything other than Synthamil. It's deeply engrained in them that real food will somehow hurt them. They resist or try to eat in secret for fear they'll be breaking the law."

"Aren't we, though?" I ask after taking another bite. "Breaking the law, I mean."

Gaia's face hardens. "What law?"

"UNPA," I say. "The Universal Nutrition . . ."

"The law of greed?" she says bitterly. "Of corporate oppression dictated by the cult of money? No thank you! Here we follow only the laws of Mother Nature."

Basil nods in agreement.

"And One World doesn't bother you?" I ask.

Gaia tosses her head back and laughs long and hard. "One World would love to get their hands on me. I'm public enemy number one. They've been after me ever since I left." She looks at us and raises an eyebrow provocatively. "In another life, I was an executive there, you know. When I left, I caused such an uproar." She holds our gaze, letting this info sink in.

Basil is rapt, but I have questions. I wonder if she knows my parents or Ahimsa and why I've never heard of her if she was a higher-up at OW, but then I think it might not be in my best interest to point out what a privy I am. "So One World doesn't know you're here?" I ask instead.

Gaia raises her chin and grins knowingly. "Oh, you're very smart, Dehlia."

"Thalia," I say, but she doesn't seem to notice.

"Do they know where I am or"—she smiles slyly—"do they keep their distance?" She holds my gaze long enough for me to feel uncomfortable. I look away and she keeps talking.

"There was a time when I bought into the whole enterprise in the Loops. Like everyone else, I was sure One World held the answers to saving humankind as they claim. Of course, the mind-numbing drugs they pump you full of make it nearly impossible to break free from those beliefs so deeply entrenched from the time your umbilical cord is replaced with a network connection!" She snorts at her own joke. "Unless you're very, very strong, like me. I could see through their lies. To me the truth was as transparent as that pane of glass." She points to the large, deep-set window looking out into the lush kudzu forest. "I know what they're up to," she says, hunching closer to us. "And if I wanted to . . . I could destroy them!" She slams her hands on the table, making our spoons jump as she shouts.

I lean far away, not sure if she's crazy or kind of awesome.

"Don't be frightened, my love." She says with a gentle chuckle. "I am here to protect you. Like a mother tiger—a large prowling cat—fierce in my devotion to my cubs. But you wouldn't understand that animal instinct because you are not yet of nature. It will come, though. It will come." She sits back and studies us. "You two are quite lucky. Do you know that?"

"So lucky that you found us," gushes Basil. "We could have been wandering around for weeks. . . ."

"Yes, obviously, but beyond that," Gaia says, waving away his gratitude. "Lucky that you found one another first." She folds her hands and cocks her head to the right. "I watched the way you reunited. You are very attracted to one another, aren't you?"

Blood rushes to my cheeks and I look away.

"Don't be embarrassed! It's perfectly normal to feel that way at your age. You're supposed to have strong passions." I peer up at her, cautiously hopeful, and see pity flash across her face then a kind smile. "I can see from your eyes that someone told you it was wrong to feel this way about another person. Or maybe about each other in particular? Someone tried to keep you two apart, didn't they?"

Basil and I look at each other, wondering how she could know so much about us.

Gaia stands up and walks behind our chairs. She lays a hand on each of our shoulders. "But you two, against all odds, found each other. Star-crossed lovers, I think!" She leans between us. "Pyramus and Thisbe! Romeo and Juliet! Tristan and Isolde! Cathy and Heathcliffe!" she whispers these names from long-forgotten novels I've plucked off Grandma's bookshelves. Gaia stands and slowly circles the table. "You two just might be the luckiest people in all the world. Who else could claim to fall in love naturally then run away and end up here where you can live freely, loving whomever you choose, starting a family, being part of the new world that I have created on the Farm? Who else?" She answers her own question in a grave whisper, "No one."

Gaia settles on the windowsill. The sun streaming through the panes of glass highlights the long graying curls around her face. "Nowhere else in the world would this be possible," she tells us. "If you were to go back, they would surely separate you. Pump you full of mood stabilizers and antipsychotics and appetite suppressants to deaden your feelings. Tell you that your desires are illegal, immoral, detrimental to the whole of society. You would be demonized. Locked up. Forgotten. It's truly a miracle that I found you. And for that we should thank Mother Nature." She closes her eyes and lifts her chin as she turns to bask in the sun filtering through the window.

For a moment, I am completely enthralled by her story. She's right. Or at least partly. I might not feel lucky given all that's happened to us over the past few days, and I'm not sure what Mother Nature has to do with it, but I am relieved to be with Basil again and not on the run. It's true that I'd much rather be here than trapped like fugitives or sent back to rehab or worse, prison, but some of what she's saying doesn't sit well with me. I look at Basil. He's got his eyes closed like Gaia, as if he's communing with Mother Nature, too. She seems to think we'll be staying here for a long time, but I want her to understand that this is only temporary. "Gaia," I say, "you know . . ."

Her eyes pop open and she asks, "Delilah, dear, when was your last menses?"

"Excuse me?" I choke on my words and wonder who Delilah is.

"Your menses. Your period. The monthly curse, which is actually a blessing," she says with a laugh.

My cheeks burn bright. "I'm only seventeen. I haven't entered the Procreation Pool yet so my hormones haven't been adjusted for that,"

I mumble, embarrassed to be talking about such things in front of Basil. "And my name—"

"Ah, I see," she says, cutting me off. "When was your last inoculation?"

"About three months ago. Why?" I ask, wondering what business it is of hers.

"Mm-hm." She nods. "So in about three more months the hormone suppressants will be out of your system, and you'll begin menarche."

I squirm, hating this conversation. Having a stranger talk about my period in front of Basil is worse than having my mother talk about my genetic flaw to Dr. Demeter. I'm so self-conscious that I can't find the words to tell her that I won't be here in three months.

"Oh, don't be embarrassed!" Gaia exclaims and rushes to my side. She leans down and hugs me around the shoulder. I sit stiffly in her arms, wishing she would stop. "It's such a beautiful thing. We'll have a special festival to mark the occasion. Everyone will celebrate you! You will be on a pedestal with ribbons in your hair."

I can literally think of nothing worse. Prison, maybe?

"And then." Gaia slings one leg over the bench so she's facing me. She gathers my hands in hers. "You will bestow the most amazing gifts."

I stare at her, completely confused. "I don't know what you're talking about."

She reaches out and lays her hand on my belly. "Your monthly contribution," she says with glistening eyes.

I flinch and pull away from her touch.

She rises and walks to Basil's side. "And don't think I've forgotten about you, my beautiful boy." She reaches out to stroke his cheek. "You have much to give, too."

He peers up at her with adoration. Similar to the way I saw him look at Ana but even more enthralled, which worries me. Especially because something in Gaia's demeanor—the way her fingers linger around his jawbone as she looks him up and down hungrily—makes my skin crawl.

"I'd really like to contact my family," I say quickly. "They should know that I'm okay and . . ."

Gaia slowly turns. She stands over me and shakes her head. "We're your family now, dear."

I feel the blood drain from my face and I get woozy.

"Now then," she says, heading toward the double doors. "I'm going to leave you two lovebirds alone. Finish your soup. Ella will bring you some lovely tea. So good for the tummy. Then we'll find a job for each of you, because everyone must earn his or her keep. Remember, there's no charity at the Farm."

❦ ❦ ❦

When Gaia is gone I whip around and latch onto Basil's arm. "Did you hear that?"

"She's completely amazing, isn't she?" he says, barely looking up from his soup, which he's plunged back into.

"No! I mean, she's certainly interesting. But some of that was weird, don't you think?"

"She can see into our hearts," he says as if it's a fact.

"No she can't."

"How else would she have known your parents were trying to keep us apart?"

"She didn't know that," I point out. "She made a general guess about why we ran away, which is probably pretty obvious when you think about it. A guy and a girl showing up together. . . ."

Basil shakes his head.

"And what the heck is my monthly contribution?" I can't even say it without blushing. "Or saying we're going to start a family! Or calling me Dehlia and Delilah? Does she even know who I am?"

"Just because everybody from the Inner Loop knows your family..."

"That's not what I meant," I snap, but my face grows warm because he's sort of right.

"Look," he says more gently. "There are probably two hundred people who live here, and she's not good with names. Big deal." He looks at my half-empty bowl. "Are you going to eat that?"

"No, I'm not hungry anymore." I push it away. "Was she part of the Analogs? Had you heard of her before?"

"No. It's crazy, isn't it? She's been here the whole time and we had no idea. If I had known about this place earlier...." He eyes my bowl.

I push my broth toward him and he digs in. "But doesn't any of what she said freak you out? Just a little? She thinks we're going to be here long enough to have a kid together!"

This gets his attention. "She just means if we want to. Eventually."

"I'm not so sure," I say, thinking about all the girls my age walking through the clearing. At least a quarter of them looked pregnant. "There are a lot of little kids running around this place."

He grins, a bit embarrassed. "I think that's what happens, Apple, when people don't have inocs and Synthamil."

"Obviously, I know that, but I don't want it to happen to us. At least not yet."

"I don't even want kids," he says as he scrapes up the last bit of liquid from my bowl.

This surprises me almost as much as Gaia saying that we should start a family. "Really? Never?"

"And end up like my parents?"

"Not all parents are that bad," I tell him. "Look at my family...."

"Yeah, look at yours," Basil says with a snort. "They stuck you in rehab then put a price on my head."

"Yeah, but . . ." I try to protest.

"How's that any different than what my mom did?"

"Because my parents thought they were doing the best thing for me."

"Are you joking? You were the first one to admit they were covering their own asses so One World wouldn't look bad."

"But—"

"These people saved us," he says, angrily. "We could have wandered around for days or weeks or months. Or we could be in prison by now because of your family. We should be grateful that Gaia welcomed us with open arms."

"Open arms? They hauled you out of the woods like you were a criminal. I saw the whole thing."

"They have to be careful. People come out here and steal the kudzu."

"Like there's not enough!" I say.

"What if I'd been a One World agent?"

"But you don't have the whole picture. Things have changed in the Loops and some of what's going on here is strange."

"Look, Apple." He turns to face me. "You've only been running for days. But it's been my whole life." Color rises to his cheeks and his eyes burn bright. "Most people here are seconds, just like me. We've lived in fear. Hiding from security. Never knowing where our next Synthamil would come from."

"I know," I tell him. "That's why we should go back and fight to change that system because there are other seconds like you and people who are hungry like me. Like us."

He shakes his head. "I've spent my life fighting a system that killed my brother and doesn't care whether I live or die, but you didn't. Now finally my life can be easy."

I look down, ashamed.

"I know this is a big change for you." He reaches for my hand. "But for the first time in my life, I don't have to worry or constantly check my back anymore. I'm sure if you give it a chance, you'll see how wonderful it is. Gaia loves us. All of us."

I shake my head.

"She sent a search party for you after they found me. They could have left you out there, but they didn't."

"I know," I mumble.

"And I was so relieved when they brought you in." He wraps his arms around me and pulls me close. "I couldn't imagine being here without you." When he bends down and kisses my forehead, I almost feel the dopamine squirting into my brain, melting away all the reasons I want to leave. "Please give this place a chance," he asks. "For me."

I snake my arms around his waist and drink in his scent. For those few seconds, part of me thinks he could be right. Then the girl called Ella pushes through the doors with another tray. When she sees us embracing, she stumbles, rattling the cups, and slopping hot liquid onto her fingers. She yelps and drops the tray, splattering its contents across the floor.

"Are you okay?" I grab a rag from the table and kneel down to sop up the tea.

"I'm fine," she says as she gathers broken cup shards.

"Let me see your hands." I reach for her to make sure she's not burned or cut.

As I hold her hands in mine, I don't look for marks on her skin. Instead, I stare into her innocent brown eyes and at her round cheeks and realize that she's very young. "How old are you?" I whisper.

She pulls away, sitting back on her heels. "Fifteen."

I suck in air and point at her belly, which extends over her thighs. "But . . . but . . . but . . ."

She lifts her chin in defiance. "But what?"

"Are you . . . ? Is that . . . ?"

She cradles her belly in her hands. "I hope this one's a girl," she says shyly. "I've already given a little boy."

"Given?" I'm flabbergasted and before I can stop myself, I blurt out, "Why?"

"Because." Ella places the broken cups on the tray. "Gaia says, 'Mother Nature wanted it to be so.'" She heaves herself up to stand. "I'll make more tea."

When she's gone through the double doors, I get off the floor and look at Basil. "Now you can't tell me this place is normal," I say in a hushed shout. "That girl is fifteen and going on her second baby."

"Maybe that's what she wants," Basil says with an unconcerned shrug.

"No," I say. "Nobody would want that if they had a choice."

He grabs my hand. "Apple," he says. "You're not even trying."

I drop down to the bench with a heavy sigh. "I don't know if I can."

"Don't say that," he begs.

"Look Basil, at the very least, I have to let my parents know where I am."

He shakes his head with disgust.

I stare down at my hands, trying to find a way to explain, but then Ella comes back with more tea. She sets the tray on the table.

"Gaia says to drink this. Then I'll show you to your work squads."

"Work squads?" I ask. "But you don't even know what we can do."

"Gaia knows," Ella says, busily exchanging the soup bowls for the teacups.

"How?" I ask. Ella doesn't answer. I try to catch Basil's eye, but he'll no longer look at me.

⚘   ⚘   ⚘

Despite being separated from Basil and stuck in a strange sparse cabin with eight girls I've never met, I sleep well that night. I'm so exhausted I would probably sleep fine on a rock. Since I have an actual bed, I wake up more refreshed than I've felt in days, and I can't wait to find Basil. But Shiloh and Wren, the girls who share the three-level bunk bed with me, have a different plan. They drag me off for the morning routine as soon as they open their eyes.

In the latrine, I notice a stack of small plastic cups with screw-top lids beside the circular hole cut in a wooden bench where we take turns relieving ourselves. When I'm washing up at a communal sink, one girl after another carries out a cup of her own urine. They take turns writing a long number on the sides of the cups with a pencil, then they place the cups on a tray sitting by the door.

When Shiloh comes out of the stall carrying hers, I say, "Was I supposed to pee in a cup?" fearing that urine shouldn't go down the hole.

"Did Gaia tell you to provide a sample?" she asks.

"Well, no."

"Then there's your answer."

"But why do you pee in the cup?" I ask.

Shiloh blinks at me as if she doesn't understand my question, then she says, "Because Gaia told me to."

I almost laugh thinking about how my grandmother used to say, *If Yaz told you to jump off a bridge, would you?* Clearly, here the answer is *Yes*. If Gaia tells you to pee in a cup, you pee in a cup.

As we leave the latrine and head toward the dining hall, a woman walks out of the pump house. A little breeze catches the door and holds it open for a few seconds so that I get a glimpse inside. What I see startles me and I quickly look away embarrassed. By the time I look back, someone has slammed the door, and I wonder if my eyes were playing tricks on me.

"Were all the women in there half naked?" I ask Shiloh and Wren.

They answer me with frowns. "Because it looked like they weren't wearing tops. Not even bras!" This makes me giggle. "What exactly are they doing in there?"

"How would we know?" Shiloh asks.

"Only mothers work in there," Wren adds. "And we aren't mothers yet."

"Gaia says, There's a reason for everything, but not every reason is for us to know," Shiloh adds.

Right, I think. If Gaia tells you to go in the pump house and take off your shirt, you go in the pump house and take off your shirt. This place is getting stranger by the minute.

⚘   ⚘   ⚘

In the dining hall, while we have our morning ration of kudzu soup and a strangely sweet, cloudy tea, I look everywhere for Basil, but I can't find him. When I ask, Wren tells me he probably ate during an earlier shift since the dining hall can't hold everyone at once. I realize then that I have no idea where he sleeps or what job he does, so I can't go in search of him after the morning meal. Instead, I follow my bunk mates from the dining hall. I'll have to ask around for him later.

We take the right-hand path out of the main clearing and stop in front of a building that's modern and sleek, made of metal and glass. No kudzu here. "Is this the hospital or the harvest house?" I ask.

"Both," says Wren.

"Do you think I could get a brace or a steroid injection for my ankle?" I ask as we enter through the front door.

Wren looks at me bewildered.

"I sprained it," I tell her.

She looks away as if none of this computes.

"Can you at least tell me where the doctor is?" I ask.

"He won't be here until the harvest," Shiloh tells me. Then she introduces me to a freckled worker named Bex who looks like her belly is about to pop and a quiet girl named Leeda whose bump is barely showing beneath her dress. "You've been assigned to help them," Shiloh says and leaves.

"Are you nurses?" I ask the girls.

Bex bursts out laughing. "Hardly!" she says. "Come on. We've got a lot to do."

We change into freshly washed blue hospital scrubs in a small dressing room near the back of the building. I never thought I would be in heaven wearing Cottonyle, but the fabric feels luxurious against my skin after the scratchy kudzu of my dress. Bex also gives me a little blue cap and tells me to tuck my hair up inside. I follow them to a clean, quiet lab with white tiled floors and walls and stainless steel surfaces, where they set to work processing pee samples that someone brought over from the latrine.

I like Bex immediately and am glad to have the company of someone chattier than Shiloh and Wren, who seem shocked every time I ask a question or make a comment. "Do you know how I would find someone here?" I ask Bex while we write down the number from each cup on a chart, dunk a strip of paper into the urine, then note the color that appears.

"Depends on who you're looking for," she says.

"The person I came with."

"That guy Basil?" She grins big. "You two ran away from the Loops together, didn't you?"

"News travels fast," I say, slightly embarrassed by what she already knows.

Bex pulls a strip from a cup. "Yeah, well, nothing much happens around here so when someone new shows up, it's kind of a big deal."

"How long have you been here?" I ask.

Bex puffs out her cheeks. "A while," is all she says.

"And did you come with someone?"

"There was a group of us. . . ."

"This is not appropriate conversation," Leeda snaps.

"Sorry," I say, stung by her disapproval. "I didn't mean to pry. I just want to find Basil—that's all."

Bex looks at me with sympathy. "You'll see him soon," she says and hands me a new tray of urine samples.

We work silently hunched over the pee cups for another ten minutes, then Bex stands up straight to stretch. "Ugh," she says holding her lower back.

"How far along are you?" I ask.

"Thirty-two weeks," she says. "And my back is killing me."

"Gaia says, 'Being a vessel is a gift from Mother Nature,'" says Leeda, barely above a whisper.

"Yeah, the gift that keeps on giving," Bex jokes. "Giving me gas, giving me hemorrhoids, giving me a fat ass! Plus, now this baby is hanging out on my bladder like it's his own personal water bed so I have to pee every fifteen minutes. If I run out of the door with my legs crossed, don't be surprised."

"Don't worry," I tell her. "I can cover for you if you need to go."

Leeda's head snaps up. "Gaia says, 'We must each earn our keep.'"

I've had just about enough of her. "So I can't offer to help someone?" I ask. "I thought this was supposed to be some kind of commune or something!"

"It's okay," Bex says as she pours urine samples into a large red bucket. "Leeda's right. I have to earn my keep like anyone else. 'There's no charity on the Farm.' Besides, I'm fine. Just complaining to pass the time."

"What are we doing, anyway?" I study the chart I've been filling out. "Checking nutrient levels?"

Bex just shrugs and continues dunking paper into pee. The crazy part is that dealing with the samples makes me miss my mom. I remember her saying the work you do when you start out as a scientist can be rote and boring—prepping experiments, reading results, entering data. But the excitement is in solving a problem in which each piece of data is part of the puzzle. Knowing that at the end you might be responsible for a major breakthrough makes it all worthwhile. Without knowing what I'm doing or why makes this work mindless, and I don't care for that.

When we're done with the pee, Leeda hauls one bucket out the door while Bex removes a tray of syringes from a refrigerated drawer and spreads them across a long table.

I pick one up but there's no label. "What's this for?"

Again she shrugs, but this time she says, "Just what the dear doctor ordered, I guess!"

"Who is this dear doctor I keep hearing about?"

"You'll meet him soon." She hands me a packet of antiseptic wipes.

"How soon?"

"During the full moon," she tells me, and I laugh, thinking she must be joking, but she looks at me quizzically and I realize that she's serious.

Before I can ask why he only comes out when the moon is full, Leeda sticks her head in the door from the hallway. "Ready?"

"Send them in," Bex says, then she turns to me. "You hand out the wipes and I'll do the syringes."

The door opens again, and a long line of girls quietly enters the room. One by one, they recite their numbers to Leeda, who makes a mark on the charts we've been filling out. Then the girls step up to the table. I hand out swab after swab and watch as the girls systematically lift their dresses, rub a clean spot on their skin, take a syringe from Bex, and jab themselves in the belly. Nobody speaks. Nobody flinches. When they're done, they drop their dresses, toss the used syringe in a blue bucket, and walk out of the room without a word.

Fifty girls must come through, including Wren and Shiloh, who pass by silently like everyone else. The whole thing takes less than fifteen minutes. When the room is empty again, I look at Bex and say, "Wow, that was . . . interesting."

"See how interesting you think it is after you do this four times a day for seven days straight. Gets dead boring if you ask me."

The last thing Leeda, Bex, and I do is clean up the lab. Once we've disposed of all the used syringes and wiped down the tables with disinfectant, Bex goes to lift the last red bucket of urine and grimaces.

"Hey," I say, rushing to her side. "Let me do that. You should rest. Put your feet up. Take it easy for a while. Make your husband do something nice for you tonight."

She bursts out laughing and puts the bucket down. "My husband?"

"Oh," I say embarrassed. "Sorry, I shouldn't have assumed, I mean, I thought . . . so you're not married?"

Bex continues to chuckle, but Leeda glowers at me. "Gaia says, 'Marriage is an outdated institution.'"

"But what about the baby's dad? Do you get to live with him?"

Bex swallows her laughter and shakes her head.

"That's so sad," I say. "Don't you miss him? Doesn't he want to be a part of the baby's life?"

"No need," says Bex. "The other mothers will help us when the time comes." She rubs her belly affectionately.

"But dads are so important," I say, and wonder how my dad is—if he's in trouble with Ahimsa for trying to help me, or if she's turned him against me? But that would never happen. My dad will always have my back. "I wish I could talk to my father," I say quietly.

Bex frowns like she's not sure what to make of me pining away for my dad. She nods to the bucket of pee. "You really going to take this out for me? I have to get to the kitchen soon."

"Of course I will," I say.

Bex directs me down the long corridor, past the dressing room, to the back door and tells me to dump the urine in the woods. When I go outside, it's quiet and peaceful. The kudzu has been cut back about twenty feet from the steps, so I take my time, wandering around under the canopy of trees. From a distance I hear something clanging, like metal against metal, and I wonder if a new building is being constructed.

When I come back inside, the hall is quiet and the lights inside the lab where we worked are out. I look inside the dressing room and see Bex and Leeda's scrubs folded neatly on a bench. I change into my scratchy dress, but rather than leave as I'm supposed to, I decide to pull a Yaz to see what I can find behind closed doors. I'm hoping for something to wrap my ankle and, if I'm lucky, maybe a screen so I can send a message to my family.

The first door I try opens easily, so I slip inside. The room is as stark and empty as the lab I've been working in all morning and the drawers only hold more plastic cups, syringes, and antiseptic wipes. I make my way down the hall, opening each door along the way, but every room is the same nondescript tile box, except for one where I can hear the hum of electrical equipment and see the faint glow of light emitted between the slats of blinds that cover the window. If there's a screen here, surely that's where it would be, but just my luck, the door is locked tight.

When I come outside, Shiloh waits for me in front of the hospital. "Come on," she says. "We're late."

"You go ahead," I tell her. "There's something else I need to do." I turn toward Gaia's house, determined to speak to my parents today.

She grabs my wrist and yanks me along with her. "If we're late, I'll be in trouble."

She drags me back to Collection House No. 4 in the main clearing, where Wren and five other women are strapping large baskets to their backs. Shiloh hands me one, then we follow Reba, our squad leader, into the woods.

"What are we doing? Where are we going?" I ask as I limp behind them.

As usual, Shiloh frowns at me.

"Can't you ever just follow along?" Wren asks.

"No," I tell her honestly.

She twists her face and looks away as if I've deeply offended her, but I don't care. If more people asked questions around here, maybe nobody would have to pee in cups and jab themselves in the belly with mystery drugs or have two kids at fifteen. Once I find Basil and tell him everything I've seen today, surely he'll concede there's something strange about this place.

Since no one will talk to me, I hang back marveling at the beauty around me. It's so lush and green. The air is like nothing I've ever breathed before. It feels crisp and clean, moist and pure. I raise my face toward the sky, letting the sun warm my skin as the faint scent of sweetness tickles my nose. It's like a place from my dreams, only it's real. In that moment, part of me can understand why Basil is so smitten.

Reba leads us off the main path to a smaller one, not cut, just trampled, and drops her basket. "This is our spot today," she says, consulting a hand-drawn map. She only looks a few years older than I am. She's tall with broad shoulders and fuzzy red hair that she pulls back into a messy knot, but she has a natural confidence that makes her easy to follow. The other girls in the group, Kiki, Jance, and Lu, look about the same age as Shiloh, Wren, and me. Only a woman named Enid appears older, with frown lines etched around her mouth and a few gray hairs spiraling from her scalp. When she takes the basket off her back, she stretches as if in pain.

"Come," says Shiloh. "We'll show you what to do."

I follow her and Wren into a thicket of kudzu. They drop their baskets. I do the same.

"There's a knife inside," Wren tells me. She's smaller than I am. Short and compact, but she moves fast, every motion like a quick jab.

I reach inside my basket and find the blade. I unsheathe it. "Good god." Sun glints off the shining surface. "That looks sharp!"

"Has to be," says Shiloh, who is as willowy as the vines and has eyes as green as the kudzu leaves. "Got to hack through this stuff. But be careful, it'll slice right through you, too."

They show me the best way to cut the vines then wrap them into coils and shove them in my basket. Although the work is tiring, I don't mind. For days, my brain has felt like one big jumble. I can't quite remember the order of events or how long I've been gone from home. But, the solitude of repetitive motion helps me unravel that knot. As I cut the vine, coil the vine, and stack the vine, I slowly go over everything that's happened to me in the past few days, trying to make sense of it all, and I wonder what the others have gone through to get here.

"So, Shiloh," I say, moving my basket closer to where she and Wren are working and chatting. "Where are you from?"

She scowls. "What do you mean?"

"I mean, where did you live before you came to the Farm? Are you from the Inner Loop or Outer Loop?"

She focuses on stuffing more vines into her basket. "Gaia says, 'Leave the past in the past.'"

"We can't totally leave our past behind, though," I say for arguments sake. "We're the sum of our experiences, don't you think? Like my Grandma Apple, she was a farmer so . . ."

"Brining up the past creates a false hierarchy," Wren huffs at me.

"Privies and workers. Firstborns and seconds. And it's obvious what you were." She frowns at me. "We left those divisions behind when we came here."

"I didn't mean it that way," I tell them apologetically. "I was just curious...."

"Well, there are better things to talk about," Shiloh snaps.

"Sorry," I mutter. They both pick up their baskets and move away, leaving me to work alone.

❧   ❧   ❧

When Reba shouts that it's break time, I leave my basket and follow the others to a small clearing with a hand pump. As we're taking turns getting drinks, we hear a man yell, "Hey ho, the vessels beat us here!"

A group of guys crash through the kudzu on the opposite side of the clearing. Most of them are bare-chested, their shirts tossed over their shoulders or wrapped around their waists. Their skin glistens with sweat.

"Shut up, Carrick," Reba tells the tallest boy who swaggers toward the pump. He is lean and muscular and walks with an athlete's loose-limbed stroll.

"You got a gift for me, Miss Reba?" he teases.

"You wish," she says, eyes narrow, but she doesn't really look mad. Shiloh stands beside her laughing.

"Who's this?" Carrick asks, looking me up and down.

"I'm Thalia."

"Fresh eggs!" he announces, which makes the other guys laugh.

"What's that supposed to mean?" I ask.

Carrick leans in close and takes a hold of the pump handle. His eyes are dark and I can smell the musk of sweat coming off him. "You hatching, girl?"

I step away. "I don't know what you're talking about."

"Leave her alone." Reba grabs me by the elbow and pulls me to her side. "She just got here, for god's sake."

"Oh, you're the one." Carrick glances over his shoulder. "Came with that boy? So your eggs are taken."

I ignore the last remark and ask, "Are you talking about Basil? Do you know where I can find him?"

"They put him in the machine shop," Carrick says. "He didn't even have to start in the fields. He some kind of mechanical genius or something?"

"Yes, he is," I say, proud of Basil, but wondering why I'm in the fields and not doing a more specialized job. "But I don't remember seeing a machine shop. Where is it?" I ask, but no one answers me.

Carrick pumps murky brown water over his head. When he comes up, he flings droplets all over everybody.

"Farm boys," Wren snorts to Shiloh.

"They're all idiots," Reba says, rolling her eyes to the sky, but I see a faint smile cross her lips, so I'm not sure she means it.

I follow the others into the shade. No sooner than we have sat down, Carrick plops beside Reba. He leans back on his elbows. "Why don't you come in the weeds with me, huh?"

Reba hugs her knees and pretends to ignore him.

He plucks a leaf from a vine and trails it gently from her ear to her chin. She swats at him but laughs. "We can plant some seeds," he tells her.

"Shut up." She bumps him with her shoulder.

"Ain't nobody plows a garden like Carrick," he coos.

Reba looks straight at him. "You're full of it."

"But you like it." He grins and wiggles his eyebrows. "Come on now. Help a farm boy out." Reba shakes her head laughing, but she relents and allows him to pull her to stand. He leads her out of the clearing and into the kudzu.

I turn to Wren, but she's deep in a conversation with a shirtless guy named Billet, who must be ten years older than she is. Within a few minutes both she and Shiloh have left the clearing with farm boys, too. I look around and realize that the only people still here are a scrawny guy named Noam, who's busy whittling a piece of wood with his kudzu knife, and Enid, who's snoring in the sun.

"Hey," I call to Noam. "Where did everybody go?"

Instead of answering me, he says, "You from the Inner Loop, too?"

I nod, surprised that he's willing to mention a place of origin. "How long have you been here?"

"About three years," he tells me.

"Really?" I ask. "Do you like it?"

He considers this for a moment. "I didn't at first, even though it was better than the alternatives facing me back at home."

"Rehab?"

He nods. "And probably jail the way things were going." He looks down at the stick in his hands, which has the vague shape of an airplane. "But, I'm pretty happy now."

"Why?" I ask.

He cocks his head to the side and smiles. "Family."

Ugh, I can barely control my distaste. How can all these people think of one another as brothers and sisters and Gaia as their mother? "So it gets better?"

"I didn't say that," he says, then goes back to working on his stick as if he doesn't care to discuss it any further.

✦   ✦   ✦

For two days, I haven't had a chance to speak with Gaia about calling home. The only time I see her is when she's on the dais in the dining hall, giving her daily address. And I've only caught sight of Basil twice, when his work squad was on their way out of the dining hall door and mine was going in on the opposite side. Both times, I caught his eye and started a crazy pantomime about us finding each other later so we could talk. He smiled and shook his head in confusion then mouthed words to me that I couldn't understand. I don't even know where his bunkhouse is, and I haven't had time to look for the machine shop. We're kept busy from morning to night, and by the time we're done with chores, I barely have enough energy to crawl into my bed, where I immediately pass out.

On the third day, I can't wait any longer. I must contact my parents and track down Basil. After I finish my morning shift with Bex and Leeda at the lab, I ditch Shiloh by going out the back door of the hospital and cutting through the kudzu toward Gaia's house.

My heart races as I climb onto the porch and knock. I hear quick footsteps inside, then the door swings open and Ella stares at me. "What are you doing?" she hisses.

"I'd like to see Gaia," I say. Ella blinks and blinks but doesn't say anything. "Is she here?"

"Ella?" Gaia calls from inside. "What's going on down there?"

"Hello, Gaia," I call, my voice shaky. "Do you have a moment? I'd like to speak to you."

Gaia hurries downstairs from the second floor, fastening a green belt around her white jumpsuit. "Who's in my house?" She stops in the middle of the staircase and squints at me as if she can't believe some person in a dirty brown dress has barged into her lovely living room. "Well?" she demands. "What is it?"

Something in the way she stares at me makes me shrink. Suddenly I don't feel like that girl who stood up on a Dumpster and admonished a mob to loot a Synthamil distribution center. Instead I've become a nervous, sweating ninny who feels out of place among the woven rugs, light fixtures, and upholstered furniture, too afraid to speak her mind. I gather my courage, take a breath, and say, "I'm sorry to disturb you, but I really need to contact my parents. I mentioned this to you when I arrived, and now I feel it's imperative. I need to let them know that I'm okay and..." I stop because Gaia crosses her arms and stares down at me indifferently.

Then she snorts as if she cannot believe what I'm requesting. "Clearly there's something you don't understand."

"I'm sorry." I wish I could shrink behind the plush red couch. "I know you'd like me to think of this as my new family, and it's so kind of you to take me in, but..."

"But what?" she demands. "You'd be happy to jeopardize everyone's safety just to have a word with Mommy and Daddy back in the Loops? Did you ever stop to wonder why we have no screens here? No network connection? No phone line straight to One World Headquarters? Why don't we just paint a big red *X* across the farm and wait for One World to send in the spies or start dropping bombs?" She pauses while I shift from foot to foot, trying to find a way to defend myself.

She grabs the railing and leans over so half her body casts a shadow over me. "Don't you know that they'd do anything to get their hands on me? Anything to denigrate me in the public eye? If they find us, they'll obliterate everything I've worked so hard to achieve. And then what would become of all these people?"

"That's not what I meant," I say, taking a step backward and nearly tripping on an ottoman. Part of me wants to reassure her that neither Basil nor I had ever heard of her before we stumbled into the Farm, but somehow I don't think that's what she wants to hear.

"Of course you didn't," she scolds with her hands on her hips. "Because you didn't think about anyone but yourself! Just marched right in here without so much as an invitation and started demanding special treatment."

My face burns and I feel sick to my stomach. I gaze at my feet in shame. "I'm so sorry. It's just that I know my parents must be worried, and if there's any way . . ."

Gaia's face twists as if she's looking at something repugnant. "You *should* be sorry," she tells me hotly. "I'm deeply disappointed. After all I've done for you, Twyla!"

I realize that she means me, but I don't bother to correct my name.

"You've completely wasted my time." She stands up tall and narrows her eyes. "Don't you have someplace you're supposed to be?"

I hurry out the front door before she has a chance to yell any more then hobble down the path toward the clearing as I fight back tears and berate myself for being such an idiot. How could I not have seen what a dangerous thing I was proposing! What did I expect? That the Farm would have some underground network that would help me contact my parents without jeopardizing everyone's safety? Wait. That thought stops me in my tracks. That's exactly what I imagined. I walk slowly, trying to reason through this. Gaia makes it sounds as if the Farm has no real-time or virtual connections to anyone. No screens. No ties to other corporate resisters. Could we really be that isolated out here? A sickening chill runs down my spine. I look all around me. The green kudzu that seemed so protective before suddenly seems more menacing, as if it could swallow me up, like it did my Gizmo, and I'd never be heard from again.

✢   ✢   ✢

I don't meet up with my work squad as I'm supposed to. Instead, I wander the paths around the Farm, looking for the machine shop. After half an hour, I've come nearly full circle and am just about to give up when I find a building I've never seen. It's tucked way back in the kudzu behind the hospital. If I'd gone a little farther into the woods when I was dumping the pee bucket, I would have seen it. It's also made of metal, and judging by the loud banging and clanging coming from inside, I'm pretty sure I've found what I'm looking for. I stand staring at it shining in the sun, shaking my head at the ridiculousness of the situation. All this time, Basil was right behind me, but I didn't even notice.

I march up to the door and tug, but it won't budge. This is strange since I've only encountered one lock in this whole place. Even the latrine doors swing freely. I try pounding with my fist, but the noises are so loud inside that I'm not surprised when no one answers. I walk around the building, looking for another way in. In the back, I see large windows two feet above my head. Discarded crates are stacked at the side of the building. I grab a couple and carry them to the rear, where I stack them up and climb on top so I can see inside.

Across one end of the large open workroom, guys in welding masks solder handles onto long metal tubes about the circumference of my thigh and the length of my body. On the other end is a table where workers fit together small, slender objects. One is pointy and the other flared like the spigot on a sprinkler. It looks like they're building showers. I scan all of the guys, sure that I can find Basil just by the shape of his shoulders and the length of his legs, but it's hard to distinguish one person from another when half of them are wearing masks and they're all dressed alike. (If Yaz were here, I would point and say, *Hey look, a guy in a brown shirt*, and she would laugh. God, I miss her.) I look and look, but I can't tell which one he is. My heart sinks.

I wait and watch as welders lift their masks to get a better look at their work before hiding behind the faceplates and firing up their torches again. Dark hair, balding, reddish brown, then finally, the fading blond curls of Basil. He steps back and wipes the sweat from his eyes. I'm so excited that I bang on the window and wave until he looks my way. Startled, he jumps, which makes me smile, but he is clearly not amused. He waves furiously for me to move away from the window.

"Fine!" I say, even though he can't hear me, and I stick out my tongue. I haven't seen him in days and this is how he greets me! As I'm hopping off the crates, a side door flies open and Basil stomps out.

"Apple! What the hell are you doing sneaking around back here?"

"I wasn't sneaking around," I tell him, annoyed. "I knocked on the door and nobody answered. I saw windows so I climbed up to look."

"You're not supposed to be here!"

"Nice to see you, too, jerk!" I cross my arms and glare at him, hurt and furious that he's not excited to see me.

"Don't get mad at me. . . ."

"I didn't come here to get mad at you!" I snap. "I was upset and wanted to talk to you, and then you act like I'm committing a crime. Forget it." I turn and stomp toward the path. "Just forget it!"

"Apple, wait!" He jogs after me and catches my wrist, but I wriggle away from his grip. "Please," he says. "I'm sorry. You just surprised me, that's all. Don't go."

I look over my shoulder and feel myself split in two. Half of me wants to throw my arms around his neck. The other half wants to punch him.

"What happened? Why did you come? Who upset you?"

When he asks me this, my anger melts a little, and the half that wants to hug him wins. "Oh Basil," I whine, trudging toward him with my arms outstretched. "I went to talk to Gaia about contacting my parents and . . ."

"What?" He steps away from me. "Why would you do that?"

My arms fall to my sides. "Because they need to know I'm okay."

Basil shakes his head and walks slowly toward a large flat rock beneath a tree as if he's exhausted. "What did she say?" he asks as he slumps down.

"She wasn't happy with me, I can tell you that much."

"Not surprising," he mumbles.

"That's not why I'm upset, though." I perch on the edge of the rock, leaving space between our bodies. "She said there's no way to contact the outside world from here."

Instead of looking appalled like I expected, Basil just shrugs. "Of course not. Think about all Gaia's done. What she's built. One World would destroy this place in an instant if they could find it."

"It's not like I asked her to call OW headquarters to speak with Ahimsa. I thought she would have some kind of underground network with the other resistance movements, who could get a message through to my family."

"What resistance?" Basil scoffs. "The Dynasuars? The Analogs?"

"Yeah, remember them?" I say. "Remember what they started in the Loops with our help?"

He shakes his head. "They don't have the answer, Apple. Gaia does."

"What do you mean, Gaia has the answer? To what?" He looks at me and shakes his head as if I just don't get it. But I'm not the one in the dark. "Maybe because you're stuck in this building all day, you don't see everything that's going on around here, but I see stuff every day that's really messed up." I pop up and begin pacing in front of him. "This dress!" I grab at the fabric and tug. "Is messed up. What's going on in that hospital"—I motion to the building behind us—"is messed up. The topless women in the pump house are super messed up! In fact, this place is so messed up that I feel like I'm going insane! Cut the vine, collect the vine, haul the vine, process the vine. We eat kudzu. We wear kudzu. We wash with kudzu. I freakin' dream of freakin' kudzu. A few days of the exact same routine, and I'm ready to run screaming for the Inner Loop again."

"Apple . . ." Basil says with disappointment.

"Well, it's true!" I slump down beside him. "Plus, no one is willing to speak up when something bonkers happens. And we're completely isolated. I can't reach my family. And I stink!" I pull my dress away from my body and get a whiff of something foul. "But at least you're building showers in there, right?" I point to the machine shop, trying to lighten the mood, but of course, I'm not even joking.

"Building what?" He looks bewildered.

"Isn't that what you're doing with the pipes and the spigots? Building showers?"

"Oh," he says. "That."

We're both quiet for a moment. The silence between us feels awkward, so I reach out to touch his knee. "I came here to talk to you about us, about our future. My god, I've barely even laid eyes on you in days! I've missed you so much."

I study his face. The work Fiyo did a week ago is beginning to fade slightly. Basil's eyes are a bit less icy and his skin has grown a shade warmer. His hair isn't quite as white blond as it was and more of the natural curl is coming back. Plus he's beginning to sprout a beard like the other men here. I reach out and push his hair away from his eyes. "You're starting to look more like yourself again."

"I feel like this place brings out the real me," he says proudly.

I withdraw my hand. "That's not what I meant."

He sighs. "I'm sorry you feel this way, Apple, but think of all the people Gaia's taken in so they can live freely as humans are supposed to. Don't you see? It's a new social order. And we're lucky to be a part of it."

I search his face, looking for the Basil I came here with. "Are you telling me that you're happy here?"

"Of course." He places a hand on mine. "And you should be, too. We're together."

"Hardly," I sniff. "I never see you."

"But nobody's trying to throw us in jail."

"I feel like I'm already in it," I mutter.

"Apple," he admonishes. "How can you say that?"

"Because it's true. The only thing I'm rewarded for is blind obedience to routine, and I don't get to make any choices for myself. This is not how I want to live."

"Apple, please." He begs me with his eyes. "Please try. I mean it when I say that I'm happy, and the only thing that could make me happier is if you were as content as I am."

My shoulders slump beneath the weight of his request. I feel like I'm back in the river flailing around, trying to find Basil, only this time he's sitting on the shore watching me drown. My chest aches at the thought of losing him to this place. This awful stupid place where somehow he feels at home and I feel imprisoned. "Basil, I . . ." I start to say, searching for a way to make him understand how I feel. Before I can find the words, the back door of the machine shop opens and a guy sticks his head out.

"You about done out here?" he calls. "We need your help."

"Sorry," Basil says to me. "I have to go back."

"Wait!" I reach for him.

"It's going to be okay, Apple." He leans over and kisses me on the forehead. "You just have to give it some time."

✤   ✤   ✤

Two more days and we follow the exact same routine. Girls pee in cups, we have our morning meal, I help with the jabbing parade in the lab, then it's out to the kudzu for collections. Every day, the farm boys meet up with my squad at the pump. And every day, the girls pair off with them, Enid passes out, and Noam whittles away at the branch that he's transformed into a little wooden airplane. The hardest part has been not seeing Basil. Reba warned me that she won't cover for me again if I shirk my shift, and I don't want any trouble with Gaia.

Sometimes during the break, I daydream that Basil comes to find me and we go off like the others. Other times I fall asleep in the clearing and dream that we're back where we found the berries, rolling across the ground, our lips pressed together, our limbs tangled up. Mostly I sit alone, annoyed and frustrated over the predicament I've gotten myself into, but today I decide I'm not going to sit here like an idiot anymore. If they're all sneaking into the woods with boys, so can I. The machine shop can't be that far. I'll just pop over, see Basil, and be back before they start working again.

The fundamental freedom of walking away from my work squad when I feel like it makes me so giddy that I scamper along the path like a naughty kid running away from her parents in a busy EA. Maybe this kind of liberty from routine is why the others head out into the woods every day. That and whatever sexcapades they're having. I'm not stupid. I know that's what they mean when they talk about plowing gardens and spreading seeds. But there's a lot I still don't understand. Like why they call some girls hatchers and other vessels and what the gifts are that they all go on about.

As I jog along, looking for a path that will lead me to Basil, I see something flutter a few inches from my head. At first I think it's just a dry leaf, floating on the breeze, but then it changes direction and glides. Instinctively, I throw my hand up to protect my face, but when the thing zips in front of me, I stop and stare, dumbfounded. A small creature with yellow and white stripes across brown wings lands on a vine curling around an old tree trunk. The flier dances from one cone-shaped purple bud to another. I try to remember from my grandmother's books what the little flier is called.

"Hello, flutterby," I whisper as I slowly and quietly move closer, trying hard to control my breath that has become shaky with excitement. The flier is so intent on the blossom that it doesn't seem to mind my giant peering eyes.

I watch it balance on wispy little legs, hinged with knees facing the wrong way. Two long flexible antennae sprout from its head above big black eye patches. Without thinking I reach out to pet its furry body, which scares the thing away. I don't want to let it go, so I follow it through the kudzu, calling, "Come back! I promise I won't hurt you!" Maybe this is why everyone puts up with the nonsense of this place. Maybe the privilege of seeing an actual nonhuman creature coexisting in this world is enough to cancel out the drudgery of the Farm. Basil asked me to give this life a chance, but I haven't really. I've been too resentful of the people to truly appreciate the place. I resolve to try harder to like it here because who knows what other wonders I might encounter, but then I trip and land face-first in the kudzu with a loud "Oooooph!"

"Who's that!" someone calls.

I scramble to my feet and see that I've fallen over a rock. Ahead of me is a tiny house almost entirely covered in kudzu vines. The only clear spot is the front porch, where an old man sits in a rocking chair. His face is obscured by a great cloud of bristly white hair, bushy eyebrows, and a long unkempt beard.

"Ella?" the man says, peering at me as I slowly climb to my feet. He closes the book on his lap and scoots to the edge of his chair then pushes himself to stand on creaky knees. "Ella, that you?"

"Sorry, no, it's not Ella," I call out. "I didn't realize anyone was out here."

He glowers at me. "What are you doing on my property? You from the damn farm? That damn woman send you here?"

"No, well, yes, well, sort of, but no." I walk slowly toward him. "I mean, I've been staying on the Farm, but no one sent me. I saw a flutterby and I was running after it and . . ."

"Flutterby?"

"Yeah, a bug with beautiful wings!" I flap my arms to demonstrate. "It landed on a flower."

The man gives a gravelly chuckle. "You mean a butterfly?"

"Right," I say, embarrassed. "That's what it's called." Timidly, I climb the steps of his porch and hold out my hand. "My name is Thalia. Thalia Apple."

He studies my hand for a second then reaches for me. "Well, at least you have some manners. Not like most of the cretins who find their way out here." He gives me a firm shake then says, "My name is Ezra Clemens."

"Nice to meet you, Mr. Clemens."

He settles himself into his chair again. "So you're staying over at the damned-fool Farm are you?"

I bark a loud, unexpected laugh. "Unfortunately, yes, I am."

That elicits a half smile from him. "Not so sure the Farm is all it's cracked up to be, huh?"

I lean against the porch railing, happy to be talking to someone who seems to share my opinion. "Exactly."

He snorts and reaches toward the table beside him for a pipe and a little red pouch with a long gray string wrapped tightly around it. "Hey," I say. My heart speeds up and my palms get prickly when I point at the pouch. "Where did you get that?"

"This?" he asks with a shrug and taps the pipe upside down on his thigh. "Someone gave it to me."

"But . . . it's . . ." I start to say, then I feel shame creeping over me. It seems so petty and privylike to claim ownership of something out here. Still my face burns because that pouch is mine, and I want it back.

"What brought you out here then?" Mr. Clemens asks. "Runaway? Sick of the corporate world? Looking for utopia? In trouble with the law?" My mouth drops open at how easily he's figured me out. He takes a pinch of shriveled brown leaves from the pouch, then packs it in his pipe with his thumb. "I heard it all before."

"I didn't really mean to get this far," I tell him, watching as he wraps the gray string around the red fabric my grandmother knit. "Now I'm kind of stuck. You don't happen to have a screen or a network connection do you?"

He squints at me. "Do I look like I have any of that?"

"No, sir," I have to admit. "You don't. But couldn't hurt to ask. It's just that I'd like to let my family know I'm okay."

"Ah," he says and strikes a match against the bottom of his chair.

"What about you?" I ask. "What are you doing out this far?"

"I live here." He sucks on the pipe, sending a little puff of gray smoke swirling above his head. "You're on my land. Those jackweeds at the Farm are on my land. But nobody seems to give a rat's ass."

"Your land?"

"That's right."

I'm not sure what to make of this so I say, "My grandparents were farmers somewhere around here a long time ago."

Mr. Clemens stops smoking and shoots me a look. "That so?"

"The Apples," I tell him. "They had a big organic place they kept through the wars."

He leans forward with his elbows on his knees, the pipe dangling from his fingers, and stares at me. His mouth opens and closes as if he's lost his voice. Finally he says, "Hector was a good man."

I stand up straight, my heart racing. "You knew my grandfather?"

He gives a curt nod. "I knew of him. He was about a hundred miles south of here. Good farmer from what I heard. Respectable. Honest. Hardworking. Died on his land, which is every farmer's wish."

My skin tingles as if the sun has come out to warm me on a cloudy day. "And my grandmother, Rebecca, did you know her, too?"

He flexes his eyebrows, deep in thought. "Her parents, your great-grandparents, had the farm first, right? She grew up there then took it over with Hector when her parents passed?"

"That's right!" I tell him, beaming happily. "My father was born there. Now we all live in the Inner Loop, but my grandma misses farming so much. She tells me all the time about how they grew things and what they ate." I'm so excited to be talking to someone about all this, but Mr. Clemens looks away.

"That was a long time ago. Things are different now." He puts the pipe between his teeth and sucks on it for a few seconds then takes it out again and says, "And those idiots over there don't have the first idea about what they're doing. They're not real farmers." His whole body shakes with fury.

Clearly this guy has a chip on his shoulder about Gaia using his land. "How do you get by?" I ask him. "What do you eat?"

After a few seconds of worrying his pipe between his lips, he says, "I can take care of myself. Always have."

Something snaps beside the porch. I catch a flash of brown scurrying into the kudzu. "What was that?" I ask.

Mr. Clemens shrugs. "Maybe a little critter. Some of them are starting to come back. I do believe I saw a mouse the other day."

From far off I hear Reba's whistle, which means that my squad's break is over. I eye the pouch on the table and debate whether to explain that it's mine. Then I think that my grandmother would probably be happy if she knew that Mr. Clemens had it. She can always make me another one when I get home. I look up at him and smile. "It was really nice to meet you."

"That so?"

"Yes. I mean it. I'd like to hear more about life here when my grandparents lived nearby. If you ever have free time . . ."

He laughs. "Girlie, all I have is time."

I shake his hand again, then hop down the steps and call, "See you soon!"

☙   ☙   ☙

The next evening when we return to the encampment after collecting kudzu all afternoon, I've lost my patience with the monotony of it all. I'm hot, tired, grouchy, and I'd like a shower—a real shower with warm water and decent soap. Plus, I want to take Basil to meet Mr. Clemens. My hope is that the old guy will be able to talk some sense into him.

I dump the contents of my basket onto the growing mountain of cut vines in the collection house then rub my back against the rough wall, trying to ease the itching. Sweating inside a dirty, scratchy dress should qualify as a form of torture. The other girls in my group add their vines to the pile, complimenting one another on how much they've collected.

I drop my knife in my basket and stack it in the corner with the others then hurry to the dining hall, hoping to overlap with Basil for a least a few minutes so I can convince him to slip off together later. My heart speeds up in anticipation as I scan the lines of people filing out of the hall, but as hard as I look, I can't find him and I feel like I might cry. Finally, I have to give up and go inside before all the broth is gone.

I grab a bowl and spoon from the level-one trough. There's a complicated system called a food chain, which determines who can eat what since people are in different stages of gastro-intestinal development. Level-one people, like me and everyone on my squad, only get clear kudzu broth and the strange sweet tea. Even though we can go back as many times as we want, my stomach still growls, and I feel hungry most of the day. The only difference here is that nobody will send me to rehab for it. I've seen what level-two people eat, and it doesn't seem all that great, either. Creamy kudzu stew with small chunks of mushy vegetables grown in the gardens and gathered from the woods, plus something they call cheese. The higher up the food chain you go, the more solid and varied the dishes become. I find an empty seat with my squad. Nobody looks up at me when I sit. Nobody talks. Eating here is nothing like the dinners my grandmother has described. It's just shoveling nutrients in like we did in the Loops, only here we use bowls and spoons instead of bottles.

Soon, Gaia rises from her place on a dais and lifts her plate. She's the only person who doesn't go through the food chain lines. Every other night she eats with our shift, and one of the domestic workers, like Ella or Bex, brings her a full plate from the kitchen. Tonight it's Leeda sitting on the chair behind Gaia, ready to jump up at her beck and call.

"Let us give thanks to Mother Nature!" Gaia booms and we all bow our heads. "Mother of the Earth, giver of life, thank you for the sustenance that you provide for us tonight. Mother, you have brought me a bounty from the forest and the fields! I dine on cooked kudzu leaves, mushrooms, corn, berries, flatbread, and cheese! What a feast of your delights. Please bless these workers. Keep them healthy and in your care so they too may someday join me in these delicacies. Blessed be are we."

Everyone around me repeats the final line, " 'Blessed be are we!' " Then we all dig in.

I slurp through my soup, miserably wishing that by some miracle Basil will walk through the door, even though I know that's not going to happen. Finally, about the time everyone is done eating, Gaia gets to her feet for her nightly remarks. I'm so preoccupied with thoughts of Basil that I barely listen to her rant about the evils of One World versus the utopia of the Farm. A few of her favorite catchphrases float by as she paces the dais, blue robe swirling "One World, the corporate enemy" and "when the others shall perish, we shall prosper" and "the answer to humankind's dilemma," but mostly I'm consumed by my sadness over not seeing Basil for yet another day.

When Gaia's done ranting and the applause die down, she doesn't dismount the stage like most nights. Instead, she moves to the middle of the dais and says, "As you all know, tomorrow is the full moon." She points to the giant wheel tracking the stages of the moon that hangs in the front of the dining hall. Each day someone turns it to reveal the moon's position that night. "Which means the dear doctor will arrive for our monthly harvest!"

For the first time, I cheer along with everyone else. I don't know what they're all so excited about. (How thrilling can it be to pick corn or whatever we'll do for the harvest?) But I realize the doctor might be my only chance to get a message to my family. If he's coming from a population center, he might have a Gizmo, and if he does, then I intend to use it.

"This month the dear doctor will bring a new member," Gaia says, which sends a murmur through the crowd.

"I know you'll welcome the new one with open arms and loving hearts. And, I'm certain that our newest member will soon know how very, very lucky she is to be here where we can live freely, loving whomever we choose, growing our family, being part of this new, better society that I have created on the Farm. Nowhere else in the world would this be possible."

I have to look into my bowl so no one will catch me rolling my eyes. She must give the exact same speech to every person who stumbles out of the kudzu. Be nice if it were true.

"As we all know," Gaia continues, "Mother Nature is a powerful force! She gives us life and snatches it away!"

I think this might be one of the only honest things she's ever said.

"But make no mistake," she goes on. "Our Mother is not capricious. She always has a plan, and she knows what's in our hearts. When our intentions are less than pure and when we question her, we anger her."

I wonder if she's talking about Mother Nature or herself.

"So you can imagine," Gaia says, stopping in the center of the dais, "how shocked I was to learn that there is someone in our midst, someone I have taken in and cared for like my own child, who does not agree."

Bile creeps into the back of my throat, and I have to swallow hard. I'm sure she's talking about me. But who would have told her about my misgivings? A wave of nausea rolls over me. Surely not Basil. I feel woozy and have to grip the edge of the table to keep myself steady.

"Who among you has questioned our Mother?" Gaia demands, suddenly fierce and unforgiving.

Nearly in unison every person in the room looks down and mumbles, "We have."

"And who has been less than grateful for the gifts she bestows?"

The room gets deathly quiet. No one will look at anyone else.

"Who among us has been so brash as to doubt the wisdom of our Mother? Who would dare to complain about the miracle of being a vessel?"

I let my breath go. It can't be me. She can call me a lot of things, but a vessel isn't one of them.

From the other side of the room, a tiny voice says, "It was me." I crane my neck and see poor Bex, standing in the kitchen door with an empty pot in her hand. "I did, Gaia. I questioned Mother Nature's wisdom. I complained about my pregnancy." I whip around and glare at Leeda who sits smugly with her hands folded in her lap as Bex walks toward Gaia on shaky legs with tears streaming down her cheeks.

"You?" says Gaia, as if she's shocked. "A person so exalted and blessed to be a vessel for our cause? How could you?"

Bex hangs her head in shame.

"Is it not enough that we clothe you, we feed you, we care for you and your child? Is it not enough that we are creating a new world for you and future generations so no one will ever again be persecuted for normal human urges to eat and procreate? Is it not enough that we protect you from imprisonment or institutionalization? What else could you possibly want from us? How selfish could you possibly be?"

All this because Bex said her back hurt and she had to pee? I narrow my eyes at Leeda, wishing I could smack her.

"You took this gift for granted." Gaia points to Bex's swollen belly. "And you angered Mother Nature."

"I'm so sorry," Bex wails. "Please forgive me!"

Gaia stands up tall and looks down on Bex, cowering at the foot of the stage. "If this harvest does not go well, we will all know why."

↯   ↯   ↯

When dinner is over, I walk through the throngs of toddlers in the main clearing on my way to my squad's evening job—turning kudzu into usable goods. It's impossible to tell which kids are boys and which ones are girls since they all wear loose fitting brown shirts down to their knees and have the same short choppy haircuts. Not that they mind, though. They seem as happy as can be playing in the dirt. Especially one little kid, no older than two, who runs in circles, making buzzing noises for the little wooden airplane in his chubby fist. I stop and watch, certain that the toy he has was made by Noam. I almost feel jealous then. Although, I suppose I should be troubled that no one ever seems to be watching these kids since all their mothers head over to the pump house after meals. I don't know why it takes so many women to get the water, with or without their shirts on.

Inside the weaving house, I join my squad who sit in a circle on low stools, making baskets and talking about the cycle that's going to start tomorrow. I notice Ella is serving the sweet tea today. She walks from person to person with a tray. Most of the girls don't even look at her or thank her when she brings them a cup. I find a place between Wren and Reba, but nobody acknowledges my presence. When Ella gets to me, I smile at her and say, "Thanks." For the first time she looks at me and the corners of her mouth turn up, just a little, before she takes her empty tray and heads out the door without a word.

"That girl thinks she's something special because she works for Gaia," Reba says as soon as Ella's gone.

"I heard she never even had to go out in the kudzu," says Kiki.

"The dear doctor brought her here when she was nine," Jance explains.

"And she went straight from Gaia's kitchen to carrying," Kiki says.

"This is her second time," Lu adds, slurping her tea.

"Girl's been sneaking off like the rest of us," Reba says with a snort.

"With who?" the others shriek, tantalized by this detail.

"Nobody knows," Reba tells them.

As I struggle to figure out what they're talking about, Wren clears her throat and says, "This will be my first harvest."

The others congratulate her.

"Does it hurt?" she asks, nervously.

"Not really," Reba tells her. "Just a little poke. And since you've been plowing fields with Billet you already know what a little poke feels like." She laughs and smacks Wren's arm.

Wren turns bright red as the others crack up. "He's nice!" she protests. "Not like Carrick anyway."

Reba shrugs her off. "Well, if I'm chosen, this'll be my sixth gift so . . ."

"Unless you're carrying," Shiloh says with a smirk.

"That boy Carrick creeps like the kudzu, spreading his seed," says Lu. "Who knows how many roots he's laid down. Maybe he got to Ella, too."

This time everyone laughs but Reba, who scowls. "He's got no interest in that scrawny little thing," she says. "And it doesn't matter anyway because I wouldn't be back in the fields after this cycle so Carrick will have to find another garden to till."

Normally, I stay out of their conversations, but what she's said surprises me, so I blurt out, "Why won't you be back?"

Reba looks up at me and blinks. "Once you've given six monthly gifts or you're carrying, you move on."

"Where do you go?" I ask eagerly. Maybe this whole bestowing your gift thing isn't so bad.

"Up the food chain," Reba says. "New job. New food. New bunkhouse."

"Oh," I say disappointed, "so that's how the system works."

Enid sniffs loudly.

"Here we go again," Reba mutters. "Every single time someone moves up, you just can't be happy for her, can you Enid? It all has to be about you, doesn't it?"

Enid stares at the strips of kudzu in her hands. Tears roll down her sunken cheeks. She clears her throat and says quietly, "I am happy for you, Reba."

"Funny way of showing it," Reba snorts.

"But I've been here the longest and . . ." Enid starts to cry.

"Gaia says it's your own damn fault," Kiki tells her. The others nod.

"Gaia says, 'If we truly give ourselves over to Mother Nature we will bestow our gifts,'" Lu adds.

"Wait," I say, "what are the gifts?" As usual, everyone ignores me and they continue to berate poor Enid, who shrinks with every accusation that she doesn't work hard enough, doesn't try hard enough, doesn't love Mother Nature enough, so of course she can't progress to the next level.

"You're always napping on the breaks!" Kiki says.

"And complaining about your back," Jance snarls.

"As if you're the only one with aches and pains!" says Wren.

Finally, Enid can't take it anymore. She jumps off her stool and runs for the door, crying, "I do everything I'm supposed to but it never works."

"Drama queen," Reba says and the others snicker. "She just needs one of them farm boys to take her out in the weeds and give her a good plow!" The others stomp their feet and laugh, but I've had enough.

"What's wrong with all of you?" I ask. Half of me thinks I should shut up and mind my own business. What's it matter to me how they treat each other? I have no intention of being here much longer. But I don't like seeing anyone picked on like that. "You're awful," I tell them. No doubt they'll snitch about Enid's transgression, then she'll have her butt handed to her in front of everyone. Well, they can add me to the list of people for Gaia to berate in public because I'm sick of this. I stand up and follow Enid out of the room.

The main clearing is nearly empty as I trail ten feet behind Enid. Only a few stragglers are out, including Ella who kneels beside the little kid with the airplane. She looks up at me and offers a cautious wave. I lift my hand then follow Enid into the latrines, where I hear her sobbing inside a toilet stall.

"Hey," I say gently and lean against the sink. "It's Thalia." She doesn't say anything so I keep talking. "Seems like I knew someone named Enid once. It's an unusual name. So pretty and old-fashioned." She continues to cry. "You know they're all a bunch of jerks, right?" I tell her. "They only gang up on you because they feel so powerless here. And of course all that crap they were spouting about giving yourself over to Mother Nature . . ."

The toilet stall door flies open, and Enid stands staring at me with a look of shock on her face. "How dare you!" she shrieks at me.

"Whoa, what?" I rear back against the sink. "I just meant that if anyone deserves something good to happen, it would be you. You're never cruel. You work hard. . . ."

"No, they're right!" she yells at me. "I don't do enough. I'm not worthy yet. Gaia says, 'We must never question Mother Nature.'"

"Yeah, well, Gaia has a funny way of picking and choosing the parts of nature that suit her best," I blurt out.

Enid's mouth drops open and she grips the side of the toilet stall to steady herself. "You horrible, ungrateful person! After everything Gaia has done for you."

"You know," I tell her, "a scratchy dress and two bowls of kudzu broth a day isn't all there is in life." Then I turn and walk out of the latrine.

ψ   ψ   ψ

I march away from the encampment, wondering how all of these people, including Basil, could be so blindly devoted to Gaia when she's clearly a lunatic. I get that she started this place and that it might be better than what most people left behind, but there's no real freedom here, as Gaia likes to claim. No one is thinking for him- or herself. This place is like a PlugIn or EA, except with kudzu instead of screens. They might as well all put their heads down and graze on the vine like one mighty flock of mindless sheep.

The really sad thing is all One World would have to do is show people in the Loops videos of this existence, and they'd probably stop protesting and head on home. *If that's life without One World then no thanks,* most of them would probably think. Of course, the protests could be over already. For all I know, Ahimsa may have won. I sigh. I hate not knowing what's happening.

When I get to the outskirts of the encampment, I decide to keep going even though the sun has begun to set, turning the sky pale pink with fuzzy, iridescent clouds. I don't care, though. I'm not going back to my squad yet, so I search for the path that led me to Mr. Clemens's cabin a few days ago. It takes me a while, but soon I find it. When I get near his place, I hear a loud snore then a grunt. "Hey, who's there?" he calls from his chair on the porch.

"It's Apple," I tell him. "Thalia Apple."

Mr. Clemens runs his fingers through his hair then smoothes his beard. "You came back."

"Yes," I tell him from the bottom of the steps. "Is that okay?"

He stares hard at me for a moment. "I don't let just anybody up on my porch, you know."

"Oh," I say, feeling chastised by his words. Looking down as I shuffle backward, I'm glad I hadn't dragged Basil out here with me. But my nose tickles like I might cry because I can't take another person being unkind to me today. "Sorry, I just really needed to talk to someone and . . ."

"Well . . ." He shifts in his seat. "Seeing as you're Hector's kin I have a feeling I can trust you."

"You can!" I assure him.

"Come on, then," he says, waving me forward.

I climb the steps, smiling with gratitude, then I lean against the porch rail like I did the other day. One side of his mouth turns up slightly as he squints at me.

"Looks like something's got your dander up, girlie."

I press my hands against my cheeks, still flushed scarlet with frustration. "Oh, you know," I mumble. "Just trying to get used to things around here until I find a way out."

"Ha!" He pulls his pipe from his shirt pocket and taps out the contents.

We sit silently, which makes me uncomfortable, so I ask, "Was all of this your family's land once?"

"Yep," he grunts and clamps the stem of his pipe between his teeth. "For over two hundred years. We made it through droughts and rotting rains, locust swarms, and corporate takeovers. War and famine. Hell, even the kudzu couldn't take us down." He sucks on the empty pipe. "Until that woman came along." He shakes his head. "She's worse than all of that combined."

"That bad, huh?" I mutter.

"You think I'm exaggerating?" He furrows his considerable brow. "Weather is just weather. It comes and goes and holds no grudges. Destroys your crops one year and lets them flourish the next. You just have to wait it out and let it pass. Same for pests. They're mindless. It's nothing personal. You can make a similar case for corporations. They might be like a swarm of hungry locusts trying to gobble up everything in the name of profit, but if you get lucky and keep off their radar, they'll pass you by. Even with the kudzu, if you're diligent, you can keep it at bay. But that woman . . ." He pokes at the air with his pipe. "She didn't come here on a whim, and she's not merely looking for profit. What she wants is far scarier." He looks at me, the muscles in his jaw twitching.

"What is it?"

"Power!" he nearly spits. "Her appetite for it is insatiable. And she'll use whatever means she can to get it."

"Why didn't you kick her off when she first came?" I ask. "It's your land."

He snorts. "Oh, believe me, I tried. Threatened to blow her to smithereens, but she's armed to the teeth and dug in deeper than kudzu roots. At a certain point, there was nothing left for me to do but slink away like a half-dead cat looking for a hole to die in."

"You didn't get far," I say, not trying to be mean, but it's true.

He snorts another little laugh. "You can say that again. This is my old sugar shack. We tapped maples around here, but of course you'd know nothing about that."

"Does she know you're here?"

He thinks this over. "The real question is, does she care?" He sucks on the pipe for a moment then adds, "If she knows, she probably figures I can't do her much harm. And she's right. What am I going to do?" He sighs. "For a long time, I thought about picking up and starting over someplace else, but . . ." he trails off and shakes his head.

"Why didn't you?"

"Well, now, that's complicated . . . but I'll tell you, if things were different, I know exactly where I'd head." He glances at me sideways.

"To the Loops?"

"Hell, no! That's just trading one evil for another." He leans in closer to me. "There's a place up north. In what used to be called Canada." He stares out as if peering into a future he'll never see. "The land is still fertile there. There's wildlife. Nobody's running the show. All you need are some seeds and a piece of land, and you'll get by. Just like the first settlers way back when."

I stare at him, not sure if he's serious or if it's wishful thinking on his part.

"It's true," he says, sensing my skepticism. "After the wars, my farm was a stop along the way for people who left the Loops and were heading for a better place. That's how Gaia got here. I was still idealistic enough to think I'd get things up and running again so I welcomed the help at the time, but then slowly and surely, she took over. Moved herself into my house." He stops as if it's too painful to go on.

"That beautiful place was your house?" I shake my head as I take in what he's been reduced to. "I'm so sorry."

He nods. "Gaia's like the kudzu. First, it's one innocent-looking tendril inching toward you. You almost welcome it because it looks so sweet and harmless, and you talk yourself into believing it could even been good. Next thing you know, she's got a stranglehold on you. The real problem is that most of the idiots who show up don't figure that out until it's too late. Except for one." He studies me for a moment. "Smart girl like you can see straight through a charlatan like her, right?"

"This place is no different than what I was fighting against in the Loops," I say.

"People finally catching on there, too?" he asks with a chuckle. "Took them long enough."

"There were protests, but all of that could be over by now." I stare into the trees, trying to imagine a place where animals scamper about and the land is fertile and no one would be telling me what to do. "Do you think people are still up there? In Canada, I mean."

"Last I heard they were, but it's been a while." He takes a few puffs off his pipe and grins. "Why? You planning on taking a trip?"

"Me?" I shake my head. "No, I have too much to finish at home. Soon as I can get out of here, I'm going back."

We sit together quietly for a few moments. I hate to leave, but I should go before it gets too dark. I cross the porch and reach out for Mr. Clemens. "I'm truly sorry about all that she's put you through. No one should have to endure that."

"Well," he says, patting my hand. "Unfortunately most of the world has had to endure far worse or die trying." He looks up at me with tired eyes that remind me of my grandmother when she talks about the wars. My chest aches because I miss her so much.

"Maybe when I find a way home, you can join me. My grandmother would love to meet you, I'm sure."

Mr. Clemens guffaws. "An old coot like me in the Loops?" He laughs until he wheezes. "That's the funniest thing I've ever heard, Thalia Apple. You're a regular comedian. Besides, I have to protect what's here."

I shake my head, strangely envious of how connected he must feel to this land. Then I say good-bye and start back on the path. When I'm near the pump, a hand reaches out of the dusk and yanks me to the side.

"Hey!" I yell and ball my fist, ready to throw a punch. I expect to see Carrick or some other farm boy sent to drag me in the weeds, but I come face-to-face with Ella who's shrinking away.

"Don't hit me!" she cries.

"What are you doing?" I ask, dropping my fist.

She looks side to side nervously then says so quietly that I have to strain to hear, "It's not over."

"What's not over?"

"What you started," she whispers.

"With who? With my squad and Enid?"

She shakes her head and looks around again. Then she leans very close to me and says directly in my ear, "Gaia doesn't know who you are, but I do. The protests in the Loops are still going."

I grab tightly to her arm. "What are you talking about? How do you know this? Who told you to tell me that?" Like the butterfly I tried to touch, Ella darts away. I run after her, but she's surprisingly fleet-footed for a pregnant girl and she must know paths out here that I can't see, because she disappears into the foliage, leaving me standing alone and at a loss.

⚘   ⚘   ⚘

After what Mr. Clemens and Ella have told me tonight, it's clear that my place is in the Loops fighting for change, not being stuck out here with a lunatic running the show. It also seems that my only hope of contacting my family or leaving anytime soon may lie with the doctor who's coming tomorrow. Of course, I'm determined to take Basil with me, if I can ever find him. The first place I try is the machine shop, but the building is quiet and dark, so I move on.

I make my way through the kudzu toward the hospital, which is also dark. When I come to the fork in the path that leads to Gaia's house, I hear loud voices. I peer down and see a gathering of women under a weak light at the foot of her porch steps. Although it's hard to tell, I'm fairly sure I see Reba's red hair and Wren jabbing her hands in the air as she talks. Gaia stands at the top of the steps looking down at a woman I assume is Enid by the way she cowers. I shake my head in disgust.

From there, I hurry to the opposite end of the encampment, where I go from bunkhouse to bunkhouse, asking if anyone knows where Basil sleeps. Door after door opens and closes, as strangers shake their heads no. Despite the small number of people who live on the Farm, I realize how isolated I've been in my squad. I recognize only the faces of girls from the lab and people in the dining hall, but I don't know a single person's name besides my coworkers'.

Finally, at the sixth bunkhouse, when I ask for Basil, a short squat guy nods curtly and calls into the darkness. Basil comes to the door, yawning and bleary-eyed, sleepily rubbing his belly under his scratchy nightshirt. When he sees me, his face lights up with a smile.

"Apple," he says, happily. "What a nice surprise!"

"I really need to talk to you," I tell him. "Can you come outside with me?"

"Sure." He stretches his arms overhead, which lifts his shirt, revealing that line of hair from his belly button to the waistband of his pants riding low on his hips. The tattoo of the seed, which he seems to have forgotten, is still on his side, but I'm determined to make him remember what it stands for. So I step toward him and slide my hands around his waist, hugging him fiercely, trying hard to bring him back to me. He returns my embrace, then we walk, arms around one another to a spot beneath the trees at the edge of the clearing.

"I'm so glad you came," he tells me as we settle onto a fallen tree covered with a soft cushion of green. "Every night when I lie down I think, I'll just sleep for ten minutes, then I'll get up and go find Apple, but I'm always so exhausted. I never wake up until it's morning again. But tonight, there you were at my door." He pulls me close and kisses me.

Although part of me wants to sink into him and stay right here until morning, I know there are more pressing things to do. "Listen, Basil. There's something I have to tell you." I lean away but keep his hands in mine. "I want you to know that I really listened to what you said a few days ago, and I've tried very hard to understand what you see in this place...."

"Good!" He squeezes my hands and beams. "So you get it now? You understand what's so great about the Farm and why we're lucky to be here?"

I shake my head and wince under his disapproval, but I don't let it stop me. "I've seen some things and learned some things that have convinced me this place isn't what you think it is. And Gaia doesn't have the answer."

He screws his face up with anger and pulls away from me.

"She doesn't," I insist. "She's not infallible the way you and the others make her out to be."

"I didn't say she was infallible," Basil argues. "But she has a vision for the future...."

"Ahimsa DuBoise has a vision for the future, but that doesn't make it right."

He looks disgusted. "How could you ever, even for a minute, compare Gaia to Ahimsa DuBoise? I've defended you so many times here. People say, 'Once a privy always a privy,' but I've told them not you. That you would get it. It would just take time. Maybe I was wrong. Maybe at heart, you'll always be a privileged little firstborn exec's daughter who cares about nothing but her own well-being!"

"You know what your problem is?" I jab my finger in his chest. "You latch on to people and blindly follow them when you think they have the answers. First Ana and now Gaia. Even if what they're saying is crazy. You can't just question authority when it's convenient. You need to question it all the time."

"Like you did when you were driving around in your Smaurto, yapping on your Gizmo for the past seventeen years?" he says. "You only became a rebel a week ago when you met me and now you act like you have all the answers."

His words sting but I don't stop. "Fine, I get it. I was a privy. I was a part of the problem. But you changed that for me. You opened my eyes and showed me how screwed up the Loops are. Now it's my turn to do the same for you. You need to question what's going on around here."

"I know exactly what's going on around here," he says with an arrogance that I find laughable.

"Enlighten me, then. Because I can't seem to figure out what stealing land and cutting kudzu and injecting girls and worshipping Mother Nature has to do with it."

"We're preparing for the revolution, Apple," he says, leaning close to my face. "Ana was too soft. She tried to make change from the inside, and look what it got her. She's dead, just like my brother! But Gaia is prepared. She's already built something that's better than the alternative. Something that's worth fighting for. And when the revolution comes, we'll be ready."

"The revolution's not coming here, Basil. No one outside of this farm knows who Gaia is or cares. The real revolution is happening without us. Back in the Loops. And I intend to get back there with or without you."

He stands. "Don't say that unless you mean it."

I look up at him with my heart breaking. "I mean it, Basil. I really truly mean it. And I hope that you'll come with me because I'm leaving as soon as I can."

Basil won't listen to me for another moment. He turns and runs.

I walk slowly from Basil's bunkhouse to mine with tears running hot down my cheeks, wondering how there could be such a divide between us? It's as if Gaia has figured out exactly what to say to a person like Basil so the Farm seems perfect and enchanting. If I could get him out from under that cloak of lies she's woven, I'm certain he could see reason again. I just have to find a way to wake him from this stupor. But I know that's not going to happen tonight. He's too angry with me to listen. The only thing I can do now is go to bed and hope I can bring Basil to his senses by the time I convince the doctor to get me out of here.

✤   ✤   ✤

I am on a kudzu leaf floating in a shallow pool. Concentric circles of water radiate out from me. Bobbing on each ripple of water are the people in my life who care about me the most. I see my mom, my dad, Grandma Apple and Papa Peter, Grandma Grace, Yaz, Fiyo, and AnonyGal whose face is obscured by shadow. I paddle in a circle, searching for Basil, certain that he has to be somewhere in this water, but I can't find him. Then my leaf starts to rock. The water grows choppy. I brace myself and understand that I'm dreaming, but fearing I'm in another flood, I sit up grabbing for something solid.

"Shhh," someone says. Hands grab my shoulders and push me back.

"What the hell!" I say.

A face gets close to mine. "You have to get out of here," a girl whispers.

My eyes adjust to the dark. "Ella?" I say. "What's going on? What are you doing?"

"They're coming for you. Gaia's on a war path. Your whole squad went to her, saying you're dangerous and you're trying to sabotage the harvest."

"What a bunch of idiots," I say and lie back down. "They're full of crap and we both know it."

"You don't have much time," Ella says, yanking me up. "There's no telling what Gaia will do when she's like this. I've seen her lock people up for days or worse." The fear in her eyes chills me and I sit up. She sweeps her hands around my floor and finds my sandals for me.

"But where am I going to go?"

"Go to Mr. Clemens. Sleep there tonight. I'll bring you some food soon and let you know when it's safe to come back."

"Won't they come looking for me?" I ask, panicked now.

"Not tonight. It's too dark, and tomorrow the harvest will distract everybody. Then Gaia will forget about it in a few days, so your squad will have to let it go."

We both stand up. I look at her and ask, "Why are you doing this for me?"

She leans in close. "I know who you are, Thalia Apple. I know what you started in the Loops."

"How?"

We hear voices in the clearing and my whole body begins to shake.

"Take this," she says and shoves something into my hands.

I hold it up and see a sheathed kudzu-cutting knife. "What the . . . ?"

"You might need it. Now, go," she hisses.

I put the knife in my pocket and run.

✤   ✤   ✤

If Mr. Clemens is surprised when he finds me banging on his door, he doesn't show it. He gives me a funny half smile and says, "Ah, Thalia Apple. Nice of you to visit again. Little late ain't it?"

"Sorry," I pant and try to catch my breath from running through the woods. "I had some trouble at the Farm, and Ella told me to come here."

"Smart cookie, my Ella," he says with pride as he ushers me in. He lowers himself into a creaky rocking chair, where he takes the pouch, my pouch, and starts to pack his pipe. Then he motions to a beat-up old chair for me. He strikes a match, lights the pipe, then a thick candle. The whole room glows yellow. I see a small table with a few simple pieces of pottery, a narrow cot with jumbled blankets, and a mantel filled with photos, but it's too dark to make out the faces in the frames.

"It speaks to your integrity that you caused a ruckus there." He chuckles. "I'd like to see Gaia's face when she can't find you."

"I wouldn't," I admit. "From the way Ella talked, she can be a real tyrant."

Mr. Clemens takes his pipe out of his mouth and jabs the smoking end at me. "Tyrant is the right word. And liar and fraud. You're too young to know spit about the past, but history is littered with people like her. Idi Amin. Pol Pot. Jim Jones. Charismatic cult leaders who worm their way into desperate people's minds with lies disguised as promises. She claims she's created a self-sufficient settlement where folks are free to live like humans ought, meanwhile she's slipping Synthamil into the soup."

"What? Are you serious? Synthamil in the soup?" I ask not sure who's crazier, him or Gaia.

"Kudzu and corn and the other meager crops she's been able to eke out of the soil aren't enough to keep all those people healthy. It'll be years before that's possible around here. There would be malnutrition out the wazoo if she wasn't supplementing everything."

"But what makes you think it's Synthamil?"

"'Cause I know where she keeps her stash." He lets that sink in for a moment while he smokes. "That doctor fella of hers brings it, and they hide it in my old corn silo just north of here."

"Oh, no," I moan. "The dear doctor is in on it, too?"

"You bet your britches he is."

I nearly cry as I see my chances of leaving the Farm dwindle with this revelation.

"I thought about smashing up all those bottles with my

four-wheeler once," Mr. Clemens says. "Then I figured I'd be hurting the little ones the most, so I didn't do it." He laughs. "Anyway, how do you think I'm still kicking at ninety-three?"

My mouth falls open. "You take the Synthamil for yourself."

"Well," he says with a wink. "I have a little helper."

"Ella?" I ask.

"She's a good egg, my Ella."

"Your Ella?" I try to work this out. "Is she your daughter or your granddaughter?"

He shakes his head. My skin prickles as I picture Ella's swollen belly. "But, wait, you're not . . . she isn't . . . ?" I can't even bring myself to say it.

"She came here so young," he says wistfully. I hold my breath as he explains, bracing for the worst. "That damn-fool doctor hauled her out here after her mother died in one of his loony bins. But she's whip smart. She saw through this place in no time. Kept trying to run away, but she couldn't get too far. I found her at least half a dozen times asleep in a little nest she made out in the woods. I knew someone had to watch over her. Wish I could have kept her here with me, but it took a long time for her to trust me, and this house is no place for a child." He shifts in his seat. I relax and let my breath go because his concern for her seems parental and not at all perverted. "I always intended to take her away from here, but by the time she would've said yes, she'd gone and fallen in love and had a baby, and now she's got another one on the way." He sighs deeply.

"But wait," I say, trying to puzzle through everything he's telling me. "If Gaia's feeding everybody Synthamil, then how did Ella and all the other girls get pregnant?"

He looks at me like I'm kind of dim. "I'm no scientist, but I seem to remember from wartime that some of those synthetic drinks had hormones so people could have babies, right?"

I gasp and smack myself in the head. "She's giving us Synthamil with Arousatrol!"

He shrugs. "Don't know what it's called, but it must be something like that."

"Oh god," I put my fingers in my hair and rub my head, which is beginning to ache.

"Darling," he says and taps out his pipe, "you don't even know the half of it yet."

"I have to tell Basil," I mutter. "Maybe if he knew, I could convince him to leave."

"Bring him to me," Mr. Clemens offers. "I'll tell him the truth, the whole truth, and nothing but the truth. He'll be ready to run screaming from here in no time!"

"Even if you could convince him, he won't go back to the Loops with me," I say sadly.

"The Farm and the Loops ain't the only two choices, Thalia Apple."

I look at him. "What then?"

"I already told you."

"You mean that place up north?"

"Yep."

"Do you really think people are farming there?"

"Last I heard they were."

"But One World destroyed the Svalbard seed vault. Or even if they didn't, they're not handing out packets to anyone."

"Heck, girlie, that's no problem. I have seeds."

I nearly fall out of my chair. "You do?"

"Course I do," he says with a chuckle. "Every good farmer keeps some back. Why? You thinking of heading up that way then?"

I snort and shake my head, flummoxed by this new information. "You going with me if I do?"

He laughs. "Girlie, I been packed and ready for years. Got a shed behind here with a wagon full of supplies," he tells me with a twinkle in his eyes. "You get Ella and her brood to agree, and I'd be out of here lickety split."

✤　　✤　　✤

I don't sleep much that night. I can't stop thinking about what Mr. Clemens told me about Ella, about the Synthamil, about Canada. I'm certain that if Basil knew all of this, he'd no longer want to stay. He'd see that Gaia is just another corrupt person looking for power at the expense of the masses. Then again, I'm not sure I can abandon the revolution in the Loops. But maybe, if I could get Basil and Mr. Clemens and Ella and her family someplace safe, I could help from afar or make my way back to the Loops then join Basil again later. The one thing I know for sure is first I have to find a way to prove to Basil what Mr. Clemens said. Then we can work on leaving.

✤　　✤　　✤

By the time the first rays of sun spill through the windows of the cabin, I've made my plan. As soon as Mr. Clemens stirs, I ask him how to get to his silo.

"You hungry?" he asks from his cot. "Ella will bring us something in a few hours or you can go out and pick some berries and tender leaves. I'll show you how to make a nice cup of tea to tide you over."

"Thanks, but no," I tell him. "I have to take care of something first."

He doesn't ask me any more questions. Just nods as if he understands and points me in the right direction.

The silo isn't hard to find. It's the largest structure for miles around, but being covered with kudzu like everything else camouflages it so that if you don't know what you're looking for, you would miss it. Inside is exactly what Mr. Clemens claimed. Cases and cases of Synthamil stacked four feet high. I open a box and pull out a bottle. The label reads, SYNTHAMIL (BASELINE FORMULA) + AROUSATROL. When I turn the bottle over, I find the warning printed in red: THIS FORMULA CONTAINS HORMONES THAT PROMOTE REPRODUCTIVE HEALTH. I tuck the bottle into my pocket, along with the kudzu-cutting knife, hoping this will be enough proof for Basil that things are not what they appear on the Farm and that he'll come with me when I go. Then I leave the silo and head across the fields toward the machine shop.

Like the first day when I followed Basil's captors, I stay hidden in the kudzu outside the encampment, watching carefully for people. I wonder if they sent a search party for me again last night, but after several minutes when no one comes or goes, I figure Ella was right—that the harvest has distracted everyone from my disappearance. So I run on tiptoe to the back of the machine shop and climb up on the crates, which are still stacked under the windows, but the place is as quiet and empty as it was last night.

I'm about to sneak off into the kudzu to hide, thinking I'm here before Basil's shift starts, but then I hear voices booming nearby, and I wonder if the harvest has started already. If so, everyone will be there. Including Basil. I move slowly and carefully through the wooded area in front of the machine shop, keeping my eyes peeled for any stragglers who might spot me, but as far as I can tell, every person who lives on the Farm has gathered around a makeshift stage in the clearing in front of the hospital and harvest house.

I creep around the edge of the crowd, searching for a place to slip in and hoping that for once, this stupid dress will help me look exactly like every other girl here. Luckily, the audience is too engrossed in applauding for Gaia as she climbs onto the stage to notice me. When she opens her arms wide and says, "Good morning to you all, it's a beautiful morning for a harvest!" everyone claps and hollers, stomps their feet, and whistles.

"Before we get started," Gaia says once they've settled down, "I'd like to take a moment to welcome our newest member." She turns to the steps and motions. "Come on up, my dear. Don't be frightened. We are so very, very happy to have you here."

A short, round girl with frizzy brown hair cautiously steps onto the stage. I squint at her because she looks vaguely familiar, but I can't place her until Gaia says, "Haza, meet your new family!"

I draw in a quick and unexpected breath as I try to puzzle through how Haza has gotten from Dr. Demeter's rehab center to this place. If there was anyone who seemed to buy into his method, it was this girl. I wonder if she escaped the same night as Zara and me and has been making her way here ever since. I have to admit, that I'm kind of impressed. I didn't think she had it in her, but I wish that I could have warned her to stay away.

As Gaia's busy spouting her nonsense about how Haza will be able to live freely now that she's on the Farm, I slip through the crowd, looking for Basil. I try to stay far away from anyone on my squad, but so far I haven't recognized a single person that I know. The next time I glance up at the stage, Gaia is walking slowly in a circle muttering to the sky. After a few seconds of her strange one-woman parade, she stands in the center and lifts her arms overhead.

"Oh mighty Mother Nature," she calls out. "Giver of all life, bestower of all gifts, have you planted seeds in our garden?" She waits, as if expecting an answer to come down from the sky, and she must get it because suddenly she smiles and cries out, "Yes! You have." She spins, arms up, happily twirling like a blue-and-white whirlwind under the morning sun. "Reveal to us, through me, your humble human conduit, the carrier of these seeds that we will harvest today!"

Gaia stops spinning and opens her eyes. "Tia Lee," she says. "Tia Lee will bestow her gift today."

A gasp and cry of happiness erupts from the crowd. People shuffle around, a wall of bodies split, and a young girl, probably fifteen or sixteen runs up the stairs of the stage. She is overwhelmed. Half laughing and half crying. Gaia opens her arms to the girl who falls into her embrace. "Blessed be are you, Tia!" Gaia shouts. "Mother Nature has made you strong. Today you will bestow upon us a gift to ensure our future!" Tia nods, reverent of Gaia's words.

Gaia begins her spinning routine again. This time when she opens her eyes she calls, "Ester Jacobi!"

Another cry. More shuffling and an older girl, probably well into her twenties runs onto the stage. "Blessed be! Blessed be am I!" she shouts and flings herself toward Gaia, who catches her and laughs.

"Yes, yes, my dear Ester. Blessed be are you. What number will this be? How many gifts have you bestowed since you came to live on the Farm?"

"This will be my fourth!" Ester shouts, excitedly.

"A worthy woman if ever there was one," Gaia tells her then blesses her the same way she did Tia and gives her a gentle push toward two domestics who lead her to a bench where the first girl sits. Gaia continues to spin, shouting names, blessing girls who run up onstage. I recognize each of the twelve girls from the daily belly jabbing. They sit hand in hand, nervously smiling like giddy winners from One World Super Celebrity competitions.

"Next, we shall welcome our donors," says Gaia. "These brave and worthy brothers of ours have been chosen for their superior intellects, able bodies, and compassionate souls. Today we will harvest their most sacred seed so that our garden shall be strong."

I've woven my way nearly to the front of the crowd, but still haven't caught site of Basil. Then I turn and see a dozen men marching up the steps to the stage, led by Carrick and flanked by Basil. "Oh no," I gasp as my stomach sours.

"Let the seeds prosper," Gaia says, beaming proudly at her flock.

"So we shall prosper, too," the group answers.

Then together, everyone says, "Blessed be are we."

I'm dizzy and near tears as I watch Basil standing placidly on-stage. How will I ever get to him now? Then Gaia says, "Our most esteemed and dear doctor would like to greet you before we have the harvest." She sweeps her arm to the side to present a man who walks up the steps waving to his crowd of ardent admirers, clapping, whistling, hooting, and hollering.

His shirt is crisp, his wing tips flash, not a single steel-colored hair is out of place on his head. I stumble back, bumping into people who stand on tiptoe to get a look at Dr. Darius Demeter.

$$\text{❧} \qquad \text{❧} \qquad \text{❧}$$

I stand, mouth open, staring at Dr. Demeter beside Gaia. My brain cannot compute how this could happen. It seems more likely that she would be squished by a falling meteor than he would show up here. Isn't this the guy who spends his life trying to stop people from eating? Quickly, I look to Basil, expecting him to be as slack-jawed and flabbergasted as I am, but he's barely flinched. Just a shadow of concern quickly passes over his face, then he stands up straight and tall, looking on as if everything is completely normal.

"I come with news of what's happening in the Loops," Dr. Demeter says once the crowd has settled down. "As Gaia has always predicted, an uprising has begun."

The crowd roars their approval of this news. The people around me slap one another on the backs and throw their arms around each other's shoulders. Again, I'm caught off guard. If they have no ties to other resistance groups, why are they so happy?

"There is much unrest," Dr. Demeter reports. "Riots and protests. Workers are striking. The privies are scared that One World will crumble. The entire economy is on the brink."

I'm not sure how much of this to believe coming from Dr.

Demeter and filtered through the crazy scope of the Farm, but given what Ella whispered to me last night, I assume some of it is true.

Gaia steps forward, smiling smugly. "I told you, my dear ones, I told you this would happen. Once word reached the Loops about our society here, the masses would rise up and revolt, demanding that they too have an existence as pure as ours!"

"Liar!" I scream, but the ovation that erupts from the crowd is so loud that it covers my shouts. "She's a liar!" I can't believe she's taking credit for what's happened in the Loops. Nobody has ever even heard of this lunatic, but she's convinced these idiots that she's causing the unrest! Unbelievable. I look to Basil, certain that by now he'll be flustered, but he's not. He stands stiff, staring straight ahead. The only thing that moves is a muscle twitching in his jaw, and for the first time I realize how tightly he must be wrapped around Gaia's crooked finger. If Gaia taking credit for what's happening in the Loops doesn't faze him, then it's possible that nothing will. And that scares me more than everything I've seen or heard yet.

Gaia lifts her arms to quiet the crowd. They are reluctant to settle down, and even when they are quiet, the excitement is still palpable in their fidgeting. "Mother Nature has chosen us, my dear ones, to carry on. We shall wait here in our Eden while the others perish, then we shall prosper because we and we alone have the answer to humankind's dilemma. Mother Nature will protect us in her infinite wisdom as we are the only ones who will be truly ready for the new world that is to come."

After Gaia's delusional proclamation of world domination, she dismisses the workers to the fields while Dr. Demeter leads Basil and the others from the stage to the front door of the hospital. As the crowd disperses, I steal around to the back of the building and slowly open the rear door then slip inside. Sticking close to the wall, I watch girls in scrubs carry trays past the line of men all with their backs to me.

Quietly, I hop across the hallway and disappear inside the dressing room.

From the neat stacks of blue scrubs, I grab a shirt and pants then whip off my dress. The bottle of Synthamil falls out of my pocket and rolls toward the door, where it makes a dull thonk. "Oh crap, oh crap," I whisper and skitter after it. As I crouch, half dressed, trying not to breathe, a muffled argument breaks out in the hallway.

"I won't . . ." I hear someone say followed by deep angry voices, then a scuffle and the sound of people running. I close my eyes and duck my head, waiting for the door to fly open. But it doesn't. Instead, I hear the back door thud and Gaia yell, "Let him go. I'll deal with him later."

It takes a moment for my heart to stop pounding in my ears, and I feel sorry for whoever just bolted, because he's going to get it after the harvest is over. I finish dressing and stuff my pockets with the Synthamil bottle and knife then tuck my hair under a cap. As quietly as I entered the dressing room, I leave.

Keeping my head down but my eyes up, I inch along the hall toward the front of the building. I see Leeda handing out small plastic cups to the line of men slithering through the open door of a lab. My heart pounds in my ears as I search the line for Basil, trying to find the one thing that distinguishes him from all the other bearded men in identical brown uniforms. *Surely*, I think, *I will know him*, but like the other times, I can't distinguish him from the crowd. With Leeda so close, I can't linger and gawk so I pass by, cutting my eyes to the right to look inside the room where I see Gaia, reclining on a bed, her blue robe wrapped tight around her body with one bare leg sticking out. She eyes the men hungrily as they line up in front of her, tiny cups in hand.

"Hey," someone says, and I jump. A girl I've never seen before shoves a tray of syringes at me. "Take these in. He's waiting." My hands shake as I take the tray, making the syringes rattle. "What's wrong with you?" she hisses. "Be careful!"

"Sorry," I mutter, panicking because I can't go in that room with Dr. Demeter.

"And where's your surgical mask?" she asks.

"I...I...I..."

She shakes her head, annoyed. "Take this one." She pulls a strip of blue fabric from her pocket and hands it to me. "I'll get another."

I hook the straps of the mask behind my ears and find the lab with Dr. Demeter. He's changed into scrubs and a mask, too, so only his eyes show. He glances at the tray in my hands and says, "Thank you, dear. You can put those right over there." I pass by the twelve women, including Tia and Ester, who were chosen by Gaia outside. They lay on gurneys, their flat bellies exposed to the bright lights overhead. Their arms are attached by thin tubes to IV bags marked meperidine and diazepam hanging on poles behind them. Bex and Ella are on the far side of the room labeling petri dishes with numbers.

"Now then," Dr. Demeter says as he snaps on a pair of sterile gloves. "If you could kindly swab the girls, we can begin."

I mimic another girl in scrubs and a mask who starts at one end of the row while I go to the other. We pull on gloves then rip open anti-septic wipes and work our way down the line. When I rub the area around Ester's belly button, she sucks in air. "Sorry," I whisper. "Is it cold?" She looks at me with bleary eyes then seems to drift away.

"Don't worry," Dr. Demeter says cheerily. "They won't feel a thing, especially when we top them off with a local anesthetic."

Bex follows him down the line with the tray of syringes that I brought in. I move away from her and pretend to busy myself cleaning up so that she won't see me. Dr. Demeter quickly pokes each girl in the belly, saying, "That should numb you up in no time." Then he goes back to the beginning of the row. "And now we'll begin the extraction."

The other girl pushes a cart of equipment over to him. He attaches a light to his forehead and puts on strong magnifying glasses then takes some small instruments from a tray. "First we'll just clip this off." He attaches two small clamps to either side of the Tia's belly button. "Raise those up ever so slightly then insert the laparoscope." He lifts the clips with one hand as he slides a long thin needle into her navel.

I have to look away because I feel faint. I lean against a stainless steel table, breathing deeply as snippets of his quiet narration float by. "When I reach the ovary, which has become enlarged . . . we being to aspirate . . . this one looks quite full . . . now I can extract the oocytes." I hear a sucking noise and think that I might vomit.

I excuse myself and run across the hall into an empty lab, panting for air, trying to wrap my mind around the truth of the situation. Haza was not insane. Dr. Demeter is harvesting human eggs! When I understand this, I think I know what could be happening to poor Basil and the other men in the room with Gaia. But I can't understand why there are so many children running around already. I know the people on my squad were having sex in the woods and since they're ingesting Arousatral in their Synthamil, they would be fertile. Surely all the girls who are pregnant got that way naturally. So why would he need the lab?

I pull the mask and cap off and wipe my clammy face as I swallow the sour taste in my mouth. Then I realize that I'm inside the one room that's been locked all week. The hum of electric generators and the eerie glow of soft light come from long tables holding rows and rows of small shallow glass dishes. Inside each dish is a thin pinkish film growing in a clear solution, which looks vaguely familiar. I try to remember where I've seen this before. Was it something online I was reading? Or in the Relics? Maybe in my mother's lab? Then it hits me. At the rehab center on the second floor. I took a picture of it with my Gizmo. I can't figure it out though. These aren't babies being grown. It looks more like human tissue. Similar to Just-Like-Skin, only not synthetic.

As I'm pondering what these lunatics could possibly be doing, the door opens. "Yes, I'll be just a moment," Dr. Demeter says. "I think I have a spare laparoscope in here." He walks into the lab muttering, "Everything breaks in this godforsaken place. . . ." Then he sees me, pressed against the back wall. "What is it?" he asks. "What are you doing in here?"

I'm too stunned to think of a quick response or to run away. Part of my brain is screaming at me to get out, but some other part of me takes over and says, "Dr. Demeter, what are you growing?"

I catch him off guard. I don't think anyone has ever asked him before because he actually smiles. "I love a good curious mind," he says. "I've been telling Gaia for years that we should groom some lab technicians who could help me." He opens a closet near me and rummages around, chatting easily. "It's not hard you know. Just follow the recipe really. And I could use help tending to these crops while I'm away." He takes a long flexible tube from the closet.

"Crops?" I ask.

"Some food can be grown in a lab, you know," he says with a wink.

"This isn't Synthamil," I say, feeling for the bottle in my pocket.

"No, no, this is the next step." When he turns to look at me fully, his face shifts into a confused stare. "I know you," he says. "You look a bit different, but I always recognize my former patients. Remind me of your name."

"I . . . I . . . I . . ." I can't think quickly enough, but before I can run, he grabs my arm.

"Thalia?" he asks. "Thalia Apple?" I recoil, trying to get away, but he pulls me closer. "I should have known you'd make your way here!" I realize then that he's hugging me. "Of course! Of course! Had I known that you were in the resistance, I would have brought you here myself." He releases me and beams. "I tried to drop hints when we were talking at my facility to see how far along you'd come in your thinking, but I wasn't quite sure you were ready. I've watched with great interest what you've accomplished in the Loops. And now I find you here! Does Gaia know who you are? She hasn't mentioned a thing."

I don't know what to do. I stand, staring at him, completely befuddled by what he's saying to me.

"Well, this is excellent!" he cries. "You can be our spokesperson! If Lily Nguyen's daughter, the One World–resistance leader tells the world that Synthamil didn't work for her, but my food supply did, we'll be able to reach a far bigger market more quickly!"

"Food supply?" I ask, still trying to make my brain understand. From the corner of my eye, I see one of the girls in scrubs step into the lab with a tray of petri dishes. When she sees us, she steps out quickly again.

Now Dr. Demeter becomes so excited that he paces in front of the tables. "Yes, you see, as I told you at my rehab center, I believe humans need to eat. It's hardwired into us. People like your mother have been able to overcome that, but not for long. The human instinct for survival is strong. The DNA is responding. You, like nearly everyone here, are one of the chosen ones."

"Chosen for what?" I ask, horrified.

"The mutation on chromosome sixteen," he says.

"Mutation? Chosen?" I clutch at my throat. "Who did this to me?"

He cocks his head to the side as if trying to understand my question, then he says, "Mother Nature. It's natural selection at play. First, we saw it mostly in second borns, but then it spread. I'm sure we'll see more and more people unable to cope with synthetic nutrition as the mutation takes root. I thought it would be years before things would shift, but now with the revolution under way and One World ready to crumble, we will be poised to offer the masses food. Real food, again. Real plants, real milk, real meat!" He motions to the table. "We will dominate the market and become the sole supplier of nutrition in the new world order."

There's so much to wrap my head around that I don't know where to begin. So I ask, "What do you mean milk and meat. There are no animals."

"Ah," he says with a smile. "There's still one."

My stomach rolls over as the pieces come together. "Human milk?" I whisper, and he nods. I remember the topless women in the pump house. The buckets of strange whitish water. The sweet tea. The talk of cheese. "And this?" I ask. "This is the meat?" I point to the dishes on the table.

"Don't you see? No one is harmed. I grow the embryonic stem cell lines from what we harvest here and create sheets of muscle fiber, which we can stack into a hearty protein source. I think your mother will be very interested in this."

"My mother?"

"And now that One World has severed ties with her, you can help me bring her on board."

"Darius?" Gaia's voice comes from the hall.

"Coming!" he calls. "Just had a bit of an equipment malfunction." He turns to me again. "After the harvest, let's sit down and have a good long talk," he tells me cheerily. "I'll explain everything more thoroughly."

As he walks to the door where Gaia's tying her belt around her jumpsuit, he points over his shoulder and says, "Did you know—"

But Gaia cuts him off. "Hurry up," she tells him testily. "The men are done. They're heading out to the fields, and I'm hungry."

"Yes, yes," he says impatiently. "Give me twenty minutes to finish up, and I'll meet you at your house for lunch."

✤   ✤   ✤

As soon as Dr. Demeter and Gaia are gone, I bolt for the door and come face-to-face with Ella, who grabs me and whispers fiercely, "What are you doing here? Why did you come back?"

"For Basil," I say and latch onto her arm. "And for you. Come with me and Mr. Clemens. We'll all leave together."

Ella shrinks from me. "I can't," she says. "My son. And Noam."

"Noam?"

She nods. "I won't leave them behind."

"Okay, fine," I whisper. "We'll take them all. We'll figure it out. Just come with us."

"How?" she asks with a shred of hope sparkling in her eyes.

"I don't know," I admit.

"What about your family? In the Loops. Would they help us?"

"Yes but ..."

"I know how you can contact them." She pulls me down the hall toward the rear door as she explains, "Gaia has a screen. If we hurry, you can call them before she gets home."

We run silently through the tangled vines. What's happening between us is so huge that neither of us dares to speak until we reach Gaia's back door.

"She's checking on the harvest out in the fields while the doctor finishes," Ella says as she leads me through a dark hallway. "You have less than twenty minutes before they'll return to have lunch here." She pulls a set of keys from the folds of her dress. My mouth falls open when she opens the door to a room as sleek and modern as any back home in the Loops. A huge screen takes up an entire wall. "Can you do it?" Ella asks. "Can you reach your family?"

"If you can get me on the system."

Ella shrinks back and shakes her head. "I don't know how," she says. "I just slip in and pretend to clean whenever Gaia's in here. That's how I figured out who you are."

"But then, she must know ..."

Ella rolls her eyes. "You'd think she would have put it all together by now, but she seems clueless. Honestly, I think she just searches for news about herself and ignores everything else. So? Will it work?" she asks me hopefully.

I swallow hard, wondering the same thing myself, but then I take a breath. "Yes," I tell her. "I can do it."

She nods and without a word, she leaves, closing the door behind her.

I assume the main screen Eye won't let me blink on, and if Gaia uses voice recognition, I'll trigger a lockdown if I speak commands, so I have to find a way to hack into the system manually. I jiggle the touch pad on the desk to wake the screen and see that she's smart enough to have encrypted her password, but I know lots of back-door tricks, including the fancy command line work AnonyGal taught me during a Dynasaur chat. I key in codes to get the system to cough up its most common keystrokes and work to decode the password, which is surprisingly simple. Username: Gaia. Password: TheFarm. Sheesh, I could've guessed it without breaking a sweat.

When Gaia's personal feed comes up, I almost fall off my chair because the first thing I see is Yaz standing in front of an EA where the portico has become a tent city. I turn the volume as low as it will go and lean close to the speaker. "Workers and privies alike have overtaken this EA demanding talks with the government and One World about the legality of the so-called Universal Nutrition Protection Act," Yaz explains as she directs her HoverCam around the area.

Below the feed, I see links to more vids by Yaz where she's visited malls that have been looted by protesters, marches that have shut down the highways, and many feeds from PlugIn 42, which has become a command center for the Dynasaurs who are orchestrating everything online. As much as I want to know everything that's happening, I must connect with my parents soon because there may not be another chance, so I leave Yaz's PRC and open Gaia's video feed.

I see myself in the small subscreen. The pink in my hair is fading, and my eyes are nearly back to hazel so my former self peeks through. I ping our house, hoping like hell that someone in my family is near a screen. "Mom, Dad, Grandma! It's Thalia. Please pick up. Hurry!" I whisper.

When my mother's face fills the screen, I nearly cry, but I hold myself together. "Thalia, is that you? Is that really you?" I nod and fight tears. "Oh thank god." She looks gaunt and tired with deep lines across her forehead. "We were so worried when we lost contact with your Gizmo."

"I don't have much time to talk," I tell her. "But I'm in a terrifying place and I need your help."

My dad jostles into the picture. His skin is ashen and his jaw is tight. "We'll come right now. Tell us where you are."

"I don't know exactly. On some crazy farm in the Hinterlands. Can you pick up a locator signal from this network?'

"I'm already trying," Dad says as he jabs at his tablet.

"Oh, Mom!" I cry. "Dr. Demeter is here, and you will never believe what he's doing!"

Mom's face grows even more pallid. "I am so sorry I ever took you to him. I've been researching day and night to understand what happened to you. I discovered that many people like you have a reaction to something in the inocs or the Synthamil that mutates chromosome sixteen on your FTO gene."

"You're sure the inocs and Synthamil cause it?" I ask. "Dr. Demeter thinks the mutation is caused by natural selection."

"My research is showing a direct link to the synthetics." Her voice breaks. "It's my fault. My fault you were ever hungry."

"I don't care," I say. "Just please get me out of here."

"It's not going to be easy," Mom says. "Things have gone from bad to worse in the Loops."

"I heard you were fired."

Her face hardens. "We've had a falling out with Ahimsa. She doesn't want to acknowledge what I've discovered."

"One World is against you, too?"

She nods then turns to my father. "Have you located her?"

"The signal's blocked, but I think we can hack it. Thalia, use RabbitHole to go into the system and reveal the IPN to me."

"How do you know about RabbitHole?" I ask, confused because it's a program AnonyGal wrote and released to the Dynasaurs years ago.

My dad looks up at me with a weak smile on his face. "I've always had your back, HP."

"Are you . . . ?" I start to ask but then I hear Gaia's voice in the hall.

"Ella, we're back!" she calls.

I freeze as a wave of nausea rolls over me. I hit the mute button on the screen and quickly IM my parents that I can no longer talk.

Dad types back, *Reveal the IPN then keep the connection open even if you have to go, kill the screen. We will find you!*

Footsteps echo through the house. "Where is that lazy girl?" Gaia mutters almost directly outside the door. I hold my breath, not daring to even type until she passes by.

Once she's gone, I quickly key in the RabbitHole code and search frantically for the IPN, then the screen begins to fade. "Dad," I whisper and IM, WHERE R U? Blackness fills the wall. I wonder if I've lost the connection until a fuzzy image takes over. My stomach drops as Ahimsa's face fills the screen. I see her mouth moving angrily but no sound comes out.

The door handle jiggles. "Stupid girl," Gaia says as she slips the key into the lock. "I don't know where she's gone off to. She knows that we're to have lunch here."

"Maybe the excitement of the harvest got her confused," Dr. Demeter says as the door swings open.

When she walks in and sees me backing away from the screen, Gaia's face contorts. First she is surprised, then confused, and finally furious. "What the hell are you doing in here!" she screams and rushes at me.

I fling myself out of the chair and run for the corner. Dr. Demeter stands in the doorway shocked.

Gaia ignores me and goes for the screen. "Were you on my system?" She sees Ahimsa's face glowering at her, so she hits the volume button and rips into her. "I know you've been after me for years! But this is too much. Sending in spies so you could learn our secrets!"

"What? Who are you?" Ahimsa shouts at her. "And why are you harboring Thalia Apple?"

"Who?" Gaia asks.

"Thalia Apple," Dr. Demeter says, pointing to me. "Didn't you know?"

Gaia whips around. "But you said your name was Natalie!"

I'm not about to argue with her about my name now. I run for the door as Ahimsa says, "Either you turn her over or you will feel the full wrath of One World Security."

"Grab her!" Gaia shouts at Dr. Demeter, who snares me around the waist. "If you want her, you'll have to come get her!" Gaia tells Ahimsa. "And when you do, I'll be ready for you. I've been preparing for this day for years!"

I struggle against Dr. Demeter's grip, trying to work my fingers into my pocket.

"I should have known that you'd come here to destroy us," Gaia screeches at me. "I'll kill you!"

"No Gaia," Dr. Demeter shouts and holds out a hand to stop her. "She's worth more alive."

Just as she launches herself at us I withdraw the knife. The light hits the blade and sends them both reeling back. "Get away from me,"

I tell them. They back away against the wall screen where Ahimsa's face begins to fade, replaced by my father.

"Thalia! Thalia!" he cries but I turn and run.

⚘ ⚘ ⚘

I sprint down the path toward the fields, screaming Basil's name. Before me rows and rows of golden stalks as high as my knees sway in the breeze. Small colorful critters, their wings flapping, flit from plant to plant. I scream Basil's name again.

"Apple!" I hear from the distance. "Apple! Where are you?"

I run toward the voice, desperately searching for him among the stalks. Long green leaves scrape at the skin on my leg, but I don't stop. "I'm over here!" I shout. "Where are you?"

Far off to my left, I see the workers, half bent over and half standing, craning their necks to see what the commotion is, but Basil is not among them because he is running toward me from the kudzu. When we meet, I throw myself onto him, gasping, "We have to get out of here. This place isn't safe. Gaia is crazy. You have no idea what they're capable of."

"I know, when I saw Dr. Demeter . . ." he says clutching me. "And in the lab . . . when she tried to . . ."

I stop and stare at him. "What? What happened to you? What did they do?"

He shakes his head with disgust. "The harvest. I couldn't do it. I wouldn't do it. I ran out and went looking for you."

"I was there. In the changing room. I heard, but I didn't know it was you." I wrap my arms around his neck. "I'm so proud of you and, believe me, you don't know half of what's going on here yet. This place is so freakin' creepy."

He looks torn, as if he's not ready to fully accept what I'm telling him. "But maybe . . ." he says.

I grab his face and make him look me in the eyes. "If you'll come with me, I'll tell you everything I know, and then if you want to return, I won't stop you."

He looks past me, over my shoulder, as if he's debating, but then his face screws into fear. "Uh-oh," he says. Slowly I turn to see Gaia marching toward us steadily but in no hurry. And why should she hurry? Where are we going to go? Basil and I grab each other.

"Infiltrators!" Gaia booms. She marches calmly but resolutely toward us with her finger outstretched. "One World spies! They've come to undo all of our hard work."

The workers from the field advance on us from the other side, eyeing us suspiciously. "Don't listen to her!" I yell. "She's a liar and she's crazy. She's putting Synthamil in your soup!" I pull the bottle from my pocket and hold it up for them to see.

"She called One World and revealed our location," Gaia accuses. An audible gasp escapes from the crowd, and Basil whips around toward me.

"Is that true?" he asks.

"No," I say. "Ahimsa broke into a call I made to my parents, then Gaia told her to come get me."

Basil's face grows pale.

"I told you all that this would happen," Gaia says. "That someday, someone would come and try to take us down. We've always known it. One World would love to destroy everything we've worked so hard for. And look at all we've accomplished! The fields. The houses. The children! The food supply! Look how we've grown. From a dozen chosen ones to nearly two hundred. They will take away our children. Burn our crops. Bulldoze our buildings. Arrest anyone who tries to stop them. And these infiltrators have come to unlock the gates for them."

Basil grips my hand tight. I think of running, but then I find my voice and shout, "She's a liar!" I turn to the crowd. "Gaia stole this land and her house from a farmer. She buys Synthamil with Arousatrol off the black market and slips it in your food so the girls will get pregnant and Dr. Demeter can harvest your human eggs and sperm, and they feed you human milk and they are growing flesh in the lab! I'm telling you, she is not who you think she is. She is a delusional power-hungry lunatic who wants to control the world. One World may not be the way, but neither is this!"

Some of the workers, especially the girls with pronounced bellies, look at Gaia, waiting for her defense. But Gaia is a master. She simply snorts, dismissing everything I've said. "We have no time for these petty accusations. We must protect what we've built. We must fight the infiltrators and secure our future."

Gaia continues ranting about how One World will enact Arma-geddon on the Farm in order to protect their bottom line. "Are you going to let that happen?" she screams.

"No!" the crowd roars back at her.

"Then we must be ready for them!"

I cling to Basil and withdraw the knife, ready to defend us, but the crowd's whoops and shouts for our blood are overtaken by a low rumble coming from the distance. Everyone looks around, searching for the source. The sound beats at the air. *Thwump, thwump, thwump.* We look up, shading our eyes.

"There!" one of the men shouts and points at a speck in the sky speeding toward us.

"I told you!" Gaia shouts. "I told you they would come for us. We must be ready. We must take up arms and protect what is ours!"

The group seems to forget all about us and instead charges be-hind Gaia toward the encampment, leaving Basil and me standing in the field alone as the noise in the sky gets louder and the dark speck grows bigger.

"We have to hide!" I yell and pull Basil toward the kudzu. From inside the tree line among the tangled vines, we watch the helicopter close in, bending the yellow stalks in the field like genuflecting masses I've seen in photos at the Relics. We cover our faces as it touches down and the whirling blades begin to slow. Then the door pops open. I expect to see armed burgundy-shirted security agents pour out, but instead a tall rangy man with wild hair and a baggy sweater shades his eyes as he peers out timidly. Another person, a thin woman with black hair, pushes in beside him and scans the area. For a moment, I'm confused. The two people look oddly like my parents. Then I realize. They are my parents. Without thinking, I run.

My father jumps out of the helicopter followed by my mother. Within seconds, I'm enveloped in their arms. They hug me fiercely, pulling me so close that I can hardly breathe. Once they release their grip on me, we all start talking at once, firing questions at one another.

"How did you find me?" I ask.

"What is this place?" says my dad.

"Are you okay?" my mother yells. "Let me look at you! Are you hurt?"

Before we can answer each other, a squat four-wheeled vehicle barrels out of the kudzu. Fearing that Gaia and her goons are on the attack, I push my parents toward the helicopter, shouting, "Go, go, go! Get in!" But my mom latches onto my wrist and yanks me along behind her. I drag my heels, trying to wrench free from her grip, screaming so I can get Basil. Over my shoulder, I see him sprinting from the woods shouting my name. The four-wheeler is closing in on him. "No!" I scream and tear myself free from my mother, certain that whoever is on that vehicle will hurt him. But then I recognize the driver and his passenger. I stop dead in my tracks. "Mr. Clemens! Ella!" I shout and run toward them.

Mr. Clemens stops near where my parents, Basil, and I stand, hands on knees, trying to catch our breath. Mr. Clemens nods to us, then says, "Looks like you got Gaia and them good and stirred up!"

I suck in air. "She's threatening to kill me, and she thinks One World is coming to destroy the Farm. She told everyone to take up arms and get ready for a battle."

"Ha!" says Mr. Clemens. "Serves her right. She's been trying to pick that fight for years, but One World wouldn't pay her no mind. Bet she's happy now. There's no leader like the martyr."

I turn to Ella. "What are you doing here?"

"After I left you, I told Noam to get our son, then I ran and got Mr. Clemens. I figured he'd know what to do."

"Told you she was smart," Mr. Clemens says proudly.

Finally, my mother can't take it anymore. "Who are these people and what is going on?" she demands.

I try my best to give her the quick version of all that has happened in the past few days, including what Dr. Demeter is growing in the lab. Then my parents explain that Dad was able to locate Gaia's IPN even though Ahimsa hijacked the call since the line was never disconnected. As soon as they had the coordinates, they hopped into the helicopter and headed this way.

"You aren't that far from home," my father tells me.

"Neither are you," Mr. Clemens says to Dad. "I believe I knew your father in passing." My dad looks at him with wonder.

"They'll be time for this later," Mom says. She grabs my wrist. "We have to get you out of here."

"Basil?" I say, but it comes out like a question as I reach for him.

"No, Thalia!" he begs. "We can't go back there."

"It's okay," my mom says. "I know you have no reason to trust me, but you must believe me. We won't take you back to the Loops. It's not safe. Ahimsa wants a scapegoat for everything that's gone wrong, so she's targeted you two. We'll do our best to protect you along with our daughter."

"Where are we going to go then?" I ask.

Mom and Dad exchange looks. "Maybe to another population center," says Dad. "You can hide there until the protests die down, then we'll think of something. But we have to leave now." He pulls out his Gizmo. "If you're right and Ahimsa found the location, security will be here soon. We can't let them catch you."

"Wait," I say. "We could go north." I turn to Mr. Clemens. "Tell them."

"I believe there are people living off the land up in Canada. I've got a trailer behind my place packed up with everything we'd need to join them. Synthamil, fuel, and seeds for when we get there."

Always the scientist, my mother asks, "What proof do you have that people can survive up there?"

"None," says Mr. Clemens. "Except that it's possible. The land around here is regenerating and the fauna is returning and things were less damaged farther north to begin with. There will be people who figure out how to start over. Human ingenuity is a beautiful thing."

I look to my mom. My father is by her side with his arm around her narrow shoulders. "No," says Mom. "It's too risky. We'd be naive to try."

"You were naive enough to try to save the world once before," I remind her.

"And look what happened!" she says. "It's my fault chromosome sixteen mutated. I ruined so many lives. Including yours." She looks to Basil and me with a quivering chin as if she might cry.

"No, Mom. We're the lucky ones." I reach out to her. "We're like the first creatures that sprouted wings." I catch Basil's eye. He nods as I recite Ana's words: " 'Now we're standing on a precipice, and we can either plummet or we can spread those wings and fly.' "

"Oh, Thalia." Mom pulls me close. Then, from a distance, we hear a loud angry buzz in the sky.

My dad scans the horizon. "They're coming."

"Get in!" my mother says. "All of you."

"Not without my son and Noam," Ella says and steps away.

Early evening shadows crawl over the crops as a fleet of helicopters low in the sky come into view. Basil latches onto my arm and points across the field. "They're bringing weapons," he says.

A group of men run out of the encampment carrying long metal tubes on their shoulders.

"The showers you were building?" I ask, unable to make sense of what I'm seeing.

Basil levels his gaze at me. "They're rocket launchers," he says, then a piercing whistle followed by a line of thick gray smoke ascends into the sky amid the One World helicopters, maneuvering into landing positions. A loud explosion rocks one of the helicopters wildly side to side. The others lift up and return fire. Something loud zips into the encampment. We hear a loud pop, then a flame shoots into the sky from behind the buildings. Ella screams and dashes toward the explosions.

"Ella don't!" I dart after her, shouting over my shoulder to my parents, "There are children in there!"

As we run, an old dark green vehicle with no top careens straight for us, with Dr. Demeter driving and Gaia standing on the seat, pointing a long, thin rifle at us.

I jump and grab Ella, sending us both sprawling in the dirt as the first shot rings out. I cover her body with mine and roll. From behind us, I hear a motor then see Basil hunched over, driving Mr. Clemens's four-wheeler straight for us. Ahead of us, Gaia's vehicle hits a large bump, which flings her up and out of the car, arms and legs flailing, rifle flying. She lands in a heap as the vehicle flips onto its side, dumping Dr. Demeter in the dirt. Basil turns sharply, encircling us. He reaches down. I push Ella up onto the seat behind him, then I scramble on and wrap my arms around them both, trying to protect her belly as best I can. He guns the engine and circles back toward my parents' helicopter where we see my mother bent over the body of Mr. Clemens, who has crumpled to the ground.

"No!" Ella screams. "No, no, no!"

Another loud whistle pierces the sky, then a bright flash erupts between us and my parents. Basil turns sharply to avoid the blast, which sprays dirt and rocks into the air. He heads away from the dark cloud of debris toward an opening in the kudzu. Above the din of helicopters now swarming the area, I hear my mother wail.

"Go back! Go back!" I scream and claw at him, trying to get him to turn around.

A man with something in his arms darts out from the kudzu at the far end of the field. "Noam! Noam!" Ella screams and I see that she's right. It is Noam with a toddler bouncing on his hip. Inside the boy's chubby hand is a stick shaped like an airplane. Ella grabs Basil's shoulders and shakes him violently. "Stop. Stop. Stop."

Basil won't listen, though. We hit a dim path leading us through the woods toward an overgrown edifice. "Is this it?" he yells over his shoulder. "Is this Mr. Clemens's cabin?"

As soon as we stop, Ella and I both scramble off. She runs back down the path toward the fields shouting for Noam. I start to follow her, screaming, "I have to make sure my parents are okay!" but Basil grabs me.

"Don't!" he yells. "We have a plan." Then he charges behind the house. A series of loud pops send smoke above the trees, and I hesitate. Basil comes around the corner, dragging a wagon behind him. "Help me," he shouts over the noise of the battle now raging. "The only hope we have is to get out of here with these supplies! Your parents will take care of the others and meet us."

"I can't leave them!"

"But that's the plan!" Basil yells as he struggles to attach the cart to the vehicle. I don't know what to do. But then I hear a deep rumble swelling. The wind whips the trees, sending dirt into my face. I wipe my eyes and squint into the gray cloud swirling to see a helicopter lifting up above our heads. I can't make out who's inside because the dust is too thick.

My parents' helicopter climbs higher and higher into the sky. "No!" I scream. "Don't leave me." I run, trying to get a glimpse of my parents, Mr. Clemens, and Ella and her boys. The helicopter swoops around, dipping right and left as if searching for us. I jump and wave my arms, certain that if they could see me, they would land, but they're too far away and the sky has become too dark with smoke. "Over here! Over here!" I scream.

Another rocket zings across the sky, narrowly missing the helicopter, which quickly ascends and darts away like the butterfly I once chased. "No!" I scream and fall to my knees. "No!"

I feel Basil behind me, his hands pressed into my back. "It's okay," he tells me. "It's alright. We'll find them."

"But what if that wasn't them? What if Gaia took the helicopter. What if they're back in the fields?"

"It was them. I'm sure of it," he says.

"But, how could they leave me?"

He reaches in his pocket and pulls out my father's Gizmo. "Before I came after you and Ella, your father gave me this. He said to get you and the supplies. He promised he'd take care of the others. Once we're all free from here, we'll get in touch."

Overjoyed, I grab the Gizmo from him and try to ping my father, my mother, the helicopter screen, but nothing happens. The Gizmo lies dormant in my hands. No signal, no life, no network with which to connect.

"We have to go now," Basils says, pulling me to my feet. "This may be our only chance."

I look down at the useless Gizmo in my hand. "But where will we go?" I ask, as my parents' helicopter disappears into the horizon.

Basil and I look at each other. "We can't go back to the Loops," Basil says, as more smoke rises from beyond the trees. "At least, not yet."

"And we can't stay here," I say.

We look out into the endless expanse of kudzu to the north. "Do you think there are others out there?"

"Yes," says Basil. "There must be." He climbs onto the vehicle and holds out a hand to me.

"But what if . . ." I look over my shoulder once more.

"We'll find them, Apple. We will."

As the smoke continues to rise and the explosions get louder, I can see no other option. "Are you ready?" he asks.

I gather my courage once more then sling my leg over the vehicle and wrap one arm around his waist. I clutch the Gizmo to my chest and consider the emptiness in my belly, the hunger in my mind, and the defect in my genes that has enabled me to love this boy. I take one more deep breath, searching for that scent from the past that I can't yet name, but am still hoping to find in my future.

"I'm ready," I tell him. "Let's go."

EPILOGUE

*"Even if I knew that tomorrow the world would
go to pieces, I would still plant my apple tree."*
—*Martin Luther*

"Look at that! Double-word score," Grandma Rebecca says as she lays down an X on the Scrabble board. "That's twenty-six points for me."

"Hmph," says Mr. Clemens, rearranging his tiles with his good arm. "You got lucky."

"Luck or skill?" she says with a laugh.

The door wheeshes open, and Dad comes in, looking beleaguered as he does every day now. Mom looks up from the screen where she patiently explains the difference between protons and neutrons to Ella, who has long since grown bored. "How did it go?" she asks Dad, who steps over the tower of wooden blocks that the boy has so painstakingly stacked on the floor with Papa Peter and Yaz. He drops onto the couch beside Grace and reaches for the baby that gurgles cheerfully in Noam's arms.

"Same old, same old," Dad tells them as he nuzzles the little girl.

"They ask me where she is, I tell them I don't know. Then I point out that they know I don't know because they're monitoring everything we do, so they'd be the first to know if she tried to contact us, which they deny. And we go around and around until they finally get tired of it, and they let me go."

Mom sits on the arm of the couch beside Dad. "I don't understand what went wrong. Why hasn't she tried? You blocked the locator right? Set the connection only to your jalopy?"

"Yes," he sighs as if he's said it for the thousandth time. "Either there's no signal where she is or the Gizmo broke or she's just biding time until it's safe. We will hear from her, you know. It just may take a while." He hands Mom the baby and smiles gently. "How was your day?"

She cuddles the girl then shrugs. "I know Mother and I could solve the problem if we had our lab and some funding but until Ahimsa accepts there's a problem with the Synthamil we don't have much hope here."

"We're thinking of going to Peter's hospital in the Outer Loop to work there for a while," Grandma Grace adds.

Dad shakes his head. "That might not be a good idea. I hear it's still pretty rough out there."

The door chimes and everyone looks up. "That's strange," says Grandma Rebecca, rising from the table. "Are we expecting someone?"

Mom's face hardens. "Probably security to go through everything again." She hands the baby back to Noam then holds out her hand for the boy. "Let's go back to the bedroom and have some tablet time," she says to him. She knows what people say about her now. About the unorthodox family she's created. But she doesn't care. Ella's and Noam's educations plus raising the little ones keeps her busy while she waits for news. Except at night. When she can't sleep and she finds Dad at the screen, scanning chat rooms on his jalopy, looking for any sign of me, but never finding any.

Rebecca opens the front door. The smell of synthetic lilacs seeps into the house.

"It's too early for lilacs," Mr. Clemens says. His hands itch to be in the dirt, rooting for the first green shoots of spring. While he sleeps, he still dreams of plowing. As soon as his arm is better, he and Grandma Rebecca will turn the dirt behind the house to see if they can coax anything to grow from the tiny seed packets he brought from his farm.

"Hello?" Grandma calls because no one is there. She scans the driveway, the sidewalk. But she sees no one. She steps out and looks down the street for a Smaurto, but everything is quiet. "That's odd," she says, and just as she's about to go inside, she sees a box on the stoop with her name, REBECCA APPLE, handwritten in neat black letters across the top.

"What is it?" Dad calls.

"A package for me!" Grandma tells them, as she carries it inside.

"Did you order something?" Mom asks.

"Heavens no," Grandma says and sets it down on the table next to the Scrabble board.

Mr. Clemens pulls out his pocketknife and hands her a blade to slice the tape. Inside the box is a smaller box that looks as if it's made of rough-hewn wood. She pries off the lid and reaches down inside the packing material, which feels oddly like sawdust.

"Smells nice," says Yaz, inhaling deeply.

Grandma feels something small and round inside. It's solid but not hard, and the surface is cool to the touch.

"What is it?" Dad asks.

Grandma pulls the object out into the light. It is red and round with a small brown stem. They all gaze at it.

"What dat?" the boy asks, pointing.

No one knows what to say for a moment, until Grandma finds her voice again. "It's an apple," she tells them. "The real thing. A perfect, red, round apple."

Mom and Dad run for the door, but Grandma knows they won't find what they're looking for. There will be no trace of the messenger outside, but still the message is clear.

"They made it," Mr. Clemens says.

"And they're fine." My grandmother brings the apple to her nose. The scent is sweet and I moan.

ψ   ψ   ψ

"Hey," someone says, shaking me awake. "You okay?"

I look around, groggy, then remember where I am. It's the same dream I've had nearly every night for weeks. I snuggle closer to Basil and pull the covers up tight beneath my chin.

"You cold?" he asks. "Want me to put another log on the fire?" Snow fell last night. The first real snow of my life. He gets out of bed, cozy in his warm red flannels.

The people up here have been so kind since we arrived. Helped us find a cabin and brought us food and clothes. They love Basil because he can fix all the machinery that's broken, and they're teaching me how to farm. Of course the thing I like best is the apple trees. When the snows are gone, they tell me, we'll be able to walk barefoot in the dirt and plant our own. If we could get a signal up here, life would be much better, but for now, we're doing okay.

I press myself up on one elbow to watch him in the glow of the embers. "Do you think they'll get it?" I ask.

"What?" says Basil, stoking the logs that warm our tiny cabin. "The apple?"

I nod.

He adds another log and turns to me. "Yes," he says. "The messenger will get it through. They assured me. It just takes time."

"And they'll know, right?" I ask and lift the covers to welcome him back into my arms. He smells of wood smoke and soap and something deeper that I can't name but it soothes me when I worry. Out the window, the stars shine bright above Basil and me and my family far away, even if they can't see them through the city haze. "They'll understand?"

He wraps me tight. "Yes," he says into my ear. "Now go to sleep."

Before I close my eyes, I look at the stars again. *Tell them*, I wish upon the brightest one, *that we'll come back for them soon.*

ACKNOWLEDGMENTS

I would like to thank all of the people in my life who helped me create the world in which Thalia and Basil exist: Stephanie Rostan, Monika Verma, and the team at Levine Greenberg for crossing all the T's and dotting all the I's while cheering me along; Lane Shefter Bishop for taking an early interest in this project; Liz Szabla, Jean Feiwel, and the fine folks at Feiwel and Friends for their enthusiasm and incredible attention to detail; and Em—as always.

Special thanks to my parents and my children for their unfailing support. And all my love to the dark-haired boy who first set my heart aflutter and still does. Any world with you is the world for me, Danny V.

Thank you for reading this FEIWEL AND FRIENDS book.

The Friends who made

HUNGRY

possible are:

JEAN FEIWEL, *Publisher*

LIZ SZABLA, *Editor in Chief*

RICH DEAS, *Senior Creative Director*

HOLLY WEST, *Associate Editor*

DAVE BARRETT, *Executive Managing Editor*

NICOLE LIEBOWITZ MOULAISON, *Production Manager*

LAUREN A. BURNIAC, *Editor*

ANNA ROBERTO, *Associate Editor*

CHRISTINE BARCELLONA, *Administrative Assistant*

Follow us on Facebook or visit us online at mackids.com.

Our books are friends for life.